BIG IF

mark costello

w. w. norton & company

For information about permission to reproduce selections from this book, write to
Permissions, W. W. Norton & Company, Inc., 500 Fifth Avenue,
New York, NY 10110

The text of this book is composed in Transit 521 BT
with the display set in Backspacer Square
Composition by Roy Tedoff
Manufacturing by Quebcor World Fairfield
Book design by Blue Shoe Studio
Production manager: Andrew Marasia

Library of Congress Cataloging-in-Publication Data

Costello, Mark, 1936-
Big if / Mark Costello.— 1st ed.
p. cm.
ISBN 0-393-05116-1 (hardcover)
1. Assassination—Fiction. 2. New Hampshire—Fiction. I. Title.
PS3553.O763 B54 2002
813'.54—dc21   2002000512

W. W. Norton & Company, Inc., 500 Fifth Avenue, New York, N.Y. 10110
www.wwnorton.com

W. W. Norton & Company Ltd., Castle House, 75/76 Wells Street, London W1T 3QT

1 2 3 4 5 6 7 8 9 0

for delia

part one

IN US WE TRUST

Center Effing is a town between the ocean and I-95, on the old and settled seaboard of New Hampshire. To the north is salt marsh. To the south is salt marsh, four square miles of state forest, and the town of Rye. It has a bit of money now, high tech and retirees, condos on the beaches and a new downtown. It was different twenty years ago when Vi Asplund was growing up. In those days, Center Effing was a town of lobstermen, dads commuting into Portsmouth, and, of course, the Air Force out of Pease.

The house where Vi grew up was your basic saltbox, New Hampshire's answer to the ranch. The house was on a quarter acre down Santasket Road, three bedrooms on the second floor, an attic and a basement and a small attached garage, with views of nothing special—on one side, Captain Cooper's house (saltbox, painted gray); on the other, Major Buckert's (saltbox, painted gray and briefly a bright orange just before the Buckerts filed for divorce). These men—Cooper, Buckert—were SAC pilots based at Pease, nine miles up the interstate. The bomber dads were gone six months of the year, deployed to forward-ready status in Thule, Greenland, and when they were away, their families always went a little crazy on the street. The older kids set fires, the younger kids went naked, the mothers took lovers (other bomber pilots, waiting to deploy). The lovers came and went in the hours before dawn and the Asplunds had a view of this as well, the craziness, the lovers, and the kids.

The front windows of the Asplunds' house overlooked a rather ordinary lawn, twin Rose of Sharon bushes and a boxwood hedge, and past Santasket Road to the wavy pampas of the intertidal marsh. Behind the house was a patio and yard, a swing set and a garden where Vi's mother, Evelyn, a sun-brown housewife, grew very tricky roses, obscure Chinese vines, and Dutch Blaster tulips, which were time-intensive and pest-prone but famous for the power of their blooms.

When Vi was six and her brother, Jens, was ten, Evelyn started forcing tulips in the den. The den was in the northwest corner of the house and sunny over the middle saddle of the day, which made it the perfect place to force a tulip bulb. She started in late winter, when the marsh was toast to the horizon, and the bomber wing was off to Greenland on a friendly weather mission, and Mrs. Buckert got up one night and started painting her house orange, and Mrs. Cooper was working on her French with the help of Major Wade, and the Coopers' oldest kid was picked up by the cops and sent to military school, and the other Cooper kids discovered streaking (which came late to New Hampshire), and the youngest Cooper girl ran away from home and got as far as Colonel Krutland's house around the bend.

Jimmy Carter was in power and Evelyn was in the Center Effing public library. She let Vi pick a book. No, two books. No, one book and a tape, and not that damn *We Sing* business either, Vi, gives your mom a splitting migraine. Vi picked her book and tape as Evelyn in snowboots looked up tulip horticulture in the card catalogs. They stopped at Monsey's Luncheonette on the rotary downtown, then at Aulette's Greenhouse down the road, where Evelyn bought three knee-high terra-cotta vases tapered to the top like antiaircraft shells, which Aulette recommended for the serious forcer. Tulip forcing, Vi later figured out, was a matter of taking the ugly, sometimes even hairy bulbs, which looked like giant bunions, something you might pay a guy to razor off your foot, and freezing them or chilling them to simulate the winter, then putting them in shells with dirt and other substances, covering the shells and leaving them in a sunny corner of the den. The bulbs, bamboozled by the dark and heat, would think that it was spring and crack into a shoot. The shells stayed in the den until the marshes came alive and Mrs. Buckert packed her kids into the station wagon and went back to Indiana, leaving her husband for not being there.

Vi's father, Walter Asplund, groused about the shells, the garden's sly invasion of the den. The den, he said, was his after-supper sanctum, the place he went to end his day with a glass of Pabst, a pipe of Borkum Riff, and a stack of old insurance journals. Walter Asplund was a claims adjuster for the Connecticut Casualty Corporation of Connecticut, which meant that he investigated losses under policies, measuring the damage, negotiating pay-outs according to a chart devised in

Hartford, this much for a hand, this much for a toe, this much for one-quarter loss of vision in one eye. He was solid seacoast burgher, a complicated man, a cheapskate and a brooder and a reader of the sort of books most people only read in college (Mill, Locke, Thucydides, *Moll Flanders*), a man who laughed at jokes but rarely told them, who got his hair cut on the same day every month, who shoveled his own driveway, ironed his own shirts. He dabbled in town politics as a Lodge Republican, chaired the C.E. bloodmobile, and was elected chairman of the Rotary, an honor he declined on the grounds that the national Rotarians required every chair to swear an oath on the Christian scripture, which Vi's father, in good conscience, couldn't do. Walter Asplund believed in many things, the dignity of humankind, the Genius of Democracy, the sanctity of contract, *The Origin of Species*, the mission of the bloodmobile, the charts devised in Hartford, poplin suits in summertime, brown bread with baked beans, little oyster crackers (with chowder, not with oysters), baseball, tennis, *The New Yorker*, travel hats he purchased from the back of *The New Yorker* (which he sometimes wore to baseball games), the pleasures of night skiing with his children on the bunny hill in Rye. He believed, that is, in almost everything but God. He declined to serve the Rotary, and announced the reason why, and after that he was known in Center Effing as the Atheist and his kids were known in school as the Little Atheists.

People said that atheism was a funny line of thinking for a moderate Republican insurance man. Walter said that people were confusing insurance with assurance when, in fact, the two were opposites. If you had assurance, you wouldn't need insurance, and if it was God's plan that your car should be rear-ended in the parking lot at Monsey's, who were you to defray His will through a no-fault auto policy? Did Sodom have homeowner's? Did Mary collect on the death of her son?

Small towns in New England will tolerate the crank, the village irritant, but Vi's father really pushed it. He wouldn't swear an oath or let his children pledge allegiance to the flag. He sat up in the den when his family was asleep, writing on his money, striking out the GOD from IN GOD WE TRUST, lest anybody think that by paying with the slogan he was buying into it, which got him kicked off the bloodmobile and defeated in a landslide for town meeting. People hated standing in the checkout line at the supermarket, opening their wallets and finding a stray five bearing Walter's personal graffiti, IN ~~GOD~~ WE TRUST. The scribble forced them to imagine the chain of small transactions which had put his money in their clothes: Walter pays Mrs. Souza, his kids' piano teacher, giving her the five; Mrs. Souza buys a quart of sherry at Townline Liquorama, paying with the five; someone else buys a case of 'Gansett and gets the bill as change, spending it on pens and gum at Rexall's; the girl at Rexall's gives the bill as change to someone buying God (or ~~God~~) knows what, anal cream or something, and this itchy person spends it on a coffee frappe at Monsey's or at the day-old-bread store on Route 32. Finding a little piece of Walter in one's wallet forced the town to see itself as a set of lives, or one collective chorus-life, consisting of piano teachers, sherry, pens and anal cream, rummy lobstermen drinking 'Gansett on bare mattresses with stains the shape of South America, stains with coastlines and dark interiors. It was bleak somehow, IN ~~GOD~~ WE TRUST, not a welcome vision at the supermarket. Vi knew that her father was never fully satisfied with his altered motto. He did not believe that we trust, or could trust, or should trust, in nothing. Some months after Walter started crossing out the GOD, Vi was at Aulette's with her mother. They were buying nitrates for the Rose of Sharon bushes and Aulette, making change at the register, gave Evelyn a bill which said, IN ~~GOD~~ us WE TRUST.

Aulette said, "Your husband's got a new one, Mrs. A."

Evelyn, embarrassed, went out of there with dignity.

People grumbled Walter's name on every shopping trip, especially the bomber dads (who were good Americans and proud to pledge allegiance), and their children, being children, picked on Jens and Vi. Bullies taunted them at recess, spitting "Pledge a legience!" as the punches flew. Jens took his beatings as a salesman takes rejection, philosophically (removing his glasses, pronouncing himself ready to be hit). Vi, who didn't take a beating, never, anywhere, fought back like a girl, the dirtier the better, kicks and bites and scratches. She fought the bullies of all grades, her brother's and her own, and though she never won these fights, she always got her money's worth. She went for the balls and eyes and lied about it afterwards because, unlike her bookish father, Vi had no morality.

She loved her father simply and completely then. She watched him as astronomers watch stars. She saw him in the house across the marshes from the sea, slippered after dinner in the den, puffing Wild Cherry Borkum Riff, leafing through *The Accident Reporter*, *Shop Safety Monthly*, and the latest OSHA circular. He said the hour after supper was the best time in the world. He said the den was civilization.

Evelyn was in the kitchen, feeding slop to dogs. They always had a pack of dogs, never any cats. They had a dog named Dingo, a string of dogs named Dingo, and when a Dingo died, Vi and Evelyn took the station wagon to the pound behind the dump, picked out another mutt, and named him Dingo too. Jens, the budding scientist, was balled up on the couch, wiping smudges from his glasses, smudging smudges, giving up and going back to whatever he was reading, pop astronomy, titles from the Mathemagic series, a battered *Best of Asimov* overdue from the grown-up library, or the monthly magazine *Ham Radio Today*, to which Jens sent penciled letters correcting the errata of prior writers.

The phone would ring, the dogs would bark. Evelyn would answer at the kitchen sink. Walter was already moving, reaching past Jens for the extension in the den. It was duty on the phone. It was Ligourie the lawyer, Boyle the mortician, the Portsmouth fire marshal, the state police dispatcher, or the morgue. Disasters were average when Vi was growing up. Her father shaved for them. She watched him shave upstairs in the master bath, the care he took about the neck, chin pointing, kissy-lipped. He tied his tie and went out to the car and was usually home again for breakfast the next day.

Jens got all the brains in the family; this was understood and not especially disputed. He was locally considered something of a wonder, a math and physics prodigy. He was often in the Doings section of the *Effing Reveille* under headlines like *Boy Wins Science Prize* and *Jr. Engineers Visit Troubled Seabrook N-Plant*. He loved his radio, a ham-bands-only Hallicrafter with a slide-rule dial. He camped out in the basement, tapping Morse, jotting Morse, the walls covered with his globe-girdling collection of QSLs, postcards hammers sent to hammers verifying contact, *Greetings from JH1VRQ-Tokyo, Cheers from 8P6EU-Barbados*. When other boys were asking Santa for dirt bikes and toy rifles, Jens was asking Walter for a new beat-frequency mixer and a half-dipole antenna.

Vi was seven when they got the powerful antenna. Jens and Walter tried to find a place to rig it. Jens said the roof wasn't high enough and they looked around the yard for an even higher place, baffled by the problem until Major Wade wandered through the trellis from the Coopers' pool. Major Wade was another bomber pilot, Captain Cooper's friend. When Cooper was in Thule, Major Wade's Camaro was often in the Coopers' driveway. Major Wade and Carol Cooper went swimming in the Coopers' pool, did the frug on the lawn, and were always wearing terry cloth.

Major Wade inspected the antenna and the roof. Carol Cooper came over too, carrying a clinking pitcher.

She said to Vi, "Ever taste a whiskey sour, dear?" and dipped a finger in. She wore a zebra swimsuit. Her breasts were true bazooms.

"No," said Vi.

"No thank you," Walter prompted.

Vi drew it out, "No thank you, Mrs. Cooper."

Carol Cooper said, "I wish my goddamn kids were that polite."

Major Wade, having a pilot's mind, saw the answer right away. He started digging through the trunk of his Camaro. He came back with a bow and a quiver full of arrows.

"Keeps me lean," he said, slapping his gut. "Little hobby I picked up in Guam."

"Jesus we're hungover," Carol Cooper said.

The bow had many knobs. Major Wade adjusted them as Walter got a fishing rod. Wade tied the line to an arrow and Walter stood back with the rod. Wade bit his lip, aiming at the highest limb of a tall copper beech in the corner of the Asplunds' yard. Everyone was watching him, Carol Cooper holding Vi by the shoulders, Jens ten feet away, clustered faces on the driveway looking up. The major drew the bow. The fishing line snapped several times and several arrows arched into the woods. Several others landed in the Coopers' yard, in the Coopers' bushes, in the Coopers' pool. The middle Cooper daughter came out and asked what was going on.

Carol Cooper said, "We're shooting at a tree. Go back inside and watch cartoons before you get an arrow in the head."

Major Wade drew the bow and let the arrow fly. It cleared the limb, the reel in Walter's hand was singing, the fishing line went taut, and the arrow fell. They cut the line at the rod, tied it to a rope, tied the rope to a steel cable, and hoisted the antenna to the tree.

Jens discovered weather through his new antenna. He monitored CONEL-RAD, the government's storm-warning band, created in the '50s to spread the word of mushroom clouds. Weather was the ghost of war, Jens said, the marching fronts, the blue high-pressure domes, or maybe it was war's original. A hurricane in Bangladesh killed half a million people, four Hiroshimas. Jens said that a hurricane was like all the nukes going off at once in terms of energy set free and he hoped to see one in the sky above the yard. When Vi was eight, Jens and Walter built a weather-watching shed, a chicken coop on stilts between the garden and the dog-house. Inside the shed was a barometer, a two-foot thermometer, and a double-bulbed device which measured dew point and humidity and was strangely named a psychrometer. On top of the shed was a mast and spinning cups. Vi could see the cups from the window where she slept. When the wind was strong, bowling down the marshes from the Gulf of Maine, the cups would spin into a halo blur.

Jens spent a year waiting for a hurricane. He checked the shed twice a day. He took his readings to the basement, where he puttered with a soldering iron, or stood in the front yard, cradling Evelyn's transistor radio, which he had rewired to pick up the static claps of thunderheads offshore. Vi remembered the summer when he rewired all their radios for practice, Evelyn's bedside AM-FM with the well-worn snoozebar, Walter's old stereophonic monster in the den, the sleek Toshiba at the kitchen sink.

The coup was uncovered in the afternoon. Evelyn was scheduled to lead a walking tour of the see-touch-smell exhibit at the Fort Odiorne Nature Center. She was in the garden, pouring bonemeal on the roses. She looked up and saw the clouds stacking on the harbor. She wondered if the tour might be rain-delayed. She wondered how to dress and whether an umbrella might be called for. She tried the Toshiba, hoping for the weather, and it buzzed—there were no thunderstorms broadcasting at the time. She played the dial and it buzzed. She tried the stereo in the den, the clock radio upstairs. She summoned Walter from the ladder—he was cleaning gutters—and they tried the cars, the station wagon, then Walter's red company LeBaron, hearing the same buzz.

Vi followed them around, getting scared. Why would all the radios fail together? Jens said that in a thermonuclear exchange, the Russians would knock out the Top 40 first. Vi wondered if the Russians had finally attacked—it would have been just like them to destroy the world during school vacation. As her father trolled the dial, sitting in the front seat of his car, Vi imagined cities disappearing. Portsmouth's gone, Nashua is gone—

Walter reassured her. "If the Russians bombed us, Vi, we'd definitely know."

She thought he meant that they would get a call from Ligourie the lawyer or Boyle the mortician. Portsmouth's been irradiated, Walt. Better hustle up there and start adjusting.

Carol Cooper was standing on her diving board in short shorts and a big straw hat, vacuuming her pool.

"See?" said Walter. "Everything is fine."

Vi was nine when her father finally let her go on his adjusting trips. They got up in darkness, preparing for the trips. Vi was in the kitchen, packing sandwiches with Evelyn, luncheon loaf and mayo, an apple for each bag. Walter was upstairs, ironing a crease into his pants. Jens was in his room, hunting for a missing sneaker, half asleep. Walter found him in the closet, curled up among the shoes, and led him like a blind man down the stairs. Vi watched her brother fake his way through breakfast, a fork clutched in his lap, one eye slowly closing, the other eye a slit, his black hair sticking up, a head of exclamation points, his face sleep-dopey and unpunctuated. Evelyn told Jens to eat something. Jens went through the motions, lifting a glass of juice to his nose, biting his waffle, but not chewing. The waffle bite would still be in his mouth as they backed down the driveway, following the inland shore of the heart-shaped marsh, a curve of misty streetlights to I-95. Fifty miles later, heading to Berlin as the sun was coming up, Vi would hear Jens chewing waffle in the front seat and know that he was finally awake.

They went everywhere one summer. They covered the whole state, stopping off in county seats and depot towns. Vi at nine saw things she didn't understand—a farmhand with one foot, a school without a roof, a golf pro dead from lightning, still grasping the flag.

They saw a paper train derailed outside Berlin. It was timber country up there on the border with Quebec. Berlin was a pulping town, her father said. The wood came in as trees or logs and left as paper by the ton, rolling south along a spur to the Gorham switches. The system went in two directions after that, east along a stony river into Maine or through the mountain notches to St. Johnsbury, Vermont.

It was hot that day. Jens sat in the front seat of Walter's car, counting seven jackknifed flatcars with his finger, until he couldn't see past them to the rest. Vi leaned out the window. She saw giant reams of paper unrolled to where they stopped, paper in the gully, on the dirt road, in the woods.

Walter stood on the embankment with the men and mangled train. The men wore suits and ties, or sheriff's uniforms, or dressed like they worked on the trains. They smoked and spat and pushed their hats back. One of them looked up the tracks and said it was a doozie.

The others said, "Uh-*huh*," and "That's a fact."

A man in a white suit said, "What do you think, Walter?" This man was the superintendent of the line. He had flown up from the Maine Central yard in Portland in a bubble helicopter—Vi was totally impressed—yet even this man waited on her father. Walter Asplund had adjusted most of the noteworthy damage around here going back twenty years and was known to be a reasonable man. He didn't say too much, but when he spoke he spoke for The Connecticut.

The super said, "What are we looking at, you think?"

Walter was looking at the paper in the woods. He said, "You got the fees and spoilage, the rolling stock—"

"Total write-off," someone said.

"Mm-*hm*," the others said.

"Two men hurt," the super said. "One fatally. Don't forget."

Walter saw it all. He would not be rushed, he would not forget. He sidestepped down the bank, laid his suit coat on the front seat of the car.

"You kids okay?"

Vi said, "We're okay."

Jens said, "What happened, Dad?"

Walter stood by the door, unbuttoning his shirt cuffs with a dainty plucking motion. "Not too hot in there?"

Vi said, "We're okay."

He rolled his sleeves up, took his time. The men were watching him.

He said, "Let me know if you get too hot. Dogs die in overheated cars, you know."

The trunk was loaded with the tools of his profession: a bulky camera with a flash, a hundred feet of tape, a wheel on a stick that also measured distance, an adding machine with a roll of paper, spare rolls of paper, a manual typewriter, a bag of flares and stakes, ledger paper, carbon paper, many pads of legal forms, a reel-to-reel recorder, coiled rope, a notary stamp, and a wide flat book, maroon leather, embossed in gold THE CONNECTICUT. Inside the book were blank checks the color of the ocean on a map. The book in the trunk was power. A check from the book was called a settlement. This was what adjusters did, settle or not settle or settle partially, after taking pictures and measuring distances and interviewing witnesses in county seats and depot towns, at train wrecks in the north. Vi felt the bounce as he shut the trunk.

Coming back from Walter's trips, they always stopped at the Boyles' house. Phil Boyle was a man about her father's age, a prosperous mortician-politician, a pillar in his parish and a power in the town. The Boyles lived above their mortuary, a mansard rampart fortress on the shady, stonewalled corner of Main and Derry Turnpike. In the summer, Walter and Phil Boyle would sit out back at the picnic table, drinking coffee in their shirtsleeves. They would talk about the things they had in common, family, taxes, politics. Boyle the mortician was her father's closest friend, but he always frightened Vi. His hair was black, his suits were black, his winter hats were Homburgs, black, and his hands were long and liver-spotted gray. He always smelled like flowers and he took his coffee black, stirring for no reason Vi could see, the memory of milk, and even the insects were afraid of him. He had served a term for the machine in the state legislature, the lower house, and even in high hatching season, with the salt pond through the pines, Vi never saw him swat at even one blackfly. She believed that he was death itself, living in her town. She stayed by her father on their visits, protecting him from Boyle's undertow.

Jens stayed in the car, reading *Mathemagic*, or he ventured out and stood on the edge of the long driveway, watching Boyle's sons play H-O-R-S-E against the three-hearse garage. Boyle had four sons, scrappy, loud, athletic boys, groomed and destined to be preppy undertakers. The Boyle boys played H-O-R-S-E and many variations, S-M-E-G-M-A, M-U-C-U-S, S-P-U-T-U-M—being sons of a mortician, they had an interest in effluvia and knew all the latest gross-out words. Jens, standing on the grass, watched the active Boyle boys. Jens looked like a Martian, like an aphid, like another life form altogether.

Peta Boyle was the mortician's daughter, a year ahead of Vi in school. Peta's full name was Petulia Marguerite, but if you called her anything but Pet (her family nickname) or Peta (as in, pet a pet), she was apt to call you something nasty back. Vi and Peta ran through sprinklers or played hide-and-seek.

The oak tree by the table was their counting place. Vi would shut her eyes and kiss the bark as Peta hid. Vi counted, *One one-thousand, two one-thousand, three one-thousand*, nonsense numbers used by children not to measure time, but to pass it. It took a second to say one-thousand, roughly equal to a Mississippi. Peta in her yellow dress slipped between the trees. She was never any good at hiding. Vi knew even as she counted (*six one-thousand, seven—*) that Peta would hide behind the metal garden shed. Vi finds her without trying, and now Peta's kissing bark, *one one-thousand, two one-thousand*. Peta searches down the yard, but Vi's already gone and now Peta's crying in the doorway of the shed. Boyle's boys are fighting, who's a S-M-E-G and who's a S-M-E-G-M. Jens hikes, slope-shouldered, up the drive, as the fathers talk about their common things, business, children, politics, undertaking, underwriting.

Vi traveled with her father in the summer and when school was out. She remembered paper trains and tractor-trailers overturned, but of all the things she saw, the fires in the houses made the permanent impression. It was always a slum bungalow by the harbor in the town. Lobstermen lived back there. Coming up the street in her father's car, Vi saw the wooden parlor traps stacked in the backyards for the winter, the trap-towers bigger than the houses.

It was always Christmas, always cold, and the fires always started in the plug behind the tree. What the fire didn't total, the firefighters did, with their boots and pikes and high-pressure hoses. Vi and her father usually arrived after the fire marshals had declared the fire out. By then, the water-slurry-foam, dripping from the eaves and the bare trees in the street, had frozen into huge smooth cookie-batter oozes, rounded, sparkling, fanciful, a wonderland in what was once the family room. They toured the ground floor with a flashlight and a magic guide named

Mullen from the county arson squad. Not that this was arson or suspicious-origin. Mullen pointed to the dangling remains of the wall outlet, noting the char-path to the stairs, black and straight, like a road. Fires are intelligent. They process information. Where is air? Where is fuel? They burn and decide. They act and choose a path.

Mullen had a scratchy cough and offered them Sucrets. He took one for himself and said the kids' rooms were closest to the landing on the stairs, one of them's at Shriners, the other one's okay. Mullen said the tree, the creche, all the window candles, and a motorized reindeer on the lawn were pulling power through extensions from the plug behind the tree, that one there—see it, Walt? Clearly fiddled with, goddamn do-it-yourselfers. Note the tool marks on the wall, wires probably heated. The drapes were made of rayon and the tree was dry.

"Poof," said Mullen quietly.

Walter asked for light. Mullen put the beam on the tool marks. Walter took a picture with a flash.

This was Christmas, growing up—a restless week away from school, the whole town snowbound, the beaches battered, empty.

Walter in the den wore his cardigan. He hunted through the dial for a single station not playing Perry Como Christmas hits.

Evelyn was in the kitchen, slow-basting a pork loin. She said, "Oh for Pete's sake, Walt, get off your high horse. Let's have a carol, just this once. It's Christmas and the melodies are pretty."

Vi stood on a chair at the kitchen table, pushing cookie cutters into dough, first circles and then stars. Jens was on the shoveled driveway, trying to enlist one of the Dingos in a game of fetch. Jens threw a tennis ball. Dingo watched it bounce away. Jens chased the ball and threw again. Dingo loved this game.

Evelyn sang along with Perry Como. *Hark! The herald angels sing glory to the newborn king...*

Her voice was light and high and surprisingly pretty. She said, "It brings me back to dear old Braintree. Push a little harder, Vi."

Vi's mother was a Randle from Braintree, Massachusetts, and Dear Old Braintree was a phrase she used to indicate a world, Boston's lost South Shore of 1951. Every family had a maid, dinner was at six, potatoes were ubiquitous and mashed.

Every mother wore a fur and every father took the Boston-Maine, which they never called the B&M, sounded smelly somehow, and Vi's Grampa Randle manned the fearless masthead of the town newspaper, battling corruption and cupidity not just in Braintree but in Hingham too.

Walter said, "It's a song about singing about nonsense. Why would it bring you anywhere?"

Evelyn was talking to her daughter now. "We used to sing those songs, Vi. I remember standing on the green with my Walker cousins. I remember Dolly Davis at the dancing school. I remember going shopping with my mother at Filene's. Their Santa was an Irish drunk, poor wretch, probably had a shameful secret on his conscience. Mother took me on the train and did it snow. They had to send a special train to get us, Vi. Us, of course, being every Tom, Dick, and Harry stranded on the platform at South Station, but secretly I thought the train had come for me. We filed on, Mother and I, with boxes for my brothers and a special box for me. Didn't know what was in it. Suspected tap shoes. Dreaded that. The train they sent was wonderful, great curved plates in front, like an ocean liner's prow, and this other thing, a huge caged fan, bigger than our car, like an ocean liner's screw. What was this special train? A ship on land with its propeller on the front, and we *blew* through the snow, and Father picked us up, and I remember how warm it was, the kitchen."

Vi said, "What was in the box?"

"A muffler," said Evelyn. "The kind you wear around your neck."

They heard Jens out back shouting, "You stupid goddamn dog."

Walter suffered Perry Como in the den. He said, "The melodies are pretty, but the words—they ruin it for me."

Evelyn said, "Don't listen to the words."

There was silence for a time as Walter tried. He called around the corner, "How the hell do you do that?"

They ate the loin for supper, bowing their heads as Walter read a short reflection by Mr. H. G. Wells. Later they opened gifts, which Walter said was their way of honoring the dignity of humankind.

"Whoop-de-doo," said Evelyn, raising her wineglass in a sarcastic toast.

Vi knew the truth—it was Jesus getting born. She had heard this from Peta Boyle, who wore a kilt to school.

Walter said that Jesus was a cherished symbol of the dignity of humankind. Peta said that Jesus was the biggest baby ever.

The day they saw the paper train derailed outside Berlin was the last insurance trip Jens ever went on. He was thirteen that year, the age when children splinter off and abandon the old loves. Jens abandoned his old loves together in a week, ham radio and hurricanes, playing ball with dogs, riding to disasters with his sister and his dad. His new love was a beaker storage closet in the science lab at Center Effing High where the teachers kept a slow acoustic modem which connected Jens to a Hexatron 1000 timeshare mainframe donated to the high school by a company in town. The rig was obsolete even then, but Jens was changed forever. He ran models of the Big Bang (which was, he told Vi, like a train wreck in the sky, vast and long ago, zillions of times bigger than all hurricanes combined). He played Zorc and Space War down the phone lines with his friends and came across a book on how to program in Beginning Glyph, which was, he said, a computer language, like logic or like math, except it's language, it's you telling the computer what to do. He spent a summer getting paler in the beaker storage closet. He came out in September with his masterpiece, a program he called JENSISNUMBER1.exe, which caused a distant printer to spit out the sentence *JENS IS NUMBER 1!!!!!!!!!!!!!*

He went on to bigger things from there. He learned COBOL, FORTRAN, C, the upper dialects of Glyph. He built his own computer from a kit, sold his Hallicrafter and his weather instruments to buy a faster modem, and would probably have taken his computer to the prom if he had even noticed that the high school had a prom. He went to high school two years early. At seventeen, he went to Dartmouth, Walter's alma mater, Walter's father's before that, the official college of male Asplunds in New Hampshire. Jens went to Dartmouth dreaming of inventions, of writing software that would change the world. Someday they would speak of the giants of computer science, Ada Lovelace, Alan Turing, Dennis Ritchie at Bell Labs, and Jens Asplund, father of the Jensatronic hyper-object language. Vi, who knew nothing about software except you couldn't wear it, was glad enough to move her stuff to Jens' empty bedroom, which was bigger and closer to the john.

When her brother went away, Vi was into other, less momentous things, basketball and soccer, tan lines at the town beach, and a lifeguard in the tower who was sixteen and too gorgeous to approach. That was the last year Vi went on insurance trips with Walter.

A cool October night, a town near Lebanon, New Hampshire, a small cement plant by the railroad tracks. Eight employees sat on vinyl chairs waiting to be interviewed by Walter and a man from the Byrnes Detective Agency in Boston. Whispers in the office. Money's missing, two grand and change. The employees readjust the blinds, smoke and push their butts into stand-up ashtrays. The town is the cement plant, the cement plant is the town, and these people have lived here all their lives, but by the close of business one of them will be exposed as an embezzler and his life in town will end. Vi watched her father find a plug for his tape recorder.

She remembered driving home that night. They saw the outline of the mountains and the stars. Her father kept it right at fifty-five.

He said, "From time to time, those cement plants explode. Especially the older ones. It's due to inadequate ventilation. There was a horrible accident in Nashua once. Six men killed, a slew injured—first million-dollar loss I ever handled for the firm. Horrible. They thought some men were buried in the rubble. They listened to the ground with stethoscopes and tubes. They asked for total silence on the scene. Your mother was expecting, two weeks overdue. I called her from a pay phone and she said, 'Come home. I feel a little woozy, Walt.' That wooziness was you, Vi, saying you were on the way, but I couldn't leave the accident. Stethoscopes and tubes—they listened through the night. They asked us to give blood. We lined up in total silence."

He looked worn out, driving home from Lebanon. Vi remembered thinking, he is old.

"Small office frauds are the worst," he said. "The pettiness, the fear, the cheap dishonesty. Doesn't make you hopeful for the species, no. Give me an explosion any day."

2

One day about eighteen months ago, Vi was driving up I-95, thinking of these things, the saltbox on Santasket Road, the child's little world, the Coopers and the Buckerts, Vi's mother in the garden pruning roses, her father in the den with his insurance journals. Exit signs were floating by, Hampton, Exeter, Eatontown, and Rye. It was a summer weekend in July. Summer meant the beaches and the beaches would mean crowds, heavy traffic on the coast road up from Gloucester into Maine. Knowing this, Vi stayed on 95.

She was twenty-five years old, a single woman living in New Jersey, working for the Secret Service in New York, Criminal Division, Treasury Enforcement. Her squad did counter-counterfeiting, though, as a trainee agent, she did everything, the scutwork of the station, long rolling tails, prisoner transport, petty counterfeiting stings, credit cards, cloned cell phones, fake ID, routine death-threat follow-up, interview a madman, finalize the time sheets, memo to the file, hot dogs in the street. She was a private in the infantry of fed-dom, a GS-5, one civil service notch above a common letter carrier, which was probably closer to the glamour level of her job.

She stopped for gas at a landscaped Mobil on the pike in Rye. She pumped it at self-serve, standing by her car, a primer-painted Bug with the ugly mustard plates of the Garden State, a gym bag and a basketball in the backseat. She wore rope sandals and a sundress and her cool Israeli shades. Her duty weapon, a Glock nine, was in her purse. The purse hung from her shoulder (a new habit—keep the gun nearby; if you lost it you were in for lengthy bureaucratic water torture, a zillion lost vacation days, and a letter from the ASAC to your file). She tapped her foot, pumped her gas, blew a bubble with her gum, pushed her shades back up her nose. The sun was hot. Traffic passed, generating breeze.

She saw two guys in a jeep with a jet ski on a trailer. The guys were putting air in the tires of the jeep. They were college boys, tank-topped, ball-capped, zinc sun-block on their noses. She saw them check her out, the sidelong glance, the nudge, babe in shades at two o'clock, or whatever was the lingo at their frat. She wasn't that much older than the guys, but she felt ancient, pumping gas.

She paid in cash and drove away. Vi didn't see herself as pretty or not pretty, though she knew that most people would have said that she was reasonably pretty. She was small and strong, an honest tomboy blond, many kinds of blond, in fact, depending on the time of year—dingy in the winter months, like a head of roadside snow, shocking corn silk in July. She had unusual gray eyes, bright and deeply gray, which made her look in winter, with the paleness in her face, a bit like Death's kid sister, the one who's always tagging along and whining for a turn, getting on Death's nerves. In the summer, with a tan on and the corn silk in her hair, the gray eyes made her kind of beautiful. It was a funny thing, her father always said, that the sun, so busy with its cosmic projects, would stop to touch his daughter in this way.

She was crying now, snot flowing out her nose. She took the exit down the hill into C.E. She had come to see her mother and her brother, to deal with the arrangements, half family and half finance, which always crop up when a father dies.

She couldn't go home crying. She drove around the rotary, past the brief commercial strip, Starbucks, Ben & Jerry's, the Easy Reader Bookstore (Deepak Chopra in the window), thank God they haven't closed down Monsey's Luncheonette. She parked along the chain-link fence at the cracked and sunbaked courts behind the purple sticker beach. Purple sticker meant town residents only. She didn't have a sticker but she had a fairly impressive Secret Service placard for her dash and a couple of the younger village cops were former high school boyfriends, guys she knew from sports. She figured she could park here long enough to get herself together.

Late morning on a Saturday. The beach beyond the fence was white. The families on the sand were townies, even whiter, dads with hairy backs, moms with cellulite, shrieking kids with blow-up water wings. The harbor was a cup between two rocky points. The ocean was a blue slap to the eyes. How she loved this coastline in July.

She wiped her eyes to see it clearly. She grabbed the basketball from the backseat of the Bug and walked around the fence to the foul line. Even in a messy state, she had the rolling, open-challenge walk of a woman who had once been very good at something physical. She was pretty good at racquet sports—squash in college, tennis with her father growing up (he played a stiff, stay-at-home, rally-from-the-baseline game; she beat him once at fourteen and after fifteen never lost), paddleball in New York (the agents in Manhattan played a lot of paddleball). She was a strong swimmer, a double-diamond skier, a high school soccer striker, an effortless ten-handicap in golf, but her top sport—growing up, in college, all along—was basketball. She had played in the summer as a kid, pickup games right here, three on three all afternoon, shifting groups of shirts and skins. She was always shirts and the only girl. She didn't have the size to post up or go down the lane, but she had quick hands, stamina, and an intercontinental jumper. She played CYO and rec league, summer nights and fall. She played for Effing High and later UNH. Her lack of height and leap caught up to her in college, where she rode the bench, coming in for garbage time, New Hampshire down by thirty-five to mighty UConn. Vi went for 0–1, picked up two assists, and hard-fouled this obnoxious power forward, and none of it meant anything.

She had joined the Service after UNH, seeking something difficult and pure. She went through basic agent's school at Glynco, Georgia, which was supposed to be like boot camp, calisthenics in the dawn, running by platoons while the DIs scream at you, sit-ups till you throw up, that whole aesthetic. The other recruits at Glynco were a mix of law school dropouts, recent Army dischargees, the kids of Secret Service dads, and backwoods deputies who wanted to be feds. They had PT every morning, classes until lunch, PT and more classes until five, evening meal and study hall until lights-out in the dorm. Everybody would be aching from the day, but Vi would bounce a basketball over to the gym and shoot around alone, trying to burn off enough energy to sleep. Vi graduated seventh in a class of twenty-seven, and was sent to New York station for a Crim Division tour.

Vi stood on the court behind the beach, the basketball tucked under her arm. She kicked her sandals off, laid her shades in one of them. She juked left, took a shot, head-faked, took a fall-away, sundress flying, bare feet slapping on the asphalt. She clanged three balls and aired the rest—her timing was for shit. She walked to center court, a white circle faded by the sun. The court was hot where it was black, but cool enough to stand on in the circle.

It was time to face Evelyn and Jens. Vi bounced the ball, hard dribbling. It was comforting, the timing and the smooth against her palm, again, again, the sound that everybody knows, basketball on asphalt, a rubberized cry, *sprain, sprain, sprain.*

It was hard for Vi to think of Jens as an adult, as a husband and a father, yet there he was on the lawn with his wife, Peta Boyle, and their son, Kai Boyle-Asplund.

"Vi," said Jens as he hugged his sister on the lawn.

"Vi," said Peta as they hugged. "I am so so sorry."

Jens had married Peta Boyle, the rich mortician's daughter, in the granite parish on the rotary downtown, a good match everybody thought. Jens, though a talented computer scientist, was scattered and erratic. Peta, an ambitious village realtor, was sturdy, warm, and sensible; she remembered birthdays, cried at sappy movies, and knew how to change the spark plugs in her car. The wedding had been Catholic to placate Peta's family. Jens was a nothing, religiously, not even a systematic atheist, and Peta, a realtor at Moss Properties in Portsmouth, went to mass at Easter for the choir. Because they didn't care, Jens and Peta had been willing to be married by a priest—if this would keep the peace, why not? Their son, Kai, had been baptized for the same reason. Do you reject Satan? Yes, said Jens for Kai. Salt on the tongue, cross of oil on the forehead, water in the baby's eyes—Jens sent Vi a funny e-mail later about how weird it was.

Vi went in the house with Jens, Peta, and their son. In the front hall, she saw her father's tennis shoes parked under the radiator, smelled his pipe smoke in the drapes, the Wild Cherry Borkum Riff—it was the only wild thing about her dad.

She spent a weekend in New Hampshire that July, beetles zzzzzing in the trees, marshes blooming almost purple, Vi sitting Yankee-style *shiva* in the kitchen with her mother. The house seemed crowded the whole time. Jens was bustling around, being strong for everyone, annoying Vi no end. Peta did the cooking, coffee, sandwiches, lasagna, which, at least, was useful. The dogs were in, the dogs were out, the dogs were getting at the food. Kai teetered through the living room, or played with pots at Peta's feet, then fell asleep upstairs on what had been Jens' bed. Boyle the mortician, Peta's somber father and Walter's closest friend, was around the house, making arrangements for cremation, pursuant to the will. Other people stopped by or called, friends and neighbors, former neighbors, a rep from The Connecticut, Mullen from the arson squad (who ate a sandwich from the platter and told Vi that no one could read scorch marks like her father). In the kitchen, Evelyn kept telling the story of the morning Walter died—how she got up, saw him lying there, head under the pillow, how she let him sleep, assumed he was asleep, how she ran her errands, came home before lunch, saw him in the pillows, how she touched his shoulder, what she knew. Then the phone would ring, or someone else would stop by, and she would start telling it again.

Vi took frequent walks to get some air. Early Sunday morning, she took a long run through the sandy trails of the state forest. When she got back, Jens was in the basement, going through old boxes, Walter's archives from The Connecticut. Jens went through the boxes slowly, file after file, reading them and tossing them into a large garbage bag.

He said, "It's therapeutic. Want to help?"

Vi didn't want to help, but she sat on the stairs and talked to Jens about his work as a software engineer. He wrote patches and utilities for a start-up in West Portsmouth called BigIf, a massive multiplayer war game on the Web.

Jens opened a folder—pictures of assorted fatal auto accidents from 1968 or so, smashed-up Cadillacs, big dented Impalas. "These are great," said Jens. "Everyone looks drugged up but the troopers." He tossed the file in the bag. "We're going public soon. BigIf is, I mean."

Vi shot water from a bottle down her throat. "That's a good thing, right?"

"That's a great thing, Vi. I'll cash out and be comfortable for life. Have you played it, the game?"

Vi had logged on to BigIf one night in New York out of loyalty to Jens. The game—or the parts of it Vi saw—looked like a giant livid desert with little cartoon people moving through it. The cartoons represented humans, teenaged paid subscribers, coming in by modem from around the world. They moved in silent, shuffling processions or milled around a deep smoking crater. There were also monsters in the desert, man-sized rats, feral dogs, vicious, spitting cats, which popped up like the targets at a shooting gallery. When a monster appeared, the cartoons ran in a herky-jerky panic, a slow stampede across the screen. Some players stood their ground and died, others fought and killed the monsters in a gory spectacle. Or this, at least, was what Vi saw in the first twenty seconds.

"I didn't get to see too much," she said. "A rat ate me."

Jens said, "Hamster. That monster model's name is Hamsterman. He's not a rat. I would never write a rat."

"Did you write the hamster?"

"I wrote his software, sure, his decision trees. That's my department—monster logic."

Vi remembered Jens at thirteen, emerging in pale triumph from the beaker storage closet, bearing his first program, JENSISNUMBER1, and later, after Dartmouth, the fellowship at Harvard, and a Ph.D. abandoned, several jobs in AI and robotics, each one a fresh start for Jens, each one the real deal (he said at the time). He lived as a grad student all those years, owning nothing more than a racing bike, a Frisbee, a backpack full of books, and a laundry load's worth of clothes. Then he married Peta Boyle. He decided, they decided, to get pregnant, buy a condo, to go corporate and succeed, and now Jens wrote monster logic at BigIf. There was a whiff of sellout and lost promise about Vi's brother. The sad thing was he smelled it too.

Vi said, "Are you happy doing that?"

"The technology is cool, state of the art. Our main software shell is eighteen million lines of beautiful cold code. It's the *Finnegans Wake* of software, Vi, except it's longer and more complicated than *Finnegans Wake*, and I wrote a good part of it. I used to think I was a genius, now I know I am. Smile, little sister, that's a joke."

"I didn't like your game," said Vi.

"Really, why? Because it's violent, cheesy, and appalling? That's just what you see. If you could see the source code, the logic of the monsters, you'd see that it was beautiful. Am I happy? When I'm creating a cool application, a sweet design, I'm happy because I don't have to think about What It All Means. I left that to Walter, my self-appointed conscience. You should've heard him on the subject of the game. 'BigIf is immoral, Jens—worse, it's amoral.' Nice distinction, Dad. Am I happy? I'll be happy when we go IPO. I'll be happy when I'm comfortable for life. Hey, check it out—"

An envelope had fallen from one of the files. In the envelope was a dollar bill, one of Walter's specials. The bill said, IN US WE TRUST.

Jens held it to the light. "Incredible," he said. "And to think"—he looked at Vi—"the man was a Republican."

Vi reached for the bill in Jens' hand.

"It's just a dollar, Vi. Do you need gas money, is that it? Jesus, don't they pay you in the Secret Service?"

Vi said, "I want it."

"Why?"

She took the bill from him. She said, "I just do."

Walter Asplund's will included instructions for cremation and a scattering at sea, a location specified by longitude and latitude, minutes and degrees. Boyle the mortician handled the cremation, delivering the urn to Jens and Vi.

They hired a pilot and a plane at the county airport, Monday morning. They flew out to the designated square of open ocean, a few miles off the coast. Jens opened the side window in the Piper Cub, brought the urn up from between his knees. Vi helped him tip it empty. They pushed the urn out too and watched it tumble to the blue.

3

That fall in Manhattan, Vi played basketball on Monday nights, a lawyers' league basi-cally, the 2-3 up to Chelsea and the Y, law firm against law firm, the lady DAs, the U.S. Attorneys. There was always lots of cheating and cheap fouls, lots of trash talk, lots of ringers (black girls from Christ the King in Queens, willowy and deadly, hired by the hired guns). There was no Secret Service team, so Vi played for Customs.

She was living in Hoboken, two bedrooms over a karate school, next to a bar called the Blarney Castle. Her roommate in Hoboken was her teammate from the Y, a Customs agent named Dawn Imperiali, another rookie out-of-towner (Dawn came from Dearborn, Michigan). They got up early, took the Hudson ferry to the World Financial Center, then walked up to Federal Plaza, unless Dawn had airport duty and had to drive out to JFK.

Vi spent three years in New York station, before and after Walter's death. She learned to love the early ferry in the summer, the Hudson peaceful in the heat, the walk up Broadway to Fed Plaza. She'd come in from a long surveillance, a day in a sedan, tailing John Doe Russians out to Nassau. She wore blue jeans and crosstrain-ers, a sleeveless cotton blouse with little roses on it, and a five-buck Yankee hat from a Chinese pushcart guy. She carried a black nylon briefcase (walkie-talkie, Glock, 40x binox, and a garlic bagel she had forgotten to eat).

Fed Plaza was a mass of slab and glass on lower Broadway. Every agency had an outpost at the Plaz, FBI, ATF, DEA, IRS, and the volume people-movers, Labor, Housing, Immigration, Social Security. On any weekday the broad lobby of the Plaz was full of wounded humans, the slag of the economy, single mothers, washer-women, refugees ashore, clients of the state who rarely went to office buildings and didn't understand how to navigate the signage. The signs were mounted overhead, airport-style pictograms with arrows, pay phones to the left, rest rooms to the right,

Information straight ahead. The symbol for Information was a *?* The arrow meaning straight ahead pointed straight up.

Whenever Vi crossed the lobby, coming in or going out, she was accosted by the old, the alien, the lame. They were almost always women, asking for directions in semi-English or through their sometimes beautiful and also thuggish sons, dragged along as translators—

"Where is Room 2000?"

"Try the second floor."

"Where is Mr. Crenshaw?"

"What agency is he?"

A shrug. "He is Crenshaw."

"Yes, but who's he with? Welfare? Immigration? What's the nature of your problem?"

—a dangerously open-ended question, which the clients could answer only by recounting the entire sequence of events which had brought them to this lobby, going back to the asbestos in the Brooklyn Navy Yard, Sinatra and the war, or a journey in an open boat from Haiti, the story always turning on some dumbfounding blunder or coincidence involving four changes of address, garbled doctor's orders, and a disconnected phone, which was why they never got the Notice of Hearing and Termination, or the Second or the Third, or any of the notices, until they got the Final Notice, a form postcard from somebody named Herbert Crenshaw, Hearing Officer, who only heard the Final Notice people. The clients showed Vi the postcard, thumbed and folded, or totally pristine, as if they had carried it in plastic all these weeks as a true communication from the Mister Crenshaw man.

Vi listened as the women gulped from respirators or paused to let their sons catch up with the translation. They finished the history of the Final Notice, insisting that Vi listen to all of it, because if she only heard one part and not the rest, the part she heard would make no sense. They would finish and the sons would finish translating.

The mothers looked at Vi expectantly. "Please where is the Crenshaw?"

When Vi was new to New York, she did her best to help. She'd be going out on routine threats, a warrant, or a vehicle surveillance, leaving with other agents from the counter-counterfeiting squad. These agents were largely interchangeable, buck rookies, past fuckups, middle managers. Her group supervisor, a GS-9 named Rocky Panofsky, organized the annual all-law-enforcement charity golf outing at the Fresh Kills Country Club Marina, Service versus FBI, DEA, and Customs, and everybody tried to beat the prosecutors. Rocky spent the year organizing a smooth and perfect afternoon of golf and gag awards, then went into a month-long funk of purpose-lessness, then roused himself and started organizing the outing for the coming year. Rocky and the other grunts would wait for Vi, who waited for the mother to gulp from a respirator, or the mother waited for her bored thug-angel son to translate some crucial bridge of information. If Vi stopped to help, other people saw her fielding queries and stopped to ask their questions too. Lines formed in front of Vi, as Rocky tapped his foot—

"Are these the elevators?"

"Where is Fish & Wildlife?"

"Is jury duty over there?"

"Miss please green stamps." A fleshy woman of indefinite ethnicity. Russian? Polish? Byelorussian?

Vi said, "Green stamps? I don't think the government does green stamps, ma'am. The nearest supermarket would be Greenwich Street."

"Please no foot," said the woman. "Foot foot foot stamps. I wish to apply myself today."

"Do you mean food stamps, lady?"

"But they say they cannot give me without green card."

Rocky broke in. "She can't help you, Mama."

The woman looked at Rocky. "Does she know who can?"

When Vi was finally free of the women, she would follow her colleagues to the cars.

"Foot foot foot stamps," said Rocky on the sidewalk. "Now I've heard every-thing."

He offered to show Vi his personal technique for blowing off the questioners, which involved grandly sweeping past, or pausing, as he sometimes did, and giving people looking for the Labor Board precise and accurate directions to the mouth of the Holland Tunnel.

They had a cycle in the Crim Division, not unlike the rhythms of a farm. Monday was for admin, routine death threat paperwork, and, after work, a subway ride to Chelsea and the Y. Tuesday was for prisoner transport, Vi at the wheel of a sixteen-seat Dodge Ram, two junkie chicks in back. Wednesday was for phony hundred-dollar bills, fake credit cards, cloned phones. Thursday was for everything they didn't finish Wednesday. Friday was an early exit for Long Island, where most of the office lived.

Threats arrived by UPS, Monday after lunch. Vi would come up from the street, burping from an ill-advised knish, and find the box sitting in her chair. The threats took every form, cards and letters, e-mails, voice mails, downloads from the Web, graffiti seen by passersby, cell phone interceptions from the satellites, flyers found in Texas gutters, things informants in Bahrain said they overhead, rumor, claptrap, speculation, bullshit, hatred, mental illness—

I will kill the president.

I will kill his Mrs.

Mr. X will take 'em down.

I heard the two men talking at a HoJo's, sir, in Harriman, and later I saw them in the parking lot with rifles—

The threats were pooled in Beltsville, Maryland, where analysts graded them from one to six for coherence, specificity, and overall heft. Ones and twos were generally handled by specialists from Beltsville. The rest, deemed random, wacky, or far-fetched, were routed to the district of origination for any appropriate follow-up.

Vi learned to judge the dreck threats from the envelopes they came in. The addresses were often sketchy, like a wild guess, WHITE HOUSE WASHINGTON, not even *The* White House, which always lost you points in Beltsville. The letters were sometimes direct —

Dear Presadent Sir

    You WILL "<u>DIE</u>." at 6:02 in the Morning on May 4th this year by GUN

       Sincerely,

             Leticia (Gomez) Jones

             Yonkers, NY

Others were harrowing accounts of persecution at the hands of Jews, Nazis, Jesuits. Every threat, even the sad and hapless sixes, required follow-up, some gesture of investigation, and this was how Vi spent her Monday afternoons, visiting nursing homes, trailer towns, half-closed state asylums, hand-delivering an oddly formal notice to the effect that threatening the safety of a protectee was a five-year felony under Title 18 of the United States Criminal Code.

She drove up to Harriman, the HoJo's on the thruway, and interviewed a waitress named Yvette who remembered the two men distinctly, the muddy 4x4 they drove. One ordered flapjacks with pineapple syrup, the other had the steakwich with the flapjacks on the side. They read the paper, yet another presidential scandal, shook their heads and said somebody ought to pop the fucking guy, put him out of our misery, they said, and laughed and ate their flapjacks. Vi interviewed Yvette at the waitress station, noting their wording, drove back to the city, and filed a report on two Caucasian males of stocky build who read the paper over breakfast and carried rifles in deer season. Most threats were like the HoJo's trip, a ripple not a fish, and half the day wasted. Vi followed threats to the point of peter-out, which was also something like infinity.

She remembered, too, a balding boy of thirty-four who signed his letters *Eric Harold Engelbrecht,* as if bucking for the three-name treatment traditionally reserved for killers of the famous. His labored-over letter was a work of many drafts, studded with references to Jefferson and scripture, the tree of liberty, the whore of Babylon. The threat was mailed from Ozone Park, addressed to ex–first lady Nancy Reagan, no city and no zip, *C/O The USA,* which the Postal Service somehow took to mean the White House. Vi skimmed Eric's letter, a crowded saga of narco-terrorists and CIA intrigue, signals beamed from Brooklyn to his brain. She flipped ahead. Several malicious misdiagnoses, rumors spread against him, a plague of staph infections. She flipped ahead. An investigation mounted, the conspiracy traced back to the China Lobby, certain unknown colonels, and the Reagans. Eric's letter had been time-stamped in the White House mailroom, stamped again by the standing detail at 1600, stamped *Rec'd Assessment Center Beltsville,* deemed nonsensitive, graded five, boxed to UPS, stamped finally by Vi's receptionist out front.

Eric Harold Engelbrecht lived with his grandmother on Cross Bay Boulevard. Vi drove out to Queens, returning the letter to the sender, like a postman in reverse.

The grandmother smoked extra-long cigarettes, the kind they called 100s. She offered Vi a lemonade. Vi took the glass and an old Mets coaster. Ron Darling smiled up at her. They didn't entertain a lot, she guessed. Vi looked around the living room, plastic on the furniture, a piano with sheet music, rocks in the aquarium, goldfish swimming circles in the murk.

The grandmother said, "Has Eric been scaring that Paltrow girl again? Her lawyers were so pleasant. I think I kept a copy of the restraining order."

Vi said, "We don't do celebrities, Mrs. Engelbrecht," and explained about the China Lobby.

Vi waited in the living room as the grandmother lured Eric down the stairs. He wore a clean white golf shirt buttoned to his throat and a bicycle helmet lined with crinkly tinfoil.

"Don't usually let him wear the hat," the grandmother said. "Not for company anyhow, but he'd be scared of you without it."

Eric seemed plenty scared as it was, sitting on the sofa, hands between his knees, knees together, each part of him shaking differently.

Vi said, "Hello, Eric. I'm with the Secret Service." She flipped her creds at him, slipped them in her jacket, then delivered the statutory warning, a letter passed across the coffee table.

Vi asked the grandmother for more lemonade.

When they were alone, Vi said, "Eric, listen up. Your thoughts are accurate. We know your thoughts, that's how we know they're accurate. If you try to shoot Mrs. Reagan, or any actresses, or anyone—if you make a move in that direction, we'll know it, since we know your thoughts, and we'll have to activate that capsule in your testicles. You know we have the power—we're the ones who changed the taste of food."

This was another Rocky trick, fuck this legalistic shit, talk to crazy people in the crazy people language. It was something agents did when they were getting burned out on threat work. Walter had been dead for two months by then.

Mrs. Engelbrecht came back with the lemonade. Vi took it with the coaster and thanked her. Eric shuffled to his room.

Mrs. Engelbrecht sat on the piano bench. She said that Eric had an IQ of 402, according to one test he had written for himself.

"Yes," said Vi. "He seems bright. Do you keep any firearms around the house?"

After the visit, Eric sent his threats to Vi, saving the analysts a step. First it was: *Dear Agent Asplund, Please inform Mrs. Reagan that unless she curtails her invidious smear campaign, I will kill her.* Later it was: *I will kill you Violet.*

Leticia (Gomez) Jones was a spookier gig. Vi never figured out her deal, except that she was a mad decrepit nuisance, well known to Yonkers 911. She lived in filth with a pack of Rotts and passed herself off as a Santeria priestess. Her letters said that she could make herself invisible and harm enemies with thoughts.

Vi went up to Yonkers, carrying a freshly printed statutory warning, banging on the screens, shouting, "Ms. Jones, Ms. Gomez Jones, I know you're in there. I'm a federal agent. We need to talk."

Vi looked through the screen into a room of magic clutter: saints' candles burning, jars of pickled roots, shrines to this and that, lithographs of the Virgin in various dolorous poses, even an eyesight chart hanging from a nail—God knows what the woman used that for. On the floor of the front room was a circle of powder, white and fine like talcum, which Vi knew from the DEA guys was a heavy-duty Santeria curse.

Vi kept banging on the screens, feeling sillier and sillier. Neighbors stopped to watch. The Rotts were barking out of sight, clawing at the walls. Then the Rotts went quiet. Fine, thought Vi, be that way. She mailed the statutory warning from her office, cc to the file, and never laid eyes on Leticia (Gomez) Jones.

Tuesday with the prisoners came as a relief. Vi worked the airports, escorting new arrests, running a shuttle from La Guardia to JFK, where the Service shared temporary holding pens with DEA and Customs. Vi spent her Tuesdays in the pens waiting for the magistrate, watching drug suspects file through booking—prints and mugs and repartee and government box lunches. When Dawn Imperiali, her roommate in Hoboken, was doing airports and Vi was doing vans, they would hang out in the pens. They watched soaps and *Oprah* to keep their spirits up. Vi thought the jail at JFK was the worst place in the world.

"Oh, it's not so bad," said Dawn. "It's just a lot of waiting. See, they smuggle heroin in their little tummies, don'tcha, ladies?"

The women, chained to each other and the wall, nodded automatically.

Dawn, being Customs, processed swallowers from many nations. "It's a ticket to America," she said. "But first they have to board the plane, survive the flight, and get to a safe house in New Jersey before voiding. If a condom breaks squeezing through the small intestines, these fucking gooms go into shock, vomit up the rest, and die. Come on, ladies, work with me. You ain't even trying. I have a date tonight."

Dawn was not allowed to give them laxatives. Fruit juice was as far as the government would go. When the contraband was finally voided, Dawn made the women pick through the stool so that she could make her seizure, type her vouchers, and punch out.

She said, "The record is two hundred and forty-seven condoms, but that was a dog."

Vi said, "What's the human record?"

"Most I ever got was twelve."

The magistrate was always running late. Dawn sat at a metal desk, doing her nails and waiting for nature. The women shifted on their hams.

Dawn glanced over hopefully. "Any progress, ladies?"

A voucher was a stat. Contraband in feces was a seizure and a stat. Wednesday was for counterfeiting and that meant a stat. They lived for stats in Criminal, cases opened, cases closed, forfeitures, arrests. This was how they judged you. You got selected for Protection or you stayed, you got to be a Rocky or you failed, based entirely on stats. Rocky would get to be an ASAC, boss of all the Rockys, if he had the squadwide stats, and the ASAC, Rocky's boss, would get to be a SAC only if he busted Rocky's balls, so everyone was driven to make arrests in volume. Good arrests were stats. Crap arrests were stats. They did not arrest the factually innocent (although it was a stat), because this was America, after all, not some fucked-up regime like the places all these people flee in leaky boats, and besides you could get caught and be someone else's stat, the bums from IAB, some public integrity attorney with diplomas on his wall, which was the point of stats, of designing the division around stats—that is, accountability.

Through all of this, all fall, Vi kept Walter's dollar tacked to the carpeted wall of her cubicle on a floor of cubicles. She tried to kill her grief with work, staying late, sometimes missing the last ferry to New Jersey. Once or twice, she even slept on the floor, her coat over her head because the lights never went out. She stared at the bill for long stretches on those nights, trying to decode his meaning: US. She knew he hadn't meant that we trust in the U.S., the United States, a unit of community meaninglessly large. No, he'd meant that we should trust in a small town, in the people of a town, or maybe just the people that you know.

Vi tried to numb herself, to lose herself in stats, the static of statistics, the dreck threats and the jail runs and the counter-counterfeiting. There were seven counter-counterfeiting squads in New York station. They broke out like the countries on a map. One team did the Asians, another did the Haitians, another did Dominicans. Vi's team, Rocky's team, did the Russian mob, the boys from Brighton Beach, avid counterfeiters from way back.

The Russians were proud of their fake paper. To Vi, it was the dumbest-looking shit imaginable. The green was neon, the gray black, as if the Russians couldn't countenance the Protestant chromatics of the Federal Reserve, and felt the need to amp the iconage. The twenties coming through the airports made Andrew Jackson look like a transvestite vampire or one of the grimmer female martyrs. She was always amazed when any of it passed.

Three months after Walter's death, Vi was in the pens at JFK, fingerprinting crackheads as she watched *One Life to Live* with Dawn Imperiali. Rocky paged her in the pens, sent her out to Nassau to claim a female juvenile caught spending phony twenties, a Russian with no green card, thus a female juvenile illegal, but sadly just one stat for all her categories.

The Russians used girls to pass their paper, thinking that no one would suspect a girl of counterfeiting. They also thought that girls would be less likely to skim, and this was probably true. Back in Russia, these girls had never seen more than ten U.S. in any one palm, but in Brooklyn they'd be handed a thousand dollars in crisp, pretty, worthless twenties. The girls were recruited by strapping young gigolos from Moscow, who drove them out to Long Island because the outerborough vendors knew the deal and wouldn't take the paper. The gigolos would wait in cars outside the Bradlees in Ronkonkoma, the Toys "R" Us in Babylon. The girls would be inside, pushing their shopping carts in air-conditioned comfort, selecting random items, kandy korn, cordless phones, menthol cigarettes, stuffed animals, hair-straightener, Michael Jordan basketballs, a senseless cornucopia. It didn't matter what they bought. The purpose of the trip was to pick out anything, pay the cashier fake money, and get real money back as change. It was a parody of shopping and a bit surreal: the change was the only thing of value.

Vi took the van from JFK. She met the prisoner, a girl from the Urals who called herself Mariah for the singer she adored. Mariah had spent an hour in a Garden City Wal-Mart, guiding her empty cart from aisle to aisle, because she was afraid to take a box from the shelves, they were so orderly, she said. Outside, her driver, her handler—who Vi suspected was also her lover—got the willies, thinking that Mariah must have been picked up, and he drove away. Mariah didn't know that she'd been stranded. She kept pushing the cart up and down the aisles, screwing up the courage to actually shop. She finally picked two items: a parakeet in a yellow plastic travel cage and a six-socket surge protector. She put them in her cart, wheeled them through the ten-items-or-less, and handed over her lurid money.

The store detectives had some laughs with the alias. Okay, *Mariah*. Right this way, *Mariah*. Have a seat while I call the wind, *Mariah*. They called the Nassau cops instead, Nassau called the Service, and Vi took Mariah to the pens at JFK.

Vi and Mariah in a roomy van. The parakeet hopped around the travel cage. The wind blew from two windows on the LIE. Mariah was a stat already, but she didn't know it yet. She was feeding Cheez-Its to the bird.

Vi asked her why she had picked the surge protector.

Mariah didn't know what a surge protector was.

Vi told her to open the box. Mariah opened the box and looked at the sockets and the cord. She plugged the cord into a socket. Nothing happened. She pointed at the picture on the box—a family of toothsome Americans, father, son, and moppet daughter, grinning around a personal computer—as if she had expected all of them to be inside.

Vi said, "Why the bird?"

Mariah said, "He sings."

Vi wanted to smack Mariah, make a fist, aim for her mouth. The feeling came from nowhere, suddenly.

Vi said, "What the fuck made you leave Russia anyway? I'm talking to you. What made you think you could survive a month in this country? Do you have any idea how much it will cost the taxpayers to deport your ass, Mariah? Why are you *my* problem? Why are you my afternoon? Tell me why, Mariah."

Mariah blinked at Vi, absolutely shocked. The blond American had been so kind till then.

Vi said, "Oh for God's sake. Here, take this bagel. Take it. It's garlic, it's good. You won't be seeing your next meal until breakfast tomorrow."

Vi explained to Mariah that she was going to the tank at JFK for pre-arraignment, from arraignment to the Marshal's and the Immigration maw.

Parakeets were not allowed in the pens and Wal-Mart didn't want it back. The bird was another refugee. After processing Mariah, Vi threw the bird and travel cage out the window on the inbound BQE.

Vi was sick of Criminal by then and disgusted with herself. She asked the Service for a transfer and they sent her to Protection, the vice-presidential team, and this was how Vi started working crowds.

part two

THE PRIMARY

the nervous system (sunday)

4

The problem with her energy was sleeping, said her doctor, Dr. Lee, and the problem with her sleeping was her weight. Dr. Lee was on the list of preapproved primary care/gatekeeper physicians for the Treasury health plan, which was why Gretchen Williams had called the doctor to begin with, Gretchen being forty-five, almost forty-six, and three years without a checkup. Gretchen was three years without a check-up because her former gatekeeper, a white guy by the name of Weiss, had retired to Palm Beach, leaving Gretchen gatekeeperless, adrift, and too busy at the time to notice.

When Dr. Weiss retired, the president was in the first year of his second term and gunning for a Nobel Prize. They didn't say which prize, but Gretchen, then a presidential bodyguard, had assumed it wasn't physics. The president was traveling to every fucked-up, war-torn corner of the world, Israel and Palestine, Bosnia and Kosovo, and other places which, though not formally war-torn, were very, very tense, Ireland and Ireland, North and South Korea, India and Pakistan (one side had a bomb named Shiva, the other had a bomb named something equally scary, much scarier than Fat Man and Little Boy and look at all the damage they had done), and going to these places with a sitting president was very, *very* tense. Gretchen remembered the flight from Islamabad to Delhi, brown earth and the running shadow of the jet. She was looking out the portholes at the roads and villages for the flash of missile-launch and wondering, how many Pakistanis want us dead? It was perfect somehow—the depth and crispness of the hate, like a big blue sky. There were other things going on in Gretchen's life around that time. She was a single mother and her son, a boy named Tevon, a fine boy and a good boy and a kind one, she believed, was having problems at his school, acting out and talking back, even, once or twice, hitting other kids, and once making fun of a girl in a wheelchair. Gretchen, returning from a peace trip, didn't know the words to tell her son how wrong it was to pick on a crippled kid, and it was the only time she ever hit him hard. She hit him because she didn't know the words. She hit him in the bedroom, in the head, and he kind of sailed across the bed, and she felt sick, watching this. Two weeks later, they went to Pakistan.

She had the kind of life in which you could easily go three years without a checkup, and so when the Director of the Secret Service called her in and offered her promotion to lead agent/chief-of-detail to the VP's team, she said no and flatly no—it was just too much. Gretchen knew that the VP would be running for president and that his entourage would be on the road six days out of seven for eighteen months on end, rallies, speeches, koffee klatches, nine and ten events a day. His campaign agents would be sleeping on the plane, working ropelines in their dreams. Pakistan was bad, but Iowa was worse. You walk up Main Street in a farm town, shaking every hand, people coming out of every shop and doorway. They mob your man, hug him, slap his back, and you have no idea who these people are.

She had worked the presidential cycle when the president himself was up for reelection and it was fairly brutal for a while, but the president didn't have to fight inside the party and they coasted through the Super Tuesday states. The travel didn't fire up until July, and then there was a crisis in the Middle East and two ugly budget showdowns with the Senate in September, and they had a fine excuse to stay in Washington, which was excellent for Gretchen, because her son had started at the special school that fall, and she could drive him there most mornings like a normal single mom, and have a little talk along the way, good and evil and don't forget your lunch.

The Director tried to talk her into accepting the promotion. He said it wasn't clear that the VP was definitely running (which was horseshit—it was clear; the guy had nine PACs by then and two different exploratory committees, and what were they exploring, outer space?) The Director sidestepped most of this and said, flatteringly, that he thought she showed great promise as a boss. There were only sixteen humans in the world under the protection of the Secret Service—the president, first lady, and first daughter, the VP and the second family, ex-presidents and ex–first family members (imagine that, the Director said, an entire agency organized around sixteen beating hearts)—and sixteen lives meant sixteen details, and, as the Director pointed out, chief-of-detail slots did not come open every week.

"I like you," he said. "You keep them dawgies moving, Gretch. I admire that. I see you as the sort of fine young female type minority supervisor who could pretty much write his or her own ticket in this Service, maybe be directress in her own right one day, given six or seven years and a well-hung rabbi, meaning me, I mean. I'd hate to see you make a shit career move here. Think it over, Gretch."

It was a remarkable speech, clever and pathetic all at once. No one called her Gretch, for one thing, and she wasn't really all that young. She had been an L.A. cop for twelve years before she took the test for Treasury enforcement, and was actually quite old for a GS-11, her pay grade at the time, and looked even older than she was, her dreads gone lank and gray, lines around her eyes, a couple extra pounds on her butt and thighs. The business about female and minority was more on the pathetic side, and Gretchen happened to know that he had given the same speech to Debbie Escobedo-Waas when he'd offered her the job of VP's chief-of-detail. Debbie was the only other woman of color above the rank of GS-10. Above GS-10 or so, the Service, like a mountain, grew white as snow and also very cold.

Gretchen thought it over in the Director's office. She was not averse to moving up. It would mean a couple pay steps, for one thing, fifteen grand a year, and she was saving nothing as an 11, but then again she had a son, a troubled son it seemed. She couldn't travel with a candidate, not ten events a day for eighteen months. Even Debbie Escobedo-Waas couldn't handle that and she was only thirty-one, and childless, and had that sexy little dress size that she was so proud of, and ran five miles on her lunch hour every day, six hundred laps of the Rose Garden. Gretchen said no again to the promotion.

"You leave me no choice then," the Director said. "I'll send you and your son back to L.A. if you don't take the job."

Gretchen learned that day just how cold it was on the white part of the mountain. She also learned that the Director was not a spineless moron as so many people thought. No, he was actually quite tough and crafty in his way, because he had somehow figured out the one thing in his power that she was afraid of: a transfer to Los Angeles. She was afraid of Los Angeles, specifically afraid, as children are afraid of basements. She was not afraid of San Diego, or anything north of maybe Oxnard or Bakersfield or something. She was a native Los Angeleno (Watts, to be exact), and growing up she had never been above Santa Monica, nor much south of Seal Beach (her mother had a nephew in the Navy there and they'd visited him once before he went to Vietnam). She had never seen the other side of the San Gabriels, the mountain bowl around her world—you couldn't see the mountains through the smog, but everybody knew that the city was so smoggy because of the mountains, and so the smog was daily proof of what it obscured. She didn't get around much as a kid and even now her grasp of geography was a little iffy. She wasn't absolutely certain that she was not afraid of let's say Chino or Simi or Snapple Valley—wasn't that a town across the mountains or did she make it up? Going down to San Diego or up as far as Oxnard, she was doing fine, but in between, the smoggy nether, she was starting to get scared. Debbie Escobedo-Waas was a Californian too, but she was the other kind of Californian, the brainless, energetic kind, the kind who didn't sense Armageddon on the way. This was probably because Debbie came from the Valley, another hazy concept, not the inner city, where the truth was like a bus line and it ran right past your house. Gretchen was old enough to remember the riots, the first riots of her life, 1965, which they always called the riots down in Watts, until they had another riot in the '90s and had to start naming them for clarity's sake. Debbie wasn't even born in 1965, and even if she had been alive and thinking, how much could she have seen from San Fernandoland? Gretchen, at the epicenter, didn't see that much in 1965. She was at her aunt's house, three bedrooms and a patch of dust in back and a dog named Goblin on a chain. Gretchen always went to her aunt's after school and in the summer to play with her cousins and the dog until her mother came back from work.

Gretchen's mother, Mildred Williams, worked in the cafeteria at Paramount Pictures, mostly on the pie line, sometimes on the drink line. She was never on the carving board, a station of prestige reserved for a man of chefly gravitas, and she never filled a salad bar. By the time salad bars came into vogue, Mildred Williams was a lunch cashier and too senior for the salad bar. There was a separate canteen for the celebrities at Paramount. Gretchen's mother fed the grips and secretaries, took their nickels, took their dimes, slapped a roll of quarters against the edge of the cash register drawer, and all the quarters spilled into the quarter section of the drawer. Mildred Williams was a stylish cashier, a saved, believing Christian, and a fixture at the cafeteria. She knew all of the celebrities, though she never fed them—Harry Belafonte, Lena Horne, even the Mills Brothers going back a ways. Mildred Williams, being the old-fashioned sort, only believed in black achievement, black success, black celebrities. To her, it was as if Henry Fonda had never happened, as if Marilyn Monroe had been a big celebrity to fish or to some other species on some distant planetoid, because the biggest star on earth was clearly Sidney Poitier, such a handsome man and so polite. Mildred Williams and her sisters and her cousins out of Houston were churchy women, all of them, and basically southern, and they got along, Gretchen thought, by ignoring everything they didn't like, or didn't get, or believed had not been made for them, and they didn't covet it, or care, or really notice in their hearts, and this was the world that blew up in the riots.

Gretchen's father, Joseph Williams, drove an airfreight truck out of LAX (some line you never heard of and the trucks were always breaking down). He had been over the mountains many times, down to Mexico on runs, up to Alaska with the Army. He knew many words in Eskimo, including "Aleut," their word for Eskimo, which means "people," because, he said, they lived up there in isolation thinking they were the only people in creation until 1941 or so. Her father did not believe in celebrities, black, white, or purple polka-dot, he always said, because the Eskimos had none and got along just fine. Gretchen thought, looking back, that her father was a smart man, a scholar of the highways, and he was not a mean drunk or a loud one. The more he drank, the less he was anything at all. She never saw him drink, or drunk, because he always went away to drink, two days, three days, a week or two at most, which was how he lost the trucker job. After that he had no job and he went away. Then he had a job cutting grass at USC, watering the grass until it needed to be cut, but he drank instead of watering, and then he went away, and then he got a job at a TV and appliance store on Slauson in South Watts, starting in the stockroom, becoming a salesman on the floor because he knew a lot and could really talk.

Gretchen was at her aunt's house with Goblin and her cousins when the riots hit. The backyard had a slat fence and the main thing she remembered was the smoke, the smell of smoke, like charcoal at a barbecue, the smell before the sight, and the sound of sirens, cops and firefighters, far away, converging on the street from six directions, then not getting closer, as if stuck in traffic, then the smoky smell became a haze, a yellow tint, barely visible, and her eyes were hurting, and by then the sirens were getting smaller, like the white dot on TV, a zip into the distance and it's gone. Her aunt made all the children go inside and told Gretchen that her mother couldn't come because the buses had stopped running.

Her mother came the next day but her father never did. Something in the riot set him off. They got a letter from him when Gretchen was in high school. He said that he'd been living in Spokane. Later, she heard that he was dead in Denver, not Spokane. She heard this separately from three different cousins on her father's side and she figured it was true. One cousin said that he was working at a dog track when he died, another said that he was living in a shelter, a third said that he was actually cleaned up and bigamously married. Gretchen thought that all of these things were probably true at one point or another.

Gretchen was an LAPD sergeant when she heard the news of her father's death. She was on patrol, a night graduate of college, still living with her mother. She was dating a detective at the time, a slick and nimble figure in the station house. They dated for three years and Gretchen thought they were engaged, in word if not in ring, from the way they always talked about a future when his divorce was finally final. Then came Rodney King, the beating in slow motion, the brutality acquittal in Ventura (which they always called the verdict in L.A., until there was another verdict later in the decade), and the second riot in 1991 (after which they named the riots), and Gretchen was standing on the Harbor Freeway with a hundred other cops, watching her city burn again, knowing she was pregnant by the slick detective. Her life became quite focused as she watched the smoke. Her sole ambition at that moment, and at every moment since, was to raise a son to manhood who would never see his city burn. She took the next fed exam—it happened to be Treasury—and came east with her mother and her baby, Tevon Joseph Williams.

She did a trainee tour in Crim, D.C.-Metro station, and was sent to Beltsville for reeducation as a bodyguard. She spent ninety days in Beltsville learning the theory and practice of what they called the Dome, the cities of security in which each protectee moves and never dies. They trained the bodyguards at the Protection Campus, low buildings on a quadrangle, the Plans Pavilion, Movements, the Threat

Assessment Center (most of it computer, cooled and highly dustproof), Technical Support, Psych Services, the Weapo School, and the mock-up parking lot (right next to the real parking lot) where the agents practiced what they did in parking lots, all of it quite modern, post-1963, when the budget for bodyguards zuptupled overnight. The campus behind fences in the corn of Maryland was the heart and soul and brain of the entire protectocracy.

The great mind of that time, the Einstein of this Princeton, was Senior Plans Analyst Lloyd L. Felker, veteran of Carter, veteran of Reagan, veteran of Hinckley, author of fifty-seven seminal white papers known collectively at Beltsville as the Certainties, the basic text on every operational topic: signal integrity, the encrypted comm, bafflers and jamming, set-prepping and site-checking, optimal bomb-dogging given crowd size n, snipers, spotters, counter-snipers, counter-sniper-spotter teams. Felker was the man who saw the Dome on long reflective walks around the quad, who saw the Dome and wrote it down over twenty years, and who watched the Service, with its budgets and its muscle, make his writing real. Felker's methodology, his quirk or tic of mind, was to work backwards, to counterplan, to imagine an assassin and defeat him in advance, to plug every hole, shore up every weakness, until none remained, and this was safety. It was a bit like lying to cover up a lie you had told to cover up your lying. Felker's tic of mind became, in a sense, the instinctive constitution of the agency, which in turn became a way of life for those who lived within it. A lot of it was jive, Gretchen decided, sitting through long lectures in the amphitheater, lanky Felker at the blackboard, chalking diagrams, cones and vectors, many little arrows, but she didn't care because the job was Washington, a world away from whatever was written in the book of urban futures for Los Angeles, some brew of earthquakes, deadlocked freeways, gangs, and power outages, and her son was safe, not just from riot or the shock waves of the riot (which had set her father on the road and had sent his daughter fleeing east), but also from the vision of a city burning—a thing her son would never see.

She could not explain her closet Caliphobia to anyone, not to her mother, not to Debbie Escobedo-Waas, native of the outerlying nowhere, so proud of her dress size and of her husband, the podiatrist (he had treated Debbie for her hammertoe from all those laps around the White House, and they had found that they had a lot in common, a love of animals and a taste for sweaters—marriage followed). She could not explain her fear to the Director, the whitest white man on the mountain (except perhaps for Lloyd L. Felker), and so she was amazed (and, later, when she calmed down, quite impressed) that he had somehow figured out her weak point, the hole in her personal Dome, which was her maternal terror of L.A.

The Director said (with a little smirk) that either she signed on as VP's lead and chief-of-detail or else he would find her something cozy in the SoCal station, chasing porn stars with fake twenties out to Rancho Cucamonga as she listens to the ticking in the sky.

Gretchen wavered.

The Director said that Debbie Escobedo-Waas, his new executive assistant, had already drawn up orders to L.A.

She wavered and he said, "I've picked the VP's team, crack agents all of them, except for Bobbie Taylor-Niles. You know Bobbie Niles, the diva of Protection? She's on the first daughter's detail presently, but there was an incident of some kind in the Lincoln Bedroom, and now the first lady wants her gone pronto. I'm sure you'll be whipping Agent Niles into shape, but let's not dwell on it, Gretch, because I have great news: your deputy lead agent will be Lloyd L. Felker."

Gretchen wavered, overwhelmed—Felker, Mr. Theory, in the field?

The Director said, "It's settled then. Someday, Gretchen Williams, when you are directress, I'm sure you'll find a way to pay me back for this."

Gretchen listened to the Sunday-morning sounds of home, her mother in the bathroom humming as she primped for church, a zot of hairspray, water from the faucet, soft gospel on the radio. Gretchen lay in bed, looking at the plaster cracks in the ceiling. With all her travel, it was always weird to wake up in a room she recognized.

Mildred Williams appeared in the doorway, her hair in curlers, gooped up with a gel that smelled like melted cheese. "When did you get in?" she asked.

"Pretty late," said Gretchen.

It was four days after Iowa, the crucial party caucus, three days before the New Hampshire primary. The VP was running even in the polls, fighting for his skin against his only rival for the nomination, a do-good former senator, the darling of reform. Gretchen had the blanket over one eye, peeking at her mother with the other.

The smell of her mother's hair was making Gretchen hungry, which made her think of eating, sleep, energy, and weight. She was coming off a solid year of food-verb events on the campaign trail, corn-boils, fish-frys, wiener-roasts, bean-bakes, salad-tosses. She snacked at these events, ate McDonald's in between, kept it going with black coffee, sixteen cups a day, and then there was the hassle and the worry and the stress, calls at three a.m. from Fundeberg, the hairy aging wunderkind, the VP's freewheeling campaign genius. Fundeberg, who never slept or needed to, apparently, never wore a coat outdoors even in Storm Lake that time just after New Year's when the mechanisms froze in the agents' sidearms and they had to warm their guns before they worked the crowd. Fundeberg would call her hotel room with some new instance of his brilliance, a way to break the figurative wall between the VP and true contact with the people. He would call at three a.m. and say, "Gretchen, are you sleeping?" and often, surprisingly, she wasn't. She would listen long enough to veto his latest proposed stunt (no, the VP can't raid a crack house with the cops; no, he can't spend a night homeless in Detroit to dramatize the plight of the homeless in Detroit; no, he can't drive in the demolition derby; no, he can't sponsor an elementary school essay contest, with the winner being "agent for a day"). Eating made her heavy, slow, and weak; coffee kept her up, which made her sleepy, slow, and weak, and over time she lost the will to veto, and Fundeberg began to take control of where they went.

Gretchen's year as chief-of-detail had been a success by the only measure that she cared about: the VP wasn't dead. There had been some rough spots in her tenure to be sure, excessive-force complaints at Epcot that one time, a bungled hoedown in Ottumwa, several others. There had also been one bona fide disaster, a visit to a flooded town in May—a photo op, Fundeberg's idea. Gretchen should have vetoed it, but she was too weak. The town was Hinman, Illinois. Gretchen lost an agent there. The agent was her deputy, Lloyd Felker, the father of the Certainties.

After the disaster in the flood, Gretchen had resolved to bite the bullet, toughen up, to lose twenty pounds. She had always been good at resolutions, making them and keeping them, even as a kid. Her father left, she loved him and he left. She had resolved to be okay with this; eventually she was. Later, as a cop, she had resolved to be a college woman, going nights and weekends, writing papers on

Tom Sawyer in a squad car (her professor said that Injun Joe represented sexuality, so Gretchen wrote this, fine), and it took eight years, but she graduated. She was dating in those days, mostly other cops, no men from the neighborhood, but she was bad at dating, bad at small talk after sex—she had no fling in her. She resolved to wait and find a special man, and she found the slick detective, who was very special to her (and pretty much divorced), and they dated for a long time, but then she missed two periods and he let her down, and she resolved to slam the door on Los Angeles and him, and she had done this too.

When she resolved to lose the weight, Gretchen had expected to succeed, but she had a Dome to run, and she forgot her resolution, moving the behemoth. The Dome could be a mile wide, a hundred cops and agents on the air together, and Gretchen was usually somewhere near the core, working with the body team, a seven-agent cordon on the man himself, the last defense they had, the worried-looking suits familiar to the nation from TV. This was Gretchen's specialty, the part she knew the best, close personal protection (as they called it up in Beltsville), a fancy name for scan the hands as the VP's shaking them, scan the hands and never stop, and take a bullet if you must. There was a joke on Gretchen's team, a joke among the macho lunkheads she was leading—Tashmo, O'Teen, Herc Mercado, all of them. The joke (as O'Teen told it) was that there were seven agents on the body team, seven and exactly seven, so that a shooter with a six-shot .32 could empty his weapon into agents, and there'd still be one agent left to tackle him. No, said Herc Mercado, it's seven for the seven dwarves.

Which made her Snow White. In a year of trying, Gretchen couldn't lose the weight. Admitting failure, she went to see good Dr. Lee, who threatened to put Gretchen on one of several diets. They reviewed the options in the doctor's office. The diets had names like important global summits, there was the Geneva diet, the Reykjavik diet, the Bretton Woods diet, and the names made Gretchen tired. Dr. Lee much preferred no diet, nothing drastic or disruptive. She asked Gretchen to exercise good common sense and nutrition habits, and exercise as well. Gretchen did her best, but she couldn't lose the weight.

Gretchen's mother was pulling at the curlers in her hair. "I'll be seeing Gullickson at church. Why don't you come too? Church is just the thing for Tev. And you can to talk to Gullickson about the banister."

Gretchen burrowed in the blankets. Her house in Maryland had a narrow, bump-your-head staircase to the bedrooms on the second floor, wear marks up the wallpaper coming up the stairs, and a shaky banister. Her mother had been after her to fix the banister for months. Mildred Williams even got the business card of a man named Gullickson, a warden in her church, who was some kind of painter-handyman, but Gretchen had never called him. Gretchen's mother was a member of the Hope Road Christian Bible Pentecostal Tabernacle, which had once been in a good stone church—Lutheran, abandoned—on Hope Road in Seat Pleasant, but then the bishop, as they called their preacher at Hope Road, ran off to Alabama with a sister from the choir and the money from the car wash, and the little congregation, bankrupt, lost its lease, and had to move to a former carpet warehouse store on Rhode Island Avenue, a rougher neighborhood inside the District. Of course, they didn't change the name to Rhode Island Avenue Christian Bible Pentecostal Tabernacle, and of course they didn't prosecute the bishop. Gretchen made some phone calls down to Alabama, found the man in Anniston living with a woman, not the sister from the choir. Gretchen knew the U.S. Attorneys and could've had the guy indicted in a minute, but her mother said it wouldn't do, indicting a man of God like that. Gretchen said, "A man of God? He stole your money, Mother. He's the reason you worship in a carpet store." Mildred Williams said, "He always preached the flesh is weak. Now he's living it." Everyone at Hope Road was a fool in Gretchen's mind, her mother too, and if this Gullickson was a leader of the place, Gretchen didn't trust him with her banister. He'd probably tear the old one out and disappear, or put in something even worse, shoddy and incompetent, or fuck it up somehow, and he'd be such a white-haired country bumpkin you wouldn't even be able to demand your money back or call the man a fool. Her mother had carped about the banister all summer, then Tev went back to school and the trouble started up again, the sulking and locked doors, giving Gretchen's mother something new to carp about.

"Oh well," said Mildred Williams. "Guess I better finish getting ready. It's a long bus down to Hope Road."

It sounded like a song, but in fact it was a hint. There was a pause.

"I'll take you," Gretchen said, pushing out of bed. She wore baggy sweats, her lingerie. She went across the hall to Tevon's room. She tried the knob.

"It's locked," said Mildred Williams.

Part of Gretchen wanted to kick the door in (Gullickson could fix it), part of her knew this was a bad idea, part of her wanted to go back to bed and do some burrowing, part of her found her fanny pack where she kept her laminated cardkey ID—Gretchen's name and rank (one word, *Lead*), Gretchen's headshot (posed against blue wall, looking somewhat leaden in the eyes), the holographic eagle (rising, tilted in the light), the five-point marshal's star of the Secret Service, filigreed and westernate, the bar code on the bottom, God knows what it said about her (weak and sleepy, lives in fear, lost an agent in the field). She slid the card between the lock plate and the tongue, popped the door, and slipped into the gloom and sour smell of Tevon's room.

He was on the bed, bellied out in a wild, semaphoric splay. His jockey shorts were white and clean—he was so finicky these days.

The TV had been on all night again. She sat on Tevon's bed, watched it for a while, the cable headline news. She saw a clip from caucus night in Iowa, the VP leaving town, sandwiched between bodyguards, Gretchen on one flank, Vi Asplund on the other. The clip was a stock vid bite, backing up the story of the Iowa results. Gretchen shut the TV off.

Tevon stirred. He saw her and rolled over, saying, "Shit."

"What's that, Tevon?"

He pulled the pillow over his ears.

"You say *ship*? Is that what I heard? Were you dreaming of a ship? Was it beautiful, a big old thing with sails? Tell your moms about it. She needs to hear a pretty thing this morning."

Punishment. Point taken, he said nothing.

"Get dressed, Mr. Man. We're taking Grams to church."

The pillow said, "Batting cage—you promised—"

She remembered calling home from Iowa, saying she was sorry to have missed his soccer game. He played indoor soccer, the worst and slowest player on the field or court or whatever you call it when there is no field. She did not remember promising a trip to the batting cage (she despised the batting cage—the crack of bats made her jumpy). Tevon knew she didn't and was probably lying, not that she could prove it.

"We don't lock our doors," she said as she left the room.

Mildred Williams was already dressed, coat and hat and bag. "He's mad at you," she said.

"I think I know that," Gretchen said.

"You missed his soccer game."

Gretchen brushed her teeth at the bathroom sink.

"He saw you on TV, out in Idaho somewheres. He's been broody ever since."

Gretchen rinsed and spat. "Iowa," she said.

"Huh?" Grams was getting deaf.

"Iowa. No one goes to Idaho. They don't even have a caucus, Mother. It would be a total comic waste of time."

"Well, it wasn't here and that's all a child knows. A child needs a parent every day."

"He has you," Gretchen said. "He's lucky to have you."

"That's what your father used to say."

Gretchen, wounded at the sink, said, "Mother," weakly, then said nothing.

Gretchen and her mother waited in the car. Tevon came out of the house and down the front steps dressed in his full replica Oriole uniform, hose and spikes and the black turtleneck, the orange bird-and-bat logo at his Adam's apple. The steps were steep concrete, tricky on the spikes.

"Uniform is foolishness," Mildred Williams commented. "What'd you pay for that?"

Gretchen said, "Too much."

"You spoil him."

"Do I spoil or neglect him, Mother? Please make up your mind."

Tevon dragged the bat bag from the garage (also Oriole, also grossly overpriced), dumped it in the backseat, and got in. They started for the church, driving through the quiet streets of suburban Maryland.

Gretchen wasn't clear on the name of the town she lived in. She said it was Seat Pleasant when people asked. She thought it probably was, though others on the street called it Capitol Highlands, which made a little sense. They were on the heights, northeast of the District, and from the pocket park near Gretchen's house you could look across the smoky riverbottom ghettoes to the tourist part of Washington. Others called the town Cap Heights, but this was confusing (Capitol Heights was a town, but not this town) and probably also wrong. By whatever name, it was the poor end of the 'burbs, the first town past the District going out East Capitol. Gretchen figured they were in some kind of quasi-independent borough of Seat Pleasant, and she figured that this was because her end of town was largely black, cops and postal supervisors, and it suited everyone, both sets of politicians, white and black, to have a line of some kind down the Prince Georges Highway. Hope Road ran east from the P.G. into Seat Pleasant proper, which was getting somewhat black these days, more your upscale buppie types, government attorneys and congressional staffers from safe seats in Chicago. The whites were slowly drifting to the Beltway farther out, except for the liberal Jews, who had just built that jazzy synagogue, looks like a spacecraft with a lawn. In the summer, someone had spray-painted a swastika on the synagogue. They caught the man, ran his name in the newspaper—it was something plain, Smith or Jones or Williams. The town was edgy until the paper ran his picture as a public service. Gretchen, like everyone, was relieved to see that he was cracker white, not black. She could almost feel the place relax the day the picture ran.

She took P.G. to the lights and went up Hope Road. Tev was looking out his window at the fast food joints and gas station minimarts. Gretchen wondered what he thought of this, his world—the safe world she had made for him.

"Where you going?" asked her mother.

Only then did Gretchen remember the bishop and the sister and the money he embezzled and the move to the carpet warehouse in the District.

She turned around, started back. "Why didn't you say something, Mother?"

"I did. I said, 'Where you going?'"

"But you waited until I was almost there."

"Don't bark at me, baby," Mildred Williams said. "I'm not the one that's all screwed up."

They wouldn't let Tevon wear his spikes at the amusement center because the indoor surfaces were rubberized, so they went to Foot Locker in the next mall down, where

Gretchen bought her son a new pair of pumpable high-tops and three sports energy bars so that he would have the energy to inflate his shoes.

Back at the amusement center, she fed a bill to the token machine and they dragged the bat bag to the bleachers. There were sixteen batting cages in the place. Four were softball only, two were out of order. The rest were being used, dads and sons, white and black. Tevon ate the energy bars as they waited for a cage. Gretchen had a pretzel from the concession stand, the big kind with the mustard and the road salt.

Tevon stretched his hamstrings like the pros and then it was his turn. He stepped into the cage. She dropped a token in the slot. His face looked puny in the helmet and it made her sad, the way he wore his uniform not to a game, but to a cage of hanging nets, one boy in a row of boys, up against these blind machines. Tevon found his stance. A red light at the other end turned green, a pitch was shoveled up. He swung and missed. Gretchen heard the big thump in the pads.

She clapped for him. "Here we go now, Tevon, keep that bathead flat."

Another pitch. He cut and missed.

The slick detective, Tevon's father in L.A., had played junior college shortstop and once had a try-out with the Padres, so he said. They were looking for the next Ozzie Smith, big range and the sweet release, so he said. Watching Tevon in the cage, it was hard to see the father in the son. Tevon was big and slow, as she was. He was often lost in soccer games, way off on the left flank when the ball was being kicked around the goal, and yet he was so serious this morning. He swung at the last ball, stepped back to stretch some more, bending at the waist, the bat across his shoulders like a yoke. He took some practice swings. He was sweating, loose. He was happy, focused on his swing.

Her pager sounded, the oscillating chirp. Tevon tightened up.

"It's nothing," she said quickly. She bought another twenty balls and walked behind the bleachers. The message was a number in the Threat Assessment Center.

"Gretchen, hey," said Debbie Escobedo-Waas. "We're sorry to bother you."

Gretchen thought, who's *we*? She didn't like the conversation so far.

Debbie said, "You're going out tonight—New Hampshire, I'm afraid. I'm wondering, we're wondering, could you shoot up to the campus on your way to

Andrews? I'm here with the Director and Boone Saxon. We'd like to have a word with you before the jumping-off."

They set a time and Gretchen walked back to the cage. Tevon was finished with his twenty balls. She dropped a token in the slot and bought him twenty more.

She said, "I'm sorry, Tev, I have to go. This afternoon, not now. We've got lots of time."

A pitch was shoveled up. Tevon didn't swing. It thumped into the pads.

"Don't be angry, son. We've got lots of time."

Tevon said, "My father's name is Carlton Imbry."

Considering everything—the pain the name had caused, and how foolish she had felt when she realized that she wasn't even smart enough to know whether someone loved her, and the other things she'd felt, the years of pointless feeling, and the sacrifices she had made to raise the boy alone—considering all of this, Gretchen, standing by the cage, was relatively steady, or so it probably seemed to the dads in the other cages.

She said, "Who told you that?"

Tevon didn't swing or drop his stance. The bat was cocked, his elbow out. His eyes were on the green light and the pitches flashing past. "There's a database on the Web," he said. "Enter name and query-field, it pulls up public records in that name."

"But who told you the name?"

"I wasn't looking for him. I was looking for me."

Boom of pads. Gretchen whispered, "No."

"You told me I was born in Maryland. I wasn't born in Maryland. I found my birth certificate, L.A. County. It said Carlton Imbry under father. I always thought my father was a bum, and that's why you protected me and never said his name. But I found him on Nexis. He's not a bum. He's a homicide detective, worked on all the famous cases in L.A. He's the one who solved the O.J. murder—he found the dog hair in the lint screen of the dryer, which matched the dog that wasn't barking. Would've blown the case wide open, if the lab techs hadn't bungled it. So I got his number, left a message. I said, 'I am your son.' I left a few messages and he finally called me back—he's been swamped lately. We've been talking ever since. He says I can live with him if I promise not to cramp his style."

The last pitch hit the pads. The cage was quiet.

Gretchen said, "You will never live with him. Listen to me, Tev, I know the man, okay? He'll hurt you, just like he hurt me."

"And you stole me off to Maryland just to hurt him back."

"Is that what he says?"

"No, that's what Brandy says."

"Who the hell is Brandy?"

"She's his fiancée. She's the coolest lady in the universe. She does traditional African massage technique at her tanning salon in West Hollywood. They've been together almost seven months now."

So this was the final blow. Brandy.

Tevon found his stance again. "Come on, put the token in."

There were four major supermarkets in Gretchen's town, assuming that her town was Seat Pleasant and not some crooked gerrymander. There were other minor super-markets and a million minimarts, but only four with everything she ever needed, whole departments for meat, booze, frozen foods, toys, pets, greeting cards. She pushed the cart along. They were somewhere in the coffee, tea, and powdered cocoas. Tevon was behind her, tarrying and loitering and up to no good, still in his full replica Oriole uniform and his pumped-up high-tops.

She remembered loving shopping with her son when Maryland was new and he was small. He would ride in the seat part of the cart, facing her, kicking her, nib-bling a cheese-and-peanut-butter cracker, the brown-and-orange kind. She always saved the torn-open package so that they could scan it at the checkout counter. But now he ran around the place, ashamed to be with Moms, and she shopped alone. She saw him down the aisle with a Ho-Ho and no package.

"Tevon! How are they supposed to *scan* it, man? Get your buttside over here this minute."

He waited almost the full minute, testing her raw nerves, then came ambling up the aisle.

She said, "Tell me what you ate so I can pay for it."

He said, "Ho-Ho."

"What else?"

"Nothing else. Just Ho-Ho."

"I saw you with Cap'n Crunch in the meat department."

"That was from the sample table. They're giving them trial-size boxes away free. They're doing a blind taste test."

"Against what?"

"Um."

"See, you're lying, Tevon Williams. They can't test anything against Cap'n Crunch. There's nothing even similar to Cap'n Crunch."

"That's not true, there's Kix."

"Kix? We'll see about that."

Gretchen found the manager, a Sikh in a bow tie. She asked him if there were any blind Cap'n Crunch taste tests scheduled. He consulted a printout and said there were no taste tests of any type scheduled until Wednesday afternoon.

Gretchen pushed the cart with one hand, pulling Tevon with the other.

She said, "If you eat things, son, and don't save the packages, they can't scan them when we leave. That means I can't pay and that's as good as stealing. Now tell me what you ate."

"I told you, Ho-Ho. The Cap'n Crunch was free."

"That's it—no computer for a month."

"I'll wait until you leave. I'll wait until the minute that you're gone."

"I'll tear it out of the wall."

"I'll plug it in again."

"I'll lock it in the basement."

"I'll bust the basement door."

"I'll give your computer to the retarded people's center."

He was quiet after that, pondering his life with no computer. Then he said, "Chill out, Moms. It's not stealing till we leave."

They went to the checkout when the cart was full. The lady scanned the Slim-Fast canisters, the tomatoes, the carrots, and the greens, the frozen dinners, the chicken parts, the cans of soup, the bread, the milk, the juice, the cereals and tuna fish. The lady totaled it.

Gretchen said to Tevon, "Tell her what you ate."

He said, "Ho-Ho."

The lady waited.

Gretchen said, "What else?"

"Nothing. Only Ho-Ho."

"Please don't be a liar on me, son. It kills me when you act like no one raised you."

She was begging. The other people in the line looked at her with pity and impatience, here's another woman who can't control her kid. Tevon saw the people pitying his mom. Pride rose up inside him. They had no right to pity her.

"Cap'n Crunch," he said.

The lady rang it up.

He said, "Nutter Butter, little bag of smokehouse almonds, single-serving Pringles."

"You must be thirsty," said the woman.

"Coca-Cola Classic. I left the bottle in the paperback best-sellers. You'll find it, aisle ninety-one."

The lady gave him credit, five cents for the return.

The thing she couldn't figure out, driving to the house, was how it all began. Why did her son go searching for himself in cyberspace? At one level, it was natural, of course—the curiosity, and Gretchen knew that she was to blame for not taking the necessary preemptive steps (she was pretty sure that you could disable the databases on a kid's account; she'd have to call AOL and ask them). So, yes, it was bound to happen sometime, but why did it happen now?

Tev was eating pizza in his lap, a gooey slice from Papa Gino's at the mall, a little slice-sized box/plate in his lap catching crumbs and drops of orange grease. She glanced at him, going down the P.G. Highway. She thought of what her mother had said that morning, how Tev had seen her on TV moving through a crowd. She thought about it for a mile and two stoplights, remembering the wet snow at the airport in Des Moines, the VP moving down the ropes, Gretchen and Vi Asplund moving with him, scanning hands and scanning hands, the blur of thumbs and palms, looking for the muzzle of a pistol coming up, or conceivably a knife or homemade grenade, or anything metallic they could not identify as not a pistol/knife/grenade, or a fist coming up holding anything they couldn't immediately see. She had the Dome in her ear when she worked a crowd, the traffic back and forth, the snipers in concealment, the fast extraction team, aircrews on the gunships overhead.

"Tevon, did you see me on TV?"

"I always see you," Tevon said. "You look pretty scared out there. My friends say you look bored, but I know it's scared."

Gretchen drove in silence. Someday she would tell him all about it, how she felt out there, hanging on the VP's flank, deep in what the agents called vacant mode, a stone defensive Zen, the mind both clean and empty except for what it sees. People leaning out, straining, almost falling over ropes. They touched his hand and took his hand, falling back to reestablish balance, and the mass effect of these human movements was to slow the VP, pull him closer, hands now up his arms and around his neck, dangerous, so dangerous. Every crowd sucked them in, a blind hydraulic suck. Gretchen's job, straddling his leg, her shoulder to the crowd, was to counteract the suck, to drive and guide him through her pelvis to his thigh, to force him down the ropes, and yes it was a bit like giving birth, the push against the suck, and yes it made her think of Tevon and the night she forced him into light, pop and burst, the openness, pain hallucination, and no man to help her there, no so-called man to help. It was brutal in that way, saving the VP. Later, on the plane, she would cramp up from the pushing. She'd be talking to some colonel, he'd be talking flight plans and MAC-hops and gunship-tasking, his lips moving, and she would be so cramped up inside that she couldn't listen to the moving lips. She'd sign off on whatever this fool wanted, then hurry to the nearest empty head, slide the latch and lock the door and sit on the pot, her skirt hiked up, fat hands between fat legs, and massage herself through scratchy pantyhose until her knots went slack and she could think again. She'd splash her face and try to picture Tevon growing up in Maryland, growing up in peace, growing up with soccer balls and roller blades and shoot-'em-up computer games and every other gift she could think of and afford. Life in vacant mode—someday she would tell him all about it.

Tevon ate the pizza, left a gummy crust. He said, "Do you love him?"

Gretchen said, "Who? The VP?"

"You're always hanging on him on the news. It's like you two are dancing."

"No, son, I don't love him."

"Is he like your friend then?"

"He's a politician, Tev, same as all the rest. He's less than a nothing. No, he's not my friend."

"Why do you go with him then—if he's not your friend?"

"It's not about friends, Tevon. They killed Dr. King, they killed Robert Kennedy. Leaders died and cities burned and everything went bad. I saw it happen, son. People tell you that it couldn't happen now. Sure, look out the window—what do you see? Houses, lawns, SUVs, everybody's rich. Well I'm not so sure. The country is a piece of supermarket meat. It looks pretty good, all tight and shiny in the cellophane, but if you break the package even just a little bit, the meat starts going bad inside. My agents are the cellophane. That's why I go with him, that's why I'm not around as much as other moms, whatever. We can't let a handgun pick our leaders, son. I refuse to see you living in that world."

This seemed fundamental to her, driving past the Jewish spaceship and later waiting at a stoplight.

Tevon said, "Would you die for him?"

"Tevon, please—where is all this coming from?"

"Well isn't that what you're supposed to do—someone shoots, you step in front?"

She thought, he's old enough to put it all together now, the meaning of the clips and what I do. He's scared that something bad will happen on the news and, as a precaution, he's preparing a new parent for himself—a new home in California, a new Dome, in case he loses what he has.

Gretchen said, "No one's gonna die."

Tevon took this in. They drove awhile.

He said, "How do you know?"

Well, this was a question, wasn't it? They pulled into the driveway. He was waiting for an answer and she knew it.

Gretchen did not believe in lying to a child except when absolutely necessary.

"Tev," she said, a little hoarse. "I'll tell you a secret, son. The secret is important and it's just between us two. Don't tell Grams, don't tell the kids at school, don't tell your little chat room pals, because it's an absolute top secret government scientific invention, and it's called, it's called the two-three-one-two-three-six-P. You can't see it on TV, this special P machine. You can't see in real life, but it's real—I swear to you, it's real—and you don't have to be afraid when I go away, because I feel it when I'm out there in the crowds, it's like a shield of energy, and it's all around me in the air."

5

Vi had lived in Tower South since coming to Protection, but standing at the window of her studio that morning, she wondered for a moment if anybody lived here. Her plants lived here, three geraniums along a dusty windowsill. Her clothes lived here, her suits and blouses in a shallow closet, her woolens still in boxes stacked against the wall. Her books lived here, or some of them, a carton's worth of fitness guides and sports biographies, but Vi herself was generally gone, and most of her possessions, the truly precious things—a box of family pictures, three unmatching chairs, a stand-up lamp with clawball feet—were taking up a corner of her brother's basement in New Hampshire.

Vi was making coffee in the kitchenette. The studio was puny, dim, and noisy through the walls, though she didn't really mind the noise. The life of Tower South was in the narrow halls, which were carpeted, generic, and bewilderingly long, like looking through the wrong end of a telescope at the faraway nirvana of the elevator bank. The complex, a multitower Habitrail on the Virginia side, was equally convenient to the Pentagon, the Metro, and Ronald Reagan Airport. Vi shared the floor with pilot-looking guys—Air Force? airline?—and their flight-attendant-looking wives. In a funny way it reminded her of the Coopers and the Buckerts on Santasket Road back home. Maybe this was why she didn't hate the noise. She heard families going and arriving, the jangling of keys, the crackling of grocery bags, the *vump* of garbage sailing to perdition down the chute. She heard the children too, laughing, shouting, sugar-rushing, the parents saying *Wait, wait, wait,* the kids not understanding that the corridors of South were like a church, a place reserved for no unnecessary noise, not home—home is when we close the door—but not the playground either, where a kid was free to scream.

Vi listened to the coffeemaker huff and start its trickling. The phone rang. It was Bobbie Taylor-Niles, Vi's roommate on the road.

Bobbie said, "I had a great idea. Let's go malling, you and me."

Malling was Bobbie's word for a certain type of shopping, not the hasty dash to Wal-Mart for a pack of razors, nor the duty-driven trudge for weekly groceries. Malling had more style, more serious intent, like going to an art museum except it's a mall. Vi didn't feel like malling on that Sunday morning, her first day off since Iowa, but Bobbie was insistent, as Bobbie often was.

"I'll pick you up," she said. "Which tower is yours again?"

"The southern one," said Vi.

"Is that the real, real ugly one right next to the Christian all-news cable network?"

It was.

"See you in an hour," Bobbie said.

Vi finished dressing for a run and took the elevator to the lobby, riding with the girls she called the Fiends, somber Arab sisters, diplomatic brats. The Fiends stood together, veiled to their eyes, holding their twin monkey bikes by the handlebars. The Fiends lived in the penthouse, up there with the weather and the blinking aviation beacons. They started on forty, racing through the corridors, taking corners at full tilt, touching every doorknob, or seeing who could go the slowest without tipping, moving down to thirty-nine when forty got boring.

Vi smiled at the Fiends and they ignored her, swapping comments in fast Arabic. Their mouths were shrouded. Vi couldn't see who was saying what. The conversation, disembodied, was sound and black expressive eyes. The elevator opened. Vi held the bucking doors. The sisters pedaled off into the lobby.

Vi stretched her hamstrings from the heel, pushing on the marble wall. She saw the Fiends circling the atrium, thumbing their bells, the doormen in pursuit. Vi kneeled to tie her cross-trainers, unbunching the tongue, looping double knots.

She set off at an easy pace from Tower South to Tower West to Tower Mezzanine. The lobbies and sublobbies and retail esplanades went on for 3.7 miles. The brochures in the rental office said so. Vi took this run whenever she was home, pounding over catwalks, weaving through the crush on weekday mornings, tenants, shoppers, office workers.

She ran through the tubes, past the drugstores, the dry cleaners, the Thai place and the MIA memorial, the BYOB bistro, the indoor junior college, the new luggage rental place for people sent on unexpected trips, the Cinema 1-2-3-4-5 and, around the corner, 6-7-8.

Vi had joined Protection out of New York station for a mix of cloudy reasons, most of which, in retrospect, seemed uninformed or misinformed or barely formed at all. In part, she had wanted to get out of New York, the grim routines of Crim, the days spent watching soaps and frisking prisoners. In part, she'd thought the travel and the challenge would drag her out of the numb and stupid grief she had felt since her father's death. In part, she saw the move as a tribute to her father, the dutiful adjuster. Insurance and Protection—a metaphor so obvious it had felt like destiny. She put in for a transfer. The transfer was approved. She was sent to the Protection Campus for a training tour in weapons, tactics, doctrine, the whole theology known as the Dome. At Beltsville, the instructors taught it as a diagram, a picture on a page, circles within circles, zones of pure control, a dot inside the circles labeled *P* for protectee. The diagram had looked to Vi more like a target than a shield, though it was an awesome shield of poised defensive force. She spent three months in Beltsville, a full winter, sleeping in the dorms, eating in the dining hall, showing her ID at every door, reading old white papers in the lamplight on her bunk, the physics of a hit and how to throw it off, dense, technical and terrifying. Then she joined the VP's team and went to work for Gretchen Williams and Gretchen's deputy, a senior special agent named Lloyd Felker.

Vi had heard a fair amount about Lloyd Felker, who had written the white papers Vi had studied on her bunk. He had been a line guy, a decorated veteran of the Reagan team. He'd earned his decorations on a rainy morning in March 1981, when a movie-addled drifter by the name of John W. Hinckley, Jr., opened up on Reagan outside the Hilton on Connecticut Northwest. Hinckley hit the chief-of-detail, Tim McCarthy, in the gut, hit a cop named Delahanty in the neck, hit the press secretary in the skull, hit Reagan in the chest, and it was Felker and another agent, Tashmo, who bundled Reagan to the waiting limousine, sped to the hospital, and probably saved his life.

Something in the mess and narrow miss drove Felker into theory. He moved up to Beltsville as an analyst in Plans. He spent the next twenty years teaching doctrine to recruits and writing his white papers. Toward the end of Felker's great career as a protection intellectual, he was asked to draft a plan for a presidential trip to Pakistan. He wrote a memo, circulating it division-wide for comments and criticism. The plan was vintage Felker, meticulous, obsessive, nothing left to chance, but it had one glaring flaw—or not a flaw exactly, more of an anomaly: it was, or seemed to be, a plan for how to *kill* the president in Pakistan. The other analysts, being thorough men, ran some crosschecks by computer simulator and concluded that it would probably work.

Felker didn't need computer simulations. "Of course it works," he said. "You think I'd circulate my fantasy?"

The other planners didn't understand. Why write a plan to kill—what purpose could it serve?

Felker said, "What purpose? We write our plans to counter plans hatched and set in motion days or weeks or months or maybe years before, or not at all—we can't know this until later, so we counterplan against the plan as if the plan exists. But what is the plan? We have no idea. We're a house of critics with no poet. Someone in this outfit needs to think along these lines. I make a plan, a murder plan; you counterplan against it. I find the holes; you plug them. It's scientific peer review. I destroy your work and if I can't, your work is sound."

Felker pitched his concept to the bosses and the bosses fell in love. They were fatally attracted to the cloak-and-dagger end of things, and besides, it was Felker pitching it, and wasn't he the *author* of the Dome? How could he be wrong on this? So they funded him, freed him from his teaching load, even gave him his own office, a vacant bunker in the cornfields on the windy ridge above the campus quad.

Felker reached the bunker in the cornfield by a long path through the stalks, and in the winter when there was no corn, there was no path. His fellow analysts would see him from their offices, a figure in the mist, loping through the stubble, scattering the crows.

He assigned himself the budget and skill level of your average terror group or one of your better survivalist militias, and he tried to make real-world assumptions. He wrote every kind of murder plot there was. He wrote clockwork operations, he wrote messy-but-effective. He wrote missiles, he wrote rifles, he wrote foreign-soil bombs. He wrote banquet poisonings (the key was fast-release, he said, deceptive symptomology, get them to mismedicate, waste those precious hours). He wrote fake policemen, he wrote gas attacks, he wrote deadly viri delivered in a child's popped balloon. Sometimes he played the jihadin, indy or state-sponsored, sometimes the white supremacists, sometimes the right-to-lifers, sometimes the Shining Path. Sometimes he played the loner in the bunker, the kid with voices in his head and a pistol in his pocket, the simplest of threats and the hardest to defend against. He didn't write too many of these kids. There was really only one of them, he said, and nothing you could do except track them out of Beltsville, build a database of faces, mag your chokepoints, weapon-sweep, and prebrief your body team to read the ropelines carefully. The murder plots were detailed to the second, to the footstep, point-of-contact and escape, and each of them, he said, was completely nonimpossible.

As he found the holes, the other planners plugged them. He studied these counterplans, wrote counter-counterplans to beat them, which forced the planners to produce counter-counter-counterplans. The Dome was getting stronger, but it was also getting bigger, more unwieldy, less controllable, and therefore weaker too, and maybe this was Felker's point from the beginning.

He circulated fifty-eight plots, one for every Certainty, plus one. They were gathered in a kind of Devil's Bible, a heavy, softbound volume—gathered, admired, and quickly classified, each page stamped in red, *Beltsville: Sensitive*. Eventually, he started finding holes the planners couldn't plug. The bosses panicked and they shut him down. The goons from Human Resources went through every safe, every in-box, every C-drive on the campus, confiscating every copy of the Sensitives. Another team of goons went through the bunker in the corn, burning Felker's files. Notes and charts and diagrams—they burned them in the dirt outside the bunker. They went a little heavy on the charcoal lighter fluid, and the fire leapt, and some of the cornstalks caught and burned like standing torches. The fire spread from ear to ear, leaping on the breeze, and the goons were flummoxed, flapping their suit coats, barking in their radios, throwing dirt like boys at play, and Felker helped them put it out. They erased his disks and the C-drive on his PC, but Felker, trying to be helpful, told them that you can't erase a C-drive—you have to overwrite it basically. He was explaining what he meant by overwrite and the goons lost patience. They took his PC to the mock parking lot and hit the thing with baseball bats until it was in pieces, then hit the pieces until they were in bits, then jumped up and down on the bits, looking like Sicilians making wine. Felker held their coats, watched impassively, and ate an ear of roasted corn he had salvaged from the dirt.

They told Felker to go back to making normal sort of plans, building on his Certainties, but he couldn't do it anymore. He asked for, then demanded, a transfer to the line, and they made him Gretchen's deputy lead agent.

Vi had heard the story of the Beltsville Sensitives from planners who had been there at the time. Later, when she joined the VP's team and started traveling, she often saw Lloyd Felker eating grapefruit and bran cereal an hour before dawn in the corner of a hotel coffee shop in Iowa or Texas or wherever they were staying. Sometimes he ate with Gretchen or with old Tashmo, Felker's buddy from the Reagan days, but if he was alone, Vi went over to him with her muffin on a tray and asked if she could sit. Felker always looked up, happily surprised—like, there are twenty empty tables in the place, why would you prefer to sit with me?

Vi liked the guy. He was lonely—she could sense it. He talked about his family, his wife and son in Maryland, and how much he missed them when he traveled. Vi asked him what had happened with the Sensitives, thinking he'd be bitter at the Service for suppressing his last, iconoclastic works, but Felker wasn't bitter.

"I was glad to leave," he said. "I was through with theory anyway. There is no theory, really. There's only what we do, day after day."

Gretchen drove her people hard, late winter into spring. They went to Iowa, New Hampshire, back and forth to Florida, stumping through the neocities of the Super Tuesday states, Raleigh–Durham, Dallas–Fort Worth, Tampa–St. Pete, all the hyphenated places, and they always seemed to put the airports in the hyphen, the perfect equidistance between centers, the linking nothingness, the land of ramps, arrival and departure, long-term parking, rental car returns, a stack of arrows on a sign, the sign floating overhead, too fast to read the options and the arrows too. Felker was a help in such a landscape; he always checked the airports on the Web and knew their maps by heart.

Gretchen was a cold and scolding supervisor, richly hated by her agents. Gretchen had her good points, Vi believed—she was brave, she was honest, she did not play favorites, she worked hard and tried to get it right—but Gretchen couldn't find her stride and settle in. Felker was the opposite: a sedative, quiet, able, slightly professorial (or not exactly so—more like your systems engineer, ready to retire after thirty years at Raytheon), tall, thin, weathered in a pleasant way, conspicuously smart about his heart, a bowl of bran for breakfast every day. Vi, eating with him, heard all about his wife and college dropout son who was learning the guitar, and his farm in Anne Arundel, somewhere near the Chesapeake. Vi could see Lloyd Felker as a modern farmer, an agribusinessman, studying the rainfall and his likely sorghum yields. They said his wife, this Lydia, was a bitch on stilts, a former TV actress of small fame in the '70s, now a faded beauty, stuck with the antique shops of Anne Arundel County, where she played the scheming moms of Shakespeare with bad rural amateurs. Vi, watching Felker spoon his bran alone, could see him as a hen-pecked farmer-husband with a loyal dog, or as an older systems engineer, or—and this surprised her—as a traveling insurance man, a guy quite like her father in a way, both men henpecked, dutiful and clueless too, but content and self-contained, their lives pared down to three or four essential elements, and for Felker, one of these was the bran cereal.

They traveled hard through March, April, May, and the crowds grew alien, unreadable, not like a page, not like a book, nothing you could ever close. It started to get pretty weird out there. First it was the pesky paparazzo whom Agent Herc Mercado nearly stomped to death at Epcot. Then it was the hoedown in Ottumwa, Iowa, where an out-of-work machinist carrying a small device got within three feet of the VP. Bobbie Taylor-Niles, working plainclothes near the fiddler, saw the machinist sliding in and put it on the comm as a confirmed grenade. Vi tackled the machinist. Herc Mercado put the boot in, Tashmo helping kick the guy (which was more exertion than old Tashmo usually went in for). The smashed device turned out to be a "portable brain-wave interceptor," built around a cheap light meter, which the machinist, who had a history of mental illness, hoped to sell to the government. Cameras caught the stomping at the hoedown and for a few days the all-news nets were running several seconds of Vi and the nutcase rolling in the dirt as Herc and Tashmo went for the extra point. Herc was proud of the beating they administered, but Tashmo had to call his wife in Maryland and tell her not to watch CNN for the next few news cycles.

They spent a week in Iowa in May. It rained the whole time. The news was pictures of the rain, the flood of Illinois, the stomping in Ottumwa, and the rain. The stomping didn't go away until they got to Texas, where everything was dry, and by then their nerves were pretty shot. Felker had briefed them on the specialness of Texas as an operational milieu. Texas was a carry state, he said. Anyone except a felon or a person judged insane by the state court system could, and did, carry a concealed handgun, and fenderbenders on the highways routinely erupted in small-arms fire. Felker said that Texas would always be the Valley of the Shadows to the Service. They had come here once with a president and had left eight hours later with a completely different president, and some things you can't live down, he said. Memory, futility, disgrace—this was what they carried through the carry state.

They worked a rodeo in San Antonio. The rodeo was in the Alamodome, where the Spurs played basketball, dirt under the lights, snipers in the rafters, dogs on every ramp, troopers in the loge, the Dome within a dome.

They came late, as always. The calf-roping competition was finishing up. The rodeo was billed by the image people as a chance for the VP to shed the cares of office and mingle with the common folk, but the only common folk permitted in his section were friendly politicians, prominent supporters, and bodyguards in leisurewear posing as the common folk. Vi sat behind the VP in jeans, Nikes, a UNH sweat top, and her earbud comm. She was fooling no one and not trying very hard. Someone gave the VP a big white Stetson cowboy hat and he waved it at the crowd to perfunctory applause. He wore the hat for twenty seconds. The photo dogs were swarming angles, what a picture, the VP in a Stetson, waving, grinning, mingling, enjoying the trick-riding interlude as the roadies got the Brahmas loaded in the chutes.

Vi scanned the house and thought about the carry state. As far as she knew, they were surrounded at that moment by twenty thousand common folk exercising their right to bring a loaded Colt to the rodeo. As the VP waved the hat, Vi made eye contact with an older lady in the first row of the next section up. The lady wore cowgirl haute couture and didn't clap. Vi looked away, looked back. The lady sat there patting the purse in her lap, giving Vi a knowing smile.

Bull riding was the big crowd-pleaser, rodeo's version of the home-run derby or the slam-dunk competition. The stands exploded at some rugged feat in the dirt ring, at the daring and hilarious bull-distracting clowns, but whenever Vi looked back the lady wasn't laughing, wasn't clapping, wasn't cheering—she was just sitting there, a cowgirl Mona Lisa, smiling at Vi.

The smile haunted Vi all night, and motorcading back to the hotel afterwards, and over pancakes the next morning. Did it mean *I got your back—homeboy's safe as a baby*? Or did it mean *I can waste him when I choose—the man exists from minute to minute only with my say-so*? They met the jet at Lackland after breakfast, bound for home by way of Andrews.

Vi remembered the long flight coming back from Texas, everybody worn out, half of them asleep. Gretchen was in front, her accustomed spot, the bench of seats next to the blast-proof door of the VP's stateroom, doing admin on her laptop like a teacher grading papers during study hall. Felker was across the aisle, munching carrot sticks, reading the national threat roundup for the day. Vi was in the next row with Bobbie Taylor-Niles, who was dozing fitfully, kicking all around, talking to three men in her sleep, a guy named Buck, a guy named Rusty, and a guy named Murph, having quite a dream it seemed. The SWATs were sleeping in formation, rather like a herd, and the snipers, further back, were deep into Nintendo. A hardcore group was playing poker on a fold-down table, Tashmo, Herc Mercado, and O'Teen.

They were almost halfway home, flying over Nashville, when Vi saw Fundeberg, the VP's campaign imageer, ducking through the door into the Service cabin, tooling down the aisle.

"Little change of plans here, Gretchen," Fundeberg announced. "There's flooding on the Mississippi. We've got to let those people know we care. We bring the balm of disaster area designation, a hundred million smackeroos. We talked to FEMA and it's all set up—a little photo op, won't take but an hour. They've got a town picked out. Hinman, Illinois."

Gretchen, to her credit, tried to fight the photo op, but she was never strong enough to handle Fundeberg. She said, "I'll talk to Plans. I'll put you there in forty-eight."

Vi felt the plane already banking.

Fundeberg said, "I don't think that's gonna fly."

Gretchen called the field, St. Louis station, requesting coverage for Hinman,

Illinois, that's Harry-Ida-Nancy-Monkey-Apple-Nixon, Illinois. The St. Louis SAC
told her she was crazy.

He said, "The whole county's underwater."

Gretchen said, "Then use a boat, I don't care. Just get some people over there."

They landed at a bomber base near Champaign, Illinois. The Army had a helo
waiting on the skirt, sixteen seats and cramped at that. With the flacks, the press
pool, a FEMA delegation, a local congresswoman, and the body team, there was no
room for the SWATs, the snipers, or the techs, and no time for set-checking or site-
prepping.

It was twenty minutes to the river, Fundeberg briefing the press pool on the
Mississippi flood and other points of interest for their readers. Herc took out a deck
of cards and dealt a hand halfheartedly to O'Teen, Tashmo, and himself, but their
minds were elsewhere and after two misdeals, they packed the deck away and rode
in silence. Bobbie looked pukey, belted in her seat. Felker, Vi remembered, seemed
to fall asleep, utterly at peace.

Gretchen spent the flight on the downlink with St. Louis. The SAC had sent
a team to Hinman, but the Alton bridge was out and his men were stranded in a
motel office, still on the Missouri side, phoning in whatever they could learn from
the PFR bands, from channel-surfing on the motelier's TV, from browsing widely
on the Web. The SAC passed along an unconfirmed report of scattered looting in
the river towns.

"And that's not all," he said. The Illinois Department of Corrections had
bused a work gang into Hinman, men convicted of light offenses only, and everyone pitched in, citizens and prisoners, their differences forgotten, building a
sandbag dike against the rising current—a human-interest story, until a length of
dike slid into the night. The water rolled and everybody fled. In Baker, down the
road, sixty-seven members of a Christian encampment had ignored all entreaties
to evacuate. The Christians never bothered anyone, but never paid their taxes
either. The local IRS had been sitting on a warrant for a year, afraid to serve it
(nobody needed another Waco). When the river started rising, three Illinois
Guardsmen went door-to-door, looking for the shut-in, the elderly, and the bliss-
fully oblivious. The Guardsmen were unarmed. They belonged to a supply bat-
talion from the East St. Louis Armory. They pulled into the commune's

compound, thinking it was just another isolated farm. The Christians hadn't personally seen any water other than the falling rain and they suspected that the whole state of emergency—complete with TV weather warnings and evacuation maps—was a law-enforcement hoax to draw them away from their arsenal, their C-rats, and their boobytraps. The arrival of the soldiers seemed to confirm these suspicions and the Christians opened fire. One Guardsman was shot through the wrist. The others were pinned down under their humvee by sniper fire from the guard towers and still the river rose.

A flying column of sheriff's men, two cruisers and an ambulance, took off down the last dry road linking Hinman to the world. No one seemed to know where the deputies were headed. They may have been going out to round up the stray prisoners or maybe they were pushing on to Baker to relieve the hard-pressed Guardsmen. Gretchen only knew that the dike was gone and the river was at eighteen feet above normal, flooding Main Street, the state forest, and some farms, and dogs and pigs and supposedly some horses, and definitely deer, and all the other animals who couldn't climb a tree, or float, or fly, were fleeing to the far side of the Baker-Hinman road. The lead car in the sheriff's column, coming down this road, hit a herd of deer crossing to the farms, killing several instantly. The deputy jammed on the brakes and was hit from behind by the ambulance and killed instantly. The tail car swerved, shearing the ambulance and striking a light pole, injuring a deputy, who later died instantly. The scene along the road was a traffic horror—doe, buck, deputies, accordioned cars, the ambulance tipped over, medicine and bandages everywhere, none of which was really Gretchen's problem, not even the Guardsmen, who were still under the humvee as far as anybody knew. Gretchen was thinking about looters, about riot, about fire and no firefighters and the end of 911.

They were bouncing through the thunderheads.

Fundeberg said, "Looters?"

"Sporting goods," said Gretchen, seriously freaked and trying to explain.

Fundeberg said, "Gretchen, get a grip. This isn't Watts. This isn't Pakistan. This is just a town in Illinois."

"Looting is a form of shopping," Felker said. "There's a pattern to it, Fundeberg. Every study shows this. Looters go for three things generally: liquor, home entertainment systems, and sporting goods—bats, knives, guns in the display case, ammo by the box. Even crossbows. There's precedent for that."

"Awesome," said Herc Mercado, who was always up for something new.

"Once they get the sporting goods," Felker said, "looters can turn themselves into a stubborn localized insurgency. How many prisoners are loose down there? Are they in possession of excessive sporting goods? We don't even know. This is not a well-planned evolution. I think this is the point that Gretchen's making."

The helo dipped beneath the clouds, flying over squares of cultivated land. The river came up suddenly on the starboard side, coffee-brown, astonishingly broad, curling and uncurling, like twenty different rivers sharing the same banks. Vi saw houses, trailers, whole uprooted trees rolling in the currents. The helo hovered over half a town.

"The school is the magnet in this district," Fundeberg was telling the reporters. "Reading scores are up, thanks to our aggressive program of Internet access."

The reporters wrote this down.

"The gym has room for eight hundred cots," said Fundeberg. "That's well over half the town."

The helo settled in the outfield of a soupy baseball diamond. A pitiful committee waited at the edge of the rotor-wash, the bedraggled mayor, a priest whose hat blew off, a two-man FEMA team. Vi and Bobbie were busy kitting up, racking Uzis, tapping ears, adjusting the straps on their body armor. Herc and O'Teen straightened each other's ties.

"Right," said Gretchen.

Quick check of the radios and they were out the door. A crowd of refugees pushed up. Vi and Felker pushed them back. Gretchen took the VP through the gap with Herc, Tashmo, and O'Teen, a box of four around him. They hustled up the hill to the magnet school with the FEMA dudes and the delegation from the town.

A light rain fell. Vi splashed across the grass, taking a position in the right-field power alley. She watched families stumble up from the town, carrying whatever they had rescued from the river. She saw young children with stuffed talking dinosaurs, men with rare and precious heirloom muskets, people saving their home encyclopedias, every family member carrying four volumes or as many as they could. She saw a woman with a small painted box marked *Recipes* and another woman in a dripping quilt carrying two goldfish in a bowl, the water sloshing as she walked. The woman held her hand over the open bowl, protecting the goldfish from the rain.

Vi heard Felker on the comm. He said that he was going for a look

Gretchen was herding the protection to the school. She said, *Look at what?*

Felker was half static. He sounded far away. He said that he was going to the town.

Gretchen said, *Felker, that's a negative. Thirteen your ass right back here.* "Thirteen" was borrowed cop code. It meant do it now.

Gretchen was hailing and recalling Felker all the way up the hill to the school, but Felker never copied back. Gretchen gave a final order before the gym swallowed her signal. She said, *Vi, go find him—bring him back.*

Vi cut through the refugees to the red clay warning track, past the scoreboard and the ten-foot foul pole, down a grass embankment. She lost her footing on the bank and slid on her ass to a gravel fire road.

The rain was pelting now. Vi was jogging down a street of prim brick homes with many family touches, trellises and flowerbeds and birdhouse mailboxes, hedges manicured. She saw a man loading a legless air hockey table into his pickup truck. She saw dogs chained in yards, barking in the rain, and others, at the windows, barking silently. She saw muddy Guardsmen coming uphill in a hurry, nearly bouncing off the back of their humvees. She saw men in denim drabs, prisoners searching for their jailers, trudging toward the shelter in the gym. She jogged, thirteening in all directions, hailing Felker on the comm, shouting *Felker* to her fist mike, shouting "Felker" at the lawns.

The river was two streets ahead, flowing like a movie, flat and wide. Vi could see the streetlights of downtown, water halfway up, the roof of a doughnut shop, and a red sign for a Texaco, *Free Travel Mug with Oil Change While Supplies Last.* She heard a burst, three rounds, from a trailer park. She jogged in that direction, splashing to her ankles, moving closer to the river now.

The trailer park was quickly flooding out. Some trailers were in place, bolted to concrete foundations. Others were half-moored, wagging slowly on an axis to the current's push. She saw men in hunting clothes with shotguns in a silver jeep. She saw a family in a metal boat being towed by a station wagon full of children and possessions. She saw men moving between trailers, men in denim drabs, many with shaved heads—the prisoners. Some prisoners were helping the homeowners load their cars and boats. Others simply fled, ignoring cries for help. She saw a few prisoners going through the trailer homes, carrying gilt mirrors and personal computers and children's bikes held high, but she couldn't tell which prisoners were looting and which prisoners were helping. She could see the street lines, double yellow, through the moving water at her knees. She looked ahead and saw Felker in a yard.

She shouted at him. Felker didn't hear or didn't look. A Doberman chained outside a trailer snapped at Felker, slashing and lunging in the water, yanking the chain taut. Felker was trying to unchain the dog and save it from drowning as the river rose, but he couldn't get around the jaws of the dog to save it. Vi watched speechlessly, Felker dancing to the side, the dog splashing at him with its jaws. The Doberman was gray. Its head was blackened, wet.

Vi heard a woman yelling from the doorway of the trailer, leaning on a single wooden crutch, holding a screaming baby in her arms. The baby was a few months old, Chinese or Korean, and wore a pink peapod suit. The woman had a cast on her left leg to her knee. She tried to pass the child out, but Felker couldn't get around the dog, so he drew his Uzi and shot the animal, one burst to the sausage-side. The dog screamed. Felker winced and took its face off with a mercy burst. The dog disappeared, then buoyed up, half-headless and still chained, floating in a water-cloud of spreading red.

Vi said, "Holy shit."

"Take the baby," Felker said.

The river pulled the dead dog in a long arc on the chain. Vi took the baby and the mother's crutch. Felker locked the trailer and carried the mom, fireman-style, up the street toward the town, staggering and dropping her, a big awkward splash, lifting her again. The baby was bawling in Vi's arms. The cast on the woman's leg was covered with signatures and messages from friends, pink and purple inks, hearts and scrawls and messages, blurring now and running down the cast. The woman was laughing and weeping and making goo-goo at the baby and thanking Jesus Christ for His sweet eternal care. Felker asked her not to move around so much up there.

They gave the baby and the mom to a group of convicts who were heading toward the gym.

Felker, unburdened, turned to Vi. "There's looters by the river. They're killing watchdogs, going house to house, taking what they want."

Vi said, "Fuck it, man, who cares?"

He started down the road, back toward the trailer park.

She followed him. "Fuck it. Felker—"

They walked into a cul-de-sac. Here the banks were gone. The trailers were coming loose from their foundations, drifting a few feet, filling with brown water, slowing to a stop. Some floated free and snagged in trees, great boxy derelicts. Others joined the current and started moving quickly as they sank, contents spilling from the open doors and windows, spice bottles, bobbing basketballs, empty plastic milk jugs saved for recycling, a trail of junk and bubbles. Vi was in cold river to her waist. She felt the loose ground slipping away under her feet.

She saw convicts wading back and forth between the trailers.

Felker squeezed a warning burst into the air. The looters turned and looked in three directions.

Felker shouted, "Federal agent. Leave this area and proceed in an orderly fashion to the gym."

The inmates looked at Felker and each other, not hearing all of what he said, and some of them decided that it was best to run. Others had guns, muskets and long rifles and some handguns looted from the trailers, and they shot into the air, warning the warner, and Felker squeezed another burst into the air, his arm stiff, like a track and field official starting the sprinters. The looters shot back, also in the air, and a few more volleys were traded in this manner, then Felker popped his clip, slid in another, and started chasing them into the river. Some looters moved away. Others stood their ground and aimed this time.

Vi said, "*Felker.*"

Bullets kicked the water, nothing very close. No one was trying to shoot anyone. Most of the inmates ran away as best they could, half wading, stumbling and dunking, swimming a few strokes, spitting water in the air, kicking till they touched the ground, and pushing up to run again.

One convict fled into the last trailer. The screen door was white aluminum and twisted off the top hinge. Felker opened the crazy twisted door using the knob.

He went in. Vi went in behind him.

It was dark inside the trailer. She was standing in a snug wood-paneled kitchen. Felker disappeared around the corner, chasing the inmate. She felt the kitchen list, the floor yawing wide into the current. She braced herself, grabbing the faucet on the sink. She heard sheet metal twisting, felt the gunshot-pop of bolts, and, through the open door, the view was moving. They were floating free. Cabinets fell open and the whole thing rolled.

She woke up in the woods, nowhere near the trailer park, vomiting and shivering, on her hands and knees. Her wallet and her creds were lost in the river. She could get replacement creds and didn't care about the wallet or anything in it, except for a folded one-dollar bill she had carried every day since coming to Protection, the bill Jens had found in an old insurance file after Walter's death.

Vi made it to the outfield and saw no helo there. She called Movements from the gym, borrowing the cell phone of the priest whose hat had blown off in the rotor-wash. She called collect. She said, "Collect me. I'm in Hinman, Illinois."

She spent the night in the gym, coughing up the Mississippi, chatting with the priest and a roofer and his pal, playing Risk with children on the cots. Some pieces were missing and the board was water-stained, but she organized a regular Risk tournament.

In the morning, she caught a ride on a medevac as far as Carbondale. They landed grandly on the roof of a hospital. Two goons from Human Resources were waiting for her there. Human Resources was the new and happy name for IAB, but no one had told the goons that they were new and happy. She asked about the others, Gretchen, Bobbie, Tashmo, and the men from Human said the team was safe in Washington. She asked about Felker and the goons said nothing.

They flew her back to Beltsville on a government Gulfstream. They took her to Psych Services, dumped her in a room with a heavy maple table, big enough for two, and soundproof panels on the walls. She asked the two-way mirror for a Coke and a few minutes later, there was a knock. It was Boone Saxon, a senior threat investigator, carrying a can of Pepsi.

Boone said, "Will Pepsi be all right?"

She touched the can; it was warm. She asked the mirror for a cup of ice.

Boone took her through the story from the helo in the outfield to the shootout with the looters and what happened in the trailer as it rolled. It was not a hostile Q&A, there were no Mirandas, but it wasn't altogether friendly either, and she didn't understand why it was Boone Saxon asking all the questions. Why not Gretchen? Why not Human? It didn't make much sense. Boone was a threat man; he only did the threats.

"Let's go through it one more time," Boone said. They went through it one more time. Vi asked for ice again, looking at herself and saying, "Can I get some fucking ice?"

They went through it many times and Boone was finally satisfied.

He turned to the mirror. "Get the ice," he said.

The Service gave her three days off to recover from the flood. Vi, not knowing where else to go, went back to Center Effing and stayed at her brother's house. It was a bad visit. She was strung out, sweaty-palmed, jumping at small noises, and she fought with Jens the whole time. By the end of the three days, she was glad to go back to the detail.

There was a rumor boom when Vi rejoined the team, and this became another way to pass the time between campaign events, the red-eyes and the van rides and the predawn breakfasts in the hotel coffee shops. The snipers said that Boone Saxon's men were looking for Lloyd Felker, the person or the corpse, a big clandestine manhunt with negative results. The bomb techs said that Felker was definitely *muerto*—Boone Saxon had found him bloated, washed up in Kentucky, and they were only waiting on the dentals to announce it. This story grew less plausible with time—how long could dentals take? Soon the bomb techs were agreeing with O'Teen, who said that Felker was alive in Mexico, working as a bodyguard for the *cocaleros*, doesn't speak the language and his memory is gone, like Charlton Heston's buddy in *The Planet of the Apes*—the only thing he remembers is how to scan the hands, and the superstitious Mexicans call him El Pantero or the Man in Pants. The comm techs scoffed at El Pantero; they had good hard rumors placing Felker in Kansas City, Denver, several shitholes in Nevada, and Duprete, Missouri. Bobbie Taylor-Niles said that Felker was alive—she insisted on a happy ending—and she even watched the ropelines for him, thinking Felker might come in from the crowd one day. Vi herself did not believe or disbelieve that Felker was dead in the river or alive, though she watched the ropes for him as well, in the spirit of a porch light you leave on.

Felker's death or disappearance affected everybody differently. Herc Mercado got a buzz cut. O'Teen gave up cigarettes. Gretchen tried to lose some weight. Tashmo bought a pickup truck (he'd always wanted one).

Herc, who lacked compassion, coined a word, *Lloydify*, which meant a total mental breakdown under pressure in the field. You could *do a Lloyd* or *pull a Lloyd* or feel somewhat *Lloydish*, and, after what they saw in Hinman, many of them did. When Sean Elias joined the team as deputy lead agent and heard his first Lloyd-word, Vi had to tell him where it came from.

Vi came back from her run, took a long hot shower, and ate a piece of toast, sitting on the futon, looking at the dusty plants along the windowsill, her home in Tower South that was never quite a home.

Most of the agents on the team had fairly shitty home lives, so Vi didn't feel too bad having none at all. There was old Tashmo, cranky, middle-aged, thirty years a bodyguard, whose wife was always after him to fix the car, fix the disposall, who didn't give him a goddamn minute's peace the one day a week Tashmo managed to get home. There was Herc Mercado, twice divorced and not yet thirty, who often slept on O'Teen's couch because his latest manic girlfriend had locked him out and he was sick of breaking his own door in. There was O'Teen himself, a balding bachelor who had tried computer dating but found that he kept getting matched up with losers, for some reason. And Felker too—he loved his wife and son; he was always telling Vi how much he missed them when he went away. But if he loved them so much, why did he walk into the flood? Was that the act of a happy man? Gretchen Williams was another story. Vi, as Gretchen's assigned driver, picked her up and dropped her off at home before and after each deployment. Every time Vi did, she saw how Gretchen and her son set each other off, the little fights, the tension in the air. Why the agents had such shitty home lives was a question Vi had asked herself many times. The pressures of the detail were special and acute—the endless travel, the need to toggle back and forth from vacant mode along the ropes (the total watchfulness, scan the hands and scan the hands, always the hair trigger) to normal people mode, whatever that might be.

Vi dressed and went down to the lobby to wait for Bobbie Taylor-Niles. Most bodyguards had rocky lives away from vacant mode, but nobody's was rockier than Bobbie's. When they traveled with the VP, Vi and Bobbie roomed together, dressed together, ate together, worked together, flirted with the newsmen in the hotel bars together. Sometimes, on the worst nights, after a big crowd, a day of overflowing crowds, they even slept together, two women in a bed sized for a king. They would get into their hotel room at nine or ten p.m., strip themselves of clothes, comm net, shooting harness, body armor. They would shower (not together), and maybe, if they were feeling wanton, slip into play clothes, as Bobbie called them, jeans and a t-shirt for Vi, pearls and a plum blazer for Bobbie, and go down to the lobby bar or up to the roof bar, wherever the hotel was serving alcoholic drinks, and have an alcoholic drink, lite beer for Vi, and for Bobbie vodka up.

Bobbie Taylor-Niles was a presence in a bar, a beauty and a bombshell and a magnet for the guys, less a woman than an ocean liner of desire, continuous and sleek, with long, knifing legs and hair a shade her colorist called *sand*, short for Streisand. Bobbie called herself the scenic route and men seemed to agree. She was not exactly young these days (she was frank about her age, which was thirty-nine-and-seven-quarters), but young men found her sexy in the older-woman way and old men found her sexy, period. This last fact was strategically important, Bobbie said, because she planned to marry a distinguished man of years and reputation, wealthy or at least well-to-do, a carnal, cynical arrangement maybe, but Bobbie had tried every other kind of marriage.

She numbered her ex-husbands I, II, and III, like movie sequels or world wars. Husband I was her first supervisor in the Criminal Division, El Paso station, a guy named Doyle Doak, who did rope tricks in his office and crossed into Mexico for eyeglass appointments, saved a couple bucks that way, no wonder he was always seasick, fucking cheap-ass dick, Bobbie said. In Washington, she met Husband II, a Senate lawyer who wrote banking regulations, who was quite a force in banking regulation, but who lost his job when he forgot to put *not* in a certain crucial sentence, accidentally abolishing all private debt in the United States. Bobbie, disappointed, left Husband II for Husband III, a surgeon in Virginia, an oral surgeon—actually a dentist, which was pretty much the same thing as a surgeon, Bobbie said. The dentist, Dr. Potter Niles, had a spreading practice in the suburbs and was certainly not poor. Vi had never met the dentist, never heard his voice, and Bobbie rarely spoke of him except to ridicule his taste in things, which was, she said, ultra–*Reader's Digest*. Dr. Potter Niles read the *Reader's Digest*s in his own waiting room and Bobbie sometimes caught him lounging in his waiting room at night, like it was a real living room. She left the dentist and moved in with an old flame, the man she called the Admiral, a two-star Navy surgeon, a true medical surgeon, the former personal physician to the president.

Vi knew that Potter Niles still loved Bobbie. Vi knew this from the support checks he sent every month. Bobbie, whose personal finances were often chaotic, asked Vi to cash these checks. Potter always wrote a little note on the memo line—*Come back to me*, or words to that effect. Bobbie got the checks in the mail, tore the envelopes, sometimes tearing the checks too in her impatience, and never read the long, anguished letters Potter included with the checks. He must have guessed this, for he wrote a Cliffs Notes version on the paper she did read. Bobbie endorsed the checks on the back in lavender ink, scrawled *No!* next to *Come back to me*, and gave the checks to Vi, who endorsed them for deposit to her NOW account. Vi's bank cleared them and sent them on to Potter's bank, which cleared them again, debiting his account, and so Bobbie's reply came back to Potter canceled with his monthly statements.

Come back to me/No!—this was the exchange for May, when Vi started acting as Bobbie's banker.

Give me one good reason, said Potter on the memo line for June. *You're boring*, Bobbie scrawled and gave the check to Vi.

July was: *But I love you/Even this is boring.*

Come back to me/I hope you find someone special—August.

I have: you/So have I: someone else—September.

Who is this Vincent Asplund, the man who keeps depositing my checks—-is he your lover now? asked Potter in October. *We sleep together yes*, said Bobbie cruelly.

Come back to me—and so on through the calendar to Christmas and beyond.

Vi knew that Bobbie would not go back to Potter Niles. Bobbie dreamed of being Mrs. Admiral, living the gracious life she saw in magazines, throwing tinkling drinks parties for the NatSecCom set. She talked about it often, drinking in the bars—her future perfect life. This was the real Bobbie Taylor-Niles. The rest of her biography—three divorces, four abortions, seven maxed-out credit cards, one personal bankruptcy—was an accident, a draft. She would quit the Service on her wedding day and say goodbye to Vi and the crowds.

Some nights, Vi and Bobbie sat alone in hotel bars, talking about men or bull-shitting with the other agents coming in, or the campaign hangers-on, the preppies of the press pool, a stray congressman or two. Bobbie, seven years an agent at the White House, a moth at the ballpark lights of power, seemed to know every man who ever had a bit of it, and it was entertaining, watching Bobbie flirt.

Other nights they stayed in the room. Vi would do her isometric exercises, pushing on the walls, as Bobbie had a cigarette and a Stolie from the minibar. Then Vi would do her crunches as Bobbie had a cigarette and called the Admiral back in Georgetown. Vi would take a shower, come out, towel down, and check her e-mails as Bobbie had a cigarette and watched a movie from the in-room entertainment menu, talking from a cloud of smoke, telling, in installments, the story of the struggle that was Bobbie Taylor-Niles.

Bobbie had grown up poor in a Tulsa trailer park. She fucked her way into the Air Force at the age of seventeen (she was a minor, her stepfather wouldn't sign, the recruiter was willing to be flexible). She joined the base police, liked the white arm-band, the way she looked in the white armband, went to college on the Vandenberg-Cal State extension program, made decent grades (Bobbie wasn't stupid), joined the Service after her discharge, did her rookie tour in Crim, married Doyle Doak (thinking he was somebody important because he had his own parking space; she was so unworldly in those days), took a transfer to Protection, trying to move up, to get closer to the real people, the ones who run the world and have the money. She spent seven years inside the White House, guarding the first daughter—happy years for Bobbie. The famously feminist first lady was busy with her teas and her causes, leaving the first daughter, a doggish teenager, completely in the dark on basic woman things (the poor kid was bursting into puberty wearing baggy overalls and cotton boxers, for God's sake, Bobbie said), and Bobbie, who loved the kid, took it upon herself to educate the first daughter in the things that every woman needs to know, how to win and keep a man, how to keep him satisfied, how to slip a condom on his hog without him knowing it, using just your lips and tongue and one index finger. The first lady caught Bobbie and the daughter in the Lincoln Bedroom covering the G-spot and its meaning to a girl, and the old witch hit the roof, sending Bobbie into exile, the Siberia of crowds.

Bobbie told these stories in the motel rooms, talking from her cloud, gray layers in the lamplight at her head, as she had perhaps another vodka for her nerves. Vi would listen as she ironed her clothes and kevlar for the morning, and Bobbie's too, and cleaned their weapons on the bedspread if she was in the mood. They talked and watched TV until one of them could sleep, usually Vi, and then they killed the lights and Bobbie watched the movie end. Sometimes—more and more, it seemed—Vi would wake up before dawn and find Bobbie in her bed, a shock the first few times, but not after that. Vi would close her eyes and drift away, and, through the night, the women found each other in the sheets, sleeping thigh-to-pelvis, sweating, flinching, jerking, dreaming of two ropelines, guarding each other in their dreams.

Bobbie showed up twenty minutes late that Sunday morning. Vi got in the car and they set out for the Galleria-at-Bull-Run, which was not a mall, but an all, Bobbie said.

"They have one of everything," Bobbie said, digging through her Fendi bag as she drove the Admiral's Lexus down the highway to Bull Run. "It's a goddamn Noah's Ark of luxury retail."

Vi took the bag from Bobbie. "You look at the road."

Searching through the bag, Vi found old charge slips from the better stores in Washington, lipstick, Chap Stick, dirt, grit and several kinds of pills, sticks of gum and foil from the gum, an empty bottle of Visine, Kleenex in a travel pack, breath mints in a roll, condoms in a gold case with a snap, a nickel-plated Smith & Wesson Ladyliner nine, and a crumpled pack of Silks, Bobbie's brand of cigarette.

"They have this one store," said Bobbie, lighting up. "Little lingerie boutique, everything's from France, shit'll blow your mind. They cater only to the most elite mistresses in Washington, cabinet rank or higher, none of them dumpy congressional oversight babes, unless, I guess, you're sleeping with the Whip."

"Why would they let you in then?" Vi didn't mean this the way it came out. She only meant that the Admiral, though rich and well connected, was not of cabinet rank.

Bobbie said, "Because they recognize in me a woman of rare taste, you pissy little cunt. We'll stop at Neiman afterwards, get you something nice to wear. Remember, Vi, there's no excuse for being plain."

"I'm not plain, I'm functional."

"Yes, but we can help you."

They saw the first sign for the Galleria-at-Bull-Run and after that they watched the signs, searching the horizon for the megamall. Exit 8 was for long-term parking and tour buses. Exit 9 was for RVs needing sewer hookups.

Vi said, "You ever think of Felker?"

Bobbie said, "I do. That poor dear, dear man. I get weepy when I think of how he risked his life to save that dog."

"No, he killed the dog. It was the baby that he saved."

Bobbie said, "Well anyway, he risked his life and that's what counts."

They rode along and Bobbie talked about her wedding plans, a full-dress ceremony in the festive Pentagon Rotunda, big names on the guest list, senators and such, drinks and dinner for three hundred, on and on and on, the band, the wine, the parting gifts, the finger bowls and napkin rings. She had every detail nailed except the year. Vi was always glad when Bobbie talked about the napkin rings. It meant that Vi could just nod for a while and not have to listen very hard. All of this—planning for a wedding, shopping, lingerie, the compulsive gabbing—was Bobbie's way of dealing with the stress of vacant mode.

"I want to get the Admiral something special," Bobbie said. "Sort of a peace offering and early Valentine, me in something sinful. I want to make that mother-fucker buckle at the knees."

"Did you guys have a fight?"

"We're adults, Vi. We don't fight, we have miscommunications."

"Did you guys have a miscommunication?"

"No, I understood him loud and clear."

They got off at Exit 12 and trolled for a parking space. Bobbie saw one in the distance, but a sports car beat her to it. She found another spot farther out. They parked and caught the shuttle bus.

The bus was standing room, packed with shoppers going to the mall or riding with bulging bags to rejoin their cars. Vi and Bobbie pushed their way to the back and found two hanging straps not far apart.

They rode the bus around the mall to the grand entrance. They strolled the indoor boulevards of the Galleria. They stopped at the mall map and, after some cross-triangulation, found the you-are-here dot.

Vi said, "Okay, we're there." She consulted the directory. "What's the name of this boutique?"

"It's a secret," Bobbie said. "Known only to the chosen few. They're notoriously discreet—they have to be, with their clientele—so they keep the name and where-abouts a secret. Don't bother with the map. I'm pretty sure it's down by Sears."

They started for the far end of the mall.

"How do they advertise," said Vi, "if it's such a fucking secret?"

"Legend, myth, word of mouth," Bobbie said. "How did people advertise before advertising?"

"Do *you* know the name?"

"Of course I know the name. The Admiral and I, we travel in those circles, Vi. We go to parties, closed parties in large houses on tree-lined private drives."

"So what is it? If you know, that is."

"I just told you that I know. Don't try and goad me into telling you the name." They kept walking.

"Oh all right," said Bobbie, "but don't tell a soul and for God's sake don't tell Herc Mercado. He'll have every stripper in the District camped out at the door."

They stopped at a pretzel cart. Bobbie whispered in Vi's ear: *"The name of the boutique is Inside the Beltway."*

"No really, what's the name?"

"Isn't it amazing, Vi? Makes me hot, just saying it. Inside the Beltway. *Inside the Beltway.* O, the way around my belt, power sleeping in my region. O, my hidden inner, my soft and rotten fruit. O, my throbbing Washington. Makes me want to touch myself, the name."

"Why's it in Virginia then?"

"The Beltway is a state of mind. Everyone has noticed this but you."

They passed Neiman's, Godiva, Pulitzer, and Wurlitzer.

"You know, sometimes I wonder," Bobbie said.

"What?"

"I wonder if the Admiral's using me, promising to marry me, promising and promising. I give him all I can, but he only wants more. Can I ask you something weird? Have you ever been with more than one man at the same time?"

Vi laughed. "I was with ten thousand men in Iowa last week."

"Sexually I mean."

Vi knew what she meant. "Can't say as I have. Why—is the Admiral into that?"

"Every man is into that—you're so fucking innocent. When I was your age, damn. I remember once in El Paso. I met these two cute postal inspectors at a weapons refresher. We went back to my place. It was nice. Even been with three men, Vi?"

Vi figured you had to be with two before you were allowed to move up. "Nope," she said.

"I remember once in Crim, we hit a warrant on the border, this big ol' hacienda in the desert. We seized eight million bucks in cash that day, a gloryosky stat, and some of us went upstairs to celebrate. I'm lying on this big old iron bed in this big adobe room, cash spread all around me. Me and these three agents—Lord, I wore 'em out. I felt sorry for those agents, afterwards. I saw 'em lying on the floor. They were young guys, they had their whole lives ahead of them, but they would never see another woman half the woman I was in that bedroom. One of the three was one of the two from the weapons refresher, just so you don't think I'm a total fucking strumpet."

They came to a cement oasis, a fountain, benches, and some palms.

"I remember this other time," Bobbie said. "Super Tuesday in Atlanta, when the president was running the first time. You've never worked Super T, but let me tell you, it's a fucking scene—six hundred delegates selected, the nomination on the line, careers are made and ruined, and bourbon is the balm. Everyone was staying at the same hotel on Peachtree, the candidates, the campaign staff, the press, and us. Georgia's coming in, Tennessee is coming in, Florida is coming in, and everybody's smashed. I'm in the hotel bar with Fundeberg, the president's Rasputin, the architect of victory, the toast of Super Tuesday. We had a thing back then."

"You and Fundeberg?"

"Why—is he so horrible? Don't answer that. We're drinking Charlie Mansons in the bar, and we go up to his suite with this twerpy little talking head from cable.

We ride the elevator and it's glass. The lobby had its own indoor jungle and we rose over it, like going up to heaven. We get to the suite and the phone is ringing. It's a well-known syndicated columnist—I shouldn't say his name."

She said his name.

Vi said, "*Him?* But he looks so owlish."

"Mr. Family Values, always calling for a moral renewal, horny little worm-wood that he is. So he shows up, flings off his bow tie and we keep on drinking and I'm feeling good, you know. I'm feeling free. Here's trashy little Bobbie Taylor from a Tulsa trailer park, drinking drinks with these big important men, and *this* is what I want and this is *all* I want, and we keep drinking and I lie back on the bed. I close my eyes and then I feel their hands on me. It's like they're searching me."

Vi said, "Was it nice?"

"Not at first. The mood was off—ringing phone, three TVs, beepers beeping, and this moaning, keening, grinding sound like a goddamn ghost in chains, which turned out to be a fax-paper jam. The talking head was talking dirty and the columnist was bragging about the opinion-making power of his weekly dozen inches, but the body's an amazing thing—I started going with it. You know that feeling, Vi? Your mind is here, your body's there. You float away. That's how Super Tuesday felt to me. The talking head's between my legs, the columnist fills my mouth, but just as I'm about to come, Fundeberg starts leaking."

"Leaking?"

"Some incredibly hot nugget of inside campaign dirt, I forget exactly what. They left me on the bed and went off the record. Deep background, they call it."

They were sitting on a bench in the oasis. Dimes shimmered on the bottom of the fountain pool, magnified by water, looking like nickels. The fountain was on some kind of timer. It rose to a halo, fell to a burble, rose again and fell.

Bobbie said, "Oh well. Someday I'll get there, Vi—the inner ring of power, sure. Come on, girl—let's find this damn boutique."

The elite boutique had no sign and no windows. They found a plain steel door under a surveillance cam.

"This must be it," Bobbie said.

Vi looked at the camera.

Bobbie said, "That's so they can peruse us and see if we're their sort of person."

She buzzed. They waited by the door.

Driving back to Washington, Vi said, "It was probably closed, that store."

Bobbie didn't say much, depressed by the rejection.

Vi said, "Let's go up to Beltsville and goof off at the range."

Bobbie didn't say much and they didn't go to Beltsville. Crossing out of Fairfax, their beepers beeped, first Vi's and then Bobbie's. They didn't check their beepers, didn't need to. They knew it was the Movements Desk. They were going out again.

In a small act of rebellion, Vi put off calling Movements for almost an hour, waiting until she was back in her apartment and alone. Her orders, when she got them, were as terse as a road sign: the VP's team was scrambled for New Hampshire through the primary on Tuesday, rendezvous and jumping-off at eighteen-thirty hours. Vi thanked the duty agent only half sarcastically and started unpacking from the trip to Iowa so that she could start packing for New Hampshire. She was thinking of Lloyd Felker—*There is no theory, there is only what we do.*

She heard the Fiends laughing by the elevators. Some days they took the stairwells down from the penthouse, headlong, forty floors, urban mountain biking. Vi listened to them as she unpacked her bags, kicking her dirty laundry in a pile in the middle of the floor, socks and pants and underwear. The Fiends came down the hall and moved off again, bumping into doors, their voices growing faint.

Vi's life was on the bed. Two suits, both blue, one dirty and the other wearable. Six blouses, five dirty and one boxed. An Uzi Model Z, black, specially modified, reasonably clean, a level three kevlar vest, folded over once, and, on the pillow, her sidearm from New York, a simple semiautomatic nine.

Vi waited, standing by the door of the studio, but she didn't hear the Fiends again. She fit the Glock into her mouth, butt up, her knuckles in her eyes.

What we do.

She wasn't suicidal. It was not that kind of act. It didn't even mean as much as self-annihilation. It was just a bored thing that you do—you have a gun and a mouth, a thing and a hole, and you're a little curious. Sex was probably invented this way. She stood there, counting *one one-thousand, two one-thousand,* thinking of the undertaker's shady lawn, the games of hide-and-seek with Peta Boyle long ago. She stood there until she was sure that she felt completely idiotic (one one-thousand later), then she tossed the pistol on the futon and finished packing for the primary.

6

There was always bullshit with the cars or actually the car, because they only owned the one and it belonged to Shirl. Shirl's car was a silver Nissan Sentra with forty thousand miles and light opera in the CD. Tashmo's car—or what she called his "car"—was, in fact, a truck, a sporty little pickup, fully loaded, cherry red. Shirl called his truck a car just to get his goat. (Tashmo knew this, and resisted, and yet it got his goat.) When she was pissed, she called the truck a toy. When she was really pissed, as she might be now—sitting in the kitchen, it was hard to tell—she called the truck a goddamn stupid toy.

Shirl put the plate in front of him, an open-faced sloppy joe with a side of shoe-string fries. The bullshit with the truck, the car, the toy, was that it didn't always start on wet mornings, especially the cool-but-not-quite-cold wet mornings which they had instead of winter here in Maryland. When it started, it didn't always brake, at least not in the velvet, mindless fashion Tashmo liked and expected in his braking. Instead, he touched the pedal and felt a leftward drag down around his balls, fleeting but distinctly leftward, which he said was like *aaagh*, like saying *aaagh*, the feeling in your throat of saying *aaagh*, except it's in your balls.

Shirl poured two iced teas from the plastic jug and leaned against the counter by the bread machine. They drank their tea from tall plastic glasses, which were pebbled to look frosted. They had once owned two sets of glasses, one for indoors, made of glass, the other for the patio. They had once owned two sets of everything, plates and flatware, various-sized bowls, and used the plastic only when they ate out back under the string of hanging paper tiki lanterns and the ever-active bug zapper, which they did, all the time, when the girls were young, sometimes just the four of them, Tashmo, Shirl, Mandy, and Jeanette, sometimes with other Secret Service families, Tashmo's pals from the Carter detail or the swingin' Reagan team, Loudon Rhodes and Loudon's wife and Kobe Rhodes, Loudon's son, who breast-fed into kindergarten and was husky for his age. Kobe Rhodes looked ten in kinder-garten and he was a sight, climbing into his mother's lap. Sue Rhodes untied her halter top, carried on with the conversation, as Kobe sucked and looked at Tashmo with one eye, like, Can I help you, bud? Lloyd Felker had been back there too, sec-tioned plastic plate in his khaki lap, with Lydia, his wife. The kids would play together, slipping on the SlipNSlide, mounting the wooden benches in their slappy bathing suits, except for Kobe Rhodes, who said he wasn't hungry anymore. The other kids ate pickles, chips, and burgers, eating as kids ate, exactly half the bun, the burger crumbled into pieces, tweezered to their tongues, piece by tiny piece, three more bites and then a treat. Three more bites? Two more? Am I done yet, Mom? Eating like plea bargaining, and the tikis swayed, filling the patio with orange lurching voodoo light and the happy smell of citronella.

Shirl said, "*Aaah?* Pay attention to me, Tash. I'm supposed to go to Generoso and say *aaah?* Like he's some kind of goddamn dentist?"

Tashmo said, "Not *aaah, aaa-guh.* From the gut, Shirl. Try it for me once."

Generoso was their family mechanic. He ran Generoso's Citgo on the Balt-Wash in New Carrollton. The truck had an appointment in the morning. Tashmo had planned to drive the truck to Generoso's with Shirl on his tail, describe the *aaagh*, the distinctly leftward drag, the sawing of the starter, then drive home in Shirl's car and let the old mechanic work his magic. But Movements had ruined a good nap, putting Tashmo on deployment until Tuesday, which meant that Shirl would have to get the truck to Generoso's on her own.

She sipped her sweet iced tea. "Goddamn stupid toy."

So it was official: she was really pissed, and he, for one, knew why. She thought that he was going north to chase other women, as he once did, but didn't anymore. He wanted to tell her that he didn't anymore, but this would have required admit-ting that he did, once, or more than once, more than once a week in fact. So he was trapped again, ketchuping his fries, a lacy, spiral pattern, as Shirl made that nerv-ous clucking noise.

Age had mugged them both, but Tashmo was defiant. His hair was gray, though still his own and thick enough to pompadour. He refused to trim his sideburns to the fashion or stop dressing as he dressed, in yoked suits with slash pockets, a style called contemporary westernwear. Gretchen Williams wouldn't let him wear the bolo ties, even though a suit with yoking and no bolo tie looked ridiculous. Why couldn't Gretchen see this? Never mind, fuck her—he loved his dudeish suits. They made him look, with the 'burns and the pomp and the zippered boots, like the carny-barking stock car impresarios he had worshiped as a kid. This was what he had planned to be when he was old, when he was young and planned for being old.

He chewed a fry and thought about a town called Falling Rock, the place where he was young, the grassland flats of eastern North Dakota. They used to hang out by the highway, Tashmo and his high school friends, drinking beer, pooling their pornography, and watching motorists mistake the city limits sign for a Highway Department warning. The motorists would brake behind their windshields, peering out for any sign of falling rock, or any height it might fall *from*. Tashmo and his buddies hunted through the grass, gathering stones, which they threw at passing cars. They gathered stones and talked about the future endlessly. One kid was going into radio, another to pro baseball, probably the Cubs, a third to the pipelines like his paw, and a fourth to glamorous stock car/funny car impresariodom, and this was the young-ass Tashmo. The kid who was going into radio already had a half-hour show on a twenty-watter in Fort Scott, beaming surfer hits—you could hear him all the way to Minnesota. The kid who planned to be a Cub could hit the city limits sign, a blue-sky peg and a satisfying *ding*. Tashmo loved the action of boys throwing rocks—the windup, the sliding sneaker-scrape, the click of elbow-wrist, the *unt* of shoulder muscle. Stay motionless until it hits, only a punk would turn his back and not watch it fall. Funny—when they talked about the future, no one even mentioned Southeast Asia.

Of the four boys throwing rocks, three went to Vietnam. Two came home, one with medals, one with legs, and this again—the boy with no medals and two legs—was Tashmo. He was in the Air Cav, '68 and '69. He saw true courage in Chu Lap and Ha Bong and decided that it wasn't up his alley. He scammed his way through the rest of his tour as a chaplain's aide, Spec 4. The chaplain was a brimstone Presbyterian from Texas. They toured the wounded tents together, passing out peppermints and reading from the Good Book. When the chaplain wasn't looking, Tashmo charged the GIs two condoms for a dramatic reading. The soldiers loved his Fats Domino rendition of the Song of Solomon, *Your breasts are like great gob-*

*lets, your eyes are like great jewels, your arms are like great boughs, and your momma
ain't around.* This was how he saved his legs in Vietnam.

He went to North Dakota State on the GI Bill, a twenty-two-year-old freshman,
majoring in Business, English, Ag, Engineering, Ag again—he had more majors
than the Army and they were about as relevant. He went to a football game in
Grand Forks that November, State v. U, the homecoming. He sat next to a girl
named Shirley Skurdahl, a one-in-fifty-thousand shot. They did the Wave and
started chatting, and quickly realized that they had a lot in common. Shirl came
from Blankenship, near Hebron, near Fort Scott, near Vercingetorix, which was only
two exits from Falling Rock, which made them neighbors, nearly. They had grown
up ninety miles and eighteen months apart, loving and believing the same things.
They both thought the sideburned, ankle-booted racetrack impresarios were cool,
the coolest, deliveries of cool from Californeeay, and even now, a lifetime and two
daughters later, Tashmo was a version of these dudes, admittedly a pension-fully-
vested, upper P.G. County, married-filing-jointly, no-thank-you-we're-quite-happy-
with-our-present-phone-provider version of these dudes, but still, he loved his suits
and boots, his pool hall El Ranchero look, and he always would. Shirl loved it too
and always would, but she didn't understand that *no one else* loved the look, east of
Forks, south of fifty. He had tried many times in the last few years to say or imply
or insinuate that she didn't need to worry when he went away, that he was finally
faithful, finally settled, finally hers, but she wouldn't let it go, this image of her husband as a stud. No woman wants a man no woman wants. She couldn't see him as
a relic of past futures, because what would that make her? Jealousy is vanity eventually, he thought.

Shirl ran the disposall. "Well I won't say *ugh*."

"*Aaa-guh*. And don't forget: leftward. Generoso needs to know."

Generoso had fixed every car they had ever owned since the microbus with the
little sink and faucets which connected to nothing and the manual in German,
making the car care tips seem all the more achtungful. Tashmo didn't like taking
orders from the Krauts, and was never big on car care, which was probably why that
piece of shit was always on the fritz. They drove it up to Philly for the Bicentennial
and had to get it towed by this real witty black guy in an afro. Mandy was a baby,
Ford was president, and Tashmo was a trainee agent, buried in Baltimore, the Crim

Division, working for a special agent in charge who liked to cut out early and watch the Orioles take batting practice.

The SAC loved Tashmo. He said, "You're a dude."

The SAC was an embarrassment, the way he brought his mitt to the ballpark, clapping for a rally, a fist into the mitt, and used it as a megaphone, *The ump is a chump!*, and knocked the kids aside for the foul balls.

Tashmo begged for orders out of Baltimore and they sent him to Protection, Carter's detail. He took Shirl and Mandy camping in the microbus to celebrate, a week in Valley Forge, where Mandy learned to walk. Tashmo was something of a history buff, a fool for dioramas and ugly observation decks. He was happy anywhere there was a gift shop selling tasseled pencils, which were much too big for the see-through pencil cases, which they also sold. Shirl called the microbus a "camper" after that, thinking *micro* made the bus sound both metric and injectable. They drove the camper/microbus to Gettysburg, Harpers Ferry, Appomattox, and all the way out to Mount Rushmore, where Shirl took his picture guarding the stone presidents in a Hawaiian shirt, but mostly they took it to Generoso, who probably fixed the microbus twenty-seven times before Tashmo finally sold it to an EPA ecologist for two-hundred dollars over Blue Book.

The ecologist claimed the bus one afternoon. He brought his wife, a tall gal named Anita. Her hair was glossy-black, straight to her ass, and she came from Winnipeg. As the husband looked for rust, Tashmo had a vision in his driveway. It came to him full-blown, as movies come to you in theaters. He saw Anita kneeling at his feet in a buckskin dress, offering him a platter of cool butter. He snuck around to the back of the microbus and stole the tire iron.

A few days passed. Carter was R&R'ing at Camp David and the detail was standing three-day rotating watches, pretty decent duty, watching Carter agonize, better than skiing with the crazy fucking Fords everybody said, except for the ticks in the woods, and the protest-hippies and photojournalists sneaking through the underbrush.

Tashmo was coming back from a rotation. He went by the ecologist's. He knew that the wife was home. He saw her car, an orange Karmann Ghia, sitting in the driveway. He didn't see the microbus. He figured the ecologist was off ecologizing. He rang the bell, spinning the tire iron in his hands, kicking at the welcome mat.

Anita opened up. She wore a long suede skirt, ferny green, a studded seam running up the outside of each thigh. He offered her the iron and started to explain.

She said, "Aren't you nice?"

And he was. He would always think of that time, Carter into Reagan, as his suede phase, remembering Anita's seam, her saddle-smelling thighs. Looking back, it seemed he spent those months commuting to Camp David, living in a bunkhouse, patrolling the dirt roads, watching Sadat take a chilly dip, then home again to Shirl, by way of Anita's.

Camp David made him horny, everything about it—the goofy swimmin' holes, the timbered dining halls, the motor court cabins done up in a thrift-store Happy Angler motif, like Mamie Eisenhower's vision of an Adirondack Berchtesgarden. The point of the place was to Retreat, clear the head of leadership in the bosom of the woods, some F. Scott Thoreau–type jazz, but the woods were rigged with the latest anti-SigInt gear, microwave bafflers under underbrush, emitting the acyclic hum of a wounded engine. Tashmo walked the fences in boots and Wrangler jeans, slinging his sixteen just like in the war, always in long sleeves and slathered in bug lotion, because the woods were ticky, and if the ticks bit you, you got this thing called Lyme disease, which was basically old age except you caught it from a deer. Walking the woods at night, Tashmo heard the bafflers, but couldn't always find them. The humming wavelength was designed to bounce between the trees and carry forever. The term was *propagate*, the techies said, the description of this bouncing, like in the Bible (he remembered Vietnam), *and Abraham did propagate with Sarah*, or like Russia, where they had propaganda instead of democracy. He tried to follow the hum, but he found himself walking in big circles, the moon between the trees, on his left, then on his right. The bafflers he couldn't find made his dick stand up. Many times on lone patrols he had to lean against a tree and jerk off in the dark just to get his mind back on Jimmy Carter.

He spent a lot of time in the duty hut, drinking rotgut coffee with Lloyd Felker, filling out the logs, watching a wall of CCTV, surveillance cameras sweeping fences all night long. They had motion sensors, infrared, scanners tuned to wide array. They tracked possum for fun and watched Johnny Carson, the monologue and guests, the smutty banter from the couches. They tracked the protest hippies, the anti-nukers trying to infiltrate from the west, saw them coming miles in advance.

Tashmo liked to interview the anti-nukers. He considered them hippies and perhaps they were. He offered them cigarettes, went easy on the frisks, gave them exciting jeep rides to the admin shack. He admired hippies, the whole Woodstock thing. They said that Vietnam was bad—he had seen it, and agreed. They advocated free love in the mud—he hadn't seen it, but he wanted to. But the hippies he met under Carter were a dreary, worried group. He asked them how often they got laid, as hippies, in an average day, sincerely curious, but they could only talk about Three Mile Island, rads and rems and cataclysmic heat-exchanger failures.

Anita was a hippie, a suburban Buddhist, and she vacuumed in the buff. He saw her twice a week, stopping by for yogurt and a blowjob when Carter was at camp. Sex with her was exercise and, she said, a brief communion with the honesty of bodies. She grew bean sprouts in the basement, quoted Joni Mitchell, and wouldn't let Tashmo smoke in the house even if he promised to blow it out the window. There was always a tension with Anita. The tension made it sexy, their little tug-of-war. Tashmo loved her clothes, her jerkins and her moccasins, and secretly he wanted to undress her partially and do the deed that way, but she was always in a rush for total honesty.

"It's all wrapped up together," Tashmo mused one day as she went down on him. "If we didn't have clothes, being naked wouldn't mean too much."

She shrieked in his lap.

He said, "What's the problem down there?"

"Your cock," she gagged. "It, it—it tastes almost like the smell of Deep Woods Off."

Tashmo said, "Oh that."

He explained about the deer tick infestation at Camp David, how the agents smeared themselves in bug repellent, how it got from his hands to his manhood when he jerked off in the woods, and how he thought of her, jerking off alone. He thought she might be flattered by this honest revelation, but no dice. She made him take a shower with the soap she cooked at home.

He came back with a towel and described his driveway fantasy, Anita kneeling in a buckskin shift, holding the ample dairy platter. He was hoping for a little role-playing, but Anita was aghast. She said he was describing the Land O Lakes logo-woman, the box the butter comes in, the ethnocentric squaw. She strode off naked to the fridge, returning with a box of Land O Lakes. Sure enough, there she was, glowing on the package, his sexual ideal, a Pochahontan princess, offering him butter on her knees.

Things were never right with Anita after that, but he didn't let it get him down. Suburbia was full of wives—wives like lawns, beautiful and useless and tended by their husbands once a week. Upper P.G. County was a civil service bedroom. The husbands in his town were civil service lifers, like the EPA ecologist, or Tashmo and his Secret Service buds, or like Tashmo's neighbor, Bo Gould, who could sing all seven verses of the Fannie Mae fight song. The wives were mostly ex–flower children, transitioning to something else, like Canadian Anita with her orange Karmann Ghia, her well-thumbed *Kama Sutra*, and her closet full of suede.

There was something in the air back then, Carter winding down, a funky sort of hope, like they were on the verge of a great discovery, and it made him horny, driving past the lawns, buying milk and fudgsicles at the supermarket, women pushing shopping carts in tennis dresses. He followed them for aisles. Shopping made him horny. Working made him horny. Breakfast made him horny—reaching for the Land O Lakes, he spread the melting squaw. Betty Crocker in the flour— what would that be like? Fishy Mrs. Paul, Aunt Jemima dripping syrup, the ripe-tomato Contadina wench. These vestals of the Pik'N'Save, always feeding others, but what about their needs?

He didn't jerk off in the supermarket. No, he was strong. He waited till he was in the car. Afterwards, he zipped his dick away, wiped his hands on a moist towelette, and had the best smoke of the afternoon, slouched behind the wheel, watching women in tennis dresses return their carts, unloaded, to the automatic doors, or leaving them to drift on wheels across the parking lot.

America. Driving home from Camp David, Tashmo passed the subdivisions speading over hills, except for one stretch of razor-ribboned fence, undeveloped blankness, several miles' worth. He passed it coming back from camp and wondered why this square of forest stood untouched as every hill around it sprouted homes. One night in the duty shack, he mentioned the blankness to Lloyd Felker. They were watching Johnny Carson and the heat-screen monitors, both of which were pretty dull that night. Felker said the thing you couldn't see behind the trees, the undeveloped heart of P.G. County, was the black budget at Fort Meade, the National Security Agency.

Tashmo said, "The spy guys?"

"Bet your ass," said Felker. "They have a fleet of satellites, biggest mainframe ever built. They can listen to any conversation in the world. They make us look pitiful."

Tashmo later realized that many husbands in his town were commuting to black budgets. He learned to spot them, off-duty at the dump, at his daughters' school plays, or at Generoso's on Inspection Saturday. The spies he knew were bearded, brainy, nervous men, good fathers and bad drivers. They would never say exactly what they did or where they did it. They always lived civilian-side cover and Tashmo tortured them for sport.

He remembered the intermission at Mandy's fourth-grade Thanksgiving pageant. Not a beer in sight and he found himself talking to a dad who said he worked for the FCC. Tashmo toyed with the man, asking intricate questions about spectrum auctions.

"Like what if, for example, I wanted my own band. What exactly are the steps that are involved?"

Shirl had made him go to the pageant. Mandy played a singing turkey and Tashmo wreaked his vengeance on this poor fake regulator.

The guy-who's-not-a-spy tried to duck the question. He said, "I don't work in that part of the shop. The Commission, as you know, is quite the little empire."

"What part do you work in?" Tashmo asked.

"The other part."

"What does your part do?"

"Pretty much nothing about spectrum auctions."

Tashmo told his neighbor, Bo Gould, about the pageant dad, forced by his position to pretend to be a bureaucrat, when he was, in fact, a different kind of bureaucrat. They were drinking Sambuca shooters in the Goulds' elaborate finished basement, playing with Bo's HO train set.

Bo was smashed that night. He said, "Want to know what *I* really do?"

Tashmo said, "You work for Fannie Mae. You sing the fight song. Sing it for me, Bo."

Bo sang a verse—

"O Fannie Mae, O Fannie Mae
You spread the credit widely. . ."

Then he waved. "Fannie Mae is bullshit. It's called cover, Tash. I don't even know why they assigned me that one. I requested the President's Council on Physical Fitness, but they said that cover was taken. I'm on the waiting list, in case a spot opens up. But my real job is listening from space. My specialty is France. I could be fired for telling you this. Hope nobody heard me."

After Bo passed out, Tashmo wandered upstairs, taking one last beer from the fridge, making himself a quick burger with fried onions.

To the living room. How do spies live? Picture-window views of other picture windows. A recliner chair, brown leather. He'd always wanted one of these. Test it out, tilt it back. They look so comfortable, but how the fuck do you get up?

Sip the beer. Where'd I put that burger?

He pushed himself up. Bookshelves always tell a story. He read the spines by the streetlights, *Principles of Radio, Birding on the Chesapeake,* Michener, Uris, von Clausewitz, *Jonathan Livingston Seagull.* He stepped back from the books and felt the burger squishing underfoot. He peeled it from the carpet and took another bite as Leah Gould, Bo's wife, padded down the stairs.

Tashmo nodded at her, chewing. "How's it going, Lee?"

Leah was a handsome woman. She played a bit of tennis at Patuxent Park and when she hit a forehand, she went *Uh.*

She stared at him that night. She wore pom-pom slippers and a forbidding nightie. She said, "Have you been *frying* something, Tash?"

It was clearly time to slide. He walked home under the trees, swinging his arms, finishing the beer. He felt it strongly, walking home, the funky hope.

He woke Shirl up, climbing into bed.

Shirl said, "Where the hell have you been?"

"Over at Bo's. We played with his train set, demolished his Sambuca. Turns out he's a major U.S. spy."

Shirl said, "It's three a.m."

"Already?"

She rolled away from him.

Tashmo said that Bo could listen to any conversation in the world.

Silence.

Shirl said, "What's it like inside? I heard they were redoing their kitchen."

When the men went out with Carter, their families got together for potluck supper on Miss America Night, or had cookouts with games and prizes for the kids by the picnic shelter in Patuxent Park. The wives of the detail made an effort to be friends, even though they had nothing in common except the fact that their husbands had been thrown together by the whim of the assignments wheel, guarding a president none of them had voted for. The wives might not have picked the same husbands again, given the opportunity, and surely didn't pick, as friends, the wives of men their husbands hadn't picked, and the kids picked no one, not Carter, not their fathers, not their fathers' coworkers, and not their fathers' coworkers' kids, yet everybody was supposed to bond at these events, and every family brought a dog. The dogs fought, humped, and ran away. The kids blamed each other's dogs and screamed until they blacked out from the lack of oxygen. It seemed like perfect hell to Tashmo, but Shirl said it was good to get together once a month, eat potluck with Sue Rhodes and Lydia Felker. It was good to get together and watch the world broadcast premiere of *The Way We Were* or the *Miss America*, root for good old North Dakoty, the brave deaf girl from Oregon whose singing was disturbing, Hawaii's always pretty but never seems to win, and what the heck is up in Massachusetts? Is Neet illegal there?

He went to a few picnics, watched the wives. He didn't jerk off at the picnics. No, he waited till he got home and Shirl was definitely sleeping. He had an iron rule: no Secret Service wives, look and lust, but don't touch. He tried to obey this rule, to masturbate the urge away, but despite his diligence—well.

He'd be packing to leave Camp David and another agent would catch him in the bunkhouse.

"Hey Tash, you going back?"

Tashmo would crack wise. "See me packing, dipshit?"

"Listen, do a favor. Goddamn wife can't change a fuse. She says half the house is dark. It's on your way home, man."

Or: "I got some dirty shirts. Hey Tash, you heading back?"

He's thirty-one, thirty-two, thirty-three, driving down the Balt-Wash in his suedest phase, smoking Trues, drinking beer, listening to Hot Country hits, pulling through the cloverleaf, heading like a missile for his buddies' bedrooms.

This happened many times: the wife is under Tashmo, cradled in his arms, his St. Olaf medal falling on her breasts. The doorbell rings, a pair of sweaty Seventh-Day Adventists. They showed up every third day in that part of Maryland.

The wife looks toward the door. "Let's not get it."

"No," says Tashmo, full inside her, "I don't think we should."

He didn't feel too guilty, cuckolding agents his own age. He figured that after seven years or so, a marriage works or doesn't, all by itself. Nothing he did when he dropped off the laundry could have any influence, and the last thing Tashmo wanted, ever, then or now, was influence. The junior agents were a different deal, Texans, Californians, and midwesterners, young husbands recruited out of Crim Division stations near their homes, where their wives could see their mothers and their sisters every weekend. The Service did these couples a disservice, he believed, bringing them east when their marriages were fragile, new and tenuous, untenured, dumping the wives in the Balt-Wash Corridor, putting the husbands on the road. The wives didn't know anyone in Maryland and along comes Tashmo with his Trues, his boots, and his impressive mastery of fuses.

The wife is barefoot, living in the dark, possibly unable to cook. She's wearing jeans cut under her belly, her frizzy Orphan Annie hair tied up in a tube sock. It's not like he came with anything in mind, but she offers to show him where the fuse box is, and her jeans and feet slap the floor as she walks, her ass going this way and that. The house smells like pot and pot pourri. He takes out the old fuse, screws in the new, and throws the knife switch. Nine lamps go on, two radios, a blender, and a blow dryer in the bathroom. Tashmo thinks this little waif must've gone around trying each appliance, thinking—what? It's *not* the fuse?

The wife's a little sheepish in her jeans. "Takes a man's touch, I guess."

Bullshit in the wicker chairs and they have a beer. She's summarizing the latest issue of *Esquire*, which is open on the coffee table next to the clamshell ashtray, the lidless jar of Noxzema, and the digital clock which blinks 7:32, 7:32, 7:32, blinking as a warning so you'll know that it's not really 7:32.

He hooks a finger in her belt loop. "These are fine. Where'd you get 'em?"

She names a store in Fresno and they tongue-kiss. Swiveling heads, all the yummy noises, the lift-off of the tank top, a joint operation, and, underneath, the blazing nurse-white glory of Maidenform bra. The jeans are wiggled out of—she turns her back shyly. Her panties are a color called mello yello. Her toenails are a color called pearl.

There are far too many items on the bed, little Chiclet pillows for decoration, others with arms for reading on, and the normal sleeping pillows, which are also in the way, and it seems he's pulling pillows from his ass.

He mounts her.

She says, "Ouchie."

Her legs are badly burned in back. She says, "I fell asleep in the sun."

They try again. She's on top, jouncing titties swinging to her rhythm, nipples circling his face, making him a little dizzy. He grabs her nipples to hold them still and she cries, "*Yes!*"

This was how he started with Lydia Felker. It was early summer, 1980. Carter was ahead of Reagan in most polls. Outside, the hired men were cutting lawns.

Tashmo ate his sloppy joe alone. Shirl was in the ultraviolet closet off their bedroom, misting her orchids. Jeanette, Tashmo's college daughter, was channel-surfing in the den.

He rinsed his plate and plastic glass, left them in the sink, and went out through the sliding doors to the patio. He sat at the picnic table, looked out at the lawn and flowerbeds.

He slept with Lydia Felker for seven months, into 1981. Lloyd, her husband, Tashmo's best friend at the time, suspected nothing. It ended after Hinckley. Lloyd became a planner and Tashmo never spoke to Lydia again.

The years passed. Then, after Felker's disappearance in the spring, Lydia called the Movements Desk, left a message: *Tashmo—call me, it's important.* She left another, left a third. Tashmo, fearing that some ball of dirty string was coming unwound, never called her back. He never called her back because it was over, Lydia and Lloyd, the green days of the suede phase, and Tashmo was now trying to rebuild a life with Shirl. How could it be good news, messages from Lydia, after all these years?

Tashmo lit a cigarette, sitting on a picnic bench. He knew that he had screwed up when he banged his best friend's wife, and he had done his level best through the intervening years to cover up all traces of the indiscretion. He was following the model of his hero, Ronald Reagan. Tashmo as a bodyguard had watched Reagan in the last years, '87, '88, beat off scandal upon scandal, Ollie North, the Contras, missile shipments to Iran, the great man diminished by a web of shredded paper. There were some who even said that Tashmo in those years began to become Ronald Reagan, to walk like him (the jaunty rancher's strut) and cock a six-gun smile in the Reagan way, and now it seemed that Tashmo was doomed to end his tenure as the Dutchman had, dodging allegations, shrewdly feigning cluelessness. It was a subtle danger of bodyguarding greatness. Exposure to that wattage of charisma seemed to hollow out the everyday. You came to see yourself not as a man with the duties of suburbia, but rather as the president of the country called your life.

The bench was cold on Tashmo's ass. He took a walk around the yard.

Spring would be coming in a month or so, and he would start his spring routine, rising early when he was home, drinking coffee in his boxing gloves, doing sixty seconds on the speed bag in the basement, wearing nasty old swim trunks. In the summer, he would go outside, still shirtless, showing off his Buster Crabbe physique. He'd pull the hose like a mule from the bushes to the flowerbed, and water slowly, making the dirt dark, cigarette on his lips, the scene slowly building toward a climactic coffee piss, Tashmo in the garden, his back to the house, the trunks tucked under his nuts. If he saw Bo Gould going off to the black budget, Tashmo would wave with the hose, thumbing off a high *Good morning!* spray, pissing with the other hand as he waved to Bo. That would be a shining time—him going, hose going, Bo going; everything is good.

Jeanette moped through the kitchen, coming from the den, going to the john, carrying a melted icepack in her right hand, the TV remote in her left. Tashmo was sitting at the table, drinking his iced tea.

She said, "I need a ride to school tomorrow morning, Daddy."

Tashmo said, "That's nice."

Jeanette went to the bathroom.

Shirl came in, fixed herself a plate of sloppy joe, and sat down to eat. She said,

"Loudon called—I almost forgot. Loudon in L.A., he said. Is that old Loudon Rhodes?"

Tashmo said, "Of course it is. How many Loudons could a person know?"

"Well I asked him and he wouldn't say. I kept saying, 'Is this Loudon Rhodes?'"

"He was probably on a cell phone. He's secrecy-obsessed."

Loudon Rhodes, the ex-Reagan bodyguard, was living in L.A., running a private security firm, making millions in retirement. His agents guarded stars and hot directors, fending off stalker fans, paparazzi, aspiring screenwriters, and divorce attorneys. He called Tashmo from his hot tub or his boat, from Aspen, Sundance, and Cannes, just to chew the fat and talk about old times. He was always telling Tashmo that he ought to hang it up, retire, join the real world.

Shirl ate the sloppy joe. "He kept saying, 'The crow is flying.' He said you'd understand. He said it twice, the crow. I said, 'Loudon, is that you?'"

Shirl had the local callback number on a scrap of paper. She gave it to her husband. She asked, "How is Sue-Bee?"

Tashmo said, "They're pretty much divorced. Loudon moved to Malibu. He's dating Malibu Barbie."

Shirl said, "I never liked that man, even when I did. What happened to Kobe?"

"Cokehead," Tashmo said. "He was working for his dad, hanging out with stars, and they got him into the cocaine. Poor Loudon had to shell out for two rehabs."

Tashmo poured another tea and sat across from Shirl, trying to come up with a way to say that he wasn't going north to bang other women, without admitting that he ever had.

He said, "Can I get you something while I'm gone?"

"Like what?" she said, still eating.

"I don't know," he said. "Something special, something nice, something you've been wanting for a long time, something they only have in New Hampshire."

"Just don't bring back the flu."

"I don't control that, Shirl. I work the crowds, people sneeze. It goes with the territory."

"Remember how sick I was the last time? I was stuffed up for a month. I missed two book club meetings. They were good books too."

Jeanette emerged from the bathroom, changed her icepack ice from the freezer trays. Jeanette was a sophomore at Martha Custis College in the Shenandoah. Her sweatshirt said CUSTIS. She closed the fridge and headed for the den, holding the icepack to the right side of her face.

Tashmo stopped her with his arm. "Let's see."

Jeanette paused, slouching. He looked up at her eye, which was puffy and purple-yellow.

He whistled. "It's a beaut."

She said, "Daddy," and went into the den.

Jeanette had rushed a southern belle sorority called Rho Rho Rho, and had come back from pledge weekend (or Hell Fest as they called it at Custis) with a fat black eye and minor kidney damage.

"God I'm proud," said Tashmo after Jeanette had left.

Shirl rinsed her plate and scraped the skillet, and slowly they returned to the business of the cars.

"If it starts," she said, "and if it doesn't crash from having no brakes, how am I supposed to get home from Generoso's? Any bright ideas?"

"I never said it had no brakes. I only said there was an aaagh."

"I can't walk home."

"I'd never let you drive a truck that had no brakes."

"You're a sweetie."

Was she always this sarcastic? He said, "It's simple, Shirl. You drive my truck, Jeanette follows in your car, and the two of you come home together."

Shirl said that Jeanette had class on Monday morning, and wasn't that what they were paying Custis for, class?

Tashmo said, "Call Mandy then. She can meet you at Generoso's."

"Who'll watch the twins?"

"There's always Nigel," Tashmo said.

Nigel was Mandy's husband. He taught comp lit at UMaryland. They were going through a trial separation.

Shirl said, "You'd trust the twins with Nigel?"

"He's their father," Tashmo said.

"He'd probably abduct them off to London and then we'd have to extradite them back. That could take years and hefty legal bills."

"The twins can ride with Mandy. They love the car. It reminds them of the womb."

"But Nigel has their car."

"You can drive my truck. Mandy can drive your car with the twins in back."

"What about the car seats?"

"What about the car seats?"

"The seats are in the car and Nigel has the car."

"I'll call Nigel and tell him to drop the car seats off at Mandy's. You can drive over to Mandy's tomorrow, early, put the car seats in your car, then you, Mandy, and the twins can drive back here, pick up the truck, and Mandy and the twins can follow you to Generoso's."

Shirl said, "It upsets the twins to see Nigel."

"He can come when they're asleep."

"They're never both asleep unless they're in the car."

"He can drop the car seats here."

"I don't want him here."

"You could pick them up at his place."

"What are we, his servants?"

Tashmo went into the bedroom. He started undressing.

Shirl cornered him. "And what about Jeanette?"

Tashmo sat on the bed and took his pants off, leg by leg. "I'm not worried about Jeanette. She's a winner—the way she took that whipping from those fancy southern belles, and told the dean of hazing compliance to stick it up his pity pot. The girl's got moxie—she'll never be a failure or a cokehead. I worry about Mandy, not Jeannette. Jeanette's a winner. She'll do just fine in life."

"Yes, but how is she supposed to get back to Custis? She can't *walk* there, Tash."

"Can't she get a ride with Shane Gould?"

Shane was Bo Gould's daughter and Jeanette's roommate at Custis. Shane had her own wheels, a puce Isuzu Trooper.

Shirl flicked the lights on. "Don't undress in the dark. I don't like the image of you undressing in some dark room. Shane isn't going back to Custis this semester— I've told you this five times. She interning at the State Department, working on the Balkan tragedy."

"What does Shane know about the Balkans?"

"She knows they're Balkanized. The question is, what next?"

Tashmo started shaving in the mirror. "Jeanette should stay home until her eye clears up."

Shirl said, "That's inane."

"No daughter of mine is going to school with a fat black eye. It doesn't look right, Shirl."

"It's not school, it's college, Tash. Your daughter is a woman now."

"I'm aware of this."

"*Shhh*," said Shirl. She looked at the wall. "Keep your voice down, Tash. Jeanette is finally sleeping."

"How in hell do you know?"

"Listen—" she said. "The channels aren't changing."

Tashmo drove his truck whenever he was home both because he liked the truck (sporty, sexy, tough—he liked to see himself in windows driving by) and because he wanted to show Shirl that it was a useful, sensible addition to their household way of life. He liked to drive the truck, but when he had to get somewhere in a hurry and didn't feel like dealing with potential starter trouble, he took Shirl's Nissan Sentra, which was more reliable. He drove the Sentra now, coming into Washington, rolling through the parking lot of a crappy public golf course. He parked between a silver van with Virginia rental plates and a second van, black, with Maryland tags and a Hertz sticker on the bumper.

Tashmo hiked up the cart road to the first tee, where Loudon Rhodes was waiting with the others from the Reagan teams of long ago, Gus Dmitri and Julius Panepinto, blowing on their hands, dressed to golf in winter, bundled up but wearing the pastels. They stood with a young man with shaggy blond hair. The young man wore a red down vest and a faded denim jacket.

The young man said, "Don't you recognize me, Uncle Tash? I'm Kobe Rhodes."

Tashmo was appalled. The kid looked like an X-ray. "Kobe," Tashmo said. "How's it going, son?"

Gus was looking down the fairway with binoculars, focused on two figures at the distant pin. The golf bags held a variety of gear, walkie-talkies, an extra set of binox, a D.C. police scanner with crystals for the feds, and a big thermos of Dunkin' Donuts coffee.

Panepinto said, "We eat them doughnuts?"

"That's a rodg," said Gus. "Yo. The crow is flying."

The crow down by the second hole was John Hinckley, Jr., the boyish shooter of March 1981, acquitted by insanity, 1982, and ever since a resident of a D.C. mental hospital. Hinckley wasn't flying. He was walking quickly with a woman, his girl-friend or his fiancée, an acquitted murderess and former fellow patient. Hinckley received periodic furloughs from the hospital. Loudon Rhodes, a nonstop operator, had a source inside the nuthouse who tipped him off to Hinckley's furloughs. Whenever Loudon got a tip, he called the boys together, Panepinto, Gus Dmitri, sometimes Billy Spandau, sometimes Larry Aaron up from Padre Island, sometimes Dusty Jackson up from Hilton Head. Loudon insisted that the Hinckley missions be professional in all respects. Panepinto, white-haired and bifocaled, walking with a metal cane after hip-replacement surgery, was still a crack logistics guy, renting vans with non-sequential plates, different rental agencies if he had the time, scaring up the kevlar vests (they wore them under the golf clothes), handheld Motorolas, and night-vision glasses, even though Hinckley had a curfew and the glasses blinded you in sunlight.

Hinckley and the girl sat down on a bench along the fairway, a little closer now. They glanced and saw the agents. Hinckley looked away, still talking to the girl.

"We're getting to him," Panepinto said.

Tashmo stood with Kobe, Gus, and Panepinto, laughing at Loudon's jokes, acting all amazed at the big-time people Loudon knew. Tashmo rarely kissed this kind of flagrant ass, but he might need a job someday and Loudon had the jobs.

Kobe Rhodes looked jumpy. He said, "Dad, which one is Hinckley?"

Loudon didn't answer.

Tashmo said, "The guy."

"I feel like going down there," Kobe said. He cupped his hands and yelled, *"Hinckley, you're an asshole!"*

"Kobe," Loudon said.

"I *do*, Dad. I feel like going down there."

"Kobe," Loudon said. "Why don't you go wait in the van?"

"But Dad, I want to help you. I want to be with you."

"Help me in the van," said Loudon to his son. "Keep an eye out for the groundskeepers."

Tashmo watched Kobe Rhodes walk down the cart path to the van. He said, "How's he doing, Loud?"

Loudon shrugged, "The kid? He says he's clean, he swears to me. He says being off the coke gives him lots of energy."

The old agents stood around, trying to look numerous and ominous, watching Hinckley as they passed the thermos. Tashmo heard all about Gus Dmitri's paddleball, Loudon's millions, Panepinto's hip.

"Larry Aaron got remarried," Panepinto said. "I saw them up in Scottsdale, Larry and the wife. She's Puerto Rican, Costa Rican, one of them. They met when she was cleaning out the house after Gladys passed away."

Tashmo took the thermos, poured a cup. "Gladys passed away?"

"It was a blessing really. She was in such pain."

Gus Dmitri took the thermos. "What's the new wife like?"

"Sweet kid," said Panepinto, "and a total piece of ass."

"Young?"

"Young."

"How young?"

"I don't think she's even forty yet. Larry's on Viagra, don't you know."

"So am I."

"Join the club."

"How's it working?"

"I don't like to brag," Panepinto said. "So, anyway, I says to Larry, 'Watch it, bunky. She'll give you a coronary on that waterbed of yours. That's probably her plan, fucking you to death. She's after your fat Tier VII pension package.' Larry says, 'I can live with that. She's earning every penny, the crazy kid.' So I says, 'Larry—'"

"Wait," said Loudon, peering through the glasses. "They're mobile."

Hinckley and his lady friend stood up. The lady stretched her legs, sat down.

Hinckley opened a book and started reading to her, making small dramatic gestures with his hands.

Gus Dmitri took a leak against the bushes.

Tashmo said, "Hey, didn't Billy Spandau move to Arizona too?"

"Sure," said Panepinto. "He rented, then he bought, but he didn't like the climate, the desert is so dry. Now he does guest protection at a Club Med compound in Chiapas. We played a round of golf in Mesa last December. Billy's born again. This was his big news. I'm lining up a putt and he asks if I accepted Jesus Christ. I'm like, 'Billy, do you mind?' I shot a ninety-six that day."

"With mulligans?"

"Without. Best round of my life. My putter was on fire."

Tashmo said, "Wasn't Billy born again before?"

Loudon nodded. "'84. He cornered me with pamphlets at Camp David. I told him to go peddle his salami somewhere else."

"I guess it didn't take that time," Panepinto said. "He backslid, got mixed up with No-Doz and his workout buddy's wife. Then he contracted liver cancer and was born again, again. He asked me if I'd noticed how many guys from Reagan had contracted the Big C. He kept saying that, *contracted*. Like it's something you sign up for."

Tashmo said, "How many?"

"Well, there's Billy. There's Gladys Aaron, Ken Howell, and Ken Ochs. Dusty lost his sister. And Reagan too, the man himself—remember, with the polyps? And Mrs., with the breast. It's a pattern, Billy says. He says the Reagan era had become a cancer cluster. We're all contracting growths, and why is this? Billy has two theories. One, cancer is secretly contagious. The other is that we were all exposed to some powerful mutagen on Air Force One."

"Like what," said Gus Dmitri, "some chemical or ray?"

"Billy didn't know for sure, but he thought maybe it was fallout from glitzy campaign advertising. Maybe ads have rads and they bombard our genes. We fill the air with glitz. It has to effect *something*."

"Billy is an idiot," said Loudon Rhodes. "I love the guy like a brother, but let's face it, he's an idiot."

The girl stood up and walked along the path. Hinckley followed her, still holding the book.

"They read each other poetry," Gus Dmitri said. "I saw that in a magazine."

Loudon shook his head. "It makes me sick, seeing Hinckley walk around like that. Look at him. Look at him. He should be in jail, the very coldest hole. Oh, but that might violate his precious little rights or mess up his precious little therapy."

"That's the problem with this country," Panepinto said. "We're afraid to punish. No wonder the young generation is walking around lost."

"Hinckley needs a bullet," Gus Dmitri said.

"*Bang*," said Loudon Rhodes.

He still liked sex with Shirl. He liked it best just before he went away. He'd find her with her orchids in the UV room and take her in the kitchen from behind, or any old way she wanted. Married couples didn't bang enough; this was, he felt, the root of many national problems. Sex with his wife made him feel patriotic.

They lay in bed, Tashmo drifting off to sleep. Shirl was bundled under covers, as she always was when naked in this room. She was talking about the problem with the car, the truck, the starter and the brakes, the trip to Generoso's, Nigel, Mandy, and the car seats, sounding very far away.

Tashmo had a crazy thought, lying there. What if Lydia Felker had called Shirl? What if Lydia had told Shirl the whole story, the old affair, all of it? Was this why his wife was so on edge?

Shirl was up and busy. She copied Nigel's number from her Palm Pilot, reaching to the night table, holding the covers to cover her breasts, like if she wasn't careful he might see one. She brought the phone to Tashmo and he dialed.

Nigel taught a seminar on plagiarism at UMaryland. Tashmo didn't like professors as a group and wasn't wild about Britons either, except for Winston Churchill, who seemed like an okay guy. Tashmo had told the guests at Mandy's wedding that Nigel taught a course *in* plagiarism, rather than *on*. Nigel, who was drunk, got pissed, saying that *in* meant he was teaching *how*, whereas *on* meant that he was deconstructing. The number rang somewhere in the District.

Nigel here. Kindly leave a message at the tone and I'll return your call.

Tashmo waited for the tone. "Hi, Nigel, it's your father-in-law, Sunday around six. I'm calling because we really need the car seats first thing tomorrow and I figure you don't need them, since you dumped your family like the scumbag punk you are, and three weeks is probably too soon for you to have new kids with someone else, I'm assuming, so *kindly* drop the car seats at the Goulds'. You remember Bo and Leah from the wedding. They live down the street, the brick house on the corner, number forty-one. Don't let us down, okay?"

The pickup started in the driveway.

Shirl said, "Hallelujah," and threw it in reverse.

They took Laurel Road to the Balt-Wash. Tashmo made Shirl drive so that she could feel the leftward drag for herself and better describe it to Generoso.

He said, "Brake."

She braked.

"Feel it?"

"No."

"It's like an *aaagh*. Tell him that. Try again."

She tried it. She didn't feel it.

He said, "I swear it was doing it before."

It was dark. They were southbound on the Beltway.

"Try it now."

She tried it.

"Feel anything?"

"A pain in the ass."

"Oh that's funny, Shirl. That's really really funny."

Shirl pulled in front of Building 00 at Andrews Air Force Base. They sat in the no standing zone and still there was this bullshit with the car.

"You mean the truck," he said. "It's a truck, a pickup truck. Say *truck*."

"I can't walk home."

"Nigel will bring the seats, you'll see. Mandy can follow you to Generoso's."

"Nigel will let us down."

The jet beyond the fence was fueled and floodlit, waiting. Tashmo knew that Nigel would let them down.

He said, "Get one of your girlfriends to follow you to Generoso's. Jeanette can take the bus to Custis."

"That's just great," said Shirl. "A girl alone on a Greyhound bus with a fat black eye. Knowing our luck, she'll be captured by a documentary photographer and become a famous haunting icon of American disaffection. How embarrassing for her—it could devastate her self-esteem."

Shirl.

"You and your book club," Tashmo said. "Besides, there ain't nothing wrong with our luck."

7

As the youngest agent on the VP's team, Vi drew the duty of driving Gretchen Williams. Vi would leave Tower South in a four-door Taurus from the government's leased fleet of four-door Tauruses, pick up Gretchen at her house in Maryland, take her to meetings at Old Treasury downtown, at the Pentagon, or out in Beltsville with the planners. Vi didn't hate the duty. It was long days of no thinking, of focus on the road, as Gretchen shot the rapids of official Washington, pestering the higher-ups for better gear, or more down time, or replacement agents. Gretchen rarely got the things she lobbied for, but she tried, which Vi thought was impressive.

Vi pulled into Gretchen's driveway around four that Sunday afternoon. She saw Gretchen in the doorway of her house, fighting with her son. This went on for ten or fifteen minutes, then Gretchen came down the steps with her suit and duffel bag.

From Gretchen's house to Beltsville was twenty minutes without traffic, and there wasn't too much traffic going northbound. In the twenty minutes, Gretchen said two things: "Hey" (as in *hello*, when she first came down her driveway and got in) and "Hey" (as in *Pass this asshole already*, when Vi was caught behind a rattle-trap Toyota in the slow lane on the Beltway). Gretchen spent the ride looking at the VP's schedule for the New Hampshire trip, a fat printout in a plain manila folder. This was another good thing about driving Gretchen Williams: not a lot of claustrophobic small talk in the car.

They pulled up to the gate of the Protection Campus, passed their creds out the window to the guard, who ran them through a reader and waited for approval on his screen. The buried sensor net around the grounds was undergoing routine maintenance. Vi saw the techies and the backhoe and the trench, the SWATs in ball caps drinking coffee, standing by the trench, everybody looking like they were making overtime. The guard handed the IDs through the window and stepped back to let them pass.

A short road up the hill, lawns on either side. Three cars at the crest, parked end to end along the shoulder, flashers flashing, two Tauruses and a big black Lincoln Town Car with a whiplash aerial. An agent saw them coming and stepped into the road. The agent was a black guy, Levi Harris, one of the Director's bodyguards. The Director, being king of all the details, had the Town Car and a driver and a detail of his own, and Levi was the weekend guy apparently.

Gretchen passed the VP's schedule to Vi. "Run this by the planners. I'll meet you on the quad when the Director's done with me."

Gretchen got out, walked around the hood, saying not a thing to Levi Harris. The doors of the Town Car were opening. Legs were coming out, followed by the bodies of three people: Boone Saxon, the threat investigator, wearing a stiff raincoat and one of his plaid vests which always made Vi think of TV Christmas specials; Debbie Escobedo-Waas, the Director's new gal Friday, so perky and gung-ho; and finally, slowly, like a bureaucratic Elvis, the Director himself, emerging from the car, pulling on his suit to straighten it.

They started down the road on foot. The Director walked in front, letting Debbie make his points, Gretchen on the other side of Debbie, Boone Saxon a step or two behind them. The driver in the Town Car swung out and followed them, pausing to let Levi Harris hop in the shotgun seat. The bosses walked slowly, talking more than walking, Levi and the driver following discreetly in the big car. Vi, uncertain of the etiquette in such situations, followed the Lincoln down the road and around the quad, Debbie talking, the Director interjecting here and there, Gretchen nodding as she walked, Boone Saxon listening in case his name was called.

The quad was a grass oval, big enough for soccer, browned over for the winter. The buildings on the quad—Threats, Plans, Movements, Psych Services, the Weapo School, and Technical Support—were of a set, if not a mind-set, red brick and cream steel, sculptural, abstract, like if you pushed them all together, they would fit and make a giant checkered cube.

Vi parked outside the Plans Pavilion, a building with a wingspan if such a thing is possible, and carried the VP's schedule upstairs to the cubicles and glass-walled conference areas. The president was flying out of Andrews in the morning and the planners were in air-raid mode, scurrying around, trying to assemble a halfway decent security assessment for a weekend in New York.

"Okay," said one planner. "We got a fund-raiser at the Waldorf followed by coffee with opinion-makers at a mansion in Bedminster. What's the safest covered route from Manhattan to New Jersey?"

"Limo," said another planner.

"Limo in Manhattan means a tunnel to New Jersey," said a third. "I don't like a tunnel."

"Limo to the helo then. Helo to New Jersey."

"I don't like a helo in Manhattan. Some guy in a building with a missile while you hover. Bingo on the helo."

"Nix the helo, do the limo. Lock the tunnel down."

"I get a Stinger missile. Bingo on your limo."

"Limo can survive a missile," the first planner said. "Cadillac assures us."

"Unless it hits the glass," someone pointed out.

"Get two limos, real and decoy. Which one do you hit?"

"Get two missiles."

"Get three limos."

"Limos just attract attention anyway. You're better off in the back of a taxicab. It's a sea of yellow in New York. Which one do you hit?"

"We can't put the president of the United States in the back of a New York City taxi cab. How would it look?"

"Or smell."

"I think we all know how it would smell."

"I'll tell you how it would look: like a taxicab. Remember Felker's Twelfth Certainty: traffic equals camouflage. I don't mean an actual taxicab, of course. I mean a special vehicle, armored like the limos, special gear, special tires, special pursuit engine, full chaff capability, the works. Surround it with other special vehicles driven by our guys, fake FedEx trucks, fake UPS, additional fake taxis, even fake messengers on special fake bicycles, whole blocks of invented traffic designed to look like ordinary New York City shit. They could even honk and call each other asshole."

Vi waited her turn, leafing through the VP's schedule, Manchester tonight, Manchester tomorrow, Rumsey on to Portsmouth tomorrow afternoon, Portsmouth Tuesday morning for a rally in the square. It would be like any other trip: three days of hotel food and hotel beds and van rides with no legroom, the dreary repetition broken only by the scattered, rattled moments of sharp focus on the ropes. Vi was jittery—a little—as she always was before a jumping-off. Her nerves had gotten worse since Hinman, and now she had to work to clear the trash out of her mind, fear and doubt and queasiness, to focus on the job of scanning hands. It was just another trip, but different too for Vi. They were going to New Hampshire; she was going home. The VP had made fifty trips to New Hampshire in Vi's time as a body-guard, crash visits to the cities inland, Nashua, Concord, and Manchester. They had been to Portsmouth several times, once to Rye, once to Eatontown, though never to C.E. itself. Vi hated the idea of going home a bodyguard, part of the armored jamboree. In a place she didn't know, Miami or Atlanta, the faces on the ropes were bar code, miles of it, and she scanned. It was hard and getting harder to stay vacant, even in a place she didn't know, but she could do it still, cram out every other thought. New Hampshire felt different to her, riskier somehow. She knew the place, her memories were there—it was more to cram out of your mind.

She said, "Hey guys—I've got a plane to catch. You want to vet the VP's sched-ule or what?"

The planners went to work on New Hampshire, analyzing each event as a series of submoves, from the limo to the hotel, through the hotel by steam tunnels, from the tunnels to the stairwell to the ballroom to the crowd. They went through the days and pages in this way.

Vi got the analyst's approval for New Hampshire and went out to her car. She waited with the motor running, watching the Director on the quad with Gretchen Williams. The Director was explaining, even pleading, making an excuse, or so it looked to Vi. Gretchen, nodding, listened for a long time, then abruptly turned away and stalked across the grass. Gretchen got in the front seat. Boone Saxon got in back.

Vi said, "Hello Boone."

Boone said, "Hello Vi."

"Questioned any agents in your sweatbox lately?"

Gretchen said, "Shut up, Vi."

The Director's limo passed them on the right and sped up the hill, heading for the parkway into Washington.

Vi's hands were on the steering wheel. She said, "Okay—where to?"

Boone looked at Gretchen, who was staring stone-faced through the windshield.

"Andrews," Gretchen said.

Vi threw it into drive and they set off.

When they arrived at Andrews, Tashmo's sporty pickup truck was blocking the no-standing zone outside the terminal and Vi had to stand the Taurus farther up the curb. Andrews was a busy place that night, the media streaming from the buses through the double doors where the base police would check their creds, sniff and search each piece of carry-on. Gretchen fetched her luggage from the trunk, following Boone into the lobby.

Vi found a parking space by the dumpsters and the storm drains at the far end of the lot. She saw Herc Mercado zipping through on his yellow motorcycle. They crossed the lot together, Herc carrying his duffel on his shoulder and his suit bag on his arm, still wearing his motorcycle helmet, which was black and speckled silver like a bowling ball. He was describing his workout of that afternoon, twenty reps of twenty each of something very heavy. They saw Tashmo in the cab of the red pickup, fighting with his wife. Herc drummed on the hood just to be a dick, startling the Tashmos as he passed.

A lone custodian ran a power waxer on the gleaming lobby floors, a scalloped pattern from the corner out. There were several stands of bolted seats, beige pillars, and tan walls. Most of the agents were already there, killing time, waiting for the VP to come out from Washington. O'Teen was standing with his bags, reading the thin parts of the Sunday *Post*. The comm techs were sitting in the chair area, working through a tricky signal-shielding problem. Gretchen was standing by the runway doors, talking on her cell phone, popping an antacid, one foot on her duffel bag, as if she had shot it in a hunt and was posing for a photograph.

Vi and Herc dropped their bags at O'Teen's feet. O'Teen was a ratty Philadelphian, a lovelorn ex-computer-dater and ruinous sports gambler. He lived alone in

Arlington, where he had full cable and his mother and his bookie on speed dial. He liked to bet the NFL and always had a few dimes down by Sunday brunch. He also bet on baseball, college and the pros, though never on the Phillies because he loved the Phillies and he said you never bet on what you love. Late winter was his fallow time, post-football and pre-baseball, and he bet on what he could, hockey, hoops, and prizefights, ice dancing and the more important dog shows. The Personnel Division was always on O'Teen for his gambling. They probably would have dumped him from the detail if they could have found anyone in Crim willing to work ropelines twenty-eight days a month.

Vi said, "What's happening, O'T?"

O'Teen chewed a fingernail as he read the sports page, checking the disabled lists. He said, "I'm fucked up, that's what. They're saying here Prince Rupprecht has the ague."

"Who's he?" asked Herc.

"Top-rated giant schnauzer. He kills 'em in deportment, a big hound with the moves of a poodle. Sidney gave me three to five at the Westminster. This throws the field wide open."

Tashmo came in grumpy from the parking lot. He said, "What's going on?"

"Prince Ague has the clap," reported Herc. "Otherwise not much."

O'Teen handed Herc the sports page, keeping Arts & Leisure for himself. He was looking at some bets on the Palmolive-Rachmaninoff piano competition in St. Petersburg. Sidney the bookie would give him three to one on a hot Korean pianist, a rookie out of Juilliard, just turning pro.

O'Teen said, "He kills 'em with impromptus and nocturnes. He's got speed, power, soft hands—the whole package. He plays these long, warm, flowing melodic lines, with brilliant stacatti, like the young Horowitz. I saw him trash a Polish girl at the Cliburns last year."

An SUV pulled up in the parking lot. Sean Elias skipped around, opening the sliding side door. Five Elias children spilled onto the curb, lining up by height, it seemed, tallest first, the baby, number six, on the end in Mommy's arms. Sean's family always drove him to the jumping-offs. Early, late, during school, in every kind of weather—they never missed a jumping-off. Sean went down the line, bending to kiss each kid, whispering a sentence to his son, his son, his son, his daughter,

and his son, a kiss and then a whisper, then the baby and the wife. There was nothing special about the Eliases, but Vi liked watching them just the same. What did
Sean Elias tell his children? *Be good. Help your mother. Help your brother help your
mother. Don't take any wooden nickels. Good luck on the test.* And to his wife—what
fit into a whisper? *I love your body and you in it. Look at what we made. Don't forget
the insulation.*

Elias crossed the lobby, suit bag on his shoulder. The SUV pulled through an
arc and disappeared.

"'Evening," said Elias, as if nothing had just happened.

O'Teen was on the cell phone. "Sidney? Yeah, it's you know who. Two dimes on
Korea at the Rach."

The waxer waxed, the agents waited, several minutes passed. Vi was worried
about Bobbie Taylor-Niles, who was always late, but even later tonight than she
usually was. Vi paged Bobbie to her cell phone. As she waited for a callback, Vi
walked between the pillars and looked out at the jet on the tarmac, blue under the
belly, white across the top, black letters on the white, UNITED STATES OF AMERICA.
Base police stood guard around the landing gear. A pygmy truck maneuvered the
jetway stairs against the forward door, carefully, by nudges.

O'Teen was reading Arts & Leisure, looking for something else to bet on. He
said, "Who here knows anything about the Venice Biennale?"

Herc turned to the scoreboard page. "What league are they in?"

"It's not a team, you mutt. It's an invitational art tournament, kind of like the
NCAAs of art. I went long last time on quirky intimate gesso washes and these
doom-laden neo-Cornell boxes, betting with my heart. Sidney gave me juicy odds."

"What happened?"

"I got killed."

The motorcade arrived, two limos, identical, and a line of Chevy Suburbans
with blacked-out windows. Agents from a transit team fanned out from the vans,
the usual close-order drill. They walked the VP through the lobby, out the doors,
across the runway, up the jetway stairs, and past the airmen, who hopped into shoe-
click salutes.

Gretchen joined her crew, folding her cell phone. "Anybody heard from
Bobbie?"

Vi said, "She'll be here."

Gretchen nodded, shouldering her bags. The agents followed her across the tarmac to the plane, zigzag single-file, listing to their duffel sides. The cold air woke them up.

"She looks beautiful tonight," said O'Teen in the wind. He meant the jet.

The airmen knew their faces, but checked their IDs anyway.

Bobbie made the jumping-off, but only barely, boarding after the press, the food, and the political riffraff. They climbed to cruising altitude, the seat belt sign went off, and Gretchen called Bobbie to the last row of the cabin. Bobbie got a *sotto voce* chewing-out as the plane banked over P.G. County, the pulsing grid beneath them.

Up front, the boys were playing poker.

"Everybody ante up," Sean Elias said. Chips were tossed. Elias started dealing.

The parade of aides began, a steward bearing dinner, a colonel bearing cables, Fundeberg bearing the latest gloomy polling from New Hampshire.

Tashmo and Elias folded after the first raise. Herc bid O'Teen up to thirty bucks, then took his money with three eights.

They were over Delaware when Boone Saxon stood up to deliver the threat roundup, a kind of global briefing to let the agents know what they might encounter in the crowds. Boone went down a list of known, suspected, or potential threats, summarizing each, the Arab specter from Quebec, the violent splinter right-to-lifers, the neo-Nazis, the militias in the north.

Vi listened from the fifth row of the cabin. Boone, a senior hand, supervised the grading of incoming threats, chaired or shared the chair of three sensitive committees, and helped run ThreatNet, a vast database of people who think the government is watching them. Most of these threats came not from organized enemies of the United States, terror groups or protest groups or hostile foreign powers, but rather from the Eric Englebrechts and Leticia (Gomez) Joneses of the world, the lost souls and lone wolves, the drifters on the road, the un- or undermedicated schizophrenics who might or might not suffer what are known as ideations, as Boone called them, or forced thought, or paranoid thought syndrome, who might or might not also own a rifle or a pistol, or have access to explosives. The might-or-might-not aspect of the thing (the *if* of it, the X factor) was the bureaucratic urge behind ThreatNet, and its full-time staff of sixty agents and ninety-two civilian employees, and its budget (classified, but sizable, Vi knew). The letters came in (the postcards and the e-mails and the voice mails and the rest), creating by their mere existence, by their coming in, a need for institutional response, if only so that later, when something happened (if it did), the nation couldn't say that Beltsville knew ahead of time and took no action. Most of what Boone described in his briefings to the team was mania, psychosis, sad mental disarrangement, people living with their parents, people sleeping under bridges, people riding Greyhounds fleeing voices in their heads, and it was easy to write these people off as merely maniacal (psychotic and pathetic, unable to organize a hot meal, much less a public murder), but then again, were any of them plainly crazier than Hinckley, who shot four men and nearly killed a president?

Boone finished the roundup and sat down. Herc played poker until the others quit, then prowled the cabin with his belt undone. Bobbie read a pillow catalog until she fell asleep. Tashmo, starved for reading matter, slipped the catalog from her lap. He turned the pages and was soon asleep.

Vi sat by the window, jutting her jaw to pop the blockage in her ears. She was thinking that she ought to go and see her brother, Jens, at some point in the next two days. The team would be in Portsmouth Monday night and Tuesday morning—maybe she could slip away for an hour somewhere along the line.

Vi hadn't seen Jens since the weekend after Hinman when the Service gave her stress-related leave. A lousy fucking visit—Vi shuddered, thinking of it. Vi's mother, Evelyn, had moved to Florida by then—a town outside of Tampa with Plantation in its name; everyone played tennis and the weather was better for her knees—so Vi stayed with Jens and Peta and their kid. Jens was working at his war game, turning out his monster logic. Vi had come home to belong, to join the crowd for once, but she couldn't stop scanning hands as they walked along the streets of the downtown that weekend. Jens caught her at it. He said, "Your eyes are always moving, Vi, like REM sleep only you're awake—it's giving me the creeps." Vi denied it but she couldn't stop, which only made her feel more like an outsider. Jens insisted that they go out to Santasket Road to celebrate Walter's birthday with a picnic in the backyard. Jens had this vision of them picnicking and telling funny stories of the Coopers and the Buckerts and the bomber dads, and Kai, Jens' son, blowing out the candles on a dead man's birthday cake. Vi wanted no part of it and said so. Jens was offended—because he had this whole idea, a plan, *his* plan. Vi hadn't seen the old house since Walter's death, and it looked so small and ordinary she wanted to cry. Jens told Kai about Major Wade, the arrow through the tree. Jens kept asking Vi to join in, help tell these stories they both knew. Vi did not remember how it started, something led to something, and then Jens was saying—shouting—"Why did you even come back here, Vi? I feel like I don't even know you."

Vi popped her ears, in and out, riding on the jet, steeling herself to work the crowds, to forget them all, Walter, Jens and Peta, to get herself to emptiness and vacant mode. Herc dropped without warning to the deck and did twenty clapping push-ups. Vi counted the claps without wanting to, staring out the porthole at the gray brainy softness of the clouds.

Shaking hands, shaking hands, shaking hands, the VP moved along the ropes outside the airport Marriott in Manchester, New Hampshire. Tashmo had the lead foot, pulling as Vi pushed, scanning as she scanned. The VP was moving at a grazing pace, reaching out, reaching in, shaking hands in bunches, reeling off a continuous greeting, *"Howyadoin howyadoin goodtaseeya howyadoin—"*

The comm was clear that night, no static and no breaks. Vi heard the pieces working, Bobbie, Gretchen, Herc, the snipers and the SWATs, all around the horn.

Shadow hands in TV lights, the VP cried in steam, *"Howyadoin goodtaseeya goodtaseeya howyadoin—"*

A woman swooned, *"Ooo—there he is."*

Vi saw a man in a Celtics' hat, two kids with air horns, a mother with a child on her shoulders, pointing. Reporters shouted questions from the darkness—

"Sir, is it true—?"

"Sir, have you considered—?"

"Sir, your polls are showing—"

Photographers snapped pictures. A cameraman walked backwards, taping as he walked. Gretchen was on the top step of the hotel entrance, watching her perimeters, talking in Vi's ear.

O'T—

Checking white male, red cap, like a stocking cap. He's about mid-crowd, ten feet to your left.

The snipers said, *We have him.*

I'm near the guy, he's homeless—this was O'Teen, plainclothes in the crowd.

Right, said Gretchen. *Can we get some troopers on him please?*

K.

K for *copy* means I hear you.

Seeing movement, roof area. Check it please, whoever's closer.

They're hotel guys, security.

K, okay. Tell 'em move back.

Let me have that female script again—Bobbie in the crowd.

Okay, we have a vehicle on the access ramp. Blue van and two males.

O'T, say again.

Do you have that?

Say again.

Female white, white ski parka, appears to be alone. She's on bush line now, really pushing forward, guys.

Van is media.

Okay.

Vi's feet and legs were pushing, her pelvis to the VP's flabby trousered thigh. If she saw the muzzle of a pistol coming up, a muzzle in the blur, she was trained to shout *Gun gun* and pivot on her outside leg and curl across the VP's chest, pushing him backwards as she did. Tashmo, hearing *Gun gun,* would be curling too, and they would shove the VP stumbling to the fast extraction team, Gretchen, Herc, and Sean Elias on the steps, who, hearing *Gun gun,* would be rushing up. They drilled the move in Beltsville, pivot, curl, and backward shove, until it was muscle memory, as fast and natural as flinching.

"Sir, is it true—?"

"Sir, does the defeat in Iowa—?"

I don't have your female, O'T—this was Bobbie.

Teenaged members of a marching band in red. The mother with the child on her shoulders. The mother slipped, trying to get free, but a crowd against a barricade will always crush its front, and the mother couldn't move. The child wailed, "Momma down. Momma *down.*"

*Okay—*Gretchen—*parka female, moving lot side now. Coming down the cars. She's trying to go around. Herc and O'T—*

"Howyadoin howyadoin howyadoin—"

They were nearly at the lobby doors when Vi saw the woman in a white, gray, or beige ski parka, fighting through the people to the ropes. The woman hit the ropes just in front of the VP. Her mouth was shouting. Vi tensed to start her pivot-curl as the woman's hands came up. She fell back in the crowd and Vi lost sight of her.

Tashmo's shudder passed through the VP into Vi. They moved down the ropeline like a beast of fable, a creature with six arms, three heads, and one nervous system.

Flashbulbs flashed, unsynchronized, a sparkling effect.

the bluffs (monday)

Coming down from Portsmouth in the clear bright winter morning, the van of canvassers passed the harbor on the river, saw the runty oceangoing tugs wearing beards of dirty ice, the long container ships pushing up the Piscataqua, the navy base across the churning straits, a tall gray water tower, a skyline of idle cranes.

The people in the van were party faithful, volunteers, here to help the VP become P. All of them were Texans, half of them were women, and all of these were active or retired employees of the Longmont-Delgado Unified School District. The other half, the men, the husbands of the women, were in carpentry, pest control, or refrigeration, except for the driver, Raymond Rios, who was twenty-four and single and taught science in the bright and gifted program at Longmont-Westside High. He taught Life Science I and II, worth four credit hours each. He also taught Life Science III, a two-credit-hour elective, which was said to be a bear.

They came around the headland, open ocean to the left. To the right was a line of bungalow motels, shuttered for the season, a line of signs, No Vacancy, No Vacancy, No Vacancy, and t-shirt shops and tackle shops and similar establishments, white and aqua-blue, and also shuttered. Farther on, they would hit the year-round condominiums, and after that the mansions, and after that the junction with Route 32. The navigatrix knew this, the woman in the front seat with the map. Her name was Jackie Kotteakis, retired teacher of ninth grade. She had worked this primary twice before, becoming over time a troop leader and den mother to the placard-covered vans of campaign volunteers, a service to her party for which she expected no reward except the excitement and the fun of it, like a camping trip with friends. These people were her friends and she felt good, riding with them on a winter morning by the sea.

The people in the van were called a pull team. The map in Jackie's lap was marked with hot pink highlighter, indicating target roads and vote-heavy condo courts. Unmarked roads were to be left alone. These orders came from headquarters. Actually these orders came from Tim, a Rhode Island lawyer who hoped to be judge. Tim was the VP's field director for Region C, boss of Jackie's pull team. Region C was basically the southern chunk of New Hampshire's First Congressional District, minus Manchester, which was split into Regions A and B. Tim had explained that Jackie's team, the teacher volunteers, had to cover the pink areas, but not, absolutely *not*, any unpink areas, thinking that this skinny bird from Texas was a newbie at pull-teaming. But Jackie was a veteran and she cut him off. She knew all about the pink. She knew that pollsters and phone-bankers and past waves of canvassers had spent months combing the streets and roads and cul-de-sacs along 1A, seeking, door by door (and call by call and questionnaire by questionnaire), the opinions of the citizens, dividing this part of the state into preference categories: the unregistered or otherwise unlikely-to-show-up, who were set aside as meaningless; the likely voters who supported the insurgent senator, the VP's rival in the primary; the likely-voters-and-weakly-leaning-toward-the-VP; the likely-and-the-strong; and, finally, the undecided. Tim had voter lists, big fanning printouts identifying residents by name, age, address, home phone, and a two-digit poll code, 01 for meaningless, 02 for rival, 03 for weak-VP, 04 for strong-VP, 05 for the undecided.

The van was coming into Center Effing. Jackie said, "Now pay attention, y'all. Today we're doing undecideds, that's your poll code oh-five, folks, a crucial group of humans—they'll decide the primary."

Jackie knew that good pull-teaming was a science and easily screwed up. She had learned the do's and don'ts on her first trip to New Hampshire when the teachers' union sent her to Berlin, way the heck up north, and the field director for that area, a lawyer from Ohio, in his zeal to serve the party, had Jackie and the other volunteers knock on every door, wasting a whole morning on the meaningless 01s, who weren't going to vote no matter what you said, who wouldn't vote for Jesus against Hitler for Pete's sake, who simply *would not vote*, and, as a result, Jackie's team failed to cover all the pink streets, rich in weak-leaners and undecided voters. Some field operatives believed in hitting the strong-leaners in the days before the primary, just to firm them up; others didn't, Jackie knew. But everyone agreed—this was the gospel of Get Out the Vote—that weak-leaners were important, second only to the biggest prize of all, the mighty undecideds. They never hit the undecideds in Berlin that year, and though they won the city, they lost Coos County, which they were not supposed to lose.

In Jackie's second junket to New Hampshire, four years later, they sent her to a gloomy woolen town called Shawgamunk, somewhere between Manchester and Portsmouth. It was the year that Jackie's husband came down with cancer, and the mills in Shawgamunk, brick, worthless, and deserted, made her ache. Her husband was the offensive line coach at Longmont-Westside, known in local schoolboy football circles as the Greek or Pete the Greek or Mustache Pete, or sometimes Nick, even though his name was Theodore, called Thea (to rhyme with *me* and *he* and *we*), and his real nickname, since Chicago as a kid, had always been Tiny, because he was enormous. Jackie didn't want to go to New Hampshire that second time, but Thea said she needed a break from her nursing duties, so she went to Shawgamunk, and the field director got his codes reversed and sent his pull team in a snowstorm to a neighborhood of 2s (strongly-leaning-to-the-other-side). The neighborhood was up and down a steep hill, dirty clapboard houses, people on relief. Jackie sensed a problem halfway up the hill. She tried to tell the field director, "You know, I've got a feeling, these people seem pretty much against us." The field director, another haggard lawyer with ambitions and bad breath, told her to knock on doors and keep her big yap shut, and she did, pushing through the snow, getting out the hostile vote, the vote against them, and they lost Shawgamunk by forty votes that year. The image stayed with Jackie for a long time—Texans in the snow, full of pep and spirit, beating themselves with each trudging step.

They were past the motels now, condos on both sides. The nicer ones, on the left, had soothing pluraled nature-names carved on hanging wooden signs, The Coves, The Glades, The Meadowlands. The cheaper condos, on the right, were smaller and closer to the road, and had names like roaring powerboats, Seaspray, Barracuda's, and Beachcomber III.

Jackie sneezed, a snippy poodle kind of sneeze, God-blessed herself, and said, "I bet it's on the left, Raymond. You better slow down."

Raymond Rios, the driver and young science teacher to the bright and gifted, didn't nod or really hear. He was thinking of the motels they had passed and the problem with the signs, NO VACANCY. This message bothered him, he couldn't decide why. Then Jackie sneezed and it came to him, the motels said no vacancy because they were closed for the season (or off-season or not-season) and were, therefore, totally vacant, as vacant as they ever got, and so the sign, NO VACANCY, was maximum-inaccurate, yet he understood exactly what it meant. This thought or chain of thoughts made him feel vacant and relaxed, done with a problem, a pleasant empty feeling driving by the beaches in the wind.

They pulled into The Bluffs, a cluster of new units, the first location of the day. They took the speed bump gently, came around the half-moon drive. Jackie was talking to the other volunteers, explaining how you pull-teamed, the purpose and the tactics of the thing. Normally, she said, they would drop a group of workers here, two or three teams of two people each. The teams would knock on doors as Raymond took the others to their respective drop-off points. Raymond would then circle back, picking up the first group, who would by then be done, and the next group, and the next, and finally the last dropped-off, who would by then be done, but many of the Texans were doing their first canvas and the pink neighborhoods were scattered down to Rye, and Jackie thought it would be best to stick together and use The Bluffs as a training ground.

They parked in front of a fenced-in playground, got out, and stretched their legs. Jackie was saying things like split up, take opposite sides, call folks by their names, Mr., Ms., don't say Miss or Mrs. (Yankee women get offended). Suddenly she stopped, struck with another image, not squandered Texas pep, the Shawga-munk disaster, futility in snow, but how this moment, here and now, was so like her dead husband teaching blocking to his linemen, pulling guards and you flare out to pick up the nickel stunt, and how she often watched him on a dusty prac-tice field, Jackie sitting in the bleachers, not liking football much, not under-standing nickel stunts, but her husband did, and he would have understood this too, check your lists and don't get lost and look enthused and let's be a team here, folks. So much depends on pep and spirit, Jackie thought, your attitude to life, and she stopped talking to the volunteers because the image of her husband teaching blocking made her glad and weepy all at once, and what the heck was that?

Raymond was pulling boxes from the back of the van. The boxes held the fly-ers and glossy issue packets, stacks of flyers tied together, which Jackie knew enough to call the literature.

Across the road, in Eight The Bluffs, a faux-weathered A-frame on the rocky point, Jens Asplund was sitting in his breakfast nook with his wife and son. Jens was tapping at his laptop, writing code. The code he wrote was destined for a file called SmoShadow.exe, which Jens needed for a meeting at his office. Jens' office was in West Portsmouth, where BigIf leased a disused building on a former Air Force base. The basement of the building, dug and reinforced in the '50s as a bomb shelter, now held a ring of mighty servers—big computers—on which the game was running at all times. Sitting in the breakfast nook, Jens was hunched in concentration, drinking his fourth mug of Glucola, a fizzy, reddish beverage, naturally sweetened, loaded with caffeine, which he favored over coffee, water, and most types of food.

Kai Boyle-Asplund, a boy of three, sat across the table, safely strapped into his booster seat, dressed for school and waiting for his breakfast. Peta Boyle was fixing oatmeal at the stove. Peta set a bowl in front of Kai.

"But Mama, I don't want the oapameal."

"You love the oapameal," said Peta. "Remember we decided?"

"But Mama, I want chewy sticks."

"No chewy sticks till later, Bimble," Peta said. "Look, I'm packing them for lunch in your power box. See? Boom, right in the box." She chopped Kai's oatmeal with a spoon to cool it. "Jens—did you get any sleep last night?"

Jens scrolled through his source code. "Why yes. Did you?"

"I woke up at three," said Peta. "You weren't in the bed."

"I probably took a pee."

"I woke up to take a pee. You weren't in there either."

"I took a pee outside," said Jens. "I find it inspiring. I love the moon at night, don't you?"

The moon at night—it was the sort of thing Peta might have said. Jens was being slightly mean, mimicking his wife, and Peta knew it.

"Make him eat it, Jens," she said.

She went into the bedroom to get dressed.

Jens did not look up from his laptop. He said, "Eat your oapameal, Kai."

Kai touched the oatmeal with the tip of his spoon. "Dad?"

"Yes."

"What are you doing?"

"Compiling a subroutine, juggling my function calls. I keep getting error flags. It's driving me insane."

Kai nodded sympathetically. "Can I have a chewy stick?"

"Sure," said Jens. "For lunch. Now eat. Come on, Bongle, we'll be late for school."

The front room was a mild mess, an hour's worth—a couch cushion and a baby blanket on the rug in front of the TV where Kai had watched a Pooh video as he decompressed from sleep, plastic blocks scattered all around, a car or two, a wooden plane, several oil tankers, and a tippy-sippy cup of mango juice, tipped and slowly leaking on the rug. Jens looked through the picture window, checking the thermometer bolted to the house. His neighbors, Sybil Hammerschmidt from Nine The Bluffs and Beth Greco from Five, were talking in the street with a group of campaign volunteers.

The phone rang in the kitchen. Peta got it. "Boyle-Asplund residence! Yes. No. No—can't you let us live in peace?" She hung up sharply.

Jens said, "Pollster?"

"Christ, they're vultures. Kai-bo, buddy, *eat*."

The phone rang again. They let it ring. Their voice mail listed their opinions on all subjects, so the pollsters wouldn't have to call them back.

Outside, the canvassers deployed, ringing doorbells. Jens, watching from the window, tried to guess their nationality. A group of college kids from Minnesota had come through the week before, followed by some autoworkers from Hamtramck, Michigan. The best day was when a van of prison guards from Buffalo had the fender-bender with the rabid tort reformers. Today's contingent had a sober, churchy look. Jens guessed they came from somewhere flat and grassy where cyclone warnings often closed the malls. A canvasser, a young man in big mittens, was coming up the walk. Jens buckled his pants and opened the front door.

"Morning, sir!" said the volunteer. "My name is Raymond Rios. I'm with the vice president. May I speak to Mr. Coakley today, sir?"

Jens said, "I don't see why not."

"Great. Is he at home?"

Jens looked up the street. "I don't see his truck. He usually leaves early."

"This isn't Ten The Bluffs?"

"No, Eight. Ten is the one that needs a gutter job. We've been after Coakley for months to do those gutters. Are you by any chance from Kansas?"

"No sir. Longmont, Texas."

Jens was delighted. "The Longmont Easter Twister, 1977. A rare Fujita five. Eighty-mile track, ten dead, forty-seven hurt. Its angry soil-darkened funnel tore the asphalt from the roads. Did you see it, Raymond?"

"Golly, I don't think so. Did it come at night? I had an early bedtime in those days."

"No," said Jens, "it came on Easter morning just as church was letting out. What do you do in Longmont, Ray? May I call you Ray?"

"Most folks don't, but what the heck," said Raymond Rios. "I teach Life Science to the bright and gifted at the high school."

Jens leaned against the door. He liked meeting canvassers and engaging them in the breezy generality of strangers meeting. He had learned many things this way. One of the prison guards showed him how to carve a deadly weapon out of soap. A tort reformer showed him how to armpit-fart. He said, "That's a lot of ground to cover, Ray, all of life and science."

"Well they're bright and gifted," Raymond Rios said. "Of course, by law I have to give equal time to both accounts."

"Both accounts of what?"

"Creation," Raymond Rios said. "We do the Big Bang in the fall, the birth of stars and planets, chemistry and physics, energy and matter, Darwin, speciation and genetics. Then we spend the spring on the first page of the Bible."

"Must go pretty quick, the Bible. Not a lot to say. God did it, class dismissed."

"We cover it in depth."

"So if one of your students wrote on an exam that we evolved over three million years from a stooped, nut-grubbing primate known as Lucy Afarensis, would that student get an A or an F?"

"Depends on the semester," Raymond Rios said. "In the fall, that's an A. In the spring, that's an F, because the whole deal only took a week."

"Want to see a cool knife made of soap?"

"I should probably hit the other units," Raymond Rios said. "Do you all need some literature? This one's about wetland preservation, this one's about prescription drug benefits."

"My wife does all our politics," said Jens. "She's a volunteer for the VP. We're pretty well stocked up."

"Petulia Boyle?"

"She doesn't use 'Petulia.' Makes her cringe, in fact."

"Says here she's a strong-leaner, but you're undecided."

Jens said, "I'm reassessing."

"*Jens!*"—Peta's voice.

Jens said goodbye to Raymond Rios, closed the door, and hurried to the dining nook.

Kai was clapping in his booster seat. Peta was standing by the fridge, hands on hips, dressed to go. A star-shaped splat of oatmeal was on the linoleum between them.

"He threw it," Peta said.

Kai said, "No I didn't. It slipped."

Peta said, "Bull-loney. Jens, I've got to run. Tell him not to lie."

Peta kissed her husband and her son, grabbed her coat, purse, keys, shades, laptop, beeper, a travel mug of coffee, a binder of new million-dollar realty listings, and went out the door.

Jens and Kai sat at the table. They looked at the splat together.

Jens said, "This is where I tell you not to lie."

"I didn't lie," said Kai. "It slipped."

Jens wet a sponge at the sink, planted Kai next to the oatmeal on the floor.

"Clean it up," said Jens.

"No."

"Clean it up," said Jens.

"No."

"Clean it up or else you'll get a time-out."

Kai wound up like a pitcher and with a leg kick threw the sponge against the fridge.

Fine. Jens carried the boy to his little bedroom on the front side of the house.

The shades were drawn. The room was dark. Jens dumped Kai on the racecar bed and stood by the rocking chair.

Kai was sobbing, facedown on the bed. Jens and Peta didn't hit, weren't hitters, did not believe in hitting. Instead they did time-outs. A child having a time-out was supposed to lie still in the dark, deprived of stimuli, and ponder the connection between naughtiness and punishment until time was in again.

Kai slid off the bed and ran for the door. Jens caught him and returned him, kicking, to the bed. Jens was never sure what to do or say when Kai made a break for it. What was the caring parent's counterthreat? Have a time-out or else you'll have a time-out? Did they really expect Kai to lie in the dark and think, this is what happens if you don't lie in the dark?

Jens said, "Kai Kai Kai. This is a time-out."

They had rules. Don't lie—this was a rule. Pretending is okay, but we never lie. We don't bite or hit or spit. We share and use our words. They were trying to communicate a moral world. Jens did not feel up to it some days. He looked at Kai, still sobbing on the bed. Something was missing. The boy deserved a lesson, a teaching, a rule for the future.

Jens said, "Son, we don't throw our sponges at the fridge."

Jens went to the dining nook, copied SmoShadow to a disk, and packed the laptop in a shoulder bag. SmoShadow was still buggy. Jens would have to clear the error flags before his morning meeting. He expected a rough meeting even with SmoShadow totally debugged; without it, he'd be dead. Jens was as that moment six weeks overdue on his last assigned project, not SmoShadow (SmoShadow was his own idea), but rather a new-series software bot, known around the company as Project Todd. Like all the monsters Jens had written for BigIf, Todd had come to him as a set of specs from the head creative, the game's chief imagineer. The specs for Monster Todd were simple on the surface, a knock-off of the target-and-attack algorithms Jens had written for prior wildly popular monsters, Hamster-man, Skitz the Cat, Farty Pup, and Seeing Eye. Jens knew that the corporate planners at BigIf considered Project Todd a high priority, a crucial counterstroke to bolster BigIf's stagnant market share.

Jens hadn't understood what was new or special about Todd until he saw the rough-up of the monster on the screen of Phoebe Rosenthal, their artist in residence. The other monsters Jens had helped develop for BigIf were preposterous, cartoonish. Hamsterman, with his saucy killer twinkle, looked no more like a hamster than Bugs Bunny looked like a pellet-chewing rabbit in a hutch. It was comfortable to Jens, this distance from reality. Phoebe's sketch of Todd, in contrast, was a boy of fifteen, slouchy, acned, callow, carrying a backpack like any skateboard kid in downtown C.E., like a million kids who played the game. There was something in this business of making monsters real or realistic which filled Jens with a deep sense of unease, as if the game were poised to cross some kind of line. He found it hard to concentrate on the code for Todd, simple though it was or should have been. His inability to finish the assignment was like a head cold which descended every time he clicked his buffers and opened a draft of Monster Todd. Jens had surrendered in frustration, turning to a program he liked working on, a problem he enjoyed, a nice bright piece of value-neutral engineering, SmoShadow.exe. He would show the shadow to his bosses at the morning meeting when they asked what he had been doing for the last six weeks.

Jens went down the flagstone walk, keys between his teeth, Kai riding on his hip carrying a peeled banana like a torch to light the way. They got in the car. Jens pulled around Bluffs Circle, waiting for a break in traffic on 1A. Kai was in his crash seat, singing to himself. Jens saw a gap and gunned it, heading up the shore to a chorus of car horns. Time was definitely in again.

Jens heard a yawn.

"Kai is tired, Poppa."

Jens slugged Glucola as he drove. Lobstermen plowed rows along the shore. Gulls attacked a Chinese restaurant dumpster, wings pumping, drifting backwards in the wind. Gypsum ships waited at the head of Portsmouth Channel, three miles out. It was clear enough to see their rust.

"Hey buddy, see the gulls?"

"Where?" said Kai.

"Right there. They're flying backwards, man. Isn't that crazy?"

Kai tried to turn and look in his harness. He said, "Where?"

"Back there. We'll look for them tomorrow."

Jens pointed out the sights as drove his son to school. He did this to pass the time, and keep Kai awake, and because Walter Asplund had done it long ago, pointing out the sights, and Jens remembered being happy in those days. After a winter storm, there were many things to see: flooded parking lots, stop signs sheared and headless, tree limbs down along the road. Today there was nothing but houses, motels, condo courts, gulls, and lobster boats, and the big ships waiting for a river pilot in the gulf. Jens liked driving up 1A—you always knew what was coming next. This was home to Jens, the commercial coastline of his boyhood, a dial tone for the eyes.

He explained about the gypsum ships and the river pilots.

Kai didn't understand. "Why do ships need pilots?"

"Because the port is rocky and the Piscataqua's fast. It's tricky getting in there, son. Your grampa used to do a lot of accidents in there."

"Do they *fly* into the port?"

"The gypsum ships? 'Course not. That's why they need pilots."

Jens pulled into the gravel lot at Li'l People and walked Kai up the handicapped ramp.

Li'l People Montessori was three years old, a mecca for new money on the shore. Tuition for pre-K was like another mortgage, but the parents paid it happily. It was a lovely school. The classrooms were sunny and open-plan. Up the stairs was music, gym, and napping mats. The coatroom was a daily scene. Mothers and a few stray dads brokered playdates and babbled last instructions to their well-dressed heirs. One kid was always finishing his muffin by the door, one kid was always screaming, at least one kid, but never Kai. He found his cubby, shed his jacket to the floor.

Jens said, "Have a good day, Kaiyawatha."

Kai was marching off. Jens followed at a distance, watching from the parents-and-caregivers' observation area, a red batter's box painted on the floor behind a half partition and the hanging spider plants. The children were already busy, one group making dolls from socks, another pounding clay, a third group on the pillows getting a story from the teacher's helper, a high school girl in baggy flame-retardant-looking pants. Kai stood unnoticed in the center of the room, rocking in his pudgy sneakers, double-jointed at the knees, no ass whatsoever, and he was just fine, a total individual, alone in the universe. Jens was proudly terrified. The teacher would spot Kai in a moment, guide him to a group, and that would also be just fine, but until then Kai rocked and asked his little questions. Why do gulls fly backwards? Why do ships need pilots? Why is music up the stairs? Why is music? Why is Kai?

The old house on Santasket Road was set back in the trees, neat-looking and well-kept, a sign hammered in the lawn, *Another offering by* MOSS PROPERTIES. Jens pulled into the driveway, cut the engine, and got out.

The house had been on the market since September, asking the low threes, which seemed like quite a lot to Jens for a nothing sort of saltbox in a humdrum part of town, but also not enough for the first place he remembered knowing well. Peta was a broker at Moss Properties, of course, but she was a mansion specialist and this house, four bedrooms on a quarter acre, was well below the bottom of her market bracket. She had farmed it out to her secretary, Claus, a purring German boy working toward promotion as a junior sales associate. Claus had arranged for regular landscaping, a paint job in November (gray, the shutters white), leaving Jens to check the place once a week, the pipes and pumps and lawn, a job he had no time for, a duty he resented, although he seemed to come out more than once a week, often for no reason, just to stand here and look up at the trees.

He looked up at the trees. When he came with Kai, Jens showed him all the bedrooms, here is Auntie Vi's (Kai barely knew her), here is Grampa Walter's (Kai knew him as a person in a picture) and Grammy Evelyn's (Kai knew her as the lady who sent oranges from Florida), and the highlight of the tour, Jens' own boyhood bedroom. Kai would climb up on the bed and bounce. "*Poppa, look!*" he'd shout and crack his little skull against the eaves, just as Jens had in the glory days of beds and bouncing. Other times, as now, Jens came out alone to walk the lawn and listen to the wind stirring in the cat grass of the marshes, a sound like faraway applause.

Jens fetched the bottle of Glucola from the car and took a walk. The grass was February brown. His mother's garden, her ex-garden, untended since the summer Walter passed away, was a patch of dirt and dried weeds down to the climbing roses, which hung heavy and would bloom again in May, though nobody would notice. Jens remembered the battle over tulips in the den, Evelyn and Walter, and Walter always lost. He remembered Evelyn feeding slop to dogs, Dingo I, Dingo II, Dingo III, a dynasty of Dingos in the yard, and Walter up late with his pipe, reading back issues of *Shop Safety Monthly*, and writing on his money, IN GOD WE TRUST, IN US WE TRUST. Center Effing didn't understand his father, the godless moderate Republican, a radical of large ideas whose life, paradoxically, was bounded by this town, by the rhythms of his habits in this town, poplin suits in summertime, a haircut every week. People understood Walter as the plodding adjuster, not as the eccentric atheist. Jens saw it the other way. He understood the atheism (Walter said, *We're merely molecules—why is that so frightening?*), but not the insurance work, Walter as enforcer of the letter of the policies, ten thousand dollars for a foot, thirty thousand for an eye. If Walter could see the lies of scripture, why couldn't he see the lies of the loss-and-compensation charts devised by The Connecticut? Why was an eye worth thirty thousand dollars, not twenty and not forty? Walter wouldn't buy into the lie of the motto printed on his money, yet he went about adjusting, serving The Connecticut, buying into a much bigger lie, or so it seemed to Jens.

Jens was looking at the beech tree in the corner of the yard, remembering the day Walter bought a half-dipole antenna, every hammer's envy, and how they puzzled over where to rig it. It was a powerful antenna, but it needed to be high. Then Major Wade, the grounded bomber pilot, wandered over from the Coopers' pool followed by good old Mrs. Cooper, the Asplunds' frowsy neighbor, whose tits and exhibitionism had hastened puberty in Jens by at least two years. Major Wade, the man who shot the arrow through the tree, came down to the basement a few times after that. He would sit with Jens at the console, drinking a beer, taking a break from Carol Cooper's conversation. Wade would fiddle with the dial and say, "Can you get Greenland on this thing?" Jens could get the world with his dipole on a good hot afternoon when the waves were skipping, a weird effect. On days like that, he could get Uganda on the ten-band, but not his buddies up the shore. It had to do with solar radiation, poison atoms in the air fifty miles up. Major Wade, as a bomber pilot, knew all about fallout in the stratosphere, although he didn't ham and couldn't fly anymore. He had a beer and a headache and an inner ear infection

and had been reassigned as base recreation officer. He enjoyed various base recre-
ations, but was finished as a bomber pilot.

Carol Cooper sunbathed on her diving board all summer. Jens watched her
brown herself all day, or swim at midnight, drunk and alone, when Major Wade was
off with other wives. Jens stayed up late, spying on Carol Cooper, or reading
weather books or his hammer magazines as he listened to the Red Sox in Anaheim
or Oakland (the games would start at ten and run until one or two). If a bomber
left at night, he'd listen on his pillow as the rumble dwindled. Jens knew the sound
of every plane at Pease, the B-52s, the swept-wing supersonic F-111s. Rumbling was
bombers, heading north and east. Listen for the sound. Was it gone? Was it
absolutely gone? Was there nothing in the room again but play-by-play and moths
against the screen and Carol Cooper, sloppy drunk and stumbling over a chaise
longue? Even half asleep or jerking off, you couldn't mistake the bombers for the
hairy exits of the fighter-interceptors, the F-111s, a sound like Christmas wrapping
tearing and the man-made thunder at Mach One. Every house Jens ever saw, or visited, or stayed in, anywhere in Portsmouth or the shore, had the same ceiling cracks
from the sonic booms. When the nights were quiet, Jens knew that the squadron
had left for Thule in Greenland, their forward-ready base under the ice cap. Major
Wade, grounded and depressed, talked about Thule, flying out of Thule, the endless whiteouts and snow-blindness, compass spinning as you hopped the pole, arc-
tic lows depressing the altimeter. You're blind and your instruments are giving
impossible readings—you're flying at zero feet and everywhere is north. The first
runway at Thule was black asphalt, but the color black stored heat from the sun,
melting the permafrost, and one day the Greenland ground swallowed up the runway. The Air Force built a new runway, bigger than the first, bigger than the lakebed
macs out west, said Major Wade, biggest on the planet maybe, five miles of paved
tundra, and it was painted white to bounce the light and not melt the permafrost,
and the pilots coming back from the Russian aerial frontier had to search for white
in whiteness, which was the same as being blind.

Jens talked on the half-dipole to a man in Kansas who was sitting in the path
of a cyclone. They weren't talking, of course. They were tapping Morse, Jens sitting
in the basement, speaker to his ear, straining for each *dit* and *dat*, jotting as he
strained. As the wind picked up in Kansas, the man keyed faster and faster until

Jens was jotting without thinking, without translating, and then the cyclone hit and the man went silent. Jens translated the last lines of dots and dashes, the last broadcast of the martyred Kansas hammer, and the man said this: *Two of them. They glow.* Jens, alone at the console, let the pencil fall. Being a scientific kid, he knew that twin cyclones were comparatively common. He also knew that cyclones did on rare occasions glow. Rustics had reported this for centuries, but scientists had written it off as terror playing tricks on rustics, a known phenomenon, until it was shown that the vicious spinning sheer of a twister system can actually create a battery in air, building up a charge, and so the funnel glows. Some weather historians believed that these freaks of freaks, self-electrifying cyclones, might have been the source of Bible stories about God-as-fire, pillars of fire, tongues of fire, burning bushes burning unconsumed. Jens let the pencil fall that day and thought, I've seen it through Morse code, I've touched the lie of God.

Ham radio and Morse—they were his two loves back then, the twin cyclones of his heart. But, looking back, he saw that they were part, one part, of a youth-long preparation for Jens' shattering encounter with the true God: software. Like the God of Israel, it went by many names, one for every face it showed: logic, code, loop, routine, algorithm, source. JENSISNUMBER1—he remembered how it made him feel, the power and control, making the computer an extension of your will. He mastered Beginning Glyph and moved up over time, climbing to the realms of high abstraction, polymorphic logic. He left Dartmouth burning with ambition to build and write cool things, beauties made of code. He went to Harvard on a fellowship to do stochastic math, but the fellowship ran out, and then he did a Ph.D. at MIT, but he fought with his adviser and left after a semester, and then there was a series of start-ups with big dreams, but one thing happened or another, and Jens found himself five years farther down the road, married with a mortgage, Peta pregnant, and Jens again without a job, and so he started writing monsters for BigIf.

Jens drove out to the house for dinner around then, just after he went to work at BigIf. Walter was alive, presiding at the table, and Evelyn was there, fussing over Peta, who was pregnant, and Walter asked about BigIf, and Jens explained the vision of a Web-based war game, of how they would build it, the overall design.

Walter said, "A war game?"

Jens explained about the monsters, how kids would pay to kill them in the game, the old joystick thrill of killing.

And Jens saw it on his father's face, a cloud of disapproval. Jens saw and felt his father's disapproval over the last months of Walter's life. Mostly Walter kept his peace, said nothing, no lying praise but not criticisms either, and Jens, sensing this, had to pick a fight.

"What's wrong with my game?" he asked his father one night at the house. "What's wrong with being a success?"

Walter didn't want to fight with his son—he wanted anything but that—and so he said, "Your game is immoral, Jens. Worse, it's amoral. It's a waste of your gifts. You must quit right now."

"Why?" said Jens. "To satisfy your idea of purity?"

"No," said Walter. "You have to quit because you'll be unhappy if you don't."

Jens felt judged and maybe he was. He went into a kind of sulk and didn't call or speak to Walter for a week, which was a long time for Jens and his father to go without speaking. When Walter called Jens, they talked about the weather, or whatever, Jens did not remember, and two weeks later Walter died of heart attack, leaving the question of the judgment unresolved.

Vi came back from Washington the summer after Walter's death. She was working as a bodyguard by then, and had come through something terrible, a bungled operation (a flood, a shooting—she didn't want to talk about it), and Jens was glad to have her home, to see her face. Vi would understand, he'd thought, she saw the things I saw, the paper train derailed, the farmhand with one foot, the losses calculated by their father. She'd known the man as Jens had known the man, and she would understand. But the Vi who came home that weekend was not his little sister, not the sister he remembered anyway. She was thin, too thin, and her eyes were vacant, gray and scary-vacant, and she seemed to scan everything, passing cars, strangers on the street, with the same alert indifference. Jens too—she scanned him like another stranger on the street. He thought at first that this was some kind of Secret Service thing, but then he realized, *No—she's judging me like Walter did, and what I'm seeing in her eyes is disapproval.*

Jens walked back to the car, thinking of the last time he saw his sister, a misbegotten birthday picnic in the yard, and how they fought and shouted, Jens and

Vi, and how Peta had stepped in to play peacemaker, *Jens! Vi!*, shouting at them to stop shouting, and how Kai, seeing the adults shouting, had started shouting too, thinking they were playing a new fun shouting game.

Jens sat in his car for a long time, looking at the house. They kept the place half furnished and the water off. Peta said that it showed bigger half furnished, as opposed to fully furnished—it was just a rule of space, the way it showed. She also said that you never showed a house *unfurnished* if you could avoid it—made the place seem lonely and forlorn, buyers caught the scent of desperation and tried to low-ball you. It was better to make them think that you were parting with reluctance.

He called Peta at the office to apologize for his mean crack over breakfast, his little imitation of her, *the moon at night*. He wanted to apologize because he loved his wife. He loved her most, or showed it best, when she was somewhere else, not right in front of him, getting on his nerves. Claus picked up on the second ring.

"I'm sorry, Jens, she's at a showing," Claus reported, pronouncing Jens' name as Yenz. "Is there any message?"

"No," said Jens. "I'm at the house, by the way. It looks fine. Any offers on it yet?"

Claus said, "The house?" They were selling many houses at Moss Properties.

"My father's place," said Jens. "Santasket Road."

"Oh yes. Offers? No—no offers yet, but spring will be a better time, I'm sure."

Jens liked to start his working day in the balcony above the server ring, watching the big gas-plasma screen, the central game-state monitor, and the smaller VDTs around it, walls of ever-changing data (current player loads, loads projected, lag time at the modem farm, kill-rate curves plotted and projected), the resting pulse rate of the network. The seats and woodwork in the balcony had come from a movie palace in Chicago. BigIf had bought the interior when the palace was demolished and rein-stalled it above the servers, a retro-reference and a gag. Jens, communing here each morning, often saw journalists and prospective venture funders coming through on carefully led tours with Reese and Reed, the twins from marketing. Today there were no tours, just six or seven slacker kids lounging in the ring, mousing around screens, feet up on their tables, keyboards in their laps. Digby, the sysop and top slacker, was conferring in the corner with Meredith Shattuck, the deputy chief technology officer, and bald Jerzy Czoll, the president and CEO. Digby did hardware and Meredith did everything, but Jerzy was more your salesman-sloganeer, the Hamsterman of deals, and he rarely got this close to the actual machines. Being close to this much logic seemed to make Jerzy nervous.

The big screen was a camera on the game, looking down, seeing all, like God or the Goodyear Blimp. Players from around the world paid a hefty monthly-and-per-minute fee to ride their browsers to BigIf, passing through the logon buffer, selecting a version of themselves from careening menus (a smorgasbord of age, race, gender, and weapon options), descending finally through trippy bluish screens to the universal starting point, a deep smoking crater formerly known as downtown Albuquerque. The object of the game was to travel safely west on foot from Albuquerque, crossing a thousand simulated miles of handsome, high-def post-apocalyptic wastes, Martian basins, mountain ranges, canyonlands, and creepy overlush forests, a trek complete with place-specific audio (three different types of footsteps—boots on rock, boots on road, boots on dirt or sand, the rush of streams, falling rain, the distant sunset cries of grazing mutant beasts), and emerge alive on the sparkling gigabyte Pacific.

Figures moved across the screen like ants, west along the interstate or north into the mountains. Digby zoomed in with his joystick, explaining some hardware glitch to Meredith and Jerzy. The figures moving on the screen were boxy and stiff-legged, with flat immobile faces. Some were human, paying customers; some were simulated humans, software bots, the helpers and the holy men, the monsters in hunt mode. The helper bots acted as guides, innkeepers, rent-a-cop bodyguards, roadside pop-up merchants selling the necessities: food, water, armor, weaponry. The holy men, the wizard monks and holy village fools, posed rhyming riddles, seven in a cycle refreshed weekly, leading players to shrines and oracles. There were initially nine shrines hidden in the desert, three branded, six generic, later upgraded to twenty-three.

When Jens came here the first time, the game was in design and the screens were still in packing crates. Over the next few months, Jens and Vaughn Naubek, another coder, wrote the logic kernel, the software brain and navigation tools for the helper bots, working with specs from the head creative, BigIf's chief imagineer.

Head demanded wizards and sent Jens a sketch of a Tolkienish creation like Walt Whitman only not as macho. The drawing had been done by Phoebe Rosenthal, the artist on the payroll (a painter of real talent, who doodled bots to support her serious work). Jens and Vaughn Naubek took the fey Walt Whitman and built a brain, a hundred lines of source and ten function calls, a good, tight piece of problem-solving, well within the memory budget for the bot. The wizards were programmed to stay in one place, a plot in the Cartesian X, Y, Z, until addressed by a human player, then nod and move toward their assigned shrine. The wizards scanned every third human second for any player within five distance tiles. If a wizard found no humans in his scan, he returned to his starting tile and waited for the next scheduled scan and the next customer. In a person, say in Walter, this pattern of behavior might be described in moral terms (stoic, faithful, dutiful), but in Jens' system it was algorithmic: new plot X^2, Y^2 equals X plus one, Y plus one, and the bot is driven to the virtual northeast. Algorithms were, as Walter had said, relentlessly amoral: the wizards scanned and moved because they were programmed to, and for no other reason.

Jens and Naubek wrote the wizard prototype together in a day and were moving to the fools when Meredith, who led all game development, pulled Jens off to work on monsters for the head creative, whose taste in chilling evil ran to conscious parody, giant hamsters, mankilling cats, and seeing eye dogs with a yen for human flesh, hunting with their handles still on their backs, a vision of suburbia gone rabid, the house pets in rebellion.

The first monster (Jens' design with Naubek's help) was the cunning, grinning, barrel-chested rodent biped Hamsterman, who became the game's first breakout star. Kids in malls on five continents wore Hamsterman t-shirts, Hamsterman high-tops, chewed Hamsterman bubble gum. Hamsterman's trademark taunt, *Majorca!* (delivered just before he sank his fangs into your carotid), became an empty catch-phrase in a dozen countries, the sort of thing everyone is saying for a week, like *Hasta la vista!* or *Cowaybunga!* Later monsters—Skitz the toxin-spitting cat and Farty Pup, that gassy nemesis—were almost as successful. Each monster class had its assigned strength scores and special weapons, peculiar to the version. Hamsterman 1.0 had fangs and claws; 1.2 had fangs, claws, sulphuric urine (the players loved it); the H2 series, 2.3, 2.4, 2.5, and the beloved 2.9, had fangs, claws, urine, throwing stars, crunchy eye scum, a Lance of Power, and a Colt submachine pistol, a model called the Sportster, with realistic kick-and-impact physics. Colt, of course, paid a whopping fee for the product placement, and again the players loved it. Skitz the Cat had claws and fangs, flesh-eating spit, later a machete and a souped-up butane lighter (a Bic until the litigation). Farty Pup had fangs, claws, gales of flatulence, flaming ear wax, a willingness to hump you, a pair of Sony PC speakers, a Cub Cadet four-wheel-drive snowblower, a Minolta office copier, a Yamaha Disklavier GranTouch piano, and a Sealy Posturepedic mattress. The latter products served no fighting purpose; they were just around.

Some monsters barred the path to certain prized locations where scarce water or power scrolls or healing appliances could be won by answering riddles, or performing quests, or by participating in member bonus-mile programs. That was later, when Jerzy put them in alliance with Visa, Sprint, the airlines, and a thousand select vendors worldwide. A human could buy a trip to Paris, real Paris in real life, earn a hundred thousand miles, transfer these as credit to the BigIf servers, travel with a holy fool deep into the Rockies, meet an oracle and cash the miles in for an amulet which gave the player added strength to fight and kill Hamsterman, Skitz the Cat, Farty Pup, or the dreaded Seeing Eye, doubling the points or better—Seeing Eye was a triple trophy kill. Other monsters roamed the roads, attacking any non-bot within a set radius, providing danger and a thrill, thinning out the weaker players, reducing server load and lag time at the modem farm.

The code behind the game provided many ways to die. A human gang could murder you. A monster could eat you. Toxic clouds drifted through the sky; the gamespace went dark beneath them, the shadow calculators taking over. The clouds were born at random intervals but moved pursuant to actual Weather Service models for the American southwest—Jens' touch, and he was proud of it. Some players who had killed monsters (or solved riddles, or completed quests, or cashed in their minute-miles) acquired power manuscripts and could predict the progress of these toxic clouds and sell predictions to newer players. If you were caught outside when a cloud passed over, the servers deducted life points until your score was zero, the binary OFF-OFF-OFF-OFF, and this was death. If you went without water or food, or lost a fight, or were duped into the bush by a false bot, life points were deducted. If you spent a night in the desert, the servers ran a hypothermia algorithm which rendered you slower and clumsier and finally immobile, as real exposure would, until you zeroed out. Life, wisdom, speed, strength, agility, time, fate, magic, beauty, death—everything was numbers crunched through algorithms endlessly.

My algorithms, Jens thought in the balcony, mine and Naubek's. Jens' code was made of IF-switches and WHILE-loops, of flow and flow-control structures. Tell the system: test for Z, a data state. *IF* Z is true, do something; *IF* Z is false, do nothing or do something else. A program runs from START to END, branching, forking, coursing forward in its runtime, or down a screen of source (*down* being *after* because we read that way). The program branches at the IF from the main run to a subroutine in memory or lying idle elsewhere in the shell. The subroutines were small programs, or big ones, often bigger than the main itself, containing their own control-of-flow conditionals, IFs and ELSEs and WHILE-loops (do this WHILE Z is true; when Z turns false, desist), their own forks into other subroutines or subsubroutines, and each subsubsub was a set of definitions (let Z equal P), a battery of tests (for Z or P, for true or false), a maze of logic gates. A trip through the maze was called a thread of execution or an execution path. Take one line of code, a single logic gate, yes/no. There are two (or 2^1), potential threads, yes or no, that's it. Add a gate, yes/no yes/no. Now there are 2^2 possibilities (or four), yes-yes, yes-no, no-yes, no-no. Add a third and there were eight ways though the maze. Add one more, there were sixteen. Twenty gates, in theory, let's say a hundred lines, an easy module (an hour's worth of work for Jens when he was working well), produced more than a million possibilities. Software was responsive, supple, thoughtlike, powerful to the extent that it could branch and pick a path in response to shifting data states, switching at the IFs, falling always toward the engineer's intended END, yet every fork was a menace to control, a potential bug and fatal logic bomb. A single slip in syntax, a semicolon missing from eighteen million lines, could send the system brute-computing to its crash, so power becomes doubt, Jens thought, which was also thoughtlike. He had built this game, written it, the IFs and potential threads. He was certain of its beauty. When Walter judged him, when Vi criticized with her scanning eyes, Jens knew they couldn't see the beauty of the IFs.

He watched the players moving west across the screen. It was rumored in the thousand or so BigIf-themed chat rooms that if you made it through the game, from the crater to Redondo Beach, with sufficient wisdom points and solved a final riddle there, you would be admitted to a new environment, which was said to be like Paradise, prepared and waiting in the database. This was rumor, not fact. No one knew for certain what lay at the end-of-play. The only way to know was to arrive. The parent corporation, BigIf Systems, owned by Jerzy Czoll and a claque of venture caps, refused to issue the customary game guides, forcing a hundred thousand players to wander the desert, killing monsters and each other, paying steady monthly fees, accumulating points, and gossiping. It was generally thought that no player had made it all the way through. A few claimed they had, by hacks and cheats, crossed into the next world, but they were exposed as frauds and mercilessly flamed. Seven humans—this, again, was rumor—had made it to the beach with insufficient wisdom points to solve the final riddle and pass through the water-door. The seven who made it were forced back into the desert to solve more riddles and kill bigger monsters, and generally pad their wisdom tallies, but all seven died when they turned back.

If the object of the game was to get to Los Angeles with wisdom, the key to playing was surviving and the key to this was money. When you entered BigIf for the first time, the shell assigned you a few days' worth of food and water and a hundred game dollars, which would buy another few days' worth from a merchant bot, but after that it was slow death from thirst and hunger unless you were robbed or scammed or ran into a pack of killer cats or got caught in a toxic downpour, in which case death wasn't slow. To stay alive and keep trekking west, you had to earn money to buy provisions. There were several software-sanctioned ways to do this. Wise players hired out as guides. Strong players worked as bodyguards. Even a new player could find a spring and sell the water, or gather firewood in the overlush forests, or make and sell bread and boots and tunics, and survive that way. One side effect of giving the game a shadow economy was that most players forgot about the wisdom pilgrimage and settled into one of the squatter camps along the way, selling simple, useful items to the new players streaming from the crater every day. You could buy and sell weapons—anything from cudgels and daggers to crossbows to fully modeled firearms. On most afternoons, when America was playing, the plains were dotted with fresh dead and the stooped figures of itinerant scavengers who moved among the bodies collecting food and water icons, stripping the dead of boots and any relatively undamaged armor. Some pickers, as these scavengers were called, waited at the crater for new players to emerge. Players who moved jerkily were new to their PCs, or breaking in a mouse or joystick or power glove or data helmet, and it was almost sad to watch them bumble as the robbers circled. Players with geek names (K00L RULZ) were generally geeks—a fair assumption, since they had named themselves—and geeks played awkwardly, often over their parents' pokey at-home modems. They stood like hapless water bags before the robbers porting over high-speed DSL or corporate T-3s. The pickers waited by the crater, following the newbies, who sometimes asked the poignant question *Why R U following me?*—the text floating in a box above their heads as the robbers struck or Hamsterman popped up and sank his fangs. Robbers sometimes killed each other over these choice victims. Pickers fought pickers for the spoils and other robbers waited, killing pickers as other pickers waited for the spoils of the spoils, and some of these were robbed. Others got away and sold the scavenged goods at stalls along the road, making money to buy weapons to stave off the robbers. Some players became prostitutes, taking players to a quiet spot for a bit of mouse-clicking and hot typing back and forth. The hookers also had off-duty chat rooms, buddy lists, and home pages, known only to them, where they ridiculed the johns, swapped investment tips, and inveighed against the robbers who posed as prostitutes, leading players to the canyons and clubbing them. Bad for business, said the whores. Some whores plotted in their chats to lure sporting robbers into the canyons for revenge, others e-mailed pseudo-postcoital thank-you notes to the robber-johns. The notes contained one of several nasty software viruses as an .exe attachment.

Some robbers worked in gangs and started moving west en masse, down the road and closer to the climax on the sea where the players were better, stronger, more experienced, but also richer, having been in the game long enough to get that far. Hunting Arizona into California took real skill, and many brigands died, straying too far west. The monsters got stronger too, and faster and hungrier, and the roads and stalls and squatters' camps, so thick around Albuquerque, disappeared coming into awesome ruined silent Phoenix, and after Phoenix there were no more helper bots. Out there, it was pretty empty. Few saw those western screens. You could travel for a day and not meet another soul. You could spend a month in real time, six hours every day, amassing strength, killing monsters, killing robbers, clicking west one footstep at a time, and, braving many dangers, earn—really *earn*—those pixel-vistas, and know, as you stared down from Mount Wilson into the basin of old L.A., that you had come farther than almost any player ever. You could do all of this, and know that you were perhaps another day's hard clicking from the gigabyte Pacific, which maybe seven pairs of eyes had ever seen, and, as you stood there and you gazed, you could be jumped by Farty Pup and lose it all.

Jens had written death. Death was zero-out, loss of name and scores and property and back to Albuquerque. To novice players—sixty seconds from the crater and you're dead—death was like losing any other game, but seasoned players had been known to grieve their own deaths, all that effort flushed, and grieve the loss of trusted friends along the way. Friends made pacts with each other: if you die, I'll kill myself; we'll meet in Albuquerque and start west again together. Jens remembered a strong player, one of the strongest humans in the game, standing alone in the cracked hardpan outside of Barstow, California, the avatar at rest. Jens went upstairs to write some code, came back at lunch, and saw the player in the desert still, logged on, but doing nothing. It took three days for the avatar to starve itself to death, so that the human could rejoin some beloved friend at the smoking crater; there was no other algorithmic way to kill yourself. The avatar collapsed, the sacrifice complete. Watching these stark moments in the server ring, Jens realized that the game, the mass of logic he had written, was growing beyond logic, beyond sense, and he began to wonder if maybe Walter had been right after all.

Money made in different ways—stripping corpses, robbery—was spent on weapons. Under Naubek's weapon-market algorithms, pistols were cheap, shotguns more expensive, while a laser-sighted assault rifle with spare banana clip cost about as much as ten years' worth of food. Players engaged in rampant brigandage to get money to buy weapons to become more fearsome brigands to get money to buy better weapons, and hire a mercenary or two, or three, or ten, or better yet a small army of mercenaries, similarly outfitted and invincible. The strongest players dreamed of becoming a warlord with a retinue. The warlords could do anything, anywhere, any*when*, subject only to the toxic storms, the hunger-thirst-exposure alg, or the danger of betrayal by your bodyguards. This danger could be cut to zero by hiring gamebot bodyguards, but the bots were considered inferior henchmen because they were, under the Asplund-Naubek template, incapable of thrill killing and did not, therefore, inspire true visceral terror in the squatter camps. Warlords plundered squatter camps, slaying hundreds of subscribers, until there were very few unplundered places left. After that, warlords plundered warlords. It was stated as fact in the BigIf chat rooms that sixteen known human players had achieved superwarlord status, traveling the space, pillaging enough gamedollars to pay off their followers. Soon, normal human players, sick of dying or living in fear, desubscribed and monthly revenues downspiked.

The VCs panicked and the IPO was canceled. The bosses ordered patches in the shell to stop the war. Many patches were discussed. One would have stopped any player from hiring more than ten mercs at a time. There were numerous conceptual problems with this. Because humans were the preferred brigands, the superwarlords who hired them were interacting with other players, not with any part of the software. They could install a twenty slays-a-day cap, but this would permit a midsized army to kill several thousand humans a day. A super could run a decent-sized genocide that way. They met and talked, managers and engineers, sipping seltzer water in conference rooms, charting counter-warlord strategies on smeary whiteboards. Why not declare a safe haven around the squatter camps? Or send the holybots through the desert spreading some kind of peace message? Or eliminate automatic weapons? Or cut the slay-per-day cap to nine or six or four? Or write a filter to deduct frequent-flier miles for each massacre? Jens was frightened at these meetings. He had come to see his great creation as he imagined Walter saw it—malignant, runaway—as a compromise one makes for money, and now they were saying that the game might die of desubscription, leaving Jens with nothing for his compromise.

The crisis peaked and passed. Superwarlords got bigger on more killing. A few became megasuperwarlords, but one after another, each of them was swallowed up by his or her own retinue, which had grown too big to pay, feed, or lead. The mercenaries, going unpaid, mutinied, killed the megas, and fought over spoils. The mutineers split into factions, slaughtering each other. Survivors were absorbed into a rival army, swelling it beyond the point of supportability and carrying the idea of mutiny like a germ, and the armies started to dry up, like a flood receding. Slowly normal players returned to the shops and roads and everything was back to where it started.

Jens looked at his watch. It was nine-fifteen, time to go upstairs. Jens heard chewing and quiet, polite spitting in the balcony. He saw Prem Srinivassan, the dapper Indian who wrote helper bots. Prem sat a few rows back, eating little purple seeds from a sandwich bag.

"See the cars?" he asked.

"What cars?"

"Out front," said Prem. "Five Lincolns at the curb, the drivers in dark suits gabbing in a circle, reading Boston tabloids to each other."

"Bankers?"

Prem ate a seed. "First three cars look bankerly to me. They usually have black cars with plain hubcaps, very understated, and at least one cellular antenna. Next one, the gray one? I'll bet that's underwriter's counsel. Lawyers do the gray or blue radio cars with wire rims. The last one, the true limo, is Howard Powers."

Howard ran the modem farm. He answered to Digby and had about twenty underlings.

Jens said, "Why did Howard rent a limo?"

"Last night was his high school's winter dance," Prem said. "His date is crashed out in the backseat. You can see right up her gown, at least you could when I came in. She may have changed position since then."

Employees checked the curbs every morning, posting sightings and interpretations to the office intranet. No cars meant that the IPO had been put off yet again. Two cars meant exploratory talks, banker-to-banker, and a sign of life. Three cars was ambiguous, but more than three cars, not counting the prom limo, meant that the bankers had brought lawyers, which even Howard's little sister Pru knew meant that they were getting close to going public.

Vaughn Naubek, Jens' fellow founding coder, passed through the balcony on his way to the employee locker room.

Prem said, "Naubek, sunny greetings. Want a seed?"

Naubek said, "No thanks, I don't like Indian food." He continued to the lockers.

Jens and Prem watched a few players die, then took the stairwell to the ground floor.

Jens ducked into the break room by the Bot Pod. Howard and Pru Powers were sitting at a formica table trying to piece together ribbons of shredded paper.

Howard wore a rust tux and a ruffled shirt. Pru was breathless, sifting through the bag, describing some lawyer-looking men she had seen outside Jerzy's private conference room. Jens took a mug from the mug hooks on the wall, found a liter bottle of Glucola in the cabinet, and filled the mug with ice.

Howard said, "How many, Pru?"

"Three, maybe four," she said. "I forgot to count."

"But you're sure they're lawyers? It's important, Pru."

"They looked like lawyers."

"What kind?"

"Thick-lipped, corpulent, pugnacious—I didn't get a good look. Prem and Digby were blocking my view."

"What *specialty*, I mean. Did they look like underwriter's counsel or a bankruptcy insertion team? Shoes are a dead giveaway. Laces mean we're going public. Loafers mean finito. Come on, Pru, *think*."

"One was in-house counsel, that midget Jaffe. The others were definitely outhouse."

"What about the *shoes*, you freaking retard?"

"Don't call me a retard."

"Don't act like a retard."

"Mom said no calling me a retard."

"Zitface!"

"Loser!"

"Scumhead!"

"Non-market-savvy zitface!"

"Oh shut up!" said Howard.

Jens said, "Hey hey hey you guys. Howard, go to your suite. You too, Pru—those MIPs won't map themselves."

Pru said, "A MIP is a type of map, not a thing to be mapped."

"Oh shut up," said Jens.

The Bot Pod was a wide and pillared space with three sealed windows at the far end. In the center of the room was a bank of low, orange, armless, foamy-looking chairs, actually a Danish Modern couch in sections, several couches probably. The sections could be reconfigured as a circle for Pod-wide thinkathons, or in twos and threes for smaller project groups, or pushed together into beds when the coders pulled all-nighters. There were enough sections to make two decent beds, or one double bed, or three short ones, or a short one and a small working circle, more like a working square. Lu Ping, the engineer, and Phoebe Rosenthal, the artist, were sleeping on the couches. Jens did not disturb them. This was their honeymoon.

The walls were lined with cluttered tables and workstations. Charlie Mayer, who telecommuted from Honolulu, had by far the neatest workspace. Lu Ping, next to Mayer, was compiling a subroutine as he slept entwined around his bride. Error flags slowly filled his screen, *Path/File access error, Bad file name, Bad file name, Bad record length, Bad file name, Input past end of life, Path not found.*

Davey Tabor, next to Lu Ping, was on vacation, supposedly trekking Nepal. Davey called in every few days from what he said was a satellite phone, telling glowing anecdotes about monks and Sherpas and the thousand-year enlightenment, but he seemed vague on the specifics, which led some Podders to suspect that the trek was a cover story and that Davey was actually doing a round of job interviews in California.

Beltran, next to Davey, was signed out to a mental health day—the company allowed them five per annum. Bjorn Bjornsson, next to Beltran, was busy grooming his screen pets, a litter of furry whatzits, and Vaughn Naubek at the next desk was making fun of him.

Bjorn said, "At least I don't carry pictures of Phoebe in my wallet."

Naubek had changed out of street clothes into his working costume, a letter carrier's summer knits, white knee socks, gray-blue shorts, a sky-blue shirt, and a U.S. Postal Service pith helmet. Naubek had taken to dressing "in character" to get himself psyched up for working on a new-series monster known as the Postal Worker. He winced at Bjorn's comment, glanced at the couch where Phoebe slept, uttered something vile in UNIX, and went back to work.

Jens hung his coat on the rack, signed himself in on the in/out whiteboard, and sat at his terminal between Prem and Naubek. He debugged SmoShadow for the next few minutes, clearing error flags, until he got it to compile. He grabbed his mug and went up to the second floor for the weekly meeting of the Spec Committee.

Meredith Shattuck, sexless, cool, and twenty-two, was boss of everybody in the conference room, Digby from the server ring, the twins from marketing, Jaffe the attorney, the head creative, and Jens, who came in late. This was the Spec Committee, BigIf's politburo of design, where system problems were hashed out, new product lines discussed, asses kissed and paddled, egos fluffed and crushed. Meredith presided in her heavy horn-rims and her pearl-gray Nehru suit, buttoned to her tiny, pointed chin. The suit made her look less Indian than Maoist, a Maoist from Connecticut, Miss Porter's School, and Harvard, where she had spent, she always said, the best semester of her life, leaving at eighteen to join and finally run the largest war game on the Web. Her hair was short and glossy brown, barbered carefully, hair by hair it seemed, and she listened to everything—the head creative ranting, mad schemes from the twins, Jaffe's dense and verbless legalese—with the same expression of polite engagement, one hand on the blondwood conference table, one hand in her tailored lap, a Connecticut Confucian, a Communist entrepreneur, a woman trapped inside the body of a woman.

"Smoke?" she said to Jens. "Are we actually talking about *smoke?*"

"No," said Jens, "smoke *shadows.*"

The topic wasn't actually smoke or shadows, but rather Jens' modest (so he thought) proposal to upgrade the blackened crater, the game's Cartesian 0, 0, 0 and universal starting point. Jens, knowing that he would be on the crush-and-paddle list for not completing Monster Todd, had planned to unveil SmoShadow as cover and excuse for his delays on the new monster bot. Jens made his pitch. The smoke pouring from the crater, as presently configured, didn't cast a shadow—a nit, perhaps, Jens said, but why not do it right?

Digby leapt in before Jens could finish. Digby pointed out that they already had shadows in the crater, moving with the sun, a phasing crater lip of gloom, adjusted for the weather, the goddamn fucking weather, Digby said, clouds and partial clouds and toxic clouds, plus other local-object shadows, helper bots and human, holybots and monsters, and all of these had to be splined and tessellated by the angle engines, giant loads of memory and throughput, batching plots to render engines, which colored plots and shaded them, laying texture maps (sand, shale, stucco wall), and turned the colors down to create a hazy fading in the distance, rounding objects in the foreground by wrapping darkness around "curves," eight or nine subrenderings, Digby pointed out, Z-sorting and MIP mapping, alpha-blending, P-correction—all of this to produce a weak 3-D illusion, forget about the loads of movement, aping movement, saving movement, everybody's moving and the game is about movement, we're heading west to destiny, and then you've got preloaded sprite routines, the mo-capture files, and the new full-polygon monsters, and all of this remembering and math-on-the-fly was carefully divided between the servers and the user's at-home RAM and vid cards, dual-ported, double-buffered, co-co-co-co-processed, and even so, Digby said, they were barely hitting three frames a second in the lulls, and now you want to enhance the *smoke*?

"No," Jens said, "the shadows. The smoke is fine, it's wonderful. I'm talking about shadows."

The crater was every player's first impression of the game and, if studies were correct, the place they saw on average 6.2 times a month (the average player died that often and was reborn from the hole—this was a post–Plague War number and a happy one; in the worst weeks of the war, players died a dozen times a day and desubscribed at the rate of ten a minute). The crater was important, Jens contended, a signature tableau, the realistic scree, the ocher tones and dusty wash, a symbol of a land returned to Bible times by Revelation 21. The crater code was very nearly perfect, Jens believed, except for this: the smoky pillar, paletted in gorgeous twenty-four-bit gray, should cast a shadow in its thickest part, and yet it didn't. Jens had written SmoShadow to track the billow's dancing shape and local densities, a function of prevailing winds. SmoShadow would upload the sun's position and throw a moving shadow on the crater wall, making allowances for rocks and rough terrain and the lip-horizon (because smoke in shadow, out of sun, would not cast a shadow of its own)—a complicated hack, and yet Jens had made it happen in a kilobyte, compiled.

"I have the mod right here," said Jens, brandishing SmoShadow on the disk. "Just give me a second and I'll get it loaded. You'll see how beautiful it is."

Jens had expected support from the head creative or at least the twins—they were always hot for new immersive graphics—but the twins were silent and the head creative said, "I think we need more dread."

Reed and Reese were nodding. They claimed to be nonidentical twins. Jens, who couldn't see a difference, suspected that the twins' parents, fearing merged identities and unhealthy personality dependence, had told their sons, falsely, that they weren't identical and the twins grew up believing in their difference, so they were relaxed and non-hung-up about dressing alike (baggy chinos, polo shirts) and driving the same car—vintage MG Spiders, a color called Champagne—and thinking the same way about how to sell the game and whip the competition, because they weren't identical, they were just agreeing, like any two smart and market-savvy people.

"I'm not sure I follow, Head," said Meredith.

Head was shaggy, fifty, ponytailed, a lamp-tanned movie refugee who kept himself by force of will on California time. Head said that Hollywood was dead, that the Web was the future of all entertainment narratives. Deep immersive gaming—this was the new movies and they should all be damn glad to be among the founding fathers, the Chaplins and the Griffiths and the Lumières, but everybody knew that Head was still in love with the big screen, still mourning the loss of the *Ohm's Law* franchise, a series of high-grossing summer action pictures, *Ohm's Law*, *Ohm's Law II*, *OL III: The Reckoning*, up to *OL VII* due out in July. Head had co-executive-produced the first *Ohm's Law*, which told the story of Joey Ohm, a tough but flawed detective, battling an asteroid. Sequels pitted Joey against other planetary threats, global warming, mass extinction, a wandering black hole, but Head was gone by then, disenfranchised of his franchise, squeezed out by his former so-called friends' attorneys.

"We need more dread," he said, coming forward in his chair. "We have these fucking early meetings, fine, I don't complain, but do I have to sit here listening to dweebs talking about fucking smoke? Smoke is not the issue. What we really need is dread."

"I agree," said Reed or Reese.

"Absolutely," said his brother. "We already have the best, most textured smoke in the business, and don't say Napalm Sunday because their smoke blows."

BigIf had two major rivals in the world of Web-based, multiplayer shoot-'em-ups. One was Napalm Sunday, set in the distant future. The other was Elfin, set in the magic past, an age of dragons, gorgons, castle keeps, warlocks, and bad spells. BigIf was poised nervously between them, set in the near future, a tricky time to work with—not exactly now, but also not the never-never of Arthurian romance or of interstellar war. The three games had been launched at more or less the same time, during the last game craze when every venture cap worth his or her corporate salt had at least one multiplayer shoot-'em-up.com in the incubator. Many games were started in the fad, all of them pursuing the same vision strategy: take the VC money, build a game, do the marketing, get the player loads up to a stable-profit, self-sustaining waterline, then take the baby public and everyone gets rich, a can't-miss plan—so can't-miss, in fact, that many game designers saw it, and thirty games were launched, more than the hard-core gamer base could possibly support, and so the can't-miss plan was the ruin of many interactivists, and a kick in the wallets of their VC backers. Remember Scoregasm, which let you, the gamer, blast your way out of a terrorist-held junior high school? Or Red Motorcade, which let you relive the murder of John Kennedy in the role of Oswald, the Cubans, the CIA, the Soviets, the Cosa Nostra, or the Secret Servicemen playing in thwart mode? Jens worshiped Red Motorcade as a design. It had one beginning, eight middles, and sixty-four endings, the nice effect of squaring possibilities, but the teens, the target audience, were only dimly aware of the real events in Dallas and the Dealey Plaza graphics were always going down. Of the surviving games, only BigIf, Elfin, and Nap Sunday were thought to have a chance of reaching steady profit, stable loads, and the sunburst of successful IPOage.

Head said, "Nap Sunday's in the shitter, but not because their smoke blows, though it does. They're in the shitter, Jens, because they are dread-challenged. What can you kill in outer space? Robots? Cyborgs? Those annoying machine poodles? I am forced to yawn my ass off. Distant future, pah. Who gives a fuck about the distant anything?"

Meredith said, "Clarify."

Head said, "We need new monsters. Hamsterman was dynamite, don't get me wrong. Skitz the Cat, Farty Pup, Seeing Eye, the piss and toxic flatulence, all the bathroom slapstick—it worked, we're here, and we owe it all to them. I'm duly grateful, but I sense a played-out trend. We've got to up the ante, folks. We've got to crank the dread. Our monsters are cartoons. Their life and death—cartoonish. We need human monsters. People want to shoot a face."

"Hmm," said Meredith. She turned to Jens. "How's the Postal Worker coming?"

Jens said, "Naubek has the Postal Worker."

"Naubek is a burnout," said Jaffe the attorney, doodling furiously, straining from the effort.

"I'll reassign it," said Meredith.

"Nap Sunday's got a droid that doesn't even kill you," said one of the twins. "If you fight it and lose, it overrides your mouse port and drags you around for an hour and you can't logoff or close the window."

"Virtual enslavement," said Head. "You know, that's not half bad."

"The problem is time," said Meredith. "Elfin has the past, Nap Sunday has the future. We're stuck in the middle."

"And Elfin's expanding," Digby said. "They're launching a new time-travel feature. Click an icon and their warlocks will send you ahead in time to the day of the Kennedy assassination. They bought a lot of code at Red Motorcade's going-out-of-business sale."

Head said, "Time travel is *so* corny."

"Maybe so," said Meredith, "but soon the wizards will be able to send you ahead to a post-apocalyptic near future, and where will that leave us?"

"Can they do that?" Digby asked. "Didn't we license the near future?"

Jaffe the attorney cleared his throat. He said, "We have a trademark on any game-related use of the word *apocalypse* and twenty-four synonyms and likely modifiers in all of the GATT languages. We own *Armageddon, chaos, plague, famine, mushroom, cloud, mushroom cloud,* and *thermonuclear exchange.* We bought *toxic, ooze,* and *mutant* from Scoregasm when they went belly up. We own *belly up, bite the dust, bought the farm.* We traded *flog the dolphin* to Sea Spawn in return for *put to sleep*—it seemed a better mammal-fit—and got it back when Sea Spawn choked the chicken. I'd say it would be difficult for Elfin to market a near-futuristic feature in any GATT vocabulary without running afoul."

"Thank you," said Meredith.

Head said, "Let them have the past, the future, the near future. That still leaves one time realm unexploited: the present." He looked around the table. "Nothing crawls the flesh like the near-at-hand. Let's draw our monsters from the nightly news. Think about it, people. What if famous serial killers made special guest appearances? I'm talking big names here, Bundy, Gacy, Gein, Manson live from Quentin. The Oklahoma City bomber, John Doe Number Two, the stocky ball-capped male they never caught. Salvadoran death squads, the Tonton Macoutes, brand-name ethnic cleansers."

"Bundy's dead," said Meredith. "Gein too, I think."

Head said, "I don't mean the actual guys, living or dead, although if Manson would play ball—wow. I mean characters like them, recognizable products of our own time. What could be more dreadful?"

"Wouldn't it get dated fast?" Digby asked. "That's the beauty of the distant future."

Head said, "We'll be gone in eighteen months, IPO'd or RIP'd. Fast is not the problem."

They covered other topics, the underbrush upgrades, the new audio fx. As the meeting ended, Meredith asked Jens to stay behind. They went into her office with the head creative.

Meredith installed herself behind her desk, a mass of spotless butcher block, a terrifying desk. "So," she said. "What the fuck is up with Monster Todd?"

Jens said, "Any day now. I just have a few kinks to—"

"Six weeks overdue," said the head creative.

"Don't blame me," said Jens. "The problem is your specs, Head. What's the concept? Who is Todd? He's just a kid. He stands there and he walks around. How am I supposed to write his logic if I don't get the concept?"

Head yawned. "Want a concept? Here's a concept, Jens. In every high school in this country, there is a quiet, troubled boy who is always thinking about murder. Maybe he is ugly, fat, or unpopular. Maybe he's a half-assed Satanist or a pimpled white supremacist angered by the failures of his skin. He's certainly a loser without normal friends or healthy extracurriculars. His parents don't understand him, neither do his teachers—who can understand a bloody-minded child? So, yes, he's misunderstood, that quaint teen complaint. He's lonely, angry, hateful. He speaks his thoughts and they are dark and other kids make fun, so he goes to Pizza Hut and buys himself a gun. He brings the gun to school one day, planning to mow down. I say let's put that kid, a trademark of our time, up on screen. The other kids will pay big bucks to hunt him through the corridors. That's the concept, Jens. Stop bucking for the Nobel Prize and write some fucking code."

Meredith said, "Are you a burnout, Jens?"

Jens said, "No." He said this very quickly.

"Because this smoke shadow thing—I don't understand. You geniuses in software, designing your cool toys, amusing yourselves. There are good, high-grossing monsters to be written, Jens, lead-pipe money-makers. There's a business plan to execute. You guys don't seem to accept this. How many coders in the Bot Pod, Jens?"

Jens said, "Nine including Mayer. He telecommutes from Honolulu."

"We fired him three months ago," said Meredith. "I meant to send an officewide e-mail."

"Eight," said Jens.

"Davey Tabor's looking for a job," said Meredith. "I don't buy this shit about trekking through Quebec."

"Tibet," said Jens.

"I think it's actually Nepal," said Head.

"Naubek is a burnout," Meredith continued. "Beltran's off on another mental health day, fifth of five and it's barely February. Lu Ping is brilliant but in love. Bjorn is clever but not solid. Prem is solid but not clever. But what do I know, Jens? I'm not down there with you. I can't see who's burning out, who's burned. All I see is a smoke shadow."

"And no Monster Todd," said Head.

Jens said, "I've done pretty goddamn well by this company. If you'd just look at my shadow, you'd see—"

Head said, "Let's fire Naubek. Tabor too, soon as he treks back."

Meredith said, "I'll tell Jaffe. He can put it all in one big e-mail."

Jens said, "Fire Naubek? That's ridiculous. Naubek wrote a big part of the code behind the game."

"So?" said Meredith. "We can fire anyone, Jens. I believe that we could even fire you."

"You can't fire me," Jens said. "*I* invented Hamsterman. *I* invented Skitz the Cat. *I* invented Farty Pup and *I* did the early work on Seeing Eye."

Jens went through several stages of reaction after leaving Meredith and Head—vigilante anger, disbelief, the giggles, outrage giving way to a simmering self-pity. He left the plant, got in his car, and drove aimlessly around the air base, slowly facing up to the practical realities. Could they fire him? What would he tell Peta if they did? What about her plan for their family future—hang on for the IPO, get the options, reassess?

Trees closed in on either side of the winding road, second growth, or maybe third, red maple and slash pine, the softwood instaforest of New England. He passed the former weapons storage area, high razor-wire fences, guard towers like a prison or a concentration camp. This was where they had stored the tunas, as the airmen called them, the long and graceful megatons. The bunkers were still out there, deep, blast-absorbing shafts driven into sandy ground. Jens had read somewhere that the bunker pumps were broken, and the shafts were slowly filling with groundwater, and it had become a cult of sorts to local stoner kids, bunker-diving, trespass on a dare. They came up from Portsmouth, gangs on racing bikes. They cut through the outer razor-wire fence, dug under the great iron doors (all of this on summer nights, smoking God knows what, angel dust or crank or crack—he had read another story about drugs coming up the interstate from the Massachusetts mill towns, Lowell, Lawrence, Haverhill, hellholes if you've been there), and then the kids, at night, confronted blackness, the blackness of the shaft, a cool wind from beneath, and the sound of echoed dripping in the depths, and being kids, and being high, some of them dove in. What the hell was in there—frogs, piranhas, one or two forgotten tunas? The bravery of kids on drugs, amazing. Was there anybody braver than a sixteen-year-old asshole from the projects of North Portsmouth? He had read a story in the paper about a boy named Suarez, missing for three days before someone called the cops. Most of the story had been about this—missing for three days, or was it longer? The boy wasn't Puerto Rican, as Jens had assumed, or Portuguese, as most people in North Portsmouth had once been, but rather Philippino, living with his mother, a cannery employee, and his grandmother, who expressed her fear and rage through an interpreter. The father was semi-in-the-picture, and the scandal was that no one, not the family, not the school, had noticed right away that the boy was missing or could state with certainty when he started being missing. It came out that the boy had been bunker-diving with his friends (Jens felt he had known this all along), and the cops sent a diver down to retrieve the body.

Through the trees along the road, Jens saw split-level houses with low-pitched roofs. He took a left and drove a loop on streets named for trees, Ash, Juniper, and Hemlock, a town of housing built for airmen in the '50s, deserted in a day after Russia fell—a brick elementary school, four softball diamonds sharing an outfield, chain-link backstops falling over, swing sets in the high grass, hydrants on the corners, streetlights overhead, a whole ghost subdivision.

Jens walked between abandoned ranches. The lot behind the school had become a lovers' lane and the woods behind the lot had become a dump, a gully full of Clorox jugs, old tires, and tumbled appliances. Kids snuck over from the malls and got fucked up in the empty houses, listening to rap, white kids throwing gangsta signs, leaving their graffiti, *Majorca!* or *Skitz is Gawd*, starting little fires for warmth and fun, and house by house the tract was burning down. Other kids, looking for their friends, wandered up here too—Jens saw them in the afternoons. Worried parents followed, cruising in minivans around the dinner hour, pausing at a corner, window rolled down, listening for music above the highway drone. Sometimes the parents followed the music to the party house, and found other parents' kids inside, kindling a fire, and kept searching. Cops arrived on noise complaints and called the firefighters. Portsmouth couldn't leave this place alone, and this was strange to Jens—so strange, he came by once a day to see who else was here.

Jens went into the house across the street from the elementary school. The door was jimmied, splintered, and the living room was bare. He heard footsteps through the ceiling. A voice called down the stairs, "Freeze, motherfucker."

Jens said, "It's me."

Vaughn Naubek said, "Come up."

Jens found Naubek sitting on a milk crate in an empty bedroom, peering out the window at the corner of the school. Naubek wore his postal worker getup. He was eating a hickory-smoked Slim Jim. He offered Jens a milk crate.

Naubek said, "I'm fired."

Jens said, "I know. I'm sorry, Vaughn."

"We wrote that goddamn game. You and me, we wrote it."

Jens said, "I know. It's wrong, Vaughn. What else can I say?"

Naubek looked at a spot on the Slim Jim for a moment, then bit the spot he had been looking at.

He said, "First computer interfaced?"

Naubek was nostalgic for the old machines, the lost technology of his childhood.

Jens said, "Hex 1000. You?"

"3000 Turbo."

"Lucky dog."

"My dad worked for the IRS in Kansas City and I snuck into the office to play on the mainframe. The Turb was a helluva machine. First program written?"

"JENSISNUMBER1.exe. It displayed the text string 'Jens is Number 1.'"

"With how many exclamation points?"

"Forgotten. Numerous."

"First modem used to access first computer?"

"Slow acoustic coupler, three hundred bips at best. Big padded cups where you fit the phone."

"Number of times you licked said padded cups?"

"Once. It tasted like a vinyl chair."

"Number of times you licked a vinyl chair?"

"None that I remember, yet I seem to know the taste."

"Number of times you put your dick in the padded cups?"

"Zero. You?"

"One. Pops caught me in the IRS computer room, pants around my ankles, cock enmodemed. Man, was he unhappy. Taxed my allowance down to nothing. But it was worth it, Jens. My cock felt good in there."

Jens shifted on the crate. "Is that a real gun, Vaughn?"

"Which one?"

"The big one in the corner by your night-vision headwear."

"True," said Naubek.

"What about the pistol in your belt?"

"No, Jens, it's a Pez dispenser."

"May I have a Pez?"

Naubek reached into his pocket and tossed a roll of Pez to Jens. Jens took a Pez and tossed the roll back to Naubek. Jens bit and Naubek sucked.

Jens said, "That's not a Pez dispenser, Vaughn. What are the guns for?"

"Why do they have to be *for* anything, Jens? Why can't they just *be*?"

The windows were sheet plastic and the room was cold. A van passed on the street below, kids getting out of school going off to party in one of the houses.

Jens said, "Should I call the cops or something?"

"You mean, am I a workplace rampage shooter on the verge? Shit, I wouldn't waste a bullet on those people, Meredith and them. They think they're so great. They think they're running a big system. Well they don't know a fucking thing. When I worked at NASA, I helped design the telemetry package on the shuttle *Columbia*. Everything redundant, triple backups, bang-paths on the mother-board—*that* was engineering, man. I wept the day she blew the O-ring."

"Aren't all rings pretty much an O?"

"*Ring* is the backup word in case you miss the O," Naubek said. "That's what I mean about NASA—they even had redundant *words*. God, I miss those days."

Naubek pretended to be interested in his shotgun suddenly, hiding his wet eyes.

Jens stood. "Think I'll take a spin and clear my head. It's been a real shitty day so far."

"Excuse me, can I help you?" asked the lady at the front desk.

Jens said, "I've come to get my son."

There was a rule at Li'l People Montessori: parents or caregivers were not allowed to go into the classroom areas when they came to get their children. Some kids were in the half-day program; some were nine-to-three; others were in full-day, which ran until six. Parents or caregivers would disrupt the classes, coming and going all day long. This had been explained in a letter from the school. Jens hated the letters from the school, the cool and therapeutic tone.

"You can't go in there," said the woman. She came around the desk. She barred the classroom door with a flabby arm.

Jens said, "I want my son. His name is Kai. He's in the full-day."

It was around noon. Jens was here six hours early.

The woman looked at Jens. "Are you all right?"

Jens saw Kai in the corner of the classroom, one head in a flock of heads watching as the teacher fed the goldfish, and explained.

Jens drove along 1A, down the rocky shore, generally home. Kai was clapping in his crash seat.

Jens felt better, driving home from Li'l People. The curving roadway straightened out his thinking. No, it was more—the road was speaking to him, a cliché come true, the white broken line, the lane divider, stretching to forever. Speeding up, he turned the faster-passing dashes into dots, slowing turned them back to dashes, and for a moment he was a hammer kid again, reading dots and dashes, writing with the stylus of speed. Other drivers honked and waved, but he didn't care.

Kai was laughing. "We're driving crazy!" he told the other cars. "Poppa, this is fun!"

Jens' life descended into code. Three dashes made the letter O. As he slowed, the road was saying OOOOOOOOOOOOOOOOO. Three dots were the letter S, four dots made the letter H. Speeding up, the road was saying *SHSHSHSHSHSHSH*.

"**We want sea views,** not swamp views, and I don't care if it's technically a marsh and part of the overall tidal ecosystem, because as I've told you, Peta, told you many times, that does *not* make it a sea view."

Lauren Czoll was standing on the wraparound terrace behind the manor house at the Silence Bell estate, homesteaded on Indian land in 1646, and priced to move at a million two. Lauren had just come from her daily boxing workout. She wore a cashmere warmup suit, soft and gray as dawn, black lace-up boxing shoes, and a mustard coat, the latest from New York, abstract outerwear, a yellow parallelogram.

"Would you like to see the kitchen?" Peta asked.

"No," said Lauren, "I would like to see *the sea*."

She was skittish as a colt and twice as pretty, Peta thought. Jerzy Czoll, Lauren's husband, BigIf's CEO, was sitting on nine million option warrant units of unrestricted BigIf common stock. When the game went IPO, if it ever did (Peta was starting to lose faith), Jerzy would become an instant millionaire or billionaire of whatever magnitude and this pretty colt would become, thereby, an instant Mrs. –illionaire. As such, Lauren Czoll was someone to be coddled at all costs. As they stood on the patio, looking down the valley at an arm of silver marsh, Peta thought the cost was getting pretty high.

Peta specialized in Lauren's type, high-strung wives (second wives or third, in Lauren's case) searching for the first true mansions of their marriages. It always went this way: the women did the looking, the footwork and the tours, treating Peta like a slave, until they found that special country seat somewhere around a million five. The husbands came in at the endgame, taking a quick tour, always on the run, sending an attorney to the closing. It was a nerve-racking jurisdiction for a realtor, new money and demanding wives, but the broker fees were making Peta the star earner at Moss Properties. She was paid to coddle women like Mitzi Hindenberg (wife of Barry Hindenberg, the screensaver visionary) and Chappie Xing (wife of Ai-Me Xing, also known as Winston, the father of the 3D e-mail singing postcard and other online breakthroughs). Peta always steered them to a closing in the end. Mitzi, after six months' hectic searching, finally found the fifty-eight-room Tudor of her dreams. Chappie, after nine months, finally bought the private island in the Oyster River. Peta was the realtor of last resort for the problem cases, the agent you send in when lesser agents fail. But she had met her match in Lauren Czoll. Peta had been searching with Lauren for almost a year.

"Let's see the kitchen," Peta said to Lauren. "It has real wow-value."

They crossed the terrace, heading for the house. When Lauren first came to Moss Properties, Peta had interviewed her over omelets and Chablis at the new French place on Market Square in Portsmouth, the pivotal initial step in a serious house hunt, the slightly boozy get-to-know-you luncheon in which Peta played the drab and understanding Cinderella, the bartender/confessor, the psychiatrist/sex therapist, the college roommate you haven't seen in twenty years—played whatever role she had to play to get the facts she needed to start looking. At that luncheon, over coffee and a ten-berry tart, Peta had teased out Lauren's list of bedrock home requirements. Lauren, prodded skillfully (Peta was the best at this), finally allowed that she needed three things: land, history, and a walk-in humidor wired for Net access, DSL or faster (Jerzy would be flexible on this). Even at the outset of the house hunt, Peta felt that she was being carelessly exploited. Peta was no Marxist (who could be in this market?), but she did believe that there was a new ruling class and a new proletariat. The rulers controlled the means of scheduling. The proles were those who bore the brunt of dithering and cancellations, who waited at the bistro when the rulers showed up twenty minutes late, as Lauren always did, mouthing stock apologies, and Peta had to smile, "Oh it's no problem, Laur." Time was the new factory of the service sector and the rulers were the ones who owned it, wasting yours to save their own.

Not that Lauren saved much time, hers or anybody's. Peta put the Czolls' price range at one-point-one to one-point-nine (she took a guess; Lauren didn't know), called up a hundred listings. The houses were on major land, and most of them had interesting histories, a link to someone notable (Fitz-John Porter, corps commander in the Civil War; David Dixon Porter, key admiral of that war; Edith Effing Dalrymple, early Mesmerist and crusading suffragette, mother of Finch Dalrymple, teenaged abolitionist and early investor in Coca-Cola Corporation) or to something notable (the whaling trade, the spinning mills, the Civil War, the paintings of John Singer Sargent, Coca-Cola Corporation). Lauren, being a new ruler, wasted everybody's time, coming late, forgetting some appointments (Peta standing on the lawn, looking at her watch), always finding fault when she saw a property, inventing new requirements, requiring new searches. First it was a helipad (had to have a helipad), then a gazebo, then a sail loft, then a bridle trail, a garden maze, and a working gristmill, plus land, history, and the wired humidor. Peta found a charming Queen Anne in Rye Crossings with humidor, gazebo, secluded bridle trails, and a Class 2 landing strip, but the gristmill was too squeaky, Lauren said, and the gazebo blocked her seaward views. Lauren was big on sea views for a time, then wanted something farmy and less windblown. She forgot about the gristmill altogether, focusing instead on music rooms and apple trees, and now we're back to sea views, Peta thought. All Peta really needed was an answer to the question What does Lauren want? What will make her happy—truly, deeply, finally happy? Why was this so difficult for people nowadays?

It seemed to be the new plague of the age, this confusion over wants and needs. Poverty was pressure, Peta knew, but wealth created pressure too. The pressure on the software wives was quiet and corrosive—if you can have anything, buy *anything* you see, why you are still nervous and dissatisfied? Peta saw corrosion in her clients and in Jens. Poor Jens was building monsters, on the verge of finally getting rich, but it wasn't good or pure enough somehow. She knew he wasn't sleeping. She pretended not to really notice, because she was afraid that Jens, confronted, would unravel. And so Peta, too, like her clients and Jens, felt that she was walking on the lip of a deep pit.

"Right this way," she said to Lauren.

Peta let them in the back door of the manor house, pausing to wipe her feet on the rattan mat inside the door. Lauren, seeing this, paused to wipe her feet as well. There were two clients here, thought Peta. This morning's Lauren was the posh, high-handed bitch. The other Lauren was the frightened child, food-disordered, lost in wealth, neurotic to the nines. One sharp word from Peta and this other Lauren would start bawling, so Peta held her tongue, just as she'd held her tongue with Jens that morning, him and his snide crack about the moon. Peta knew that Jens was jealous of the love and care she wasted on her clients' whims, of the Saturdays she spent touring mansions with Lauren, or the nights she spent at the office, eating takeout sushi as she did her listing searches on the Web. It was a crock of shit, of course—Peta didn't love her clients any more than a doctor loves her patients. Jens' panic and self-pity were among his least attractive traits, ranking right down there with his lacerating tongue. He turned it on himself ("Even my best monster is a failure," he would say), and—less often, but more often lately—on her as well.

"Here we are," said Peta, leading Lauren through the spacious, eat-in, center-island kitchen, newly renovated. The Bell Estate belonged to a man named Geoff Rishman, a Bell by marriage, twice removed, a pushy Boston asshole (they called them Massholes up here) who had lost the last of the Bell fortune on a team gymnastics league. His franchise, the Boston Swans, had crushed the New York Attitude in the title meet, but Geoff couldn't get a TV deal and the league collapsed. Geoff was asking one-point-two, but Peta thought he would gladly entertain high nines.

Lauren worked the faucets as Peta did her spiel. The pattern for the house, she said, came from thatch-roofed cottages of Lincolnshire, that's England. It came not in blueprint but in the eye of the first Puritans, who adapted the design to the colder winters and abundant timber of America. The walk-in fireplace was actually a pyramid of Flemish bricks, brought across as ballast, 1638. The stove was Viking, high-output, as in the best restaurants.

"No more waiting for the pasta water," said Peta hopefully.

Lauren touched the oven door. "Who was Silence Bell?"

Portsmouth brokers knew their history. The big-ticket properties were the registered estates, the landmarks on the headlands down to Rye. Selling them was telling them, Noel Moss always said. Peta knew her history better than most.

"Silence Bell," she recited. "Born 1616, left England at the age of twenty-one under a Stuart death warrant. Elected captain of Winthrop's militia, 1644. Came north to quell the Indians that year. Bell was related to the Mathers on his mother's side. He was little Cotton Mather's favorite cousin and was best man at Mather's wedding, most historians believe. Cotton Mather, son of Increase, is regarded as the last important voice of—"

"I know who Cotton Mather was," Lauren said. "He was a racist dick. Was Bell a racist too?"

"No," said Peta mildly, "he was a moderate, a Puritan Eisenhower. He stopped the wanton massacres of the Onomonopiacs through a judicious policy of mass deportation to the Jamaican sugar fields, and presided in old age over the later Salem witch trials, voting against several of the hangings and many of the pressings. His personal narrative of the Puritan experiment, *Covenantum Bloodcurdlicum*, was written in this very house."

"Really?"

"Upstairs, in what's now the TV room."

They did the dining room, the drawing room, the music room, the den. Peta pointed out the period appointments, the Hepplewhites, the Chippendales, the Sheratons, the Sonys. They came to the game room, a blast of garish '70s—rugs like body hair and vanilla leather couches, obelisks and orbs on every table. Geoff was sleeping with his decorator and it showed.

Peta said, "Ignore the LeRoy Neiman prints."

Lauren winced. "I'll try. The listing mentioned paddocks. Can we see them?"

They went outside and down the lawn, past the brick barbecues, the teak cabanas, and the tarpaulined pool.

Peta said, "The paddock's just ahead."

There was one horse at home that morning, a vermin-ridden thoroughbred named Locomotion, also on the market. They watched the horse munch squash rinds for a time.

Lauren said, "Is this paddock winterized?"

"It feels pretty winterized," said Peta, losing patience. "I'm warm, Lauren. Are you?"

"Check and make sure. This horse looks sick. I wouldn't want my horse getting sick out here."

"Do you own a horse?"

"No, but if I did the poor thing could freeze to death out here in this drafty paddock."

Locomotion flicked its tail.

"Lauren," Peta said. "May I make an observation? I think we're going at this backwards. Heated paddocks, bridle paths, gazebos—that's crossing t's and dotting i's, fine tuning. That's detail, Lauren, and detail should come last."

"What comes first?" Lauren asked.

"The dream. We're searching for a home, Lauren. Home, I know, is a loaded concept for people of our generation, us feminists in particular, given the historic subjugation of the female in the domestic scheme, as you were explaining to me last week, but on the other hand, it's just a goddamn building. And I know, as we've discussed, that in many ways the quest, the journey home, is more important than the destination, but on the other hand, Lauren, you are supposed to buy something eventually. Commit and post your earnest money, move to closing—"

Lauren turned away. "You know I hate that word. You're rushing me. I thought you were my friend and here you're rushing me."

"I'm speaking as a friend. Listen to me, Lauren. The search for home must begin in dreams—one dream, one constant dream, not all this compulsive running around. Face it, darling: you are rich. You can have anything you want, housewise. All you need to do is tell me what you want. Don't cry, baby—it's all right. You are Odysseus, trying to get home, and I am, I don't know, his real estate agent."

Lauren took the Kleenex Peta offered, blew her nose resoundingly. She said, "Lately I've been thinking about lighthouses. Can we look at some lighthouses?"

"No more of that," said Peta, firmly now. "I'm afraid it's time for drastic measures."

It always came to this with the Mrs. –illionaires, the woman lying on the couch, Peta standing by the door, dimming the lights. As a realtor, Peta rarely used hypnosis, preferring less invasive means of clarifying what her clients needed in a home. When Mitzi Hindenberg was "blocked," Peta used aromatherapy. Mitzi, sniffing almond oil, had a sudden vision of a fifty-eight-room Tudor on the beach. Peta, armed with Mitzi's vision, found the place exactly as described; it was kind of eerie actually. Peta tried everything on her toughest clients—inkblots, bong hits, long runs, sometimes even prayer. Chappie Xing said the Act of Contrition with Peta (who, being a Boyle, knew the Act backwards and forwards, *God our Lord the to me for*—this was backwards). They prayed and said amen, and Chappie drew a picture of a Georgian mansion with cathedral ceilings surrounded by these little squiggles, like 3s on their sides. The squiggles puzzled Peta (they had seen several Georgian mansions with cathedral ceilings and Chappie didn't bite). Then Peta realized that the sideways 3s were dream-symbol water and that what Chappie deeply needed was an island of her own. Again Peta found the place exactly as dreamed of, the old Honus Steadman house on what was now Xing Island. The moment Chappie stepped over the gunwales of the longboat and saw the house up in the rocks, she collapsed in Peta's arms, saying, "Oh Peta, oh Pet, you have brought me home." There was much for Jens to sneer at here, but some human feeling too, and Peta was happy for the Xings.

Lauren was lying on the couch in the game room. Peta dimmed the lights, took a CD from her purse, split the case, and handled the bright object. The CD was called *Voices of the Rain Forest, Vol. III*, Peta's headache music. She fed a string through the doughnut hole (the string was carried for this purpose), blew on the shiny data side, and wiped it on her blouse cuff.

Lauren said, "This couch is less comfortable than you might imagine."

"Never mind the couch," said Peta.

"I can't be hypnotized. A doctor told me that. He said I'm in the five percent that can't be—"

"Just relax. Watch the CD, Lauren. It's swinging back and forth, back and forth, back and forth. Your eyelids are growing heavy, heavy, heavy."

Soon Lauren Czoll was very, very hypnotized.

"Lauren, do you hear me?"

"Yes."

"You are standing on the lawn of your dream house. The home of your dreams and inner peace. Do you see it, Lauren?"

Lauren nodded tentatively.

"Tell me what you see."

Lauren spoke in a deeper voice. "Light," she said. "Airiness."

People needed urging. Peta said, "Go on."

"Space and line and form. A sense of—"

"Yes?"

"Destination. Old and new in balance. A stately Greek Revival with up-to-date conveniences."

Greek Revival—this was good. Peta made a mental note.

"Turf, trees, wet bricks, a self-mulching garden. But through the windows— sea. Light abundant. Not just that. No, abundant change. Each room dapples differently. Winter is a tone. Easter, a tone. I watch the gales roll in. I see my children growing up—I look forward to nostalgia, a parent's job well done. This is mine. This is mine. Time is not an arrow."

"Does it have a garage?"

"I see the neighbor's house."

"Let's stick with your house for the moment. Are you seeing a garage?"

"I'm standing on my lawn looking at the neighbor's house across a lake or bay. There's a party going on, show people and a dance band. I see a green light on a dock. I see a hooker and some Dutch sailors. They've come for the orgy too."

"It's probably a rental," Peta said. "Now turn around on the lawn. Are you turning, Lauren?"

"Yes."

"Now go in your house. Tell me what you see."

"A music room upstairs, a glass conservatory. Fretted ironwork, a cage for a singing bird. A chest of drawers with room for all my keepsakes. I see Jerzy in the driveway with our daughter. I'm standing at the window, looking down. The year is twenty years from now. They hug. The car is packed. Our daughter is beautiful and golden-haired and Jerzy is so pleased. She's going off to college, off to Yale. No, wait—she's going off to Wheaton. She got dinged by Yale and wait-listed by Wellesley."

"Breathe deeply, Lauren. Good. Just tell me what you see."

"Jerzy's hugging her goodbye and—wait, that's not our daughter. Why's he kissing her?"

"The house, Lauren, come back to the house."

"I see a chest of drawers. Room for all my pretty things. I keep a gun in there. I go down and teach that tramp a lesson on the lawn."

Motherhood was pressure (Kai would live on chewy sticks if Peta didn't nark him every minute of the day); marriage was pressure, watching Jens slip off the edge,

Peta feeling helpless, saying nothing; and then there was her job at Moss Properties, which used to be so fun, like being paid to shop with other peoples' money.

Coming up I-95, Peta felt a headache hatching in the swivel of her eyeballs. She found a bottle of Excedrin in her purse and chewed a pill dry-mouthed as she drove. Peta had two jobs at her company, and this was the problem—she was spread too thin. Noel Moss, the dapper laird and heir at Moss Properties, marveled at her talent for the million-dollar sale. He said the way she had steered crazy Mitzi Hindenberg to a closing on the Tudor was a masterful performance, like a seasoned pilot landing a crippled jumbo jet on an icy runway, and he could only doff his cap in admiration. Noel called her the Realtrix, a play on dominatrix, a playful play Peta knew because Noel was more or less openly gay and certainly not flirting. Noel was grooming her for partnership, which Peta wanted badly, but the elder Mosses—Noel's father, grandfather, and three uncles, hardshell Yankees to a man—were against it. Peta was a crack mansion-mover, they admitted, but she had never worked the other side of the family's business, the lucrative if dreary realm of building management. The Mosses owned or managed under contract a healthy coastal empire of retail/office space, ten strip malls, six office blocks, a quarter million square feet of light industrial. The agents at these properties advertised the vacancies, dealt with bitchy tenants, got the carpets cleaned, rode herd on the supers, a succession of small pesterings for which the building agent received nothing more dramatic than the rent.

Noel had put it bluntly at a lunch in November to discuss Peta's prospects for a partnership. "Managing these buildings is a crashing bore," he told her. "It wouldn't be so bad if the spaces themselves were pleasing or distinctive, but alas we're talking Kmarts here, we're talking sneaker stores. I'm almost ashamed to be profiting off such ugliness, except it's so damn profitable and I'm so damn greedy. And that's the problem, Peta. You are used to the grand, the exquisite, the historic. You have a gift, there's no denying it. The question that my family has is, can you handle dull?"

Peta, eager to make partner, was sure that she could handle dull. She even welcomed dull—it would be a break from the pressures she was feeling, Jens, Kai, and Lauren Czoll. Noel proposed a test, a chance to show the elder Mosses that she could excel at being bored. The Mosses owned an office block in Portsmouth Harborside. The property was called the Dental Building, a two-story box of unconvincing brickface, plexi windows, white vinyl stripping, matching vinyl gutters, a smallish lobby with a potted palm.

"Manage it for us," Noel had said. "Manage it *sans* drama and we'll make you the next partner in Moss Properties."

Peta had been managing the Dental since November. She had rearranged her schedule, carving out an hour at the end of every day to attend to whatever tedium the building might present. She toured the space with the super, Frank Horan, forcing herself to pay attention to Frank's monologue on pest control and upcoming ventilation maintenance. She read the building files, reviewed the manuals on the water pump, the burglar alarm, the HVAC unit on the roof, and went through the bank statements on the operational accounts until she felt on top of every detail in the place.

Then the problems started, real tricks on the Realtrix. They started with a little thing, a single roofing nail Peta found in the parking lot one winter afternoon as she was coming in to hold her office hours. She held the nail in the palm of her hand and looked at the pavement. She saw another nail on the ground, then another and another, and realized that the lot was sprinkled with the nails. She told Frank Horan to sweep the lot, and wondered briefly why a roofer would have been in their parking lot, since there was no roof work scheduled.

Two days later, Frank Horan called her to the roof and showed her the HVAC plant, a big fan-and-pump unit enclosed in sheet metal. Frank pointed to the freon lines, coils up the side of the machine. Peta, squatting by the coils, saw marks like a dog's jaws on the soft aluminum.

"Looks chewed," Frank Horan said appraisingly, "but that's impossible. No mouth could touch it, man or animal. Freon'll maim you—it's so cold, it burns. So maybe it was pliers or a hacksaw or a dull pair of pinking shears."

Peta touched the torn aluminum. It was somehow terrible, a common thing destroyed. She looked up at the super. "Frank, what's going on here?"

Frank Horan crossed his arms. "You'll have to ask Mr. Moss."

That afternoon, she cornered Noel in his office and demanded an explanation of the curious occurrences at the Dental Building. Noel closed his door and told her the story of a doctor named Soteer, a former tenant at the Dental, an MD-OBGYN, some part of whose practice involved, or had once involved, performing safe and legal abortions at various fully accredited clinics in New England.

Peta remembered sitting in Noel's office at Moss Properties. Noel's office was a comic place (the handsome oaken paneling, the oriental rug, the sea charts and the brass telescope on legs)—it looked like Nelson's stateroom at Trafalgar—but it wasn't very comic when he said the word *abortion*.

Noel poured himself a coffee at the sideboard. He said, "There's a war going on apparently. I call it a war, the cops call it a war—you can call it anything you like. Doctors shot, nurses shot, clinics bombed and firebombed. But there's also a low-level conflict, an endless war of nerves. Protesters haunt the doors of clinics, screaming at women hurrying in. The staff is harassed, every day, everywhere. They are followed to the movies, to the mall, to the dump. Pickets go up at the end of their driveways. Shouting and chanting all night long. Crank calls at five a.m., tapes of babies crying. The buildings themselves are sabotaged. People chain themselves to the doors or chain themselves to cars, which are towed to block the doors. Power is cut, water is cut. Butyric acid is sprayed over the ceiling panels, producing a vomit smell of Biblical intensity. Cutting the phones is a favorite tactic; another is flooding the phones with bogus appointments, booking weeks of doctor time for imaginary patients. Nerf balls in the sewer line create another kind of flood, but the goal is always this: to stretch the nerves until they snap, to make the normal impossible and vice versa.

"Soteer never saw patients or performed procedures at the property. He used the space as a hideyhole, a quiet place to do his paperwork. He was evidently followed there and our address appeared on some nutball wanted-poster website and the harassment began soon afterwards. First it was the roofing nails in the parking lot. Frank Horan swept them up, it was no big deal. One assumes the normal, after all. A roofer has spilled nails, sweep them up, it's done. This is called sanity, by the way—the habit of understanding life's little glitches as the unusual result of the usual phenomena. None of the tenants gave it any thought. Except for Soteer. He saw the nails and never came back. What does one conclude? Connected events—nails and Soteer's disappearance? No, the nails are sloppy roofers and Soteer is just another rent-jumper, which is why God created the two-month security deposit. Then came the superglue in the locks. What does one conclude? Prankster kids.

Made sense to me. I never liked kids. When I was a kid, jerking off to pictures of Gore Vidal, I didn't like me. Now I like me and I *still* don't like kids. Then came more nails and more nails. It was raining nails in Portsmouth. So I called my good pal the district attorney. He called his colleagues in the FBI, who recognized the MO. Violent splinter right-to-lifers, they said. So now I gather they've destroyed the HVAC. It's a natural progression, in a sense."

Peta said "Why didn't you tell me this before?"

"In part because I'm selfish," Noel said. "In part because—well, selfish covers it, I'd say."

"You promised me boring. You're a bastard, Noel."

"I promised you a crashing bore. Just the phrase, don't you agree?"

"Roofing nails in the parking lot are *not* boring."

"Not the first ten times perhaps," Noel admitted cheerily. "Everything is boring, Peta. You just have to give it time."

"But Soteer's gone."

"What's that, dear?"

"You said he left. They're harassing the building pointlessly."

"Do you mean it's *irrational*? What a blazing insight, Peta."

"Maybe we could let them know that the guy they're trying to harass is gone."

"How does one do that? Erect a sign, *Soteer: Not Here*? Or maybe a post to MossProp.com or a mass e-mail to everyone on Earth. *Sorry to bother all of you, but we're realtors proudly serving Rockingham County and the seacoast since 1917, and we'd like a dozen wackos to know that Soteer is not here.*"

"Did he leave a forwarding address? Maybe we could put them on his trail, get them off our backs."

"Did I mention these were killers? Really, Peta, show a little spine."

"But we're realtors, Noel. We're neutral in this thing. We just want to live in peace."

"Your cowardice appals me, Peta Boyle. Besides, I thought of that already. No forwarding address."

The clock ticked in the office. Noel milked his coffee.

"As a Moss," he said, "I'm conservative, of course. I'm quite prominent in several organizations of New Hampshire gay and lesbian conservatives. These are not large organizations, which is nice in a way—we all get to be quite prominent. But it's odd too, Peta. Because, you see, I love—really *love*—twenty people in the world. I made a list the other night. I couldn't sleep, so I made a list. This is what they call middle age. Don't glower at me, darling, I'm busy being wise. One set of the people on my list, Gramps and Dad, my uncles, find my quote-unquote lifestyle choice repugnant. The other set, my lover and our friends, find my Tory politics repugnant. And yet I love both sets, and they love me, and as I grow older I'm increasingly sure of the fact that I just can't handle coffee in the afternoon. Burns the stomach tubes. God knows why I drink it."

He burped lightly and went on: "It seems to me the central question is: when does life begin? I've given this question some thought lately. Strenuous, nonironic, pro bono thought—unusual for me, but then so are roofing nails in my parking lot. It comes down to a sub-question: what is life? In one sense, my life began the day I was born. In another sense, it began on the afternoon of July the tenth, 1970—my junior year abroad, his name was Jacques. I saw him on the channel ferry, Peta—I saw him and I knew a truth about myself. I'll spare you the details of our week in Amsterdam, poignant though they are. Life, living, being human in your skin, is something one comes into over time—with effort or by accident, a meeting on a ferry—or never, as the case may be. But life, breath, pumping blood, is obviously something else. When does *that* life begin? The best answer I've come up with is: I don't remember. One day I was here, conscious of myself, a Moss and son of Mosses in New Hampshire. Before that—well, all I have is rumor in the end."

He put the coffee down. "I don't think we'll be posting any notices or sending any e-mails to the world. I don't think we'll be doing much of anything, Peta, except what we always do. Because, you see, it's *my* goddamn building, my family's goddamn ugly building, and that is why you are going to keep it open. That is why you will sweep the nails and de-Nerf the pipes and take whatever extraordinary steps are necessary to run an ordinary, boring, mid-market office block in Portsmouth."

So the siege began. During Peta's first week as the Dental's manager, Frank Horan found epoxy in the locks when he came in. He drove up the street to call an all-night locksmith from the phonebook. After making the call, Frank discovered that two of his tires were flat from roofing nails. He changed the tires as the tenants were arriving, parking in the lot, ruining their tires, demanding to know why their keys weren't working. There were seven tenants at that point, a lawyer, an accountant, another lawyer, a dentist, a psychiatrist, a speech pathologist, and a Web designer. Each tenant had customers arriving with their problems, a toothache or a lawsuit, a stutter or a lisp, a web to be designed, a delusion to be cured, and these clients didn't need tire punctures too. That night, Noel authorized a nine-thousand-dollar anti-vandal fence. The gates were padlocked each night at dusk, unlocked at seven-thirty.

In Peta's second week as manager, the padlock was sawed off, nails scattered, and the door locks glued again. She got a new lock for the gates, heavy-duty tempered steel (uncuttable, the locksmith said—you'd need a welder to get it off). Frank came in two days later, found the gates secure, the padlock uncut, and a second lock, behind the first, also tempered steel, equally uncuttable, and Peta had to call a welder to get the building open. The tenants were frantic, waiting for the welder as their customers arrived. A patient of the dentist, moaning from the pain, begged him to pull a molar on the sidewalk. A patient of the shrink, a struggling agoraphobe, had a good cry by the dumpsters.

In Peta's third week as manager, the Web designer found a Nerf ball in the sewage line. Several people found the Nerf ball more or less together, flushing toilets on both floors, flushing again, as people do. The wastewater overflowed, soaking the carpets. The smell was pungent for a time, shit and wet acrylic. Peta had to call the plumber, a radio-dispatched carpet-cleaning crew, and the police. Noel was determined to fight on. They put cameras on the building, in the lobby and the hall. They put spotlights on the fences, codepads on the bathrooms, and new alarms on all the outside doors. The psychiatrist complained that his patients were unhappy and regressing. Noel responded by hiring a guard dog to stay overnight. The dog attacked the lobby palm and left scary paw marks on the glass of the front door. They got a different dog and a few nights after that, the lawyer on the first floor, working late on a brief, was mauled outside the bathroom. He hired the other lawyer to sue the building and the psychiatrist moved out.

Over Christmas, they lost power—someone cut the line. Over New Year's, someone shot the floodlights with a pellet gun, put a new lock on the gates, and threw nails over the fence. Noel made the move to the armed guards. The guards sat around the lobby, pistols on their hips, reading fishing magazines. Peta dealt with the guards, the dog guy, the police, telephone security, the power company, and—most strangely—a man who answered his phone, "Threats."

This man was Brian Ryan, U.S. Secret Service. Peta never fully understood why the Secret Service cared about the Dental Building. As near as she could figure, Brian Ryan was an anthropologist of threats, doing his fieldwork, building up some file in the sky. Peta reasoned that the agents needed to know the local terror scene, who was active, who was quiet, who was up to what. Even so, there seemed to be a big connection missing, two ends with no middle, misdirected Nerf attacks (her end) and a real threat to life and limb (Agent Ryan's). Peta tried to ask Brian Ryan about the missing middle, but he kept saying it was all routine. Well, it wasn't *her* routine, goddammit. Later, however, it became almost routine, roofing nails and sewage in the halls. It was as Noel had promised: even terror becomes boring if you give it time.

Driving up the interstate, chewing her dry aspirin, Peta was talking on the cell phone to her secretary, Claus. Claus was a fine secretary, Prussian and efficient. Noel had met him on a cruise ship to St. Bart's.

Claus said, "And how is Lauren?"

"She's impossible," said Peta. "Get a pen. I need a listings search—"

"Again?"

"Just get a pen. We need Greek Revival, sea views, humidor, gazebo, and a music room, fretted ironwork a definite plus. Also a self-mulching garden."

"What is a self-mulching garden?"

"I don't know, just search for it. Any messages?"

Claus read from a pad. "The VP's campaign called, a rude man named Tim. He wants to confirm you as a volunteer for tomorrow morning."

"Call him back, confirm it."

"Agent Ryan called at ten. Is he that new cute boy who works at Impact Realty?"

"No. What did he say?"

"Please call. Want his mobile number?"

"I have it," Peta said.

"Also Jens. He was at the house, Santasket Road."

"Why wasn't he at work?"

"He didn't say."

"Is everything all right?"

"He didn't say it wasn't."

"Goddammit, Claus, what *did* he say?"

"Nothing. He said the place looked fine."

Nothing and more nothing—this was Jens the last few months. Peta rubbed her temples. She knew that he had fallen behind on his latest project, Monster Todd, and that he left his office for long stretches during the workday. He called her sometimes from the road, either to attack her for coddling the wealthy or to apologize for a past attack, a cycle of attack and regret, itself a form of self-attack, which only led to more attacks on her.

She said, "I'm sorry, Claus—I'm a bit wound up today. Do the listings search. If you find something good, set up a showing ASAP. Let's find a fucking house for Lauren Czoll."

She was coming to the beaches exit. The cars were doing seventy, a few feet from each other. A FedEx van was braking in her lane, slowing to a stop. She tried to pull around, but there was a Honda on the driver's side, braking to a stop. Ahead, she saw cars slowing, brake lights going red, or already stopped, a line of shimmer to the crest of the next hill. She cut into the breakdown lane and tried to nose her way up to the next exit—it was just ahead—but others had the same idea, a blue SUV, a black pickup, two guys on motorcycles, moving till they slowed and finally stopped. She thought about backing up in the breakdown lane to the beaches exit, but even as she put the car in reverse other cars, coming north, filled the lanes behind her, slowing to a stop, and Peta was sealed in, stranded between exits.

She said, "Fuck." She looked through her bag for *Voices of the Rain Forest*. She tried to untie the string, finally had to bite it. She called Brian Ryan's mobile.

"Threats."

"Agent Ryan? It's Peta Boyle from Moss Properties in Portsmouth."

"Ms. Boyle," Brian Ryan said. "Thanks for calling back." The voice was smooth and young-official with a western twang. "Any new developments at the Dental Building? It's just routine. We like to keep abreast."

"Yes of course," said Peta, who had grown to loathe and fear this word *routine*, the way the cops and guards and agents used this word. She told Brian Ryan that there were no new developments, everything was normally abnormal at the Dental, as before.

"There's something I don't get," she said.

Brian Ryan said, "What's that?"

"I don't get how my routine relates to your—routine. I don't get the connection between the Dental and whatever it is you're looking for."

"Oh, I doubt there's a connection," Brian Ryan said. "We track eighty thousand threats a year from Beltsville, Ms. Boyle. The vast majority are blips and nothing more."

"Blips?" said Peta. What the hell was he talking about?

"They're nothing, they lead nowhere, they don't connect to anything. Still, the only way to know for sure is to act as if they lead somewhere, do your follow-up beforehand. We can't afford to wait until the ball drops. Are you in Portsmouth now, ma'am?"

"Heading there," said Peta, still pondering the blips and dropping balls. "I'm stuck in traffic."

"Me too," Brian Ryan said. "Traffic's bad up here. That's the big surprise. I always thought New Hampshire would be pretty traffic-free."

"It's not always bad," Peta said defensively. She blamed it on the primary, like some kind of bomb test or mass evacuation drill, this staged craziness, three months every leap year.

"What's your Portsmouth ETA?" he said.

"My ETA," she said, "is not known at this time. I'm stuck on 95."

"Me too. Whereabouts are you?"

"Just past the beaches exit."

"Me too. What cars are you near?"

"FedEx truck, some motorcycles, and an SUV."

"You must be right around me," Brian Ryan said.

She saw a young man two cars over, talking on a cell phone. The young man wore a necktie and a white straw cowboy hat. She waved at him.

"I see you in that hat," she said.

"What hat?" he said.

The man was waving back.

"You must be up ahead somewhere," said Peta, sinking low behind the wheel.

She promised to call Brian Ryan with any new developments. Including peace, she thought—that would be quite new.

Traffic moved, rolling a few feet. The motorcycles revved, rolling to a stop. In the distance, Peta saw the source of the delay, a bus spun out on the grassy strip between the northbound and the southbound sides. The passengers were gathered by the bus. Trooper cars were pulled up, domers strobing, a harsh flicker in the daylight. The accident was not obstructing traffic and yet the cars slowed as they passed to inspect the crash. The highways were the place of straight ahead, lanes and lines, signs mounted high for visibility so that motorists wouldn't have to make decisions at the final moment, all together—a place of architected flow, rails and information. Any break in flow, any accident, was doubly engrossing because the eyes were starved for something jarring. The first car slowed out of curiosity. The next car slowed to avoid rear-ending the first car. The next car, recognizing rubbernecking, tarried long enough to see what they were rubbernecking at, saw the bus on the grass and looked for the ambulance, the fire trucks, the bloody body on a gurney, pausing long enough to make the cars behind them pause and start rubbernecking too. By the time the back cars were braking to see, the front cars, which had started it, were gone, flying north through normal traffic. In fact, Peta thought, there couldn't be a back because even after the wreck was towed away, the cars delayed by cars delayed by rubbernecking cars would pause to view the cause of the delay, and if the cause was gone, the motorists would only look longer, seeing nothing, searching disappointedly. Crashing bore, thought Peta.

Traffic started moving. Space opened between cars.

The phone rang.

Brian Ryan said, "We're moving!"

Peta said, "I see that, thank you."

The bus coming up on Peta's left didn't look damaged and there was no ambulance, no skid marks on the pavement, no deep ruts in the grass. It was nuts, she thought, a thousand cars delayed by this? It wasn't even a good bus crash. Where were the EMTs, the flame-retardant foam, the line of snap-light flares?

She could see now that the bus belonged to the senator's campaign. She paused, taking her turn as lead rubbernecker. As the daughter of Phil Boyle, the mortician-politician, Peta was solid for the party, the Rockingham machine, and the machine was solid for the VP. If she didn't hate the dashing senator (she didn't—she disliked him, she mistrusted him, and gave him high negatives whenever she was polled), she hated him a little for causing this delay. She only saw his bus, a knot of campaign workers, and reporters with boom mikes, but she knew that he was in the center, totally at fault. Someone honked at her.

"Keep your shirt on," Peta said.

Peta was driving to meet Lauren Czoll at their second showing of the day when she got the call from Li'l People Montessori. The headmistress said that Jens had shown up around noon, barged into Kai's classroom, dragged him out to his car, breaching several rules of Li'l People, all of which were spelled out quite clearly in a letter to the parents, the headmistress pointed out. Peta apologized, soothing the headmistress (the woman had connections to the admissions people at all of the best private schools in the county and could make or break Kai, come kindergarten time—she was nobody to fuck with, Peta knew).

Peta said, "I'm sorry. My husband's been—sick."

"Sick parents are not allowed in school," the headmistress said. "Children pass these germs around."

"It's not a germ-type sick," said Peta. "It won't happen again, I promise."

Peta called the house. The voice mail picked up, Peta's rich-as-toffee phone voice playing back at her: *You have reached the Asplund-Boyle residence. If you are a pollster, please press one for our opinions, and do not call back; if you are a human being, please press two and leave a message. Have a great day. 'Bye!*

Peta was tempted to press one, thinking that a roll call of all the things she believed might be calming or confirming, but the sound of her own voice was good enough. She called again and again, knowing that Jens would eventually pick up.

He answered on the fourth call.

"Jens," said Peta, trying to sound like the impressive woman on the voice mail. "Did you go to Kai's school today?"

"I don't like that school," said Jens. "They practically tackled me. I have a right to see my kid. That headmistress is a psychopath, I'm telling you."

"Where is Kai now?"

"I took the day off. I was driving. I went by the old house and I thought, well, it's a nice day, and I felt like seeing Kai. You'd think the headmistress was president of Harvard from the way she carries on about her rules. Christ, it's not even a school. It's a *pre*-school."

Peta drove along a beach road. She saw Lauren's silver Jeep parked on the shoulder up ahead. Peta counted to three, another trick to calm herself. "Tell me where Kai is now, Jens."

"He's in his bedroom. He's having a time-out."

"I'd like to speak to him."

"I think he's asleep," said Jens. "I haven't heard him moving in awhile."

Peta and Lauren Czoll stood on a blasted dune facing the Atlantic. Behind them, on the landside of the dune, a stately Greek Revival home was sheltered in the pines.

"Asking one-point-six," yelled Peta to the wind. "Three acres to the road. Walk-in humidor. Semiprivate bridle paths. Gazebo with an indoor-outdoor disco ball."

The facts didn't go together. She could feel the wind inside her mouth as she talked. She stopped talking.

"So bleak," Lauren said. "So beautiful. I could watch the gales roll in."

Peta tried to rally. "It's perfect for you, Lauren. It's just what you described under hypnosis. Let's make an offer, darling. They'll take one-point-five, I'm sure, so let's offer one-point-two and see what happens."

Saw grass swirled around their knees.

Lauren bit her lip. "No," she said, "it isn't right at all."

In that moment, Peta Boyle, mother, wife, and Realtrix, finally snapped. She started up the path. The path wound through the grass, down stone steps into the quiet of the pines. Lauren hurried after her.

"Maybe you're not ready," Peta said.

"Not ready?" Lauren said. "What are you saying?"

"You can't just go on looking forever, Lauren. I have other clients and new responsibilities and I'm not sure we're making headway here."

The wind seemed to chase them, whipping Peta's coat.

"Maybe I've failed you as a broker," Peta said.

"No," said Lauren. "*No.*"

"Or maybe you're not ready. There's no shame in that."

"I'm so ready I could scream," Lauren screamed. "It's just that I get nervous when you talk about the closing. It sounds so final, like the closing of the casket." She grabbed Peta by the elbow and jumped in front of her. "Are you leaving me? Is that what you're saying?"

Peta shook her off. "We'll always have the memories, Lauren. Now get out of my way before I knock you on your ass."

There was a little struggle on the path, Peta pushing past, Lauren holding her. Then Lauren went limp in Peta's arms, and Peta saw the other Lauren Czoll in full fragile glory, not the cashmere bitch, but the codependent six-year-old within.

"Sometimes," Lauren sobbed, "I think you're the only one who really cares. Jerzy doesn't listen, and all our friends just pretend to like me because of Jerzy's money. I guess I'm scared that if I go to closing, we'll drift apart, you and I. You've become more than a broker to me, Peta. You've become my best friend in the world."

Lauren grabbed her in a hug. Peta stood there, being hugged.

The surf crashed in the distance.

Peta said, "I see."

the wave (monday afternoon)

Leaving the big luncheon at the steak house in Pinardville, the VP and his entourage started for the mountain towns. It was early afternoon and the clouds were moving in. They had covered eight events since dawn: the VP's morning jog/photo op, a carefully "impromptu" drop-in at McDonald's (the VP eating Egg McMuffin like An Ordinary Guy surrounded by a crowd of journalists), three cold ropelines outside crumbling mills in central Manchester, a quick visit to a Hooksett kindergarten (the VP reading to the kids as the cameras whirred), a tour of the shop floor of a fiber-optics firm (the VP nodding in a hard hat as the cameras whirred), and finally the luncheon in Pinardville with the New Hampshire State Association of Police Chiefs.

Heading east, they came to Severance, a pretty lakeshore village (a photo op with trees, apparently—they were collecting the Sierra Club endorsement). In Severance, Vi and Tashmo were detached for special duty, Gretchen's orders. Gretchen told them to report forthwith to Boone Saxon at Threat Assessment's local outpost, a few miles down the highway from the lake. Vi and Tashmo, glad to be excused if only for an hour, borrowed a sedan and set off to meet the threatmen.

Vi drove and Tashmo rode. They were passing malls and bowladromes and home improvement superstores. Boone Saxon and his trainee agents tracked local known, potential, or suspected threats from a shabby rented office on the second floor of the Bank New Hampshire building. The building had two floors, drive-through teller windows, a night deposit slot, three glassed-in cash machines, and a parking lot with shrubbery and about ten spaces. Vi parked by the cash machines. She was crossing the lot with Tashmo when Peta Boyle called.

Vi walked and talked to Peta on the cell. The two women exchanged pleasantries, the usual: how are you, where are you, how is Jens, and Kai is fine. Peta was in Portsmouth, calling from her car. Vi hadn't talked to her sister-in-law in many months and hadn't seen her since the visit after Hinman. Vi knew that Peta had a point in calling—Peta, unlike Jens, always had a point. At first, Vi thought that something was wrong, that somebody was sick or hurt, but Peta assured her that it wasn't so.

"Really," Peta said. "Everything is A-Okay, we're chugging right along!"

Vi heard a woman sobbing in the background. "Is someone crying there?"

"Just a client," Peta said. "*Lauren, honey, hush now—Peta needs to hear.* Vi, are you there? I understand the vice president is coming this way, and I know it's probably impossible, but do you think you could come down to the house at some point? We'd love to see you, Vi. Jens would really love to see you."

The VP would cross the state that afternoon with a stop along the way, spend the night in Portsmouth, and work Portsmouth in the morning. Vi doubted that she could squeeze an hour free to see Jens and Peta. She'd have to go to Gretchen for permission, and Gretchen wasn't free and easy on these things.

Vi said, "I'll try, Peta, I really will, but they keep us pretty scheduled."

"Of course—I understand," said Peta. "It was just a thought."

The call ended as Vi and Tashmo clomped up a set of narrow stairs to the second floor of the bank building.

Boone's office was done in a certain style—Vi thought of it as Late War on Drugs, except (she knew) the War on Drugs was timeless and endless, and for all anybody knew it was still Early yet. Boone's desk and chair on wheels and glued-plasterboard credenza had been built by prison laborers at Unicor in Leavenworth and sold at a profit by the government to itself, part of some half-abandoned crackpot scheme to make the Bureau of Prisons self-supporting, like Alabama penal farms of yore.

Boone was on the phone when Vi and Tashmo came up from the parking lot. They waited for him as he flipped his desk blotter calendar, last month, this month, next month, making an appointment with the Concord FBI. The calendar was also jail-made and featured rousing productivity slogans, a different one each month, *Think and Suggest* for February, *Always Foster Quality* for March. Vi had seen this very calendar in every federal outpost she had ever visited or worked in, or worked out of, the Crim Division in New York, Psych Services in Beltsville, the ATF in Newark, even once the embassy in Moscow. She found it vaguely sinister: inmates jailed by the hard work of the agents being forced to print slogans rooting these same agents on to even greater feats of busy-beaverism.

"Coffee's on," said a trainee agent, padding by the office in his socks. The trainee was named Christopher, a tall soft sofa of a boy, two months out of threat school. Of the eleven trainees, only Christopher was here. Two were out with flu; one was up in Concord, checking with the doctor of a man who blamed the pope on the Jews; two were down in Nashua, battling the flu, checking on a recent theft of fertilizer from a city golf course (a year's supply, a hundred bags, just shy of four tons); one trainee was busy infiltrating a militia sect in the northern forests; one was on a flight to Montreal where he would liaise with the RCMP, rattling the cages of known Moroccan jihadin; one had gone across the highway for a sandwich; another was in Portsmouth, working on the violent splinter right-to-lifers.

Tashmo was sitting on the edge of Boone's credenza, his long legs stuck out, jiggling his little zippered boots, like a kid who needed to wee. He was looking at a picture of Boone's wife, June, a stolid, freckled woman in a pageboy and safari jacket.

Vi took the picture from him.

"Know her?" Tashmo asked. "Helluva nice woman, Mrs. Boone."

Vi had met June Saxon once at a Beltsville function, chatted with her about her work at the National Zoo, where she was a staff psychiatrist. June had diagnosed the depression of the Chinese panda pair, Ling-Ling and Hsing-Hsing, the marquee mammals of that zoo, which had finally explained the pair's extended failure to mate in captivity. You couldn't ask a panda how it felt, June told Vi, and so she had relied on long observation of the pandas, noting their listlessness compared to pandas in the wild, and their odd behavior, clawing at one spot in the dirt, tearing at one shoot of bamboo, empty, pointless, repetitive patterns of activity, for hours every day. June had watched them for hours before arriving at her diagnosis. Vi put the picture back on the credenza. Pandas and psychotics—Vi thought Boone and Mrs. Boone were perfect for each other.

Christopher returned to the office with a plastic tray of mugs, sugar packets, milk in a little pitcher, and a pot of coffee, but no one felt like coffee. Christopher seemed bummed.

"Apologies," said Boone, getting off the phone. "Housekeeping—one must always kiss the butt of the sister agencies."

Vi thought this saying would look good on a calendar.

Boone said, "Tashmo, how's it going? How's Shirl? She good?"

Tashmo said, "She's fine. How's Jane?"

"June. She's doing great. Her panda memoir came out last year. You'd love it. It's a touching story of friendship and depression."

"I'll wait for the movie," Tashmo said.

Boone said, "I'm afraid you already missed it. It was in the theaters for about a minute. You can still see it on some airlines, Thai Air and maybe Continental. Tash was on the Reagan team, Christopher."

"Is that where you guys met?" asked Christopher, all wide-eyed. The Reagan team was famous in the Service, like the '27 Yankees of Protection.

"Boone wasn't on no Reagan team," said Tashmo. "Boone, have you been telling this poor kid that you were on the Reagan team?"

"I *was* on the Reagan team," said Boone.

Tashmo said, "We let you hang with us because your wife was—nice. But that doesn't mean that you were on the team."

"What do you mean, nice?"

"Cheerful. Pleasant. Always a kind word."

"I guarded Ronald Reagan," said Boone through a tight jaw.

Tashmo said, "You guarded the ballet-dancing son."

"His legal name was Ronald Reagan. He was often with his father, and when they were together I guarded both of them. I stood ready with my life."

"They were not *often* together," Tashmo said. "The father didn't even like the kid. He used to say to me, 'Ballet.' Just that word, ballet. It tore him up inside."

"That's a lie," said Boone. "They had the special bond of son and father."

Vi said, "Let's not fight about it, Christ. Yo Boone, why are we here?"

Boone was sulking. "You had a screamer at the Marriott last night. Female white, brown hair, medium height, medium build, beige or tan parka. This is the script we got. You and Tash were on the body, closest to the woman. I thought we'd take a gander at the vid feeds, pool and Channel 9, see if we could pick her out."

Tashmo said, "We get a lot of screamers, Boone."

Christopher drew the shades. They watched two clips from two angles of the ropeline at the Marriott. The pool press covered every event, no matter how routine (it was called the death watch), but they didn't always cover all of each event. They often got their requisite ten- or twenty-second clip, a rough cut for the uplink to New York, later trimmed to nothing or two seconds. At the Marriott, the cameras took the VP almost to the end, but Channel 9 cut out at three minutes eighteen seconds and the pool went black just after that, ropeline still in progress.

Vi said, "No, it's later. She's closer to the end."

They watched the video again, Boone working the remote, fast-forwarding through the tight shots, looking for the woman in the pans.

"We could look her up on ThreatNet," said Boone, "but we'd need a name or KA. If we can get her picture, I can probably trace it to a name."

He walked between the cubicles to the file room, talking over his shoulder. "She came early and she waited till the end. That's what I don't like. Gretchen said no gloves, she wasn't wearing gloves. I don't like, she waited in the cold night with no gloves."

The file room had steel walls, deep shelves, and stacked boxes. Boone ran a hand along the boxes. "These here are the closed threat investigation binders going back several budgets. I'd say there's fifty feet of threats and follow-up back here. More recent stuff, the working files, is parceled out to my guys. We'd have to go cubicle by cubicle. I've got a master printout in my desk, but it'll just have the basic information."

He disappeared down an aisle, returning with a box. The box was filled with books like photo albums. He was looking at the spines. "This is Arabs. This is neo-Nazis. This is white supremacists and a few tax protesters. This is the militias and the violent splinter right-to-lifers. This is schizophrenics. This is miscellaneous. It's not the perfect system, because, for example, most neo-Nazis are also white supremacists—it's a question of emphasis—but I guess it's better than no system."

He picked a book from the stack. The book thumped on the tabletop.

"This goes back to July," he said. "Spring is down the hall. I can get it for you, if you want."

Vi sat at the table in the corner and started going through the book, turning the heavy album pages, picture after picture, summer crowds in shirtsleeves, crowds and smaller groups, twos and threes. She saw two men in a pickup. The driver had sideburns and a hairy forearm. The passenger was in the shadow of the cab.

"Those two," said Christopher, looking over Vi's shoulder. "They kept hanging around the courthouse up in Concord. One of them we traced back to the tax protesters, or maybe the car. I think we traced the car. We have a file on that car some-where. They saw us taking pictures and never showed again."

Tashmo asked for the little agents' room. Christopher handed him a key tied to a ruler.

Vi saw a man in a bathrobe taking out the trash, a man and a woman crossing a street, two men at a pay phone, one man pumping gas as another walked away. The weather got colder as Vi turned the pages. The people wore shorts and shirt-sleeves, then jackets and pullovers, then coats and hats and boots. Vi saw a man scraping ice from a windshield, two men outside a Dairy Queen, two men and three women standing by a park bench on the fringe of some protest. Vi looked through seven books in all.

"I don't know," she said, closing the last book. "Maybe she's in there. I didn't really see her face."

"No," said Boone, "you never do. Drives me nuts, personally. You never know until later that this face—in a wall of faces, *this* face—will turn out to be signifi-cant. Not that your screamer will turn out to be significant, because, I mean, chances are, statistically, she won't. But you can't know this until later and now you're kicking yourself for not knowing at the time that she might turn out to be important."

Christopher came back with a large manila interoffice envelope. "These are loose," he said. "We'll file them when everything dies down."

Vi started through the color photos in the envelope. Outdoor protests, placards and human chains, riot cops in helmets, people kneeling. Vi pointed at an old man with white hair, his face half obscured by someone else's blurry hand. The picture was stamped *SP-Harrisburg.*

Vi said, "I've seen that guy somewhere before."

Boone said, "Are you sure?"

"Definitely yes."

Boone looked at the picture. "Oh, him. He's in the other books."

Another picture: a woman, a brunette, and a young man with a boot-camp haircut getting into or out of a green car, something with a hatchback, a Pinto or a Mazda.

"No," said Vi.

Another picture: another protest, wintertime. Vi saw the same brunette, now in sunglasses, a scarf over her head, with another woman, also in a scarf. The women were walking up a street. The picture was taken from a car; Vi could see the doorframe in the corner of the shot. The first woman, the older of the two, carried a cardboard mailing tube. The picture was stamped *Erie PD.*

Vi said, "Maybe."

Christopher said, "Which?"

"Her," said Vi, pointing to the younger woman, the one without the mailing tube.

"We could do a flyer," Boone was musing. "We could do a sketch, pass it out to the cops, in case she tries to crash your perimeter again. That's worked in the past. We've got a super artist on retainer. He does wild seascapes and all of the offi-cial gubernatorial portraits—you should see him work. Holds the pencil like this, eraser like this, and his hands are like a blur, incredible. I think he's on vacation, but I have his beeper. We could do it over the phone. He could fax the sketch back to us for corrections. His name is Ed Talty, and I like to kid him. I say, 'Ed, where in the hell—'"

Vi pointed to her maybe, the woman in the picture. "What's her name, Boone?"

Boone looked the women in the picture, the face just out of focus, frozen in the frame. "I don't know," he said, "but I know someone who might."

"The informant's name is Little Flower," Boone was saying. "Or that's her movement name. She has a real legal name, of course, but we don't use it, do we, Christopher? She's been working for us since the fall—we got her from the FBI in a multiplayer trade—and if you call her anything but Little Flower she gets all bent out of shape and it takes an hour to get her back on topic. So that's the first thing to remember when we get there, Vi: call her Little Flower. It'll save a major hassle."

Vi said, "What's her deal?"

Boone said, "She bombs things."

They were following the motorcade away from Severance, east on a state high-way through the low, eroded hills.

"She started as a biker chick," Boone said. "She was with a gang up north, some lame Hell's Angels spin-off. They roared around the timber towns, sold guns and fake ID, smuggled speed from Montreal. Little Flower's specialty was rental cars. You steal a credit card, run up some ID to match the name, rent a car from Avis, chop it up for parts, not a bad racket all in all. The Bureau popped her at Logan with a stack of Vermont driver's licenses, her picture with ten different names. They sent her to Memphis for that. She met some Christians in the bing. They recruited her, converted her, whatever. She came out loving Jesus and reporting to Probation. Last winter—I don't know, you maybe saw the press—her group blew up the Whole Woman Wellness Center down in Erie, Pennsylvania, with a two-ton fertilizer bomb. The cops found Little Flower sleeping in a rest stop on the Pennsylvania Turnpike. The van was stolen, she was wanted by Probation, and the van seats tested positive for nitrates. The Bureau tried to flip her on the clinic. She said no, I'll never talk, this is my religion now, blah blah blah blah blah, so the Bureau went to work on her. They showed her pictures of the watchman in the rubble. She said it was a big mistake, there wasn't supposed to be a watchman, that's why they blew it up at night. The Bureau said, 'There's always a night watchman, Little Flower.' They showed her pictures of the man, his family, his wife of forty years, his eleven grandkids, his ribbons from Korea, and his bowling trophies. They said, 'This was a life. You took a human life.' They kept it nice and simple. I'm told she fell apart and started giving names and that's how she became a confidential source. She's still pretty touchy about the night watchman. Don't ask about Whole Woman, don't mention bowling trophies. She gets all worked up and then you have to calm her down again."

They stopped for gas at a two-pump country store in a town called Willingboro. Christopher did the pumping. Vi and Boone stayed in the car. Vi watched the motorcade get smaller down the road.

"She isn't always stable mentally," said Boone, two hands on the file in his lap. "She needs to be focused. She's funny with her lies. She'll admit to murder if you phrase it right, but not to the little things. She's like a child, only worse. Kids can't tell the difference between truth and lies, between what happened and what should have happened, fact and wish get all confused. That's why you can't polygraph a child."

Christopher came back from the store carrying a white plastic bag. He got in, threw the bag on the seat. They took a side road out of Willingboro. There were signs along the road for deer, the leaping silhouette, shot up with little holes, rusting from the holes.

Boone said, "She was a minor Bureau source, not the mother lode. She did names and faces—adequate for background. The Bureau talked to the judge, got her home confinement, electronic monitoring, the ankle radio. The Bureau says her head was fairly clear at first, but you know how it is with these historical informants—they sit around, all cooped up, getting grilled by teams of strangers about what happened on a certain date a year ago, two years ago, three years ago, until finally they lose track of what day it is today. The Bureau sucked her dry and we did a deal. We gave them two spent dope informants and they gave us Little Flower. One of the dopers died of OD after that and the Bureau tried to renegotiate. They said, 'You never told us he was an OD candidate.'"

Christopher said, "We were like, '*Duuh.*'"

Boone said, "I told 'em, 'Hell, the girl you gave me doesn't even know what year it is.' Last deal I do with them whiny bastards. I let my guy, Brian Ryan, run her for a while. These kids need experience and I feel a duty as a mentor. Bri did a nice job and then I figured I'd give Christopher some hands-on, which was a bit of a bum deal, I'm afraid, because she's really going soft on us."

"I don't mind," said Christophe, driving. "I learn from everything."

"Tell Vi about the time you caught her lying on the rock."

"It started with Bri."

"But you're the one who caught her. Tell the story."

Christopher said, "She was obsessed with the EM unit on her ankle. When the Bureau got her home confinement, Probation came out and installed the hardware at her house. They explained it to her, and she kept explaining it to Brian like it was the seventh wonder of the world, this whole moronic explanation. 'The ring on my ankle is a radio, Brian.' He's sitting there, listening to this. 'My ankle radio sends a weak signal to the receiver in my phone jack.' Bri is nodding, yeah, whatever, Little Flower. She's says, 'The weakness of the signal is the key. It will carry one hundred feet, no more. If I get more than one hundred feet from the unit in my jack, the absence of the signal will cause my jack to dial Colorado, where a mainframe will page my PO in Portsmouth. He will get the page, call my house to see if there's a malfunction, and if I don't answer, he'll show up here or maybe ask the cops to send a car. If the cops don't find me here, my PO will notify the judge's clerk to get an absconder warrant. The warrant is the point of no return. Once they find me, boom, I go to Memphis.' Poor Brian must've heard this rap twenty times. It was like hearing a child explain thunder."

"It's not that she lies exactly," Boone said. "Half her stuff is on the money, half is in her head. Our job is to figure out which half. She gave Christopher a murder plot last month."

"Said she knew a man named Gib," said Christopher, "an ex-biker, who knew another man. She said this other man worked in a factory where they mill casino chips, Bally's, Harrah's, and, I think, Trump's. Said the man had skimmed and stolen a million bucks in chips a little at a time from the assembly line. The chips were buried in a field outside Troy, New York. The thief himself had disappeared. Two brothers had killed each other looking for the chips. Hoodlums dug the fields at night, playing hunches. This whole vignette. She was great on detail, that's what half-convinced me."

Boone said, "My kids are good young agents, Vi. They spent twenty man-hours running down the lead, and it checked out, to a point. Yes, there are casinos and they issue chips, and yes, some chips go missing. We found the factory. It's not in Troy, nowhere near, but there *is* a Troy and Gib exists, we know this for a fact. Then Christopher was watching cable one night at his place."

"I saw a rerun movie," said Christopher. "*Ice Heist*. Ben Gazzara, Nipsey Russell, Barbara Eden. I've always been a Ben Gazzara fan."

Vi said, "Let me guess. Casino chips, buried in a field."

"But not in Troy," said Boone. "That part was invented. Now, whenever she gives us information we check the TV listings before acting on it."

They came to a small lake dammed between two hills. At the far end of the lake was a motel cabin court, seven wood-frame cottages on a dirt pullout in the pines. The cabins were dark brown, shingles green with age. Each cabin had a little saggy porch facing the highway and the lake. The road to the cabins was half washed out and deeply rutted, rocks and roots exposed. They parked in front of the last cabin.

"Little Flower's parents bought this place in '51," Boone said. "She says it was really nice when she was a kid. They had perch in the lake, sunnies too, and families came to fish from as far away as Worcester, same families every year. They had their favorite cabins and reserved them in advance. They showed outdoor movies on Saturday at dusk. Don't get her started on how nice it used to be."

Vi saw the curtain move in the cabin window. "She knows we're out here."

"Yup," said Boone, relaxing.

"It's good to let her stew," said Christopher.

"That's right," said Boone.

"The key to Little Flower is to make her think that you already know the answer to your question. If she thinks you don't know, she'll go off on a tangent. That's why we always bring a file when we see her. She thinks we keep the answers in our files. Sometimes Bri forgot to bring a file and he had to stop at Staples, buy an empty folder and some typing paper. He wrote 'Little Flower: Facts' on the file, just for the intimidation value."

Boone said, "That's exactly right."

"Another thing we do is sit in the car and talk before going in. She sees us and assumes we're talking about her. She thinks we must know plenty, if we have this much to say."

Vi saw the curtain move again.

"Lake is pretty," murmured Christopher.

"Yes it is," said Boone.

"I understand they dredged it."

"Really?"

Vi said, "I think she's pretty focused now."

Boone banged on the cabin door. "Little Flower, Little Flower, it's Boone Saxon from the Secret Service. Open up."

They heard a woman's singsong voice. *"I'm in the shower—"*

They waited on the porch. Vi saw fallen tree limbs in the straggle grass, pinecones everywhere, and rusted lawn furniture, separate little groups of chairs and tables in odd parts of the yards, two chairs facing each other over by the road, three chairs in conversation by a flaking silver propane tank. Vi didn't hear a shower in the cabin.

Boone said, "Let us do the talking, Vi, and remember: don't mention Erie, bowling trophies, or how beautiful these cabins used to be."

"And the date," whispered Christopher.

"That's a good point—avoid the topic altogether, Vi."

"What's up with the date?"

Boone said, "Her home confinement time ran out last month. Legally she's free. Probation came out and took her bracelet off. We came in as they were leaving and put a new one on. It connects to nothing, of course. We never said it did. On the other hand, we never said it didn't."

"We don't lie to her," said Christopher. "Everything we say is strictly true."

The door opened and there was Little Flower, dressed in stretch slacks and a red-checked flannel shirt. Her hair was dirty, brown, and straight, wet-looking though not wet.

Boone said, "I thought you were in the shower."

"I didn't say it was—*turned on.*" Little Flower said this as she inspected her visitors, first Christopher, then Vi, a quick look up and down. As she said "turned on," her eyes came around to rest, coquettishly, on Boone.

Boone said, "We don't have time for your silly games. This is Agent Asplund out of Washington. Let's have a little chat."

"What have I been doing? What have I been *doing*? This is a question, Boone?"

They sat in the front room of the cabin, Vi in a rocker at one end of the coffee table, Little Flower on the couch between Christopher and Boone. The little room was packed with bric-a-brac, glass poodles and glass dishes, an older woman's taste, Vi thought. She wondered if Little Flower's mother was alive and living here, or whether the bric-a-brac was posthumous. Christopher got up and roamed around the cabin, looking in the closet, pushing coats around to see behind them.

"Lately, I've been listening," Little Flower said. "My ankle unit makes a noise, a high-pitched *eeeek*—it does, Christopher, I don't care what you say, or Bri either, you're both a pack of liars in my book. I can't sleep, listening for it. When I can't hear it, I get scared and think my bracelet is malfunctioning, and the cops are coming for me, and I panic in my bed. I can only sleep when I hear it nice and steady. Wait—there it is."

"It doesn't make a noise," said Christopher. He was looking through the closet. "I told you that before."

"You also said the ankle rash would go away, but you were wrong there too."

"Use the ointment," said Christopher, moving to the kitchen.

"Did you bring me some?"

"No, I brought you chocolates. They're in the bag. Go ahead, indulge."

"I don't feel like it," said Little Flower, asserting her authority. "Where is my probation officer? I called him fifty times. I demand to speak to him."

Boone was spreading photos on the coffee table. "He's a busy guy."

Little Flower turned to Vi. "Busy guy, my ass. He was always after me to get a job. 'Get a job'—that's all he ever said. He said, 'I need to check the box next to you're gainfully employed, or else I catch hell from my supervisor.' I said, 'How can I get a job? I can't *go* anywhere.' He said, 'That's not true. You can shop for necessities, one hour, once a week, and attend the religious observance of your choice.' I said, 'What if I choose the Church of Blown-Up Buildings?' He said, 'What the heck is that supposed to mean?' He said, 'You can find a job that lets you work from your house.' I said, 'Like what? President?' He said, 'I know a man in phone solicitation. He's reputable and desperately needs help.' He said, 'Most of the people who call you selling things are actually sentenced federal prisoners earning money from the comfort of their home confinements.' So I called the guy and tried it. Turns out I suck at phone solicitation. They give you a written script, but I can't read and talk and listen and think of a response all at the same time." She itched her ankle rash, then picked a chocolate from the box, bit it, something white inside—she forced herself to finish it. "Yesterday, or I don't know, it could have been last week—anyway, pretty recently I measured a hundred feet from the jack in my wall."

Vi said, "Why?"

"Signal from my ankle, my wall dials Colorado, computer pages my PO—it doesn't sound quite real to me somehow."

Vi said, "You thought it wouldn't work?"

"I *knew* it would work—honey, it's the government. It's just that I thought it wasn't real. So I stood ninety-six feet from my phone. I marked it off exactly and I stood there waiting for the cops or my PO to come bombing down the road. Maybe I was lonely, I don't know. I waited hours, standing there, and nobody came. Then I tried ninety-seven feet—nothing. Ninety-eight, ninety-nine—nothing. Then I got the courage—I tried one hundred feet. I was out there half the day and no one came. I laid out on this big rock and watched the clouds. My ankle was a hundred feet from the phone jack, so the rest of me was even further."

Boone had his pictures set. "We're doing names and faces, Little Flower."

Vi recognized the pictures—rallies, protests, people in the street.

"We did these guys a million times," Little Flower said. "That's Dick Laurent. That's Mater with him in disguise. Dick again. There's Gordon, Gordo. That's the kid with the Jesus Rocks tattoo. That's Martin from the Army in the back. He's the one who brought the fertilizer. What happened to Martin?"

"I told you," said Christopher. "Shot by troopers in Nebraska. Routine traffic stop."

Little Flower shook her head. "He wasn't even twenty yet."

Boone turned the pictures.

Little Flower peered at them. "That's the kid, sometimes we called him Thad and sometimes Baxter, sometimes Jesus Rocks. That's—him, I never knew his name. That's Dick again, behind the car. We had that car when we lived in the cabin in Vermont. It was a pretty cabin. We were sad the day we torched it for insurance."

Boone turned the pictures. "We're doing names and faces, not cars and cabins."

"That's Dick again. That's Baxter and that's Mater with him. Is Mater dead too?"

"No," said Boone. "Death row."

"That's Gordo with a beard. Is Gordo on death row?"

"No, he's doing life."

"That's Baxter. Is he doing life?"

"No, he's doing seven hundred months in Terre Haute."

"That's Dick. Is he in Terre Haute?"

"No, he's on the Ten Most Wanted, presently at seven. We'll get him, Little Flower, don't you doubt it."

"That's Gordo, God I can't believe it. That's Martin, who you cruelly blew away. That's Thad and Baxter. That's Claudio and Norbert. That's Timmy Tuckahoe. That's Johnny Poopooface."

"Stop it," Boone said. "There is no Timmy Tuckahoe."

Vi started for the bedroom down the narrow hall.

Little Flower said, "Where the fuck is she going?"

Vi turned and said, "Relax yourself."

Little Flower's bedroom was a miniature wilderness, limp curtains in the window, the mattress flopped over, clothes and pennies on the rug, jars of Vaseline, a TV on a milk crate, a lamp with a badly dented shade. Vi took out her cell phone.

Little Flower was standing in the doorway. She said, "My prison is weak signals."

Vi said, "Let me make a call here, Little Flower. I'll just be a sec."

Little Flower whispered, "They come out and rape me. This is not my fantasy. Boone cannot control them—he has no idea. Brian was bad, but Christopher is worse. You have an honest face, lady. Help me. Help me."

Vi looked at Little Flower. She said, "Yeah okay, just let me make this call."

Little Flower went back to the living room.

Vi called Gretchen Williams, who was on the way to Rumsey Moose Lodge with the motorcade.

Gretchen said, "How's it going there?"

Vi said, "This is bullshit."

Gretchen told her to meet the team in Portsmouth.

Vi said, "If I get to Portsmouth before the rest of you, can I take an hour off? I want to see my brother. He's just down the road from Portsmouth—it won't even take an hour."

Gretchen said, "What is this, Vi, a college road trip? Thirteen your butt to Portsmouth and stay there, got it?"

"Fine," said Vi. "And Gretchen?"

"What?"

"Thanks for everything." Vi punched END.

Boone was down to his last picture in the living room. He pointed to a picture on the coffee table, two women side by side at a rally. Boone pointed to the woman Vi had picked out as a possibility. He said, "Who's she? Lady on the right."

Little Flower glanced at the picture. "I have no idea."

Boone pointed to the woman on the left. "Okay, who is that?"

Little Flower looked a moment. "I don't know."

"That's you, Little Flower. With the mailing tube."

"No it isn't."

"Look again."

Little Flower looked again. "God I was a blimp. Is my butt *that* big? I thought those slacks were slimming. What a fool I was."

"The point is, you're with this other woman here. We know the lady's name. We just want you to confirm it."

"I told you, I don't know her."

"Come on, Little Flower—what are the odds that two women would both go separately to the same hate rally in the same type of disguise *and* just happen to wind up standing next to each other?"

Little Flower squinted, concentrating. Then she shook her head and said, "I give up, what are the odds?"

"Little Flower."

"Okay, okay, okay. Her name is Linda. Linda, Belinda. We called her Linda mostly. Also sometimes Lindy."

"What's her last name?"

"Linda. Linda B. Linda."

"What's her last name, Little Flower?"

"Johnson."

"Christ," said Vi.

"Jaw, jaw, Joe, Jones. She used that name sometimes—Jo Jones."

Vi said, "That's the fakest fucking name I ever heard."

Little Flower saw it then. She said, "You don't know." She looked at Boone accusingly. She looked at Christopher. She said, "You're asking me and you don't even know."

13

The motorcade continued east, heading to the next event, a brief speech to a small crowd at the Rumsey Moose Lodge. Tashmo and O'Teen, working the advance, got to Rumsey first, running twenty minutes ahead of the others and almost ninety minutes behind schedule.

Tashmo, looking at the town (a superette, two houses, a blinking yellow light, and a ghostly depot with no tracks), felt the need for some confirmation that this was, in fact, the Rumsey listed on the schedule, and not some other hill-and-hollow crossroads in New Hampshire's Appalachia. He sent O'Teen off to ask a local. Tashmo, as the senior hand, stayed with the vehicle, ran the heater, had a smoke. He was in a foul mood by then, getting on toward five, the sky going pale behind the clouds, late winter in New England and he hated it, there's no such thing as afternoon up here, it's morning then it's getting dark, and anyone with half a brain has moved away or is getting loaded in a bar, except they didn't seem to have a bar in Rumsey.

Tashmo knew he couldn't fairly blame his mood on Rumsey, or the weather, or the hour. No, he had been feeling dumpy since the session with the threatmen. He had called Shirl from Boone's office, hoping, honestly, that she would be out having salads with her book club. He had planned to leave a message asking if Mandy's sneaky English husband had dropped off the car seats at the neighbors as requested, so that Mandy and the twins could follow Shirl in the truck to Generoso's. He didn't need to know if this had happened (he assumed it hadn't and he didn't really care), but he needed to act like he cared, and a message would have done the trick quite nicely. But his strategy had backfired (why was he surprised?). Shirl had answered fast and said, "Oh Tash! I'm glad you called." There was no plausible way to avoid a conversation at that point, so he asked her if she got the truck to Generoso's. Shirl said, "Oh yes, and it worked out just like you said, Nigel left the car seats at the Goulds', but we didn't even need them as it turned out, because we left the twins with Leah Gould—she was overjoyed to baby-sit—and Mandy followed me to Generoso's." Several questions sprang to mind, the sort of tiny story-flaws Boone Saxon would have jumped on, but Tashmo, spooked by Shirl's good cheer, didn't want to probe. He asked if Jeanette got off to school okay with her swollen eye and slightly damaged kidneys. Shirl was, again, disturbingly upbeat. "Everything is great," she said. "Jeanette rode the bus and no one took her picture as a disaffected icon of cauliflowered innocence, at least that I know of. Heck, I *hope* they took her picture, Tash. She looked great, so adult, going off like that." Shirl closed the conversation with a kicker: "I love you and I trust you, Tash," she said. "Everything is going to work out for us, you'll see."

Listening to Shirl, and thinking of it as he smoked and waited for O'Teen, Tashmo felt a slow-unfolding system-wide alarm, like coming to acknowledge and admit that you definitely need to piss without delay. *She loves me and she trusts me, Nigel brought the car seats, everything worked out.* What the fuck was going on? He wondered if his prostate tests had come back negative or positive or however they came back when you've got cancer on the glands. He wondered if Shirl was banging old Bo Gould and feeling the guilts about it. He doubted it (Bo was such a square), but what else would make his wife be so—pleasant?

He went into the superette and found O'Teen talking to a guy behind the counter.

"He says it's Rumsey," said O'Teen.

"It's all Rumsey," said the counter guy. "Which Rumsey are you looking for? There's Rumsey Corner, Rumsey Crossing, Rumsey Bridge, and Rumsey Depot."

Tashmo said, "We're looking for the Moose Lodge."

"That's in Shawgamunk."

"It says Rumsey Moose Lodge," Tashmo said.

"Well, it's in Shawgamunk. Go to Rumsey Bridge, take a left, follow the signs."

"Are there signs before the bridge?"

"Yes, but don't follow them. They go back to Willingboro."

They motored up the road to Rumsey Bridge. They were pretty late by then, but Tashmo figured the motorcade was at least as lost as they were. They passed one of the press buses going the wrong way, heading for the superette.

O'Teen found the Moose Lodge off the highway, ten minutes past the bridge, a cinder-block building, a sign hanging by two bike chains from a rusty pole. The cops were there, sheriff's men from Portsmouth, and a gang of campaign volunteers. Tashmo did a walk-through with the deputies. There was a beer hall in the basement where the VP would address a gathering of eighty Moose and invited guests, a side door to the parking lot, stairs up to the ground floor, a hallway in the basement going back to the latrines. The furnace room was locked, as was the door upstairs (O'Teen checked them both), so Tashmo put a deputy on the side door, another on the stairs, told O'Teen and the other deputy to set up a choke point at the entrance to the beer hall.

The Army truck arrived and the bomb dogs went to work as Tashmo watched the volunteers drape the basement walls in crepe and campaign placards. The volunteers had come up from the VP's Portsmouth operation. Their leader, an officious prick named Tim, started asking questions about when the VP would be here, and which door he would use, obviously scheming to be in the VP's path, to pump his hand and press his application for a judgeship, or whatever it was that Tim had in mind for Tim, post-election.

Tashmo, who knew Tim's type, eyed the volunteers. "How many people did you bring?"

"Ten or so I guess," said Tim. "We have two vans."

"And you know them?" Tashmo asked.

"Well, of course—what do you mean?"

"You know them, you know who they are. We don't like a lot of strangers in the room. The rest of these people here are Moose."

Tim said, "Oh, I get it. We have a group of Texas teachers, and three women from Mothers for the Truth About Gun Violence, it's an issue group, strong for the VP, and two lobbyists on leave from the—"

"I'm just saying, do you know them?"

"Sure I do," said Tim. "The Texans came in yesterday, the women from The Truth came in last night, and the others have been up here even longer. So what about it, buddy, which door will he be using?"

Tashmo didn't like the *buddy*. He said, "We'll use the furnace room. We'll stage it all from there."

"Great," said Tim, hurrying off to the furnace room.

The Moose had been waiting in the basement, drinking beer and coffee, eating doughnuts by the dozen, and the line to the bulls' room, AKA the crapper, wasn't short. O'Teen rechecked every Moose returning to the beer hall from the loo, the mag wand bleating at their watches, keys, and coins.

"Anything metal," said O'Teen, holding out a tray.

The Texas teacher volunteers worked quickly in the hall, unrolling bunting in the colors of the flag. Tashmo watched them closely, checking to see if any of the teachers were young and hot and possibly worth putting a move on later, at the hotel. Not that he would actually put a move on anyone, not that he was even up to it. He hadn't banged a volunteer since Super Tuesday in Atlanta the last time around, and even that had been a stretch. Tashmo had hooked up with some old corporate broad who said she worked for Coca-Cola, who claimed that she had never cheated on her husband, had never even *thought* about it, until Tashmo swept her off her feet at a victory party, and yet this never-cheating woman had a room at the Hilton, and what the fuck was that, good luck? He figured he would play it smooth and soulful, tell his stories of the war, his adventures with Dutch Reagan, act like this was not about fucking, but rather about two people having an intense spill-your-guts type personal encounter, thinking this would be the right tack, but finally, in her room, the woman said, "For God's sake, just shut up and *do* it." She handed him a condom wrapped in foil, like a chocolate from a restaurant, and the whole scene was so beat, so threadbare, that Tashmo had to will himself a boner, which he was able to maintain just long enough to get the condom on. He lost radio contact with his boner the minute he was in her, felt himself go rubbery and small, and he had to fake a climax, pulling out, panting like a terrier, and when he did, the condom stayed inside her. The woman was nice—or mortified—enough to pretend that it hadn't happened. She got up, got dressed, said she had another gala function to attend. They left her room, rode the elevator down, talking about the new mass transit system in Atlanta. She was smiling and talking, all Coca-Cola corporate, the little latex ring inside her the whole time. And that was it—Tashmo's last illicit piece of ass, like the final sad at-bat of a fading slugger. Tashmo, disgusted, walked over to the choke point.

O'Teen was rattling his tray and watching an old man deloop his belt.

Tashmo told the man to go ahead.

O'Teen protested, "But I didn't wand him yet. Everyone who leaves the room gets checked when they come back."

Tashmo said, "The codger took a piss."

"He left the room and came back, Tash. Maybe he hid a gun behind the toilet. He's clean when he arrives, nips off to the bathroom, comes back with the gun. How do we know he didn't?"

"Search the bathroom," Tashmo said. "Bet you don't find a gun. Me, I'm going for a smoke."

Tashmo climbed the basement stairs to the parking lot. He called Sean Elias, who was with the motorcade.

Elias said, "We're running late, we got a little lost. Turns out there's four different Rumseys."

"Of course there are," said Tashmo. "Can't you people read a map? We never had these problems on the Reagan team. Which Rumsey are you in?"

"We aren't. We're in Shawgamunk."

"Keep going. If you hit a bridge, you've gone too far. I think we passed a press bus coming up here. You guys missing one?"

"Stand by, let me ask." Elias hailed the press section on the radio. As he did, the lost bus pulled in from the road.

Tashmo said, "Hey Eli."

"What?"

"Never mind, they found the place."

Tashmo had a smoke in the dusk of the rural parking lot, brooding over Shirl, the disturbing conversation of that afternoon. *Everything worked out like you said. I love you and I trust you.* His inner threat investigator went to work on the known facts: Lloyd's disappearance in the flood; the calls from Lydia since Hinman, unwanted and unanswered; the iffy starter on his pickup truck; the black eye and the mild kidney damage inflicted on Jeanette by her sorority sisters; Shirl, his wife, his ball-and-chain of thirty years, in a liberated mood. *I love you and I trust you.*

There was definitely something going on. The black eye and the pickup were probably unrelated, but the other facts were probably not so unrelated. He reached three conclusions as he flicked his cigarette away: 1) that Lydia Felker had talked to Shirl, and therefore (1A) that Shirl knew about his old affair with Lydia; (2) that his wife and former mistress, bonding over this, were now in league against him; (3) that all of Tashmo's past was crashing in on him; and (4) that he needed to piss immediately.

He thought about weeing in the parking lot, but if the motorcade came in and Gretchen saw him in the headlights, watering a wall, he'd catch a lecture about Secret Service dignity, so he went down the stairs, moving through the crowd of Moose. People sat in folding chairs or stood in the aisles or were laughing at the bar, the flower of the Rumseys, oldsters most of them (which meant, to Tashmo, anybody older than he was). Tashmo heard Gretchen on the comm and knew that the motorcade was in range, coming down from Shawgamunk. Her signal grew stronger as the motorcade drew near and weaker as it passed the lodge without seeing the sign on the pole outside. Tashmo called Elias on the cell (the vans were crossing Rumsey Bridge by then), and gave him directions back from there.

The funny thing, the spooky thing—the thing most beautiful—was how it all came back to him, and how it always did. Just close your eyes and think of it: the last malaisey summer of the Carter presidency and Lydia, a frizzy waif in faded jeans. She is gorgeous, she is sleepy, she is sunburned on her legs. Her ass is white, however, a moon to be landed on, and her arms are deeply tanned. Her front is deeply tanned except for her bush and boobs, and Tashmo (in the bedroom, gazing at her bush and boobs) can't work out how she came to have this grab-bag pattern of tan, burn, and total white.

He faced the dirty urinal in the men's room at the Moose Lodge, feeling tense, trying to relax the special peeing muscles in his dick. His eyes were closed. He was seeing her again, naked, slick, and sleepy after sex. He felt at once relaxed and aroused, the twin sides of comfort, his dick releasing pee at last (he heard it drill the urinal), and getting hard a little in his hands too.

"*Shit.*"

He jumped back, dabbing at his pants above the knee.

Easy, big guy. Start again.

He coughed and started peeing. How it all came back, those delicious trysts, summer into fall. They got together at the house, the house she shared with Lloyd, and later at a motel in northeast Washington, the hilly ghettos around Catholic U. They weren't Catholic, they weren't black, they weren't college students; nobody would know them there, they figured. They trysted at the house and the motel, and yes it was betrayal, Shirl betrayed and Lloyd betrayed, but Tashmo did it anyway. He was seeing Lloyd every day on Carter's team. They worked the late watch in the shack at Camp David, a wall of screens, drippy eco-hippies trying to sneak in, and Lloyd could only talk about his wife.

Lloyd drinking coffee, watching screens: "I don't know, Tash—I worry about Lydia. She needs some outside interests. Maybe if you sat her down. She still talks about the time you changed the fuse. I think she looks up to you."

Tashmo didn't squirm. He tried to be a pro about it. He said, "She needs a change of scenery, that's all, Lloyd. Go back to Fresno, have a kid. I bet they'd make you a group supervisor in Crim, bright young guy like you."

But Lloyd, the trusting geek, said he couldn't leave. He loved Protection, the idea of the perimeter, the science of the thing. He said, "She was an actress, Tash, did you know that? She was on TV in supporting roles. She was in a two-part *Harry O*."

In fairness, Tashmo had tried to end it after a few weeks, his thing with Lydia. The record, he was thinking, should reflect this. The sex was unbelievable, yes, but Lydia, the actress, was into melodrama, which spooked him in his sober, nontumescent moments. Shirl was pregnant with Jeanette that summer—Tashmo had a family to consider. Lydia was risky for a hundred reasons. So he made his move. He called her from the White House and arranged a lunch-hour meeting at the Tomb of the Unknown Soldier, a good place to remember their duties, Lydia to Lloyd, Tashmo to his family. The Tomb was Tashmo's favorite place to end his love affairs. He had dumped many women in the pillared amphitheater over the years—it was the perfect setting, strategically and otherwise. The Tomb was always awash in out-of-towners, nobody he knew, and always hushed, the awesome, marble hush of fatherland and sacrifice. Even Lydia would find it hard to shout obscenities at him in such surroundings. He planned the breakup like a Secret Service op, doing the advance work in his mind. If she wept, a fifty-fifty bet, the tourists around them would assume that she had given a loved one to America's defense and respectfully ignore her sobs. He had a whole plan for cutting Lydia loose—a sleazy, craven plan, brilliant in its way, but it was raining when he met her in the amphitheater, and they had to make a run for it. They wound up in the front seat of his government sedan. He tried to deliver the speech he had prepared. *You know how much I care for you, that's why this is so hard.* It might have worked at the Tomb, but in the car it sounded phony. She was drenched through her blouse. Steam rose from both of them, fogging the windows. As he spoke, she slowly put her seat back, and unbuttoned the top button on her blouse.

Not a success. The next plan he came up with (equally craven, though less brilliant) was to never call her, never see her, never return the coded messages she left at the White House switchboard. *Tell him he's got a dentist's appointment, Tuesday, say threeish, the usual place.* He was guarding Jimmy Carter, going down the ropes, knowing she was elsewhere in the city, waiting for him on the greasy sheets of the ghetto motel.

He was saved by the elections. He traveled double hard with Carter, volunteering for every trip, keeping temptation far away. He came home in November 1980. Carter was defeated and good riddance to the pious little party-pooper. Jeanette was born and Lydia wasn't calling anymore.

Ronald Wilson Reagan was Tashmo's new beginning, his clean slate. Tashmo loved the Dutchman as a father, as a pal and fellow dude. He loved the team, Loudon Rhodes, Felker, Gus Dmitri, Billy Spandau, Panepinto—Reagan's boys they were, and would always be. He loved the trips out west, door to door, coast to coast, the South Lawn to the California ranch, six hours in the air, three touchdowns in between, Memphis, Phoenix, LAX. They crossed the time zones like an arrow, nearly made the sun stand still, bringing Reagan west. They worked prepackaged rallies at the airports, shirtsleeve crowds, clapping hands, low rolling chants, music from the marching bands, tiny flags, red, white, and blue, a blizzard of these tiny flags, like unfalling confetti, and it was Reagan who did it, and Reagan who made it, word chanted into manglement, name chanted into stadiums of sound, *A-gihn, A-gihn, A-gihn.* They jumped from LAX to Point Mugu Naval Air, met the helo on the tarmac for the final leg, rising with the mountain walls to the Western White House, the Rancho del Cielo, which Lloyd Felker (bilingual and showoffish) tried to say meant the Ranch of the Ceiling, a concept of fixed limits, of you-can-go-no-higher-than, but which Tashmo and the other boys knew meant just the opposite, the Ranch of Heaven and no limits.

Shirl was always after Tashmo to come home. She got him when he was at his weakest, after sex and sloppy joes, after soapy hand jobs in the tub, when his daughters were asleep, when he kissed them both asleep, just before he went away. She'd be at the bathroom sink, washing the jism and soapsuds off her hands. His bags were on the bed, packed and zippered for a month in California. He'd be at the mirror, styling his pompadour, waiting for the burning sensation in his dick hole to die down.

"You should watch your daughters grow"—this was Shirl's argument back then.

Tashmo thought the best way to watch a child grow was to see the kid something like once a month. That way you really noticed the progress. He didn't share this insight with his wife.

Shirl said, "Men do projects around the house. That's what a husband does. Look at Bo Gould. He redid their kitchen with his own two hands."

Tashmo tied his tie. "He did not."

"Did so."

"Did not."

"He paid the men who did. He paid them with his own two hands. Tash, it's not for me. It's for Mandy and the baby. Don't you think they deserve a dad?"

Well, he thought, they had a dad. He had done his bit, sent his little cowboy DNAs along.

Shirl was stuck in Maryland—that was the problem. She didn't understand how it felt, crossing time, taking Reagan west. Half a day of sunset, boys. We're at the peak—

Heaven was a ranch in California. Who was more American than Dutch?

Reagan went riding most mornings at the ranch. He went out with Laxalt, his pet senator, or Charlton Heston, or with Mrs. Reagan and the Annenbergs. The Service bought a stable of used horses to cover Reagan on these rides. The horses had appeared in Mexican westerns and were trained not to buck at gunfire. Agents who could ride formed a mounted subdetail. Tashmo's father had run a bar in Falling Rock and Tashmo grew up shooting pool, throwing rocks, pumping gas. He wasn't any kind of rider, but he was a skilled and supple liar, and he bluffed his way onto the saddle squad. Reagan always cantered to this one high-country meadow, which looked like a set from *Bonanza,* the perfect tableau west, but only from one angle. Every other angle took in the sprawl beyond—snarling US 101, booming Santa Barbara, miles of arroyo burning for years, some vast drought management fuckup, which Reagan always blamed on too much government. Against this modern backdrop, men on horses looked hemmed in, endangered, asinine. But Reagan had a gift for making cameras see him as he saw himself, and in the thousand wire service photos of the meadow on the ranch there was never any evidence of 101, the city, or the smolder in the hills. In Tashmo's memory they were really cowboys at the ranch, packing Uzis, wearing chaps and creaky Tony Llama boots. He was with the Reagans and the Annenbergs on the semifamous morning when someone's horse kicked up a rattlesnake. Tashmo drew his Uzi and fired at the dirt, the muzzle exploding in his horse's ear. The nag forgot its training and Tashmo fell backwards, emptying his clip into the sky. He landed on a stump, still firing, and nearly put a hole in Mrs. Reagan. All the agents opened up on the snake threat, a ring of blazing Uzis in the meadow. They couldn't find the pieces later, but Betsy Annenberg swore it was a rattler.

Just another day in heaven with the Dutchman, and when it was all over, the posse had a story to bring down the mountain into Santa Barbara on their day off. The journalists and generals hung out at the Biltmore. The agents commandeered a London-style pub with forty-seven beers on tap and dollar bills tacked to the rafters. The pub was up the coast a bit, near the county trauma center, and often full of nurses getting off. Tashmo dated many nurses from the pub and learned a lot about the nursing profession. Like they don't wear white and look down on those who do. Like they spend every December in Reno dealing blackjack—the money was better and you skied. Like every pit queen in Nevada is actually a California trauma nurse, thinking about skiing as she deals. These were things you could only learn in a beachfront pub, cheating on your family back home.

He went to the pub one afternoon during his second evolution to the ranch, just after the inaugural in 1981. The pub was dead, he remembered that. The other men were on the mountain guarding Reagan. Tashmo sat at the bar and had a Foghorn by himself. The bartender was a new guy, a fill-in. Tashmo asked for the darts. The new guy said he'd have to take a credit card impression as security.

Tashmo said, "I'm in here all the time."

They went back and forth about the darts, the policy, the credit card impression. Tashmo turned on his stool and saw a woman in a booth across the bar. It was Lydia Felker, eating a bleucheeseburger, reading *TV Guide*.

For a moment, he thought that she had stalked him all the way from Maryland. He considered walking out, or ducking in the men's, but she saw him at the bar and waved. It wasn't a fraught wave. It was just a *Hi there* sort of deal and back to her reading.

He sipped his Foghorn, thought it through. Felker's mother lived in Fresno, a few hours north. Lydia was probably staying with the mom and had come down to spend the weekend with Lloyd. It was just the thing Tashmo himself had recommended, a change of scenery to shoo the housewifely blues. He could even imagine Lloyd's therapeutic itinerary, a visit to the painted caves, the Itty-Bitty Railway, and maybe, if there's time, the aquarium. Tashmo figured he was in the clear.

"Want them darts or not?" the bartender said.

He took his stein of Foghorn across the London pub and said hello to Lydia. He remembered how she offered him the radish garnish on her plate, how she tore a match from a book of matches and used it as a bookmark when she closed the *TV Guide*. He remembered how he took the pungent radish in his fingers. It was cut like a flower. He ate it as a gesture—look, I'm cool, I'm non-hung-up, I'll eat your garnish—and he remembered how he suddenly remembered that he hated radishes.

She looked at him and said, "I guess you dumped me, Tash. I waited for you in the motel, three weeks in a row."

The radish was burning in his belly as he started his Unknown Soldier speech, the speech he never finished at the Tomb.

She cut him off. "Did you lose your nerve?" she asked.

He tried to be Reaganesque about it, mimicking his hero, grinning like he didn't hear the question.

"Nerve—did you lose it? I thought we were having fun."

The Reagan thing didn't work for him, so he tried Carter. He pulled a quivery, conscientious face. "I'm married, Lydia. There are long-range issues requiring much study. I have lusted in my heart."

She said, "That's your trip," and pushed her plate away.

He remembered how the pub slowly filled that afternoon, nurses coming in, surfers playing darts in flip-flops, the hour creeping toward the shift change on the mountain. He drank stein after stein, but couldn't wash the taste of radish off his tongue.

She said, "I was supposed to spend a month in Fresno. Ever try to spend a month in Fresno? Mother Felker didn't really see me at my best, I fear. She claims I shoplifted. Claims she saw me shoplifting. Says the Felkers of Fresno have a name to protect. I said, 'Let me tell you something, Mother Felker, there's no way you saw me shoplifting.' So I drifted over here. I don't care about your wife. I don't care about your kids. How are they, by the way?"

"Good," said Tashmo.

"I don't care."

She said Lloyd had tickets to a brass ensemble, an all-atonal program at the hanging gardens. Lloyd would be on the mountain until four-o'clock. It was half past two.

Lydia said, "What do you want to do?"

He was out of presidents. He answered as himself.

She was living toward Oxnard in a rented trailer in a colony of trailers in a parking lot along the PCH. They got there, he gargled with cheap scotch, and they made love.

He would come to know the trailer well. Reagan spent fourteen days at the ranch after the inaugural. Whenever Lloyd was in the hills, Tashmo was living in the trailer with his wife. Tashmo connived the duty charts, putting himself on when Lloyd was off, off when Lloyd was on, becoming, in effect, the anti-Lloyd. He drove the canyons from the ocean to the ranch, switchbacks like a ladder, headlights below him in the night, many sets, crawling back and forth. He drank Sanka at the trailer from the same chipped mug, standing in the open door, watching the morning surf pile up a mist. His eyes traveled down the coast and up the mountain walls. The beach outside the trailer was duneless, hard-packed. He dumped the dregs and the wind took them. He was thirty-three years old, had saddle sores, a bite mark on his calf, and rashes from his radish allergy, and had never felt stronger in his life.

They walked the beach at sunset, played Scrabble in the kitchen, drove to Montecito for cheap Mexican. She scrambled eggs at midnight and talked about her television days.

She said, "I was Quinn Martin's favorite for a few seasons. He threw me a ton of work. Quinn has a reputation, but he was sweet to me."

She wore a big sweater, faded jeans, and no underpants.

Tashmo said, "Quinn Martin?"

"*Harry O* and *Cannon, Barnaby Jones*. A certain pulpy gravitas. Act I, Act II, Epilogue."

Tashmo asked her if she missed the acting.

"No." She thought about it. "No. I was typecast. It's every actor's dread. I was always playing frightened witnesses. That's how I met Lloyd. I was sick of the type-casting, I wanted to break free, so I went to Fresno. *Buried Child*, summer stock. I was Shelly, the girlfriend with the heart of gold. One night, Lloyd came to the show. He was into cultural self-improvement even then, poor bean. He sat in front, a scratchpad on his knee, noting his emotions with a penlight pen. After Shelly ditched the shitheel, Vince, Lloyd asked me out to the half-priced matinee at the Fresno Planetarium. The wheeling Milky Way got me hot and bothered, so I unzipped his fly. He resisted—momentarily. Lips and milkiness, I guess I blew his mind. Within a week, we were engaged. I called my agent in L.A., told him I was through. He begged me to reconsider. 'Give it two more years,' he said, 'we'll get you other roles. You won't always play the frightened witness. I just saw a casting call—you'd be prefect for it. It's called *Hill Street Blues*, you'd play the captain's wife. She's basically the star of the entire show.' I told him no, I was getting while the getting's good. He said, 'No one marries their agent, Lydia. It's always a disaster, and besides, *I'm* your agent. You signed an exclusive with me.' I told him Lloyd was not that kind of agent. He said, 'Oh my God, you're marrying a *literary* agent? What will you do for food?' I told him Lloyd wasn't literary, he was literal—utterly and totally, heroically literal. He was clear—Lloyd. In his head. His mind was a perimeter, and *clear*, and, God, I thought I wanted that after television. So we got married and came east to Maryland. And the rest, as they say, is histrionics."

They lay in bed. She traced his scars.

She said, "Movie lovers do this, Tash, but I never did. Lloyd is scarless, of course."

A slice above the hairline. She traced it. "What's this?"

"Kid hit me with a rock," Tashmo said. "I was fourteen. It was strictly accidental. Poor kid went to Vietnam, died with the Marines."

"And this?"

An old gash down the lifeline of his palm.

"Bowie knife, jungles of Chu Lap, 1968. I was opening a jar of Skippy peanut butter. They're vacuum-sealed and—"

"This?"

Stitches on his buttock. "A snake. My horse. Betsy Annenberg."

"And this?"

His calf. He said, "You bit me."

She doubted this.

They listened to the ocean and the radio and polished off the scotch.

She said, "I've been four places in the world, counting all of California as one place." She said the others were: Maryland; Muncie, Indiana; and the Punjab.

They were in the trailer the night before Reagan headed east again.

"What's in Muncie?" Tashmo asked.

"My innocence, my growing up. I told you that whole story."

"What about the Punjab?"

"*Sepoy!* My big shot at feature film. I was Lady Adelaide, frigid baroness and bitch extraordinaire, trapped in the seething tumult of the 1854 Raj Mutiny. The producers were three dubious Hindus with underworld connections. They planned two endings, one for export, in which whitey wins and I marry Major Smuts, the other for India, in which I die quite badly. The producers asked if I could do a British accent. My agent said, 'She doesn't have to. She's a native Londonian, as English as the queen.' The producers said, 'But she seemed so American on *Barnaby Jones.*' My agent said, 'I told you, she's a genius!' We shot all the scenes involving elephants and the backing collapsed. I later heard the movie was cover for an arms deal, an excuse to import rifles and light artillery. The extras were actually members of a Hindu terror group. Big things afoot in Bangladesh, I gather."

They drank the scotch and listened to the wind across the parking lot. She didn't own a television, but she read TV Guide—to keep abreast, she said. She bought it every week, but didn't subscribe.

He asked her why. He said, "It's always cheaper to subscribe."

She said, "This way I can stop at any time."

She brought the eggs to the table steaming. He was getting ready to climb into his car and drive the switchbacks up to Reagan's mountain, where the helo would take them to Mugu, on to Washington—the world.

"Stay," she said. "We could live this way forever."

Did he fall in love with Mrs. Felker? He thought he loved her, coming east on Air Force One—loved her more than Shirl, more than the girls, more than all his other mistresses combined. He loved her, maybe, even more than he loved Ronald Reagan.

When the team got back to Washington, Tashmo started sleeping in the ready room, a line of cots in the basement of the White House for agents pulling back-to-backs. He couldn't face Shirl, Mandy, and the baby, and the shitty new construction in upper P.G. County. This went on for days. Shirl tried to find him. She fed the kids and watched the nightly news for any sign of her AWOL husband. Shirl knew that Reagan was in town, meeting with the cabinet and the Contras, and she knew that Tashmo was somewhere in the presidential wake. On the fourth day of no Tashmo, Shirl showed up at the East Gate, bawling at the guards, Mandy in the backseat of the station wagon, Jeanette screaming from the bassinette.

The guard said, "Well, you know, they're pretty busy in there."

Shirl said, "Pretty busy? We're a family in crisis here. Step aside or else I'll run you down."

A line of cars behind her. The guard made a call, trying to find the husband of this loon. The wall phone rang in the ready room. Tashmo picked up, heard the guard and Shirl cursing in the background. Tashmo said he hadn't seen Tashmo in awhile.

Shirl stayed away after that. A silence. From Lydia, a silence. His wife and mistress were saying the same thing with their silence: this is the X that marks your life, the cloverleaf of choice.

He couldn't choose. He slept on a cot five nights in a row, trying to decide: his mistress or his family? But he was back in a suit, official Washington, endless prayer breakfasts, bill-signing ceremonies, a rack of pens handed out afterwards as mementos of the law, the Pro-Family Export Amendment, the Glad and Happy Tidings Act of 1981—no posses, no horses, no thrilling vistas of not-101, just Tashmo standing post again, waiting for nothing on the pavement, a crowd of gawkers gawking at the limo with the Seal of Office on the door.

The X that marks your life. Reagan's in the ballroom of a luxury hotel, address-ing labor leaders. Tashmo is outside, underneath the overhang, a curving wall of poured concrete, roughened, the faux-sandstone look. Light rain falling in the street. Tashmo hears the detail coming out, Reagan through the doors, waving at the gallery, agents weaving all around him, Felker, Loudon Rhodes, chief-of-detail Tim McCarthy. Tashmo sees it happening: a distant sodden popping sound like hunters, cornfields, boyhood, Reagan stumbles as if bumped, Tim McCarthy falls, a cop falls to his belly. Tashmo's like a movie extra playing Streetman when Rodan appears, one face in a mass reaction shot of faces, *Oh*. In the time it takes to star-tle and de-startle, bloody Reagan's bundled past him, wrapped in Felker's bulk. The door handle's ripped from Tashmo's hand, which is how he knows the limo's off and safe. The blond boy with the pistol crumples under a humping, grunting pigpile of terrified plainclothesmen.

For the next two days, the agents kept a vigil outside G.W. Medical Center. Inside, Reagan quipped and wavered at death's door. Loudon had to be sedated, Tashmo couldn't eat, Felker didn't shave, and none of them could sleep. The Ser-vice tried to send the agents home. The deputy director told them one by one to get some sleep, but they didn't sleep or leave, they wouldn't go, they couldn't. They were Reagan's boys. They had seen a nation at sweet zenith, and they had fucked it up, fucked it up, they had bungled something precious on the sidewalk at the Hilton, and Hinckley's bullet, fired in the rain, was still killing Ronald Reagan as the doctors operated. Reagan's agents lived in the lobby of the hospital, pissing in the men's rooms and the shrubbery outside, Panepinto in the chapel lighting can-dles, bumming money to light candles, Gus Dmitri in the chapel, offering his prayers. Billy Spandau in the chapel offering his life, *Dear God please take my life, but spare my protectee*, offering his life and Panepinto's too, if this would tip the scales. They couldn't sleep or leave until the word came down from the man himself, from Ronald Wilson Reagan: *Go home, boys, I'm in the clear—I want you to go home.*

Tashmo left the hospital that day, drove back to P.G. County, the shitty house, the yard, the screaming baby and his wife. He never saw Lydia again.

Tashmo stood by the back wall of the Rumsey Moose Lodge, waiting for the motorcade to show. He was watching the loose crowd of Moose and friends of Moose, the volunteers, the press pool from the lost bus. O'Teen was busy at the choke point, shaking his tray, "Anything metal—"

Tashmo was thinking, Shirl—this is my apology, my last full accounting. This is what I did and didn't do. I'll skip the others, Shirl, because they're not important—the barmaids and the bridesmaids and the campaign volunteers, the eager phone bank coeds and my Christmas party conquests, too numerous to count. This is what I did—and I lied about it too, and I know that I'm supposed to say that the lie is worse than the lay, a bigger, more polluting sin, and I'll say it, and believe it. I know I'm supposed to say that I never loved a one of them. Loving them is even worse than laying them, I know, somewhere well below lying about laying, and so I'll say that though I laid and lied, I never loved. I loved them all, of course. I loved them as a concept, as a demographic, but I don't think that counts as love, do you? But I know I cannot lie in my apology, and so I have to say: maybe I loved Lydia a little.

The motorcade arrived outside. Tashmo heard it on the comm, Gretchen in the parking lot, telling the snipers to spread out.

A runner came in from the vans and whispered to the emcee of the event. The emcee, a ranking Moose, climbed onto the stage and stood behind the podium, tapping the microphone. "This on? This on?"

The entourage was coming in, a rush of noise, a clatter on the stairs. The crowd stood up. A cheer.

And so they came to Portsmouth, that early haven of the English-speakers, that former spice-and-whaling port, that faded base of long-range bombers and ballistic
submarines, that host of now-ghost throw weight, that pretty harbor city voted
third most livable by the editors of a well-known in-flight magazine, that swing of
state elections, that home to fifty thousand souls (including the down-county
towns), that target of the pollsters and perfect microcosm of the—

"What's the opposite of microcosm?" asked the wire service woman, pausing
at her laptop as she typed her lead. She was sitting at the bar of the renovated inn,
the Old Governor Weare, which wasn't pronounced "weary" but rather "wear," she
had learned from the snippy concierge. It wasn't very renovated either, from the
looks of it, except for the roof bar itself, which revolved slowly, offering successive
views of, first, a steeple like a candlestick on Market Square and, later, the black
channel of the Piscataqua River, a ribbon of no light between the populated banks.

The wire service woman asked the question of the tall, graying gentleman to
her left, thinking he was a fellow journalist or columnist or possibly a speechwriter
or in-house campaign memosmith, a word-worker of some sort.

The tall man popped a salty cashew from the dish. He said, "Opposite of
microcosm?"

"And don't say 'macrocosm,'" said the wire service woman. "Micro is a little
version of the thing. Macro is a bigger version. I'm asking, what's the thing?"

"You got me," said the man, scoping out her blouse. "They call me Tashmo, by
the way. I'm with the VP's detail. May I buy you another flavored vodka or would
you care for a mixed drink?"

The wire service woman suddenly remembered an appointment down the bar,
leaving Tashmo at the taps, one cheek on the stool, drinking Bud from a pewter
tankard. The bar was crowded, network men and beat people, producers and politi-

cos. O'Teen, Herc Mercado, and Bobbie Taylor-Niles shared a table in the middle of the room, where they were working on a round of drinks.

The barkeep slid another Bud in front of Tashmo and fiddled with the bills by the cashew dish. Tashmo drank in the manner of old cops. Put a fifty on the bar when you sit down, leave it there all night, watch it go, fifty turning into twenties, twenties into tens and ones and fives, as the barman does subtraction, wet fingers in the pile. This was how you drank, paying as you went. It was more a custom than a law, like throwing rocks in Falling Rocks when he was a kid—stay motionless until it hits, only a punk would turn his back on a falling rock. The Bud arrived and, with it, the thought: he was endangered here, tonight. He saw the wire service woman at the far end of the bar. He thought, I guess the word is "cosm"—as in "cosmos," a word containing every other word except, of course, "macrocosm," which was a bigger version of the cosmos.

He drank the beer, left a tip, left the bar. There were six floors at the renovated inn. The VP was on six, just below the bar. He was always on the top floor, whatever that floor was. The elevators were, of course, locked out of the sixth floor. There were troopers in the stairwells, in the lobby, on the roof, cops and K-9 in the parking lot, guarding the vans against a bomb plant. The vans would be bomb-dogged in the morning, a full sweep, but the Service stored them under guard just to be certain. The planners always rented out the entire floor the VP was staying on, or the entire wing in a very large hotel. The rooms in the secure zone (the whole top floor tonight) were parceled out to the VP (he got a suite, empty rooms on either side for anti-eavesdropping purposes), his military attachés and close civilian aides, his top politicos, the agents on his detail, the aircrews on his jet and helicopters, which often left a lot of empty rooms, and gave the secure floor a creepy and deserted feel, tense and dead all at once. Tashmo knew the feeling well.

He shared a room with Sean Elias. He sat on the bed, watching Elias carefully unpack his undershirt supply. Tashmo had come back to call Shirl and confront her on her statements of earlier that day (*I love you and I trust you, everything is going to work out*), but now that he was here, sitting on the bed, he felt the danger again. Lydia and Shirl. He decided not to call.

Elias tidied up the tabletops. Elias was perhaps the only man on earth who felt the need to tidy up a new hotel room.

Tashmo hung his cowboy suit inside the bathroom door, ran the shower hot to steam out the wrinkles for the morning. He dressed himself in sporting clothes, slacks, loafers, and a short-sleeved turtleneck.

He said, "Fuck it, Eli, let's go grab a pop."

At the table in the middle of the bar, Herc Mercado was splitting an order of Cajun chicken fingers with Elias and O'Teen, and trying to figure out if they had ever stayed in the Governor Weare before.

Herc said, "This is Portsmouth, right?"

"Look around you," said O'Teen. "Or better yet, just look and let the building move."

Bobbie said, "The building's moving?"

"That's a rodg," Elias said.

Bobbie looked relieved. "I thought it was me."

Tashmo, feeling dumpy still, nursed a beer and listened to them talk.

Herc said, "I don't think I've ever seen this bar before. When were we last here?"

"October," said Elias. "We stayed in this hotel. We always stay here when we come to Portsmouth. It's on the list of Plans-approved dignitary lodgings. I think they gave it two stars."

Herc said, "Did we drink in this bar?"

O'Teen said, "Hell yes—don't you remember, Herc? I scratched your pager number in the men's room. I've never seen you so irate."

"I was getting paged for days," said Herc. "But it was a different bar, I'm pretty sure of it. The bar we drank in had a buccaneer motif."

The agents looked around the room, risking motion sickness. The waitresses wore tight white breeches, low-cut bodices with big puffy sleeves, and shoes with big square buckles. The barmen wore a similar getup with cockaded tricorner hats. The imitation fireplace was six feet wide, hung with pots and kitchen implements of hammered brass. There were crossed oars on the walls, hanging sabers and muskets on pegs.

Elias said, "It's fairly buccaneerish, Herc."

Herc said, "No it isn't. Check the menu."

The menu was seven heavy pages cased in plastic. Every drink was dubbed, of course. Vodkas-by-the-glass (in a spate of flavors) were listed as the Shots Heard 'Round the World, Bloody Marys were called the Boston Massacre, martinis were known as the Midnight Ride.

Herc said, "That's more your revolutionary theme."

The waitress appeared, a pert coed in breeches, pen ready at her pad. She said, "Hi, my name is Kelli. I'll be your server for the evening." She looked at their suits. "You all flight attendants or something?"

Bobbie said, "What happened to our other server? She was nice, I liked her."

"She had to cash out early," Kelli said. "Her psoriasis was acting up."

Herc said, "Did this bar have a different theme before?"

"No," said Kelli, "we've had this theme all night."

"How about October?"

Kelli said, "I'm new."

"Well," said Herc, "how would you describe this theme?"

Kelli looked around. "Oh, I don't know—Roaring Nineties?"

Elias said, "Is history required at your college, Kel?"

O'Teen said, "Ignore them, Kelli. I'll have another."

Kelli said, "Another what?"

Everyone had beer except for Elias, who had another Schweppes, and Bobbie, who had a Shot Heard 'Round the World. The agents pondered dinner, reviewing the menu.

Kelli said, "We also have our specials for tonight: old New England baked spaghetti in a spaghetti sauce; the hearty Yankee pot roast with creamed spinach, buttered bread or a popover; our signature baked ham with your choice of the house salad, a popover, the steamed green beans with slivered almonds; the cod, which you can have baked, grilled, poached, or deep-fried in a popover; roast turkey with the cream-a-corn, or your choice of two, creamed spinach, maple carrots, Uncle Jesse touched me, or a steamy crock of our famous onion soup."

"Cheeseburger," said Herc.

"Ditto," said Elias.

Tashmo said, "Uncle Jesse what?"

Kelli blushed. "I usually get away with that—no one ever listens to the specials."

O'Teen said, "Do you have baked spaghetti?"

"Yes sir, it's a special."

O'Teen got spaghetti, Bobbie got the cod. Kelli took the orders to the kitchen. O'Teen left to see if Herc's number was still in the men's room and ran into Gretchen Williams. Tashmo watched her cross the room, pushing O'Teen along.

Gretchen stood over the agents at the table. No one said hello to her.

Gretchen said, "Where's Vi?"

Bobbie said, "She's sleeping."

"She was yawning," said O'Teen.

"I've never seen someone so tired," Herc observed.

They were obviously lying. Tashmo knew that Vi had left the hotel without orders. The VP's team wasn't a close group, like the glorious old Reagan team, but at least these half-assed kids had the decency to lie and cover up for a fellow agent, even if they did it badly. Tashmo was proud of them, a little.

Gretchen said, "It's curfew time, you're finished here. We've got an early pre-brief in the morning. Everyone to bed."

"But we just ordered dinner," Bobbie said.

Gretchen said, "Bobbie, shut your trap. Herc, locate the waitress, cancel that last order. Elias, don't pay with plastic, makes us look like fucking flight attendants—Jesus, Eli, have some pride. The rest of you to bed except for Tashmo. Tashmo, follow me."

Every night on the road, Gretchen's last official act before she went to bed was a tour of the hotel from the lobby to the roof. She took this tour alone most nights, double-checking normal, making sure that nothing was undone or overlooked. She crossed the lobby of the inn that evening, Tashmo at her elbow.

She said, "Where were you when you were called for this deployment, Tashmo? I was at the batting cage with my son, seems like a million years ago. Then I get beeped by Debbie Escobedo-Waas. She says the Director needs to see me. Fine—Vi comes by and we go up to Beltsville. When we get there, the Director takes me for a big walk on the quad. 'Gretch,' he says, 'everything pertaining to the life and works of Lloyd L. Felker is secret now, and triple need-to-know, and you don't need to know so I shouldn't tell you, but I will. Because I know it bothers you, what happened in the flood. Felker was your people, Gretch, and you left him on the ground. You left the Asplund girl too, but we were able to recover her substantially intact, so it's no big whoops. But Felker—that was a *big* whoops. Not your fault, of course. You lost a man, Gretch. Cost of doing business. And in the end, it's not your fault that the man you lost happened to possess, in his legendary memory, all-clearance knowledge of every plan and tactic in the cupboard, every plug in every hole, every hole in every plug, every Certainty and Sensitive. I'm not here to dwell on your fuckup in the flood, because I admire you. You keep them dawgies moving, Gretch, and I see you as directress of this Service in a few years. I'll be out to pasture then, an eager, hungry, slightly desperate, business-lunching corporate security consultant, probably working for that goddamn Loudon Rhodes, assuming he's not in prison for shooting Hinckley, ironically enough, not that I object to shooting Hinckley, sauce for the gander in my humble book, but I *don't* condone hiring ex-Mossaders to plan such a hit, and I have in my office, Gretch, at this very moment firm evidence of contractual discussions between Loudon Rhodes in Hollywood and a shadowy global headhunter with offices in Crete and Lake Success, New York—*firm* evidence, I tell you: wiretaps, *wiretaps*—well, not wiretaps because everything in Hollywood is cell phones nowadays, so these are mostly wireless taps, but shockingly explicit nonetheless, and when the time is right, evil Loudon Rhodes will be facing a grand jury if he doesn't give me a really good job when I retire. You don't need to know what I'm about to tell you, Gretch, and I shouldn't fill you in, but I will. Because when I'm retired to the cold, unfeeling private sector, and you sit in my twirly chair of power, and are in a position to give out certain lucrative consultancies, I want you to remember me as one who knew you felt responsible for Hinman and had the decency to fill you in.'"

Tashmo said, "Did he ever actually get around to filling you in?"

"They found Felker," Gretchen said.

There were troopers on the couches by the lobby doors. They got up as Gretchen approached and sat down again as Gretchen went away.

"After Felker disappeared in Hinman," Gretchen said, "Boone Saxon's guys put a watch on his Diners Club card. Two days after Hinman, the card came alive in a burst of charges, St. Louis, K.C., Denver, and Las Vegas. The rate and spacing of the charges indicated a man driving west, steady progress, but not headlong flight.

Most of the charges were for gas, barbecue, or Asian-only escort services, and the tips, I'm told, were staggering. Boone traced the card to a casino-motel-massage complex in Laughlin, Nevada, a southward jog from Vegas, which made the Director think of Mexico, of Felker running for the border, not quite the Director's worst nightmare, but up there anyway. Because what if Lloyd went into Mexico and sold his knowledge of our weakness to the drug cartels, to Castro at his embassy, to the Shining Path? What if he made the jump from Mexico to the Middle East and sold his mind to the Iraqis? We'd have presidents in bunkers for the next twenty years. It was therefore deemed imperative to catch Felker before he made the border. The Director sent a troop of SWATs to Laughlin. They covered the casino and found the Diners Club card in the hands of a car thief from Chicago. We'll call this person Earl."

There were two banquet halls off the lobby at the inn. The first, the West Wind Room, had been rented to the campaign and transformed into a cavernous press center. Gretchen walked between the rows of folding tables, watching people type at laptops, talk on cell phones, type and talk and chew their pencils, looking at the ceiling.

"Before the flood, this person we call Earl was a guest of the State of Illinois, doing the back nine of a seven-to-fourteen, working in the barber shop, studying for his GEPh.D. in boxing history, hoarding marijuana, snitching on his friends, abusing his free access to the law library, pestering the overburdened courts with nuisance suits complaining of various ills, slights, and due process violations—in other words, living the life of your typical mellow prison inmate.

"Then it rained and rained, and the river rose, and the person we call Earl was sent to Hinman with a work gang, throwing dikes against the flood. He was separated from the others when the levee broke. He wandered through the town, in no special hurry to find the nearest guard. Earl claims that as the water swallowed the lower-lying trailer parks he was bravely engaged in a volunteer salvage operation, rescuing televisions, sporting goods, and women's underwear from the sinking trailers. As he was salvaging everything that wasn't bolted down, he looked up and saw an apparition, nothing less—a crazy white man in tacky flight attendant clothes, wading through the water, telling Earl and his co-salvagers to disperse to the designated refugee processing center. The man was with a spindly-ass little white girl, who seemed to work for the same airline. When Earl and the other salvagers did not disperse as directed, the white man came up with an Uzi. Earl flees into a trailer, the flight attendants follow. Shots are exchanged inside the trailer as it slips into the river.

"Everything is dark and they are under water. Earl pushes through a window and pops to the surface, spinning in a nasty sucking current. He can't see the banks. He thinks that he will die and opens negotiations with the Creator of the Universe, making certain promises: If You let me live, dear God, I promise I will never, never, never joyride or set poor examples for the youth of my community. He fights to keep his mouth up. He kicks and promises. He weakens and begins to fade. At that moment he is bashed in the face. He looks up and sees the old white flight attendant clinging to the roof of the floating trailer home. Felker—and of course it's Felker—is trying to push a ladder to Earl, striking Earl in the face and head. Earl grabs the bottom rung and climbs to the roof, where he promptly vomits.

"They rode the house downriver. The trailer was small and vinyl-sided, winterized, airtight against the kind of drafts which can balloon your heating bill, and therefore semi-watertight. This is Earl's version. I'm not saying I believe it. Boone has consulted home-buoyancy experts and even staged a secret reenactment with scale models in Nevada. The conclusion reached by Threats is that a fully winterized, vinyl-sided domicile could, if weighted properly, float and not capsize, but only in no current, not the monster wet stampede Earl has described, and even in no current, the house could float for, at best, some hours, not the day and night and dawn Earl has described, and so there is good cause to doubt the heart of Earl's account. I don't care about the floating house, myself. My question is, what did they talk about, Felker and the car thief, clinging to the roof? I assume there was some conversation. Be awkward without conversation, wouldn't it?"

Gretchen left the press center in the West Wind Room. There was a complementary coffee bar by the front desk in the lobby, two steel urns, a sleeve of cups, little baskets holding sugar packets and half-and-half containers. Gretchen stopped to pour a cup. She took it black. Tashmo passed on coffee.

"The house was always breaking up," she said. "What happens is, the stripping glue becomes unstuck. Water seeps into the drywall, the drywall swells, the plastic staples blow, panels float away, and the house begins to sink. First Felker and Earl had the house and roof, then part of the house and all of the roof, then a corner of the roof. They floated, clinging to it, and Earl again made final preparations. 'Dear God,' he said, 'it's me again—we spoke earlier today, and you'll notice that I've thus far kept the promises I made, and haven't joyridden or set a poor example for the youth, and so I'd like to propose that we continue with our mutual understanding about me not dying or joyriding.'"

Gretchen sipped her coffee, blew on it, and sipped again. "Prayer, it seems to me, is like a voice mail—you can get quite detailed, anticipating all replies, though it's still basically a one-way conversation, until you hear the beep. My mother prays a lot. I never really saw the point of it."

They moved on to the second banquet hall, called the Nor'easter, rented out that night to a wedding reception. Tuxedoed groomsmen spilled into the lobby, ties unclipped, cummerbunds askew, and formed, improbably, a human pyramid, a frat stunt and a tribute to their brother getting married. The pyramid collapsed in a welter of low-fives and booty checks. From the ballroom, Tashmo heard the rising *tink-tink-tink* of forks hitting goblets, guests calling for another kiss. Tashmo thought of several things: marriage, getting married, his wedding day in North Dakota, which was practically the last time he was ever in a church on his own time, and how Shirl's father, a shrewd Jew-hating wheat farmer named Arne Skurdahl, was too choked up to give a wedding toast, standing there babbling, *My daughter, my Shirley, my daughter, my girl*, just full and overcome with love on his daughter's wedding day, and Tashmo, who didn't like the old blowhard all that much, liked or understood him for a moment at the wedding. Tashmo thought about fraternities, sororities, all that useless brutal energy, and how the girls at Rho Rho Rho beat his daughter up and called it a ceremony, how they beat his daughter, his Jeanette, his number two, his future and his past, the kid he raised from spit and sperm, how they blacked her eyes and made her pee blood instead of pee, and who were they to lay a hand on his Jeanette? And shouldn't he be mad instead of somehow *proud*?

Gretchen moved along. "Earl says he woke up in some reeds on the Missouri side. He pulled Felker from the water, felt him cold, believed him to be dead, and went through his pockets, finding Felker's empty holster, a billfold, and the creds. Earl took this—plausibly, I think—as a sign from God. He rented a big car and started west, charging every pleasure, posing as Lloyd Felker, Deputy Lead Agent.

Earl had the best three days of Felker's life. He tipped impressively, didn't joyride, and tried to set a good example for the youth. When the SWATs tackled him in the casino, he was giving a staunch antidrug lecture to a cigarette girl.

"The searchers got this story out of Earl. They believed it or they didn't— either way, they hit Missouri that night, towns around New Snively and Duprete. The river was itself again by then, but the wreckage spread for miles, a great curving rat's tail of debris. The SWATs went from hospital to hospital, tent city to tent city, searching through the refugees for any sign of Felker. The refugees were battered and looking for their children and their families. People, searching, moved around, which made them hard to search through systematically. In one camp, the SWATs would hear of a man like Felker in another camp, but when they got to the second camp, the man who was like Felker had moved on. They chased a dozen phantom Felkers who were always moving, conducting their own searches.

"They finally found him, nine days after Hinman, doing volunteer crowd control at a first-aid station in German Gap, Missouri. Felker admitted being Felker, but he didn't want to leave until everyone was bandaged, and, in the end, the goons had to get a little physical. They forced him on a plane, flew him back to Beltsville, the special-access area of Threats, and tried to figure out what the fuck to do with him. They couldn't send him back to the ropelines. High-stress duty—one never knows. On the other hand, they couldn't forcibly retire him because of what he knew, the bible in his head. Best to keep him in the family, right? So they had a problem: where do we store Lloyd?

"So they put their little heads together, the Director and Debbie Escobedo-Waas, and they came up with a plan. Felker was reassigned from Protection to the Technical Assistance Unit of the Data Administration Group of the Personnel Division, Boston station. His title was Leave Specialist. Felker meekly went to Massachusetts with his family. They leased a house in Concord, outside Boston, high suburbia."

Gretchen and Tashmo rode the elevator to the bar. By the time they got there, the bar was past last call. Kelli, the waitress, wiped tables with a rag. The barman hung his tricorner hat on the tap pulls and washed his tankards with a spray gun. Herc Mercado was sitting at the bar, explaining the true meaning of "La Vida Loca" to Kelli as she wiped.

Kelli said, "Isn't that a street in Italy?"

"No," said Herc, "it's about a woman and a man and the music they can make."

Gretchen came up behind Herc. "I told you to go to bed."

Herc said, "I went to bed. Now I'm up again."

Gretchen stared at a spot in the air three inches to the right of Herc's left ear. Herc slid off the stool, blew a kiss to Kelli, and slunk out.

Gretchen left the paper cup of coffee on the bar. Tashmo followed her to the gray steel fire door. They marched up the stairwell to the roof, the echoes of Gretchen's footsteps merging with the sound of Tashmo's feet.

"Now we're into Lydia's version," Gretchen said. "Because, you see, I called her, Tashmo. Had to, once I heard Earl's story. I'm the one who led her husband to the flood. She's a real piece of work, Miss Lydia. She told me the part of the story nobody else knows—you and Lloyd, you and her. I gather you were all quite close way back in them Carter days."

Tashmo said, "I should explain."

"Yes," said Gretchen, "but not to me. So there they are in Massachusetts, Lydia, Lloyd, and their son. It was a happy life, if you believe Miss Lydia. Lloyd got up every morning, ran three miles in the nude, stepped off the treadmill, showered, dressed in clothes he had laid out the night before, went off to work. He left the house like any good commuter but never made it to the office."

Tashmo said, "Where did he go?"

"Everywhere but work. He'd scout for coffee shops offering free refills. He'd stand on commuter rail platforms, waiting for discontinued trains. He'd tour the homes of Concord's famous authors. He took these tours repeatedly, staring at the furnishings. He fell asleep in Emerson's boudoir and was asked to leave the Hawthornes' on several occasions. He went to the Battle Road Visitors Center, the shrine to the Minutemen, sat through the twenty-minute slideshow more than twenty times. The rangers remember him. He seemed to be a busy and important man stealing time from a pressing schedule to learn about his heritage. He was always calling someone on his cell phone, always being paged—he waited for the pages, called back, and was paged again, an epic game of phone tag as he walked the storied mile where liberty was born."

"Who was he calling?"

"This was the Director's question. 'Did this goddamn Felker sell our secrets to A-rabs?' Boone pulled the billing file on the cell phone. Turns out Felker was fever-ishly paging himself from the cell, entering the pager as the callback. This went on for weeks."

"What did Lydia think?"

"She thought they were happy in Massachusetts. She said he seemed more excited, more engaged, and they were having sex again. Don't make a face. They were having sex like never before and he was finally talking about work. For years, she said, everything he did was secret and Most Sensitive, plans and counterplans—he was totally absorbed, she was totally left out—but now he talked about his job in minute detail, all the tittle-tattle from the water cooler, who was up, who was out, who was kissing butt, who was fighting for a better parking space, what Ned said to Fred about Ted, all the dull, intricate arcana that makes working in a large, collegial office like being wait-listed for Purgatory. And Lydia, hearing it, felt a self-ish joy. He was talking, they were talking after sex. He was asking her opinion, like they were a team, like he valued her input and advice. Should I put my name in for the parking space? Should I tell Ted what Ned said to Fred? She listened and she tried to give the best advice she could. It made her happy, and he saw this, so he told her more."

Gretchen pushed the roof door open. A sniper with a nightscope turned, star-tled. He saw the chief-of-detail, touched his helmet with his glove, and looked off to the east.

Gretchen walked to the edge of the roof, a little close for Tashmo's comfort.

She said, "Imagine the energy, the sheer creative will, required to invent, day after day, a new day's worth of tedium. Can you imagine loving somebody so much that you would do this every day for months just because it gave them a certain amount of pleasure?" Gretchen shook her head, looking down six stories at the parking lot. "Ever loved someone that much?"

"No," said Tashmo.

"Ever been loved that much?"

"I don't know," he said. "Have you?"

"Not so far," Gretchen said.

She turned back from the drop. "Let's go."

"Where?"

She said, "To my room."

"Felker had a favorite ranger at the Battle Road—a woman, as it happens. Her name was Ranger Nguyen. She isn't Vietnamese, despite the name. Her parents are, of course, both of them, but Ranger Nguyen was born in Baton Rouge, and she knows everything there is to know about her heritage, falling bombs at Fort McHenry, American guerrillas in the Massachusetts woods, a people mobilized, an arrogant empire hurled back across the sea. The pride she takes in Bunker Hill, the way she reveres Paul Revere—she's thrilling, somehow, this young and deeply clueless girl. I can see why Felker fell for her."

They were coming down the hallway of the sixth floor of the inn. A cop was tilted in a chair, reading the want ads.

Gretchen said, "What's doing?"

"Quiet," said the cop.

A brace of cops stood outside the VP's door. It was shift change for the cops. Three were going on, three were coming off. Gretchen walked past them down the hall.

"Felker took the tour with Ranger Nguyen seven times a day and asked her many questions afterwards. Was there a stamp tax on stamps or just on tea? Why was it One If by Land and Two If by Sea? Didn't the redcoats come by river, which is neither? He asked his questions and she answered brightly, missing part of her lunch hour. It pleased her to be quizzed on her beloved subject and he thought up new tough questions to please her further. She went back to work after lunch and he was there again. This went on for several days and after work one night he was waiting by her car.

"He said, 'I am here to protect you, Miss Nguyen.'

"She became afraid. He followed her to Cambridge in his car, staying very close. He stood outside her apartment building and was still there in the morning. He followed her to work, staying very close. He took her tour again, again, again, asking no questions now, watching the crowd, as he had been trained to do at Beltsville long ago. He followed her to lunch and home again that night. She called the cops and they arrived, two meatheads in a cruiser. Felker flashed his creds and said he was a fed working on a case. The cops looked at him and saw a guy who looked exactly like a fed. They looked at Nguyen and saw a somewhat strung-out gook. They said, 'Have a good one, Agent,' and got in their car. Nguyen, by now a weeping mess, called her dad in Baton Rogue. Her father called an army buddy from the war. I'm not sure which army they were buddies in. I'm assuming it was ours, I mean theirs—our theirs, if you know what I mean. The father's army buddy owned a string of Boston pizzerias. The pizzeria owner also owned a nickel-plated .forty-five, not the Double Eagle, but the next Colt up the line, I think it's called the Binding Arbitrator. He crept into the parking lot of Nguyen's building. Felker stood alone by the entryway, faithfully on post. The army buddy came around the dumpster, shouting at Felker to leave the girl alone. Felker saw him, saw the gun, and shouted something very similar. The army buddy fired, hit Felker in the chest. As they loaded Felker into the ambulance, Ranger Nguyen was beside herself, covered in his blood."

Gretchen and Tashmo were standing at the door to Gretchen's room. Gretchen knocked once, quietly. Tashmo saw the knob turn from inside.

"Why did you tell me all of this?" he asked.

"Because she wants to see you one last time."

The balconies on Gretchen's side of the inn looked across the parking lot at a river pier. It was a cold night by the ocean and Tashmo felt the cold, leaning against the railing, hands and wrists dangling over. Lydia Felker was standing at the end of the balcony, six feet away, as far away as she could be without jumping.

"Lloyd's dead," she said, "and I accept it, and though I accept that most of what he told me toward the end was imaginary, I think that it was true in a different way. Ted and Fred and Ned, the battle over parking spaces—I think we could spend the rest of our lives decoding what he meant."

She was older. She was gray and shorter, which Tashmo knew was a certain filling out around the midriff, which looked like shorter on a woman. He saw troopers smoking in the street. This made him think of smoking, which made him think of sex, which made him think fleetingly of butter.

"We'll be fine, me and the boy," Lydia said. "Your Director has promised to see about Lloyd's line-of-duty pension, and there's always my residuals. They rerun my *Cannons*, my two-part *Harry O*. Seventies crime drama is in vogue again on cable. The college kids just love it, the ties, the Fords, the facial hair. I get puppy-dog e-mails from sophomores at Caltech saying, 'You are the greatest frightened witness ever.' They ask me on dates, like I'm still the girl I was on television. So innocent, these kids. They ask me for a lock of hair. It's like something from a Brontë sisters novel—a lock of hair, a token, a remembrance. It's touching, this innocence, so I pluck a hair for them, dye it, and send it along with a form letter I've developed. Did you ever love me, Tashmo? Tell me, yes or no."

"No," he said.

"You're a coward to deny it. Remember the day it rained at the Tomb of the Unknown Soldier? You tried to dump me that day, but I was undumpable. Remember Reagan at his ranch and you so sexy with your saddle sores? Remember the trailer on the beach? We made love and scrambled eggs. Then Reagan went to the Hilton, dragging you and Lloyd to a rendezvous with Hinckley. I know you loved me in the trailer. Tashmo, tell the truth."

Helplessly he said, "What difference does it make?"

"I conceived a son the night we scrambled eggs. I named him Jasper Jason Felker, and we raised him together, Lloyd and I, and he has been nothing but a source of total joy since the first morning he made me puke from the womb, through pregnancy and birth and babyhood. Even his sullen adolescence was a gift to us. Jasper is a brilliant, soulful boy, an artist and a vagabond, and we loved him, Lloyd and I, and he is your son."

She was an actress. This was the first thing Tashmo told himself.

He said, "I thought you used protection."

"Ironic, no? It's always the small flaw which leads us, unwillingly, to something wonderful."

"Did you tell Lloyd?"

"How could I tell Lloyd that you—of all people, *you*—had betrayed him? Lloyd admired only two men in the world: you and Ronald Reagan. He thought you and Reagan were the same, or similar, as pets resemble masters. He said you and Reagan had an easy way of living. He meant this as a compliment. He said it was an admirable knack. He always said, 'Sure, intelligence and a glimmer of self-knowledge are attractive in a person, but there's something to be said for simply *living*. Cowboy Tashmo simply lives.' I think he always wished that he would some-day find a way to escape his brain and simply live. No, I couldn't tell him, not for many years. I waited until Jasper was a man. Then I told Lloyd about you and me, and he took it beautifully, as I knew he would. He said he didn't care. He said a father is someone who's around. He said he was at peace with his achievements. Then he quit the Plans Department or whatever you call it, and after that—well, we know what happened. Gretchen says he left the detail and walked into a flood. Did you see him when he did it? Was he happy? I think he was happy, Tash. He was simply living. Step outside the Dome. Step into the glorious and accidental world."

"Did you tell the kid?"

"No, and I don't plan to. Jasper shouldn't lose his father twice."

The river slid by.

Lydia said, "Jasper's waiting in the Windstar."

The Ford Windstar minivan was parked in the turnaround outside the Governor Weare. Tashmo paused, one hand on the door, looking back at the women on the curb. Lydia looked exultant. Gretchen, next to her, looked merely hard.

Tashmo climbed in the front seat.

Jasper Felker sat in back, strumming a guitar, listening to a CD through ear-phones. The CD was called *Learn to Play Guitar*.

Tashmo said, "They call me Tashmo. Your father was my best friend a long time ago. I'm sorry about what happened. I'm sick about it. And I want you to know that if you ever need to talk to someone—to a guy, an older guy, someone of your father's generation, I'd be honored to be that guy for you. I can't replace your father, Jasper. No one can. But maybe, I don't know, you might feel the need one day to hash out some life problem with a man of the world, and I want you to know that you can always count on me."

Jasper took the earphones off. "What's your name again?"

"Tashmo. Got a pen?"

"Not on me, no."

"Never mind, I'm in the book."

Jasper returned his hands to the guitar, touching but not playing. He was long-legged, as Tashmo was, and his hair was black, the blue-black of comic-strip characters, as Tashmo's had once been.

Tashmo cleared his throat. "So. Do you like sports?"

"I prefer modern dance."

"Oh yeah? Which ones? When I was your age we used to do the Funky Chicken. That's probably not considered very modern anymore. You're in college, right?"

"I dropped out," said Jasper. "Maybe I'll go back someday."

Tashmo said, "You should. College is important, son. It's the foundation of the rest of your life. I went to Vietnam and I got to college late. I wanted to drop out a million times, but I stuck it out, and you know what? I'm glad I did, because it's been the foundation of my life ever since."

Jasper said, "I'd like to hitchhike to Vancouver. That's my plan right now."

"Well, don't do anything hasty. My daughter is in college and she loves it. She just pledged a top-notch sorority, Rho Rho Rho. She's a beauty, my Jeanette, a real firecracker. You should meet her. I think you guys would really hit it off, and who knows? You two might even—no, wait a second, never mind, forget I said that. She only dates black guys anyway."

This wasn't going well. Tashmo tried to think of sons and fathers he had known, to summon all his knowledge on the subject. His own father, the North Dakota tavern keeper, was never one to overdo the father thing. The best advice he ever gave young Tashmo was to steer clear of college girls, on account of most of them were lesbian, or worse. Tashmo thought of Loudon Rhodes and the cokehead, Kobe Rhodes—not a model either. Then he thought of Ronald Reagan, Tashmo's hero in all things, and Reagan's ballet-dancing son. Tashmo remembered how Reagan's aides used to have to tell him that his son wasn't in high school anymore. This was in '86, when the son was nearly thirty. Maybe Reagan wasn't such a hero after all.

Tashmo blundered ahead. "But you do like girls, right?"

"Some," said Jasper. "Some I don't."

"I mean, generally."

"Are you trying to ask if I'm gay?"

"Of course not," Tashmo laughed. "Why—is that a question in your mind?"

"Not until you showed up."

"Well," said Tashmo, "if you ever feel the need to talk sexual preference, give me a call. We'll drink a beer, hit some wiffle balls, discuss the pros and cons. Or not. I leave it up to you."

The minivan went down the hill. Tashmo watched it go.

Gretchen was waving from the curb. She smacked Tashmo on the back.

She said, "Don't just stand there. Wave."

Vi had meant to go to Center Effing earlier. She had no right to go at all, of course (she had asked Gretchen's permission, which Gretchen had refused), which was why she had wanted to go that afternoon, when Gretchen and the detail were still mired in the hill towns. Vi had thought that she could hitch a ride with Christopher and Boone as far as Portsmouth, borrow a spare Taurus, visit Jens and Peta, and get back to the inn before the detail made it down from Rumsey, but this had proved impossible. After the lengthy (and, in Vi's view, pointless) Q&A with the informant, Little Flower, Christopher and Boone took Vi into Portsmouth, stopping at a Denny's on the highway, where they met two other threatmen coming up from Nashua with new bulletins concerning the recent theft of nitrate fertilizer from a golf course in that city. They had coffee at the Denny's, four agents in a banquette booth, comparing leads, discussing threats, this one's kind of interesting, this other one's played out. Vi, who didn't want to be there, spent half an hour listening to Boone work the phones as the two guys in from Nashua ordered cherry pie and Christopher called Beltsville to run a check on the names and AKAs Little Flower had supplied, Linda (also known as Lindy or Belinda) Johnson, Jo (for Josephine?) Jones, the threat men looking to the world like weary salesmen out hustling for customers.

From Denny's, the threat guys took Vi to the inn. By then the motorcade had come down from Rumsey, and Vi couldn't slip away until sometime after eight, when she bummed a pool car from the comm techs and started driving down the shore. She was flouting regulations, leaving the hotel, and risking a rip, or formal command discipline, a major rip at that, ten or twenty lost vacation days, Vi estimated, which Gretchen would administer only after a stiff, humiliating dressing-down. Gretchen believed in leadership by fear, but Vi was not afraid of rips or Gretchen anymore. The day had somehow lost its weave, its forward-moving order. Maybe it was leaving the motorcade in Severance, or maybe it was seeing the informant Little Flower imprisoned in her cabin by imagined signals. It made Vi think of her Crim Division time, her New York City tour, watching soaps and *Oprah* in the pens at JFK, tailing John Doe Russians from Brighton Beach to Queens, the endless, inconclusive tails, or running out to Nassau to collect the girl who called herself Mariah who had bought a bird with counterfeit to get real money back as change. (*Why the bird?* Vi asked; Mariah said, *He sings.*) It was tired, the scene with Little Flower, and later, in the Denny's—tired in the way New York had felt tired in the months after Walter Asplund passed away. Vi's solution in New York had been a transfer to Protection. What was her solution now? A transfer back to Crim? For the first time since leaving her hometown to join the Secret Service, Vi did the math and figured out that she was fifteen years and three months from retirement with pension.

1A came around the headlands into Center Effing. She saw the ocean by the road, beaches under streetlights, graffiti on cracked seawalls. She saw the gates to The Bluffs and signaled for a left.

Kai Boyle-Asplund was sitting, Indian-style, in the front room of the house watching the last scenes of a video called *Earthmovers!* The video consisted of muddy, grainy footage of large pieces of road-building equipment, graders, backhoes, and front loaders, being operated in a skilled and stylish fashion by burly, bearded men in yellow hard hats. Rolls of soil driven forward, boulders dropped like sugar cubes from bucket cranes into waiting dump trucks—Kai was transfixed.

"It's his porno," Peta said, pausing in the kitchen to look at her son. "He could watch it for hours."

Peta brought the pot of coffee from the counter to the table in the dining nook, where Vi and Jens were sitting surrounded by a homey clutter: sections of the morning *Union Leader* piled at the end, some bills, some torn-open window envelopes for bills, a dirty sippy cup, and a large blue bowl of oranges. Vi was drinking coffee, Jens was drinking some sort of reddish soda pop.

Vi had been there for two cups of coffee, maybe twenty minutes, and in that time, she and Jens and Peta had talked about nothing really, catching up. Jens sat across the table, pale and work-obsessed, saying little. Vi thought that he had lost a lot of weight.

Vi and Peta talked about Brian Ryan, the trainee threat investigator Peta had to deal with in connection with the Dental Building. Vi didn't know Brian Ryan personally, but she knew threatmen as a group.

"Ignore them," Vi advised. "They're paid to be obsessive. Eventually they go away and bother someone else."

Peta washed the sippy cup and left it in the dish rack. "I asked him why he cared," she said. "I mean, what's the connection? He said they couldn't wait until the ball drops. What the hell does that mean?"

"Different things," Vi said. "You guys paint this kitchen?"

Jens said, "It means a goddamn *bomb*, Pet, what do you think it means?"

Vi said, "Really, Peta, it's always nonsense with those guys. Was this kitchen yellow last time I was here?"

"Yes," said Peta, "but it was a different yellow. We got it painted in October. This yellow's called Morning Lemon."

Kai's video was ending.

Peta said, "All right now, Kaiyahoga. Book and bed, you know the ritual. Let's go, buddy, *up*."

The credits rolled as Peta hauled the boy onto her hip with a grunt and carried him into the small bedroom at the front of the house. Vi had slept in that bedroom when she came here after Hinman. She had slept on Kai's racecar bed, surrounded by Kai's toys and books and blocks and stuffed animal collection. Kai had slept between his parents in the master bedroom. Sleeping with the toys was part of what had made it a disorienting visit, Vi thought, waking up to see twenty pair of dolls' eyes staring into space.

Peta and Kai came out of the bedroom, laughing about something. Kai wore a pull-up and spaceman pajamas. They settled on the couch to read a book.

Vi listened from around the corner. She thought, I'm never in a home these days, a real home with real people living in it. Tower South, Vi's cubicle/studio near the Pentagon, didn't count as home. Little Flower's squalid prison cabin wasn't a home either—it was closer, in spirit, to the sinking mobile homes Vi had seen as drifting derelicts in Hinman, Illinois. But this formica-bright condo in The Bluffs was a real home to a real family—a sample of the country the bodyguards defended. Vi thought, that's the problem—I've lost touch.

Peta said, "Book time! What shall we read?"

Kai wanted *Look Out for Lollipops*, but this was a baby book, Peta explained. "You're not a baby, are you, Kai? You're a big guy now. Now here's a big-guy book— *Bomb-Dog Bob*. This was a special gift from your Auntie Vi."

It was typical of Peta to make a point of reading Vi's book when Vi was there, a thoughtful little gesture. Vi knew that *Bomb-Dog Bob* was a creepy and not exactly age-appropriate choice. She had bought it just before she had cleared out of Beltsville for her mental health leave in May. Coming home, she'd felt she ought to bring a gift for Kai, and *Bomb-Dog Bob* was the only kid's book they sold at the Protection Campus gift shop.

"I don't want *Bomb Bob*," said Kai on the couch. "Momma, I want *Lollipops*. You read it."

"That's not such a nice way to talk," Peta said. "What do we say when we want something?"

"Read it, Momma."

"*Please*. The magic word is *please*."

"Please Momma please I want please *Lollipops* please."

"But that's a baby book, Kai. Your Auntie Vi's book is more for big guys like you. It's the story of the Secret Service, which is where she works. Look, Kai, there's a dog. His name is Bob. Can you guess what he's looking for under that big limousine? When he's done, he gets a special treat."

Vi heard something hit the wall.

Peta said, "We don't throw books, Kai." Her voice was controlled. "That book was a gift from somebody who loves you a whole lot. Pick it up, son."

"What's the magic word?" asked Kai.

"Pick up the damn book."

Vi couldn't hear what Kai said.

Peta said, "I'm counting, Kai. One— Two—"

Jens said, "He loses his nerve around three usually."

"Thank you," Peta said. "Now get back on the couch."

Vi listened as Peta read to Kai.

"'Licky was a lollipop,'" Peta started bouncingly. "'One day he asked his daddy, "What's this big stick for?"'"

Kai said, "You're skipping the beginning."

"This is the beginning," Peta said. "See Licky with his daddy?"

"Read the first page—Momma look."

"Oh all right," said Peta. She read, "'*Look Out For Lollipops*, by Nancy Klein-felt and Joan Melissa Oates. A My First Reader Book. London. New York. Sydney.'"

Kai turned the page for her.

Peta read, "'*Look Out for Lollipops*' by Nancy Kleinfelt and Joan Melissa Oates. All rights reserved. Printed in the United States of America. No part of this book may be reproduced or transmitted in any form or by any means—'"

Kai sighed. This was his favorite part of every book—his mother's voice, the certainties.

"'—electronic or mechanical, including photocopying, recording, or any information storage and retrieval system without written permission from the publisher.'"

Kai said, "I love you, Momma."

Peta said, "I love you too. Now let's read about Bob. I'm curious, aren't you?"

Kai said, "No—more *Lollipops*."

"'Licky was a lollipop.' God I hate this book. 'One day he asked his daddy, "What's this big stick for?" His daddy said, "That's so they can lick you, son—"'"

Kai turned the pages as Peta read them. Together, they followed Licky's journey of discovery to the candy emperor and finally to the belly of the boy who loved him best of all. They came to the last word on the last page, which was actually *all*.

Peta said, "The end." She closed *Lollipops* solemnly.

Peta carried Kai past Jens and Auntie Vi for a round of sloppy goodnight kisses. The boy climbed out of Peta's arms into Vi's lap. Vi hugged the child, arms around his neck. His little hands patted her back and he pecked a kiss on her hair. Vi felt weak suddenly, her nose in the boy's shoulder. Tears started in her eyes. She did not know why. She barely knew this child.

"Go," she said, lifting Kai to Peta. "You go and have a good sleep, Kai, okay?"

Peta carried the boy down the hall to his bedroom. Kai bounced on the bed. Peta snapped the lights off.

"Sleep well, Kaiyo."

"Momma, stay—" said Kai.

"There's nothing to be frightened of," Peta said.

"Momma—"

"All right," Peta said, "I'll lie down with you, Kai, but only for a minute."

Vi heard Peta climb into the bed next to the child, the creaking of the wooden frame, a luffing of the sheets.

Jens said, "She'll be asleep before he is, just watch. We go through this every night." Jens looked at the wall, listening. He said, "She works too hard."

Vi said, "Peta."

Jens was nodding. "She's always a zombie by eight thirty."

Vi took an orange from the bowl. She wasn't hungry for an orange, but she liked the rough, cool feel of it, the rounded weight, the pleasingly astringent cleaning-product smell of a ripe orange. She couldn't get over how it had felt, Kai patting her back, those tiny hands.

"Mom sends us those oranges from Florida," said Jens. "She enrolled us in a fruit club of some sort. Once a month, oranges. Also sometimes grapefruit. Never lemons, though. We have the walls for that."

Evelyn Asplund had moved to a tennis-themed community between Tampa and Dade City. She played doubles every morning, volunteered for her good causes, visited her Boston cousins who had settled in surrounding towns. Rumor had it that she was dating a man from her development, a retired Navy captain, a widower named Burt. Burt had five grown children and a sailboat named *The Escapade*.

Jens said, "Want a knife to cut that?"

"No," said Vi, rolling the rough orange in her hands. "I'm not hungry."

"Take it for the road," said Jens. "Take six. We're almost due for the next shipment anyway. I always feel a bit of pressure when the fruit arrives. You feel like you have to eat all of them before they go bad, especially since there's a *club* involved—certain obligations are implied. It's a race against rot, getting all the fruit consumed. We freeze it and make smoothies, that's our fallback."

"What's the word on Burt?"

"They're just good friends," said Jens. "Don't you get the e-mails?"

Evelyn, a New Englander in exile, had taken to e-mail with the fervor of a Concord Transcendentalist. Her e-mails read like the letters of Louisa May Alcott, thoughtful, trenchant essays filled with observations about race relations in mid-Florida, and the country's moral soul, and the cruelties she saw doing volunteer work at the local shelter for battered and abandoned pets. Cats were brought in starving, dogs were brought in with broken ribs. Evelyn said the problem was that people saw their pets as consumer goods, like shoes or a new hat The towns of Florida coughed up a lot of surplus weirdness in the form of abused pets. The deputies brought in exotic Burmese ferrets, terrified to viciousness, yaks half dead from dehydration—even once a baby Shango monkey (a gentle jungle breed) with strange symptoms, lolling eyes, bleeding gums, a racing heart. Fearing the outbreak of a new disease, a primate version of mad cow, the shelter vets did blood work and it was determined that the monkey's former owner had gone to the trouble and expense of addicting it to methamphetamines, apparently thinking it was funny to see a monkey stoned and crashing into furniture. Evelyn said that pets and how we treated them were the secret index of our soul, and you could see the future of the nation at any shelter in the land. Her dark e-mails notwithstanding, Evelyn had clearly made or found a happy final phase of life in Florida, healthy from the tennis, busy at the shelter, and Burt was a good man, she said, who had no expectations for their relationship.

Vi said, "I get the e-mails, but I don't always read them. They pile up when I'm away. The one about the monkey, though—that was truly fucked. I've told that story to a lot of people. Everyone gets mad about that monkey."

"Yes," said Jens. "But still, it's pets. There's something about spilling out that much compassion for a *pet*. It's trivial somehow."

Vi thought of their father, suddenly. She remembered Evelyn and Walter fighting over the mutts Evelyn adopted from the pound. Walter grumbled every time the dogs dug up the lawn, or came home smelling like the Effing River, or barked at something in the marshes at four a.m. and started every dog within a quarter mile barking. Evelyn said she had no choice but to adopt the dogs. "They gas them if no one claims them in a month," she said. "I can't bear to see a poor, innocent dog gassed." Walter, being Walter, marshaled Aristotle, pointing out that gassing wasn't punishment, that animals in general were neither innocent nor guilty, that her use of these terms was, in this context, incoherent—a bad thing to be guilty of in Walter's universe. The soft love of pet owners was beyond him. He said, "They gas the innocent cats too. Why aren't there forty rescued cats running around here?" And Evelyn said, "Because the dogs don't like them."

These were probably the worst fights in what was otherwise a quiet, serviceable marriage. Vi remembered watching from the stairs, hiding behind a banister, as Walter and Evelyn went at it in the front room, the basic opposition, Mom and Dad, a cats-and-dogs-type thing, with Walter very much the dog, ironically, relying on the sheer weight of his reason, and Evelyn the cat, clawing, unpredictable. Evelyn said, "I do what I can. I don't save every animal, or even most of them, but I do what I can, which is more than you can say, Walt. All your arguments add up to No. No, there is no God. No, there'll be no Christmas carols in the house. But what have you ever actually *done*? You scribble on your money. Cross out God. I watch you. But what does that accomplish, other than getting your children beat up in school and creating pointless controversy with a bunch of Air Force bozos?" Vi at the age of eight or nine had felt a nauseous thrill, watching her mother try to wound her father with a word like *bozo*—it was thrilling, silly, terrifying, in the way a really scary horror movie is always close to being totally hilarious. Vi always took her father's side as a child. He was Walter, after all, a stubborn, odd, quixotic figure in their town; he seemed to need the protection of a daughter's loyalty more than Evelyn, who was more like other people, more at home in groups. Vi rooted for her father, watching from the stairs, but thinking of it now, she saw Evelyn's side too. Vi hoped that Burt the sailing widower was the lighthearted type.

Vi said to Jens, "The monkey isn't trivial to her. You sound like Walter now."

Jens stood up and said, "Let's take a walk."

"I don't think about him much. I'll bet you think about him all the time."

Jens and Vi were walking down the lawn, a slight slope to a drop-off, beyond which lay the rocks of Effing Head, the crashing surf, the bay. The condo blazed behind them, threw their shadows down the lawn. Their shadows were absurdly tall, gunfighterish somehow.

"Why?" asked Vi.

"Because you were always closer," Jens said. "You and Dad. You were his favorite."

Vi said, "That's bullshit. I remember you guys in the den after supper. He's reading about how to adjust a toxic spill. You're reading about ham radio. Two peas in a pod. You were smart, Jens, and Dad respected smart. I was like his little buddy mascot, which was cool with me, I'm not complaining. But you, Jens—you were *smart*."

They had come to the end of the lawn. There was no moon. Vi saw the odd flash of whitecap, but otherwise the bay was absolutely black.

Jens was looking out. "You know what he said to me? It was practically my last conversation with him. The game was going great then and the monsters were like runaway best-sellers. So we were talking about the monsters, how I write them, all of that, Hamsterman and Seeing Eye and Farty Pup, except I could never bring myself to say *Farty* to Dad, so I called him Poopy Pup, whatever. Now, Dad's a well-read guy, but he doesn't know a goddamn thing about large software systems, and how hard it is to make something run within x kilocycles or a y-sized byte group. You know what Dad says? He says, essentially, it's trash. It's immoral or amoral. All my work. I know the game itself, the stuff you see, the monsters and the plugs for snow blowers and the frequent-flier-mile tie-ins—well, it's pretty bad. But the code, the engineering—that's *totally* different. I don't expect him to understand the beauty, or frankly the *honor*, of the engineering. But I do expect him to trust me, trust my judgment. A parent's attitude should be, if my child's doing it, it must be worth doing."

Vi laughed. "We'll see if you're still saying that when Kai's sixteen and getting high off Vicks VapoRub."

"I wasn't sixteen," Jens said. "I was a grown man with a child of my own. He told me I had to quit. *Quit?* This game is my chance to make some real money. I'm not greedy, but I'd like to get out of the rat race, have more time with Kai, maybe see Peta not have to work so hard, so she's not a zombie every night. I'd like to do some pure research—and, yes, maybe really leave my mark with something great. Are these *wrong* things to want?"

"No," said Vi.

"I made a compromise. Dad thought I wanted the money 'cause I wanted yachts and sports cars. And if that's your motivation, then sure, working at BigIf is probably pretty shameful. But I've never been that way. And that's what hurt me when he said I had to quit. I looked at him and thought, I'm your son and you don't even *know* me. You know how that felt?"

"Pretty shitty probably."

"It felt lonely. Isn't that strange? Then I thought about it and it made me mad, and then he died, and that made me even madder, because now I'm stuck being angry at him forever." Jens turned and looked around the yard. "Remember last time you were here? We went out to the old house, had a picnic for his birthday. I thought it would be good for you, because you and he were so close, and frankly, Vi, you looked like you needed help that weekend. You looked like you'd just come from a train wreck."

"No," said Vi, "a flood."

"So I figured, this will be good for Vi, and she's my little sister, and she's the only thing I've got left, really, from the old days, so let me try and help her out. But that whole weekend, Vi, and especially at the house, you were giving me these looks, this blankness. I thought it was because of whatever you had just come through."

Vi remembered the weekend after Hinman, how she couldn't stop herself from scanning.

Jens said, "Then I realized—no, it's about *me*. She thinks I'm a sellout asshole, just like Walter did—of course she does, she was always his favorite. I thought, where does Vi get off judging me?"

Vi said, "Listen, Jens—that's all in your head. I was all fucked up back then. It had nothing to do with you."

"You're telling me the way you look at me has nothing to do with me? Does that sound like it makes sense to you?"

"Well," said Vi, "it's true. Not everything in your life has to do with you. It's easier once you realize that. Give Walter a break. The guy was human, big surprise. If you're happy in your life, what difference does it make?"

gotv (tuesday)

No movement was simple, but jogging was especially complex. Gretchen would have outlawed jogging altogether as an unacceptable security environment (the dawdling perimeter, the cover of the trees, the problem of thru-traffic, the exposure in 360 of a slowly moving man), but Fundeberg wouldn't hear of it. The point of jogging, Fundeberg believed, was to beam the people images of a vital, active man, fit for every challenge. This was important anywhere, and more so in New Hampshire, where the VP was losing droves of undecided voters to the senator, a younger man with fresh ideas and much better hair.

Gretchen tried to compromise—let's jog in a stadium, I can lock it down—but Fundeberg demanded neighborhood backdrops, typical and scenic, and would not consider tracks of any sort. Tracks are laned and banked, he said, a theater of speed. People think Olympics. Our guy, with his pudding-muscled, fiftyish physique, would look pathetic gasping on a track, a disappointed loser reliving high school glory, hearing nonexistent cheers. No, they needed neighborhoods, Fundeberg believed, houses, hedges, and parked cars, a line of picket fences, bikes on the sidewalks, hopscotch chalked out on the driveways. A man jogging past this scene looked disciplined yet friendly, at peace with his surroundings, open to the day. Gretchen hated running through a neighborhood. Cars meant car bombs to the Service, people in their houses couldn't be evicted, garages and backyards, all those dormer windows—an uncoverable layout. Some nut could be sitting in his living room, eating cereal, oiling his carbine, letting the entourage draw near.

Because the jog was especially complex, Gretchen was up early, making the arrangements. By half past six, she was showered, dressed, and eating breakfast with Elias in the hotel's coffee shop. Elias had the traffic plan for the jog route. They reviewed it one more time, then Boone Saxon came in and ordered scrambled eggs, and Elias left to prep the route. Boone and Gretchen went over the day's schedule, the jog, a drop-in photo op at a McDonald's on the turnpike, a big speech at a rally, then a motorcade to Manchester for seven more events, a brutal campaign day. Rain had been predicted, but it wasn't raining yet.

"Be snowing by the time we get to Manchester," said Boone, shaking hot sauce on his eggs.

Gretchen knew a few things about Boone, and one of these was that he liked hot sauce on his eggs, though not on any other food she had ever seen him eat. She had watched him eat a lot of meals over her year as chief-of-detail. Boone briefed her over breakfast on the road and it was usually a scene like this, Gretchen buzzing from the coffee, limited by diet to a toasted bagel (dry), Boone across the table, shoveling his eggs, and talking with professional dispassion about car bombs, right-to-lifers, released mental patients who were former Marine snipers, and whether it would snow in Manchester that day. His voice was comforting, a drone.

Another thing she knew about Boone Saxon was that he had led the search for Lloyd Felker after Hinman. She had learned this in the course of her long talk with the Director on the quad in Beltsville, and it had surprised her at the time. Boone was based at Beltsville, where Felker had spent his prime. Boone, hunting Felker, was hunting a friend. If the job had bothered Boone, he didn't show it, and it probably didn't bother him. It was duty, number one. It was logic, number two: Felker on the loose was a giant liability, as Felker himself would have been the first to understand. Knowledge of the Dome was a weakness of the Dome if turned against it. Which meant that Felker, as the father of the Dome, had been consumed by his own creation. Gretchen was still looking for a lesson in the mess, the rise, glory, and destruction of Lloyd Felker, senior analyst in Plans. She wanted to ask Boone—maybe he would know. Boone knew Felker's story too, or part of it, and the parts he knew he knew better than she did. He was there the day they found Felker at the first-aid station. Boone could tell her how he had looked and talked that day. Was he really nuts? Or had he simply shed a skin of contradictions in the river? Would Boone know the difference? Gretchen doubted it.

In fairness, Boone only knew the official story: how Felker wrote the Dome and how, in his twilight, he had tried to make it stronger by *un*writing it, by writing murder plots to give the planners something real to plan against; how the Service shut him down; how Felker, seeking freedom from the thing he had created, did something risky and quite foolish, it now seemed, which was to go out in the field and *join* the Dome as deputy lead agent. He saw what Beltsville never saw—that there are no theories in the field, no zones of pure control, there is only waiting, boredom, preparation, and the crowds are always out there, a seascape of potential threats, waves in all directions, cresting and receding and re-forming somewhere else.

The official story, though not inaccurate, missed the other side of every agent's life, your marriage or your lovers, your kids and lawn and dog. For Gretchen, this meant her son, asleep at that hour (she looked at her watch). For Felker it meant— what? All the years he worked in Beltsville, commuting from his farm, building a grand structure on his Certainties, he went home again each night to a mirror-set of certainties: this is my house, this is my chair, this is my wife, Jasper is my son. Gretchen thought the real unraveling of Felker had begun not when he started stalking/protecting Miss Nguyen, nor before that when he left the Dome in Hin-man, nor before that with his murder plots in Beltsville. She thought the crackup started on the night Lydia told him that his son was not his son. How did Lloyd, then a planner of unquestioned orthodoxy, process this new data? Several options were available. One: denounce his wife and leave her, the macho option—but what about Jasper? Two: forgive, forget, move on—you'd have to be Jesus to do that. Three: accept, acknowledge, roger-copy, keep the family whole, outwardly forgive, but, inside, brood and wonder—if my life has been based on lies, if nothing that I thought I knew has turned out to be true, if uncertainty is queen, what does this imply about the Dome? Gretchen thought the breakdown started there, Felker ask-ing the first, forbidden question and following the answers where they led him. They led him to dead ends, reversal and inversion, Felker guarding Nguyen, scaring her with "safety," a fine and final paradox.

Boone droned on, summarizing threats. Gretchen listened, or tried to. She was thinking, that's the story, fine, but what's the lesson? Maybe that's not the ques-tion—maybe it was lame to expect a lesson. So, what *is* the question? There can't be no lesson *and* no question, right?

Tashmo and Elias drove the chosen length of river road twice in each direction with a Portsmouth traffic captain, watching the odometer, measuring a mile. The mile ran from a rotary, down a hill, around the bend, around another bend, past nine quiet

side streets, and up a gentle grade to a four-light intersection. There were houses
on one side, woods on the other, sloping to the river's edge.

Coming back the second time, Elias stopped the car. He spread a city map on
the dashboard and told the captain to close the rotary to all traffic for a distance of
a quarter mile and the four-light intersection southbound only. The side streets
would have to be secured in both directions for at least five blocks.

"Five blocks?" said the captain. "How are these folks supposed to get to work?"

"Four blocks ought to do it," said Tashmo from the backseat.

"What about the woods?" Elias asked. "They worth sweeping, do you think?"

The captain said, "There's nothing down there but the river, junky cars and old
refrigerators. Sometimes in the warmer months you'll get hobos living in the cars."

The captain was an oldster, many times a granddad from the looks of him, and
he made the homeless sound almost picturesque. Elias went over the traffic plan
again, making sure the captain had all the arrows in his head, no flow going this way,
no flow going that way.

The Army trucks appeared and Tashmo led a group of soldiers to the river
woods. Another group of soldiers took the bomb dogs up the street. The dogs ran,
ass-waggling, snouts to the pavement, sniffing the tires and the tailpipes of the
trucks they had arrived in, finding no explosives, moving on to the parked cars,
sniffing trunks and tires, the mailboxes, the trash bags on the sidewalk, the
hydrants on the grass. One dog paused and took a leak.

Cop cars started showing up, parking on the shoulder around the Army trucks.
The captain went up the street to seal the intersections, leaving a young sergeant
to liaise.

Tashmo came back from the woods. "Hobo check is negative," he said.

Elias called Gretchen at the coffee shop, reporting the all clear.

Tashmo was standing with the young sergeant, looking at the map spread on
the hood. The sergeant came from the motorcycle unit. He wore a leather jacket,
blue jodhpurs, and white helmet, chin cup unsnapped and dangling.

"Where's the nearest trauma center?" Tashmo asked. "Show me on the map
here, Sarge."

The sergeant pointed to the map.

"What would be the quickest route, trafficwise?"

The sergeant traced a route.

"Where's the nearest place the gunship could put down?"

The sergeant pointed. "That's a little city park. Not too many trees."

"Where's the nearest halfway decent breakfast place?"

"Right up here," the sergeant said.

"What is that, McDonald's? 'Cause I'm sick of McDonald's. Eli loves McDonald's, but I'm sick of it."

"It's a diner," said the sergeant.

"Is it any good?"

"They say it's pretty good."

"The coffee or the food? Because some diners with bad food have excellent coffee. The coffee fools you into ordering the food."

"They just say it's generally good."

"Do they do a breakfast sandwich? Hey Eli, want a breakfast sandwich? Never mind, I'm sure he does."

"I assume they do," the sergeant said. "We could call them when they're open and find out."

"When they're open?"

"I don't think they open until later."

"How about a halfway decent breakfast place that's *open*?" Tashmo said. "What do you think, this is some kind of academic inquiry? I'm *hungry*, Sergeant."

The sergeant pointed to the map.

Tashmo said, "What's that?"

"McDonald's, but they do the Egg McMuffin."

"Fuck it, never mind. I'll just get some coffee."

"Should I wait here then?"

"Why, do they deliver?"

The sergeant left to get the coffee. The sniper vans unloaded, the bomb dogs finished with their sweep. A campaign van parked on a side street. Several aides piled out, Fundeberg's young minions. They started an inspection tour, making sure the street was typical and scenic.

Tashmo was sitting in the front seat of the Taurus. He watched the campaign workers frantically chalk hopscotch squares on the sidewalk as Elias scanned the housefronts through binoculars. The snipers on the rise were scanning the same housefronts. The gunship overhead covered the backyards and the river woods. Tashmo, rooting through the glove compartment, came out with an orange. He bit the skin to get a start and peeled it with his thumbnail.

"Eli."

"What?"

"Who had this car before us?"

"I think the comm techs brought it down from the Moose Lodge. Why?"

"No reason." Tashmo finished peeling. "Want some orange?"

"No, I'm good," Elias said.

Up the road, two cops blocked a driveway with their car and argued with a man in painter's pants who was sitting in the cab of a large luxury pickup.

The captain hailed Elias on the comm. "I'm with this painter guy down here," the captain said. "He wants to know why he can't leave his driveway."

Elias said, "Explain the situation."

Tashmo said, "And tell the guy, nice truck. That rig goes for thirty Gs, Eli. I priced it when I got my little Jap."

Tashmo ate the orange like an apple, in big bites, sucking juice and spitting seeds as he chewed.

"Hey Eli."

"What?" said Elias, still scanning the housefronts.

"How long you been married?"

Sean Elias smiled. "Seven blissful years."

"Out of how many total?"

"Nine," Elias said. "I've been very blessed."

"You ever cheat?"

"On my wife?"

"No, your taxes, dopey. Of course your fucking wife."

"I don't cheat on either, Tashmo, actually."

"Ever come perilously close?"

"Well, it's hard to say—it's so subjective nowadays. How do you depreciate a timeshare on a sailboat? I took a guess, but maybe I was cheating without knowing it."

"How about your wife?"

"We file jointly."

"Ever come close to cheating on her?"

"Never," said Elias.

"Why the hell not?"

"Well," Elias said, "I have my faith. Also, I stay sober at office parties. What's on your mind there, Tash? Something wrong with Shirl?"

"I'm just asking," Tashmo said. "I have this buddy, see? He cheated on his wife a long time ago. He cheated with this one woman in particular, the wife of his best friend."

"This anyone I know?"

"No—it's just a guy from my Bible study class."

"You're doing Bible study, Tash? Good for you."

"Yeah, thanks—anyway, now the husband's dead and the lady's saying that her son with the husband is actually my buddy's son and has been all along. It could be pretty messy, if it all comes out."

"Sounds like it's already messy," said Elias, looking up the street. "It's nearly J-hour—where's the goldang motorcade?"

The motorcade had left the inn thirteen minutes late and lost more time along the way. The roadblocks coming north were less than textbook, two intersections not locked down, two others locked down partially, and for at least a quarter mile there they were actually *in traffic*, surrounded by non-decoys, by true ordinary cars, part of the world's commute, which Gretchen didn't like one bit. She hailed Tashmo on the comm and gave him a good reaming for fucking up the roadblocks. This wasn't fair. She knew it; Tashmo knew it too. While the intersections coming north were on the master traffic plan, this aspect of the jog had been farmed out to the locals. If anybody was to blame, it was the traffic captain or maybe Sean Elias, who, as deputy lead agent, was the ranking man on scene. It wasn't a big deal, though it created more delay, and even if it was, it wasn't Tashmo's fault, but Gretchen let him have it anyway. She was thinking about Felker, still looking for a lesson (or at least a question), and she was mad at Tashmo. She wanted him to suffer for the role he'd played, betraying Felker in the good old Reagan days, fathering the son who wasn't Felker's. Few things made Gretchen madder than men who tried to slide through life. Thoughts of Jasper Felker had led her back to Tevon, and to Carlton Imbry, Tevon's father in L.A., another slick-ass law-enforcement Casanova, a black Tashmo almost. She gave Tashmo a tongue-lashing for the two blown roadblocks. Tashmo, to his credit, took it like a man, not finking on Elias or the captain.

Gretchen signed off. It was seven fifty-five. She dug through the pockets of her overcoat, looking for her cell phone. Every morning on the road, Gretchen called her son in Maryland. It didn't sound like much in the mothering department—a phone call, what was that? Pathetic—especially with Tev at such an awkward age and with all the trash out there, drugs and gangs and thievery and evil on CD, computer, television, movies, drops of poison in the well. She tried to protect him from the poison in the well. When she was home, she took him to the movies at the mall. She let him pick which one, PG, PG-17, she'd even do an R. She knew that movies got R ratings for sex, violence, or explicit language. Explicit language didn't worry her; kids heard worse in schoolyards. The violence scared her, but the sex scenes were the worst—damn embarrassing to sit through with your kid right next to you. She let him pick the movie because he wouldn't go to any movie she had picked, and wasn't that the purpose of the cineplex, the batting cage, the sneaker store, Tevon-time, son-and-mother bonding, all of that? Tevon liked cop movies, so they saw a lot of them. Often she was so worn out from the road that she fell asleep before the first burst of small-arms fire and missed the scene, somewhere toward the middle of the movie, where the cop rivals became buddies, and she woke up to explosions at the climax, throwing herself on the person sitting next to her, screaming in the dark, *Tashmo, Felker, gun gun gun!* The ushers would hustle down the aisle and eject them and Tev would be so angry and embarrassed, riding home.

Gretechen knew her morning phone calls weren't a substitute for mothering. She could only hope that Tevon understood that it was a major pain in her ass to line up five private minutes at exactly seven fifty-five each day. The jogs, generally scheduled for eight, were small invasions to bring off; she couldn't really stop the show to call her house and tell her son to get out of bed. Seven fifty-five was an awkward time for Gretchen, but she was stuck with it. If she called before that time, Tev would be in REM sleep and a SWAT team couldn't rouse him. There was no point in trying to do battle with her son's biological clock. Tev's clock was more like a biological Stonehenge, mute boulder, enduring and immovable, slow cycle of the seasons, spring planting and the harvest, Tev wakes and lies there for a time and slowly, very slowly does he reach to scratch his buttcrack. If she called much past that time, Tev would be awake and still in bed, but already behind schedule, not yet showered, much less dressed. The school bus left at half past eight and Tev would have to go through at least four outfits, careful self-inspections in the mirror, before he was ready for his cereal and the daily hunt for the missing backpack, which contained the undone homework and a certain crucial comic book he'd be needing if they sent him to detention. Her phone call set it all in motion—shower, dressing, breakfast, the dead run to the bus—and if she called at eight, say, or five minutes past, Tevon's morning went to hell from there. She told him what a pain it was to call on his schedule, not to make him feel guilty, but to let him know that he was fully worth it.

The vans pushed through traffic. Gretchen got her mother first. Mildred Williams was her usual fount of small complaints involving joints and poor digestion. Gretchen asked her to get Tevon—*it's late, Mother, for chrissakes put him on.*

Tev picked up in his bedroom. "Hello, Moms."

Gretchen said, "It's late—you should be in the shower."

But Tevon was relaxing like a pasha in his undies. "So how's the P machine?" he asked.

The what? Then Gretchen remembered the lie she had told him in the driveway Sunday afternoon, the secret weapon of Protection, the two-three-one-two-three-six-P, the ring of energy around her in the crowds, the reason why he didn't have to be afraid for her.

"It's fine," she said. "It's great. They're getting it off the truck right now."

Tevon said that he had been thinking about the P machine. He'd figured out that it was a lie.

"Like Santa Claus," he laughed.

Gretchen said, "Oh yeah? Well, I'm looking at the P machine right now, pal. They've got the extension cord out and everything. Come on, Tev, it's late. Get your butt into the shower."

Tevon said that he had been talking to Carlton Imbry in L.A. —just talking, no big deal, they were having some good talks.

"You can't stop me, Moms," Tevon said. "I can talk to my father if I want."

Gretchen felt tired and afraid, hearing this—Tevon plunging into the uncertainty of fathers and of love.

She said, "I can stop you, son. You don't think I can? Wait'll I get home—we'll see who can't stop what."

Tev said nothing. It wasn't a long call.

She said, "Take a shower, Mr. Man. Let's try and make the bus today."

The vans were out of traffic, coming up a hill. She looked out at the neighborhoods. Typical and scenic, she thought bitterly. She was starting to have fundamental doubts about herself. Not about her job, her methods as lead agent, the way she drove her people. The whole team had heard her ream out Tashmo and most of them understood traffic plans well enough to know that the bungled roadblocks were not Tashmo's fault. Tashmo wasn't beloved by the other agents. They saw him for the selfish civil service schemer that he was, but they also knew that when you gave him an assignment, it usually got handled (usually by Elias—Tashmo had Elias wrapped around his finger). If Tashmo handled it, he handled it on Tashmo-time, complaining the whole way, but in the end the thing got done. The agents knew that Gretchen wasn't in the right, blasting Tashmo for the roadblocks, and they probably chalked it up to She's a bitch.

Gretchen didn't want to be a bitch. She wanted to be an asshole, a bastard, a ball-buster, but she had to admit that she was sometimes bitchy too. She knew that every slipup, every lapse, could lead to Tevon in his room watching an assassination on TV. This was another thing she had lived through as a kid (Dr. King in Memphis, Robert Kennedy in L.A. —blood looked black on the black-and-white TV her mother had in '68, when the country went to hell). Tevon was her country now, the only country Gretchen knew, and he wouldn't see the VP die on television, not while she was chief-of-detail. She drove her agents to protect her son, and if they didn't like it, well, they could fuck themselves and go back to Crim, in more or less that order. This was Gretchen's way, maybe not the best way, but she didn't doubt that it had to be her way. Riding in the van, she was doubting something else. Was she a good mother? She thought of Tevon searching for himself in cyberspace. She saw him at the terminal, typing the same lonely search, *Tevon Williams*, *T. J. Williams*, *Tevon Joseph Williams*, trying it all-caps to see if this picked up some hits—it broke her heart. The search had led him to back to L.A. and to Carlton

Imbry, and now they were talking, son and father, though she had forbidden it. She couldn't let Tevon come to know his father because Carlton Imbry was one of those handsome, talented, weak men who hurt you in the end, and she couldn't watch her son get hurt. She also didn't want him to grow into that kind of man—she couldn't watch that either. She had built a Dome named Gretchen Williams all around her son, his promise and his future, but she was tired and she couldn't stand the fighting, or the silence on the phone, or the locked doors at the house, and maybe it was time to let it go.

The motorcade took the last corner like a centipede, in segments, van after van, arriving at the top of the jog route only twenty minutes behind schedule. On Gretchen's order, the rotary was sealed by flashing cruisers. Traffic started backing up in three directions. Some commuters, running late already, tried to go around, following the side streets, which were also blocked. The VP and his party stretched on the shoulder. Gretchen watched them stretch, cell phone in her hand. Through the trees she saw the river, a blue police boat midstream, frogmen jumping backwards off the deck.

Gretchen took a deep breath. She punched a number in L.A.

A woman's voice: "'lo —?"

Soft as a kitten's, Gretchen thought. She stiffened. "Is this Bambi?"

"This is Brandy. Who is this?"

"This is Lead Agent Williams of the U.S. Secret Service. Is Carlton there?"

"He's sleeping."

"Is he sleeping there?"

"Yes but—"

"Wake his slick ass up, girlfriend. Tell him Gretchen's on the line."

There was fumbling and whispering in California. Brandy's voice said, "Carl, Carl, *Carl*—" Gretchen heard what sounded like a drinking glass knocked over and a mattress being bounced on.

"Gretchen," Carlton Imbry said.

Same old midnight DJ voice. He said her name a certain way, made it musical, a breathy sort of *Gre*, you barely heard the *tch*. It was as if no time had passed. Ten years had passed.

"I've been meaning to call you, Gretchen—damn, wow, how you been? Kind of *early* to be calling the West Coast, but, hey, it's really great to hear your voice. You been good? You sound good. Tevon—well, I'm sure you know that we've been talking. He's a great kid, Gretchen. He knows all about my cases. I really get a kick out of talking to him. Of course, the phone bills are a little steep, but it's worth it, and Tev says you have a real cheap calling plan, so it's not a big deal. You know, I think it's time for you and me to sit down together, discuss a couple things, don't you? I'll be out east in a few weeks. I'm retired now. Over Christmas. We had a nice affair at Spago's, the mayor came and everything. I've got a couple jobs lined up, reality consulting, *Law & Order*, and this new show, *Black Dragnet* for BET, which is based on me, on some of my big cases over the years. Anyway, you don't want to hear all this. I'll be in New York, let's see, the week of the twenty-third. I thought I might bop down to Washington on the twenty-fifth. No, wait—I'm looking at my book—I've got dinner that night. What about breakfast, the twenty-sixth? My treat, you pick the place. What's the best and most expensive place for breakfast in D.C.?"

"You're a failure," Gretchen said.

Carlton Imbry sighed. "This is about Tevon. Let's try and think about what's best for Tevon. He wants to come out here in the summer, spend some time, and I'd like to get your input. I mean it's fine with me, it's great, depending on some shoots we're looking at for *Dragnet*, July and maybe August. How's breakfast on the twenty-sixth look for you?"

Gretchen said, "I don't want to eat with you. I don't want to be sitting in a restaurant and say 'Pass the salt' and have you pass the salt. I don't want a normal minute in your presence. 'Cause I'm past that now. Tevon can go to California in the summer if he wants. But I'm warning you, Carlton: if you hurt or disappoint that boy in any way, if you are for one lousy second anything less than the hero he's created for himself, I swear to God I'll come out there and burn your house down."

It felt good, pressing END.

They were ready to start jogging on the river road, waiting only for the second press bus, which had missed a turn. Gretchen sent a cruiser for the bus as the comm techs in van four went operational, activating jammers to disrupt nonauthorized signals, including point-to-point voice communication, radio-controlled bombs, radio-controlled toys, cell and cordless phones, broadcast television, TV clickers, and automatic garage doors for a radius of about two thousand yards. The press bus appeared without the cruiser. Reporters piled out, cursing at the driver, who cursed back at them.

Two motorcycles led the way, crawling down the river road, followed by two cruisers, dome lights flashing. Van one, behind the cruisers, had the rugged look of a war wagon but inside the blacked-out windows it was empty except for a driver and a sideman looking out. Van two, next in line, held a driver, a sideman, backup troopers, and the SWATs. One SWAT was crouched low, pointing a .50-caliber machine gun out the side door at the woods. The other SWATs were kneeling on the last bench, pointing their machine guns out the back doors, keeping a visual on the bodies jogging in their exhaust. Herc and Bobbie were flanking the VP, who wheezed. Vi was at the VP's heels, keeping to his awkward pace, not quite running, not quite walking, fending off photographers and cameramen who danced around the party, shouting "Over here!" and "Look this way!" and "Can I get a wave?" A few reporters followed too, shouting questions, holding their tape recorders in the air. Van three, behind the joggers, carried the extraction team for this event, Gretchen, O'Teen, and the troopers, Tashmo and Elias standing on the bumper, gripping the luggage rack. Behind the comm techs in van four was an ambulance followed by a cruiser and two motorcycles.

They came up on the first quarter mile. People watched from driveways, sidewalks, porches, lawns. They watched from upstairs windows, from carports and garages. They stood there holding mugs, folded newspapers, car keys, crullers, muffins, and the garbage. They stood alone, amazed, unsure of what to do. Some heard the muffled *wud-wud-wud* and looked for the gunship overhead. Others went in and got their families, spouses, kids, excited dogs, and the families stood together, watching. Motorcycle cops were parked along the road every hundred feet. They twisted in their saddles, watching too.

One curve fed into the next. Two paperboys on mountain bikes kept pace with the joggers, jumping curbs, tossing papers at the houses, yelling to each other, slaloming the street. Gretchen saw the paperboys and spoke into her fist. Tashmo and Elias, hanging from the van, touched their ears and stepped off to the street. They tried to shoo the paperboys. The boys evaded them with ease, laughing, pedaling ahead.

The leading cruiser had almost disappeared around the second bend when the press bus came around the first, and for a moment the whole slow strobing spectacle was visible, complete. Somewhere in the center was a jogging man, hips rolling, feet shuffling. He wore a ball cap from a local high school hockey team. He waved the cap at the families in their yards as the paperboys popped wheelies up the hill.

The rain predicted for that morning started falling, stray drops, then a downpour for an hour. The VP finished his jog just before the heavens opened. He motorcaded to West Portsmouth for a breakfast drop-in at McDonald's.

Half the press corps covered breakfast. The rest, bored with photo ops and mindful of the rain, had stayed at the inn, calling sources from their rooms or mobbing the lobby coffee shop. The press hall, off the lobby, was a trading pit of tips and inside dope, journalists from twenty nations running, shouting, hunt-and-pecking at their laptops. Three assistant innkeepers were at the front desk in gold blazers. Six New Hampshire troopers were lounging among ferns. In the hotel's business center, the VP's volunteers were getting a pep talk from their leader, Tim the lawyer, field director for the region.

Tim was speaking to a circled group of fifty people, local and imported, one of whom was Peta Boyle. She was dressed for work (corporate pearls, Italian pumps, a houndstooth suit showing off her knees), and she had a businesswoman's day ahead of her. She had no time to volunteer, but she had made the time. She was here because her father, Philip Boyle, mortician of C.E., was a figure of some tonnage in the county party structure, and Peta had inherited his talent for the practical. It wasn't lost on Peta that Moss Properties did a fair amount of business with the city—vacant lots auctioned off, little whispers about zoning—and it never hurt to hold a chit or two, or many chits, with the mayor's office. When the county chair, a man named Thomas Monahan (criminal attorney and a family friend), asked Peta to work for the VP, she was glad to be a name he could circle on his list. She had a deep, near-glandular belief in the concept of a party as a tribe, of we pick a guy and back a guy and get him into power—otherwise, what are we doing, thumbs stuck up our asses, while rival tribes get power. The VP, as the choice of the machine, was entitled to support; it wasn't complicated. Plus, she liked the guy. From what she saw on TV, there was nothing major to dislike.

Tim started the pep talk with a poll. "Who here has done GOTV before?"

Many hands went up. Among the volunteers, there were three hungry-looking women from Mothers for the Truth About Gun Violence, an Oregon school safety group, several tort reformers, two global-warming Deadheads, a smattering of action-seeking retirees up from Sarasota, ten boys from the UMaine football team (earning gut credits for a class on governmental processes offered only to prize athletes at that university), and a dozen bleary Texans from the teachers' union. When Tim asked the question about GOTV, Peta raised her hand, as did the Deadheads and the tort reformers, and several of the caravanning retirees, and two of the ten football boys (who had somehow managed to flunk the gut class as freshmen the first time around and were taking it a second time in hopes of graduation). The others—the women from Mothers for the Truth and all of the Texans—didn't raise their hands.

One old woman was a little hard of hearing. She cupped her hand to her ear and said, "What did he say?" This was Jackie Kotteakis, the retired prairie school-marm, the captain of the Texas volunteers.

"Who's done GOTV," Peta paraphrased for Jackie.

Tim was pacing like a general. "We could win or loose this thing by a thousand votes statewide. GOTV will be essential. Do you have a question, ma'am?"

"I've done GOTV," said Jackie Kotteakis.

"You can put your hand down," Peta whispered.

Tim continued pacing. "Our goal for today is one hundred percent turnout of our base. Now, how do we do that? Well, we have a plan."

The plan, like Gaul, consisted of three parts or three subassignments. One group of volunteers would man the bank of phones along the wall, calling the base and generally urging it to vote. A second group would do visibility, pumping signs at intersections, *Honk for the VP, Honk If You Love Reform, Honk If You Hate Dead Seas Due to Greenhouse Gases*, the purpose being both to flash a last message to the eyeballs of the electorate and to deny prime intersections to the forces of the senator, who would also be asking motorists to honk. A third group would be assigned to GOTV.

"Now," Tim said, "who here knows the meaning of GOTV?"

GOTV meant get-out-the-vote, the eternal ground game of elections. It meant sending vans of volunteers out into the countryside armed with lists of voters needing rides to the polls. Done properly, GOTV was a satisfying exercise, raw muscle, group effort, people pitching in. Peta knew the meaning of GOTV, but she didn't raise her hand (Tim's Q&A routine was getting on her nerves). To Peta, it was more than satisfying. It was the system vindicated, the world working as it was supposed to work.

A volunteer was handing out maps and voter lists, as Tim explained GOTV.

"G," he said, "stands for Get. Who can guess what O stands for?"

Peta felt like raising her finger, but raised her hand instead.

They took the back roads out of Portsmouth, avoiding the slow death of 95, Peta and four volunteers riding in a placard-covered van. Jackie Kotteakis sat up front. The women from Mothers for the Truth sat in back. Peta, driving, finally felt a purpose, the gathering momentum of the day.

Jackie Kotteakis wore a button on her coat. Peta read the button: *Kiss me—I'm a teacher*. The button was designed to say a lot about the wearer, to convey a certain sassiness, irreverence, pride in one's fill-in-the-blank profession or ethnicity (Peta had seen many variations, *Kiss me—I'm Irish, Kiss me—I'm Slovakian, Kiss Me—I'm a roofer*). On anyone, the button would have made a statement, but on Jackie the effect was particularly striking, Peta thought. Jackie's skin was deeply wrinkled, lightly powdered. Her hair was silver, flapperishly bobbed. Her shoes were cushioned nylon, an orthopedic sneaker with aggressive arching. Jackie's manner in the van suggested many things to Peta, the patience of great age, kindliness, good posture, but not sassiness or kissing.

"You from around here, honey?" Jackie asked.

"Yes," said Peta. "C.E. —Center Effing. Born and raised."

"I can tell by how you drive. You know your way around."

"You're from Texas? Your whole group?"

Jackie nodded. "Longmont, north of Denton. You know Texas at all?"

"Not really," Peta said. "I went to Houston once. I had to take this two-day ethics seminar for my realtor's license. They give it all around the country, but Houston was the place that fit into my schedule."

"You like it?"

"Houston? It seemed like a weird place to learn ethics. It was really humid."

"Oh, Houston's *super*-humid," Jackie said. "It gets humid up by us, but not that Houston kind of humid."

They ran out of things to say about Houston and the conversation flagged. Peta glanced in the rearview at the women from The Truth. She was trying to decide whether to ask them about their group, its positions and beliefs, the problem of gun violence and school shootings generally (the scariest thing going, Peta thought— the phrase itself, *school shooting*, made her kind of sick). There had been a rash of shootings that year and the year before, one in Oregon, one or maybe more in Southern California. Peta saw the stories in the paper, on TV, children shooting children after study hall, parents asking why. There was always at least one hero story in the mix, the brave teacher who disarmed the kid or led the other kids to safety through a locker room.

Peta wanted to ask the women from The Truth why children shot children, why there was, or seemed to be, a trend, and what could be done to stop them in the future, all the talk-show questions one might ask. But the women from The Truth were kind of spooky, Peta thought, the way they scrunched together on one bench, even though there were three benches in the van. One of them was named Hilly, or it sounded like Hilly when she said her name. The second was named Shannon (Peta heard it clearly) and the third one didn't say her name, or did, but mumbled it, or mumbled something. The women from The Truth came from Oregon, different parts of Oregon. They had driven east together in a battered little camper to save money. They parked the camper at the inn, slept in back, and didn't go out for pizza with the other volunteers, eating nothing or buffets. Peta had seen them that morning before Tim's pep talk, feasting on the wreckage of the continental breakfast in the pressroom, obviously starving from the night before. They had a wounded, disemboweled look, and a Moonie farawayness in the eyes. Peta saw many people like these women in grassroots politics, victims-rights types, AIDS activists, ghost-souls brought together by some awful loss or tragedy. Peta guessed or suspected that what bound the women to The Truth, and to each other, was that they had all lost children in school shootings. It fit together suddenly, the gypsy life, the camper, the cultic closeness, the harrowed gaze. For a moment Peta felt for them. It's Kai ten years from now who dies in the hallway with the others. It was fully real to her for as long as she could stand it, a moment and no more. Peta wanted to learn about gun violence, how to stop it, a truth, The Truth, anything at all, but she was afraid that if she asked the women about their group's proposals, they would come out with something crackpot, angry and extreme, and Peta, feeling for them in one part of her brain, would be disagreeing with them in another part, and thinking they were crazy too.

The rain was thinning to a drizzle as they came into C.E. Hilly and Shannon got out at the Gateway-to-the-Wetlands Nature Center, the polling station for the area. Hilly took some signs, Shannon took a box of leaflets. Tim had assigned them to visibility. They would wave the signs and distribute literature, staying at least a hundred feet from the doors, as required by state law.

Peta took Route 32 to Belvedere Estates, a low-end subdivision in the hills above C.E., new houses by the hundreds, saplings wrapped in burlap, gutters without curbs. Peta, Jackie, and the quiet woman from The Truth tried to find the first address in their action packet, but the unit number was evidently wrong. Two voters weren't at home—Jackie rang their doorbells, waiting on the stoops, drizzle running down the bricks. They moved on to voter number four, a man named Leonard Nichols, a fat mechanic with a bushy Fu Manchu.

"I appreciate the ride," he said as Peta pulled away.

"That's no problem," Jackie said.

Leonard Nichols wore a too-small leather jacket and a concert t-shirt for a heavy metal band, WORLD TOUR '98, with the names of forty cities listed in small type, none of which were outside of the United States.

He said, "Is there any way you could run me up to Willingboro when I finish voting? I've got a job interview up there and my Buick's fucking totaled in the shop."

"Willingboro?" Peta said. "That's halfway to Manchester."

Jackie was more diplomatic. "Another van will pick you up at the polls, Mr. Nichols."

"Call me Leonard."

"Leonard. Maybe they'll have time to drive you up to Willingboro."

Leonard Nichols seemed to buy this. Peta heard him pawing through the ice and free drinks in the cooler, looking for a beer, settling for a juice box. He sipped and started a long rant about the builder's broken promises, town water and town sewer, the builder had promised, but everything is shoddy-like in Belvedere, he said.

The next successful pickup was a man named Bob Mangano, out on disability from the navy yard in Kittery, who was listed as a four, strong for the VP, because he felt the VP would do more for people who were out on disability from the navy yard in Kittery.

"Could you get my buddy?" Bob Mangano asked. "He votes religiously, but he lost his license over Christmas. He's three-time DUI."

"Where does he live, Willingboro?" Peta asked.

"What's that supposed to mean?" Leonard Nichols said.

Bob Mangano's buddy wasn't on the list, but he lived nearby and Jackie thought it was probably okay. The buddy trotted down his walk, climbed into the van, and introduced himself to everyone as Al. He was a sociable old sport, dressed entirely in tan. He sat in the backseat, next to Leonard Nichols and the free drink cooler, and soon they were discussing the shoddiness of Belvedere, the sewer lines and water lines.

"What street are you on?" Al asked Leonard Nichols.

Leonard said, "Tippecanoe."

"Over in the battle names," said Al. "I hear you're having problems with the deer pest over there. They come out of the state forest after dark, eat your shrubbery, I hear."

"Not lately," Leonard said. "They put this box up on a pole, makes a noise the deer just hate, drives 'em down to Rye. Our problem is the water pressure. I haven't had a shower in three days. It's more like a dribble, what I got."

They passed a van from the senator's GOTV operation. It was bigger and nicer than their van. As the two vans passed in the street, the senator's van veered playfully at them.

"Assholes," Peta breathed, swerving to the right.

The last stop in Belvedere was a deluxe unit, a steep-roofed palazzo with numbers slanting down the door. Peta pulled into the driveway, honked the horn, and flashed the lights. Two men in fur-lined raincoats came out of the house and approached the van. One was Boone Saxon. The other was the trainee agent, Christopher. They flashed their credentials, a practiced flip and back in their pockets.

Boone Saxon said, "Do you know the woman who lives here?"

"No," said Peta.

"We're a pull team for the VP," Jackie explained. "These are his supporters. This lady's name was on our list. We're taking voters to the polls."

Boone Saxon was distracted, reading Jackie's button. He said, "'Kiss me—I'm a teacher'?"

"Yes," said Jackie.

"Does that mean you're a teacher?"

"Yes," said Jackie. "I'm retired."

Boone Saxon said, "Okay. Let's see this list."

Christopher walked around the van, looking through the windows at the carpet on the floor as Boone inspected Jackie's action packet, turning several pages, flipping back. Satisfied, Boone gestured to the house.

A thin woman scurried down the steps, zipping a jacket. She climbed into the van and the agents stepped away. Peta backed down the driveway and headed into town.

The woman sat in back with Al and Bob Mangano. Leonard Nichols offered her a drink. The woman took a juice box, pierced it with the straw, and sucked thirstily. She was trembling.

"What was that all about?" Peta asked.

"I'm Belinda Johnson," said the woman. "They're questioning all Belinda Johnsons."

They dropped the Belvedereans at the polls and went down Santasket Road, past the glittering new developments, Sandy Point and Breezy Ridge. The next group of likely voters lived in Grassy Knoll, the development past Breezy on the right. Grassy Knoll was the latest, best, and biggest retirement community in town, a mini-city of units and subunits, care levels ranging from affordable to posh. Peta drove past curving roads and maple groves and multiuse fitness paths, streams and little ponds ringed by tall grass and low willows, the homes and lawns and wild dales blending into greens and roughs and undulating fairways. Jackie didn't even notice the golf course until they were in it, and Peta pointed out the cedar wheelchair ramp down into the sand trap.

"They're making millions," Peta said.

They collected Nadine Clanksy, a litigator's widow from Cohasset, Massachusetts, who lived in a cookie-cutter cottage in a line of cottages facing a tricky little meadow, a par four.

"I never have to leave," said Nadine Clansky, explaining why she'd moved. "Everything I need is here."

"It's incredible," said Jackie.

"I'd like to live here now," said Peta.

"Minimum age is sixty-five," Nadine said, "and they enforce it strictly. Every so often, they'll get some yuppie couple ready for the quiet life, trying to move in, pretending to be their own parents. Least that's what I heard. It might be urban legend."

"You have urban legends out here?" Peta asked.

"We have everything," said Nadine. "Rock-climbing too. The golf course is the big draw, though. It won two awards."

"Do you golf?" asked Jackie.

"No," said Nadine. "You?"

"Tried it," Jackie said. "Didn't grab me."

"Seems so boring," Peta said. "Just seeing it on TV. Why is the announcer whispering?"

Nadine turned. "How 'bout you?"

The woman from The Truth said, "I'm sorry, what?"

They pulled up to the Big House, as Nadine called it, a fifteen-story cube of brown reflective glass.

"That's full nursing," said Nadine. "You don't mind if I wait out here. That place gives me the creeps."

Jackie, Peta, and the woman from The Truth went into a creamy lobby. A guard watched them through a break in the trees. They heard the sound of water falling but saw no waterfall.

Jackie took the bottom floors, looking for the three names. A woman, who polled as a strong supporter, had died over the weekend, and a man, another four, was having a nap and the nurses wouldn't wake him. Jackie woke him anyway.

The man's name was Arthur Freilinghuysen. "'Course I want to vote," he said. "I haven't missed a vote since Roosevelt in '40. Help me find my pants."

Jackie let Arthur Freilinghuysen dress. She went looking for the next name on her list, a Mr. Grosjean. She found him being fed his breakfast.

Jackie knocked. "Mr. Grosjean, I'm Jackie Kotteakis from the vice president's campaign. Would you like to vote today?"

"He's absentee," said the orderly.

Jackie said, "He's on the list. Mr. Grosjean, hello. Would you like to take a ride with me today?"

Peta walked the middle floors, looking for a voter named James Patrick Fagan. She stopped at a nursing station where a black man in a smock and stethoscope was picking through the pill drawer.

Peta said, "I'm looking for James Fagan. He's a resident."

The man gulped some pills and closed the drawer. "You got him."

"You're James Fagan?"

"All day long," he said.

"Aren't you a little young for a place like this?"

"That's what I tried to tell my daughters," James Fagan said. "They said, 'Dad, you're going through some changes. It's not your fault, you're getting older now.' They got all worked up because once—once—they came to my house and I didn't recognize them. They said I didn't recognize them because I was getting older. Truth is, I didn't recognize them because *they* were getting older. I remember my daughters blowing out the candles on their kiddie birthdays, going off to proms. These girls, my supposed daughters, were fat and gray and had those tiny spider veins. Of course, I didn't say this, knowing how sensitive women are. Next thing I know I'm living in a cube. This is what I get for being nice. Let's roll. I've got a chat-room date at noon."

They rendezvoused in the lobby, Jackie with Arthur Freilinghuysen and Mr. Grosjean, Peta with James Fagan, the woman from The Truth with Mrs. Souza, the old piano teacher from C.E. They got the voters settled in the van, Nadine Clansky pushing over to make room.

Peta headed into town.

Arthur Freilinghuysen said, "Who's running this year?"

"The VP," Jackie said. "You support him."

Arthur said, "I do?"

"That's how they get your name," James Fagan said.

"Well okay," said Arthur, not too sure of this. "Is anyone else running?"

"Not really," Peta said. "The VP is a solid choice."

"I don't know," said Arthur. "I never trusted Tricky Dick."

"He's not running," Jackie said.

"I never trusted any vice president, Humphrey, Agnew, Mondale, Bortlund."

When they pulled up at the Gateway-to-the-Wetlands Nature Center with the second load of voters, Leonard Nichols was fuming in the rain, water running from the fangs of his mustache.

"Where's the other fucking *van?*" he shouted at Jackie. "I been waiting half an hour. Is this your strategy? Get my vote and then it's Leonard who?"

"At least you got a shower," Peta said.

"I've been here before," said Mrs. Souza, looking with suspicion at the nature center.

Peta often saw flocklike delegations from Grassy Knoll visiting the nature center under heavy chaperon. She said, "Yes, Mrs. Souza, the horseshoe crab exhibit's really interesting. Can you get out, dear, or do you need a hand?"

"No, I mean I was here this morning," Mrs. Souza said. "Some nice men in a van—they asked for my help."

The voters from Grassy Knoll assembled on the curb, popping their umbrellas, everyone but Mrs. Souza, who had already voted for the senator, apparently. The woman from The Truth went around the back and helped Mr. Grosjean with his folding walker.

Leonard Nichols said, "Don't vote for their lousy candidate. I did and look where it got me."

Nadine Clanksy said, "I'm too old to walk home."

Jackie said, "You won't be stranded, Mrs. Clansky. We'll wait for you, I promise. Now all of you get in there and do your civic duty."

Voting was a careful process in New Hampshire. You stood in line as the ladies from the League of Women Voters checked names on the print-outs, then you waited for an open booth, then you pulled the big lever and the curtains closed behind you, and you pressed the little button by your candidate's name, then you got a cookie and a cup of juice from the women who did juice and cookies. It was like giving blood and took about as long.

Peta, Jackie, and the woman from The Truth waited in the van with Leonard Nichols, who had calmed down a bit, and Mrs. Souza, who had brought her knitting bag and was working on a sock.

Peta called the campaign office. Tim said the C.E. pickup van had been reassigned to Rye when the Rye van went to Eatontown. The van for Eatontown had thrown a rod on 95, and the van from Portsmouth, dispatched to get the stranded voters, took them by mistake to Rye.

"But everything's on track again," said Tim, "except for Exeter."

By then it was clear: the VP's operation was a shambles.

Peta heard snoring. It was Mrs. Souza.

The senator's van pulled up, unloaded, and pulled out again. The senator's brisk and chipper volunteers made three trips while Peta and the others sat there waiting.

Leonard Nichols said, "Maybe we should send somebody in, tell them to hurry up."

"They're voting, not shopping," Peta said. "You wait in line, you vote, you get a cookie and you leave. There's no way to 'hurry up.'"

The van was beginning to feel cramped.

Leonard Nichols said, "You promised me a ride to Willingboro."

"No we didn't," Peta said. "We said the pickup van might *possibly* have time to go all the way to Willingboro, though it isn't very likely when you think about it, Leonard, because Willingboro's *thirty freaking miles* from here. Jesus, buddy, take a bus."

"I missed the bus to vote," Leonard Nichols said. "I can't be late for this interview. I really need this job."

"Want a fruit drink?" Peta asked.

"No, I want a job. I'm a skilled mechanic. I can break an engine out like nobody's business. Don't roll your eyes at me, you stuck-up bitch. I'm a piece of shit, I guess, until your Saab breaks down."

Jackie said, "Enough of that. Leonard, I'm surprised at you."

James Fagan came down the steps of the nature center. He said that Nadine Clanksy was almost finished. "I saw her with a cookie. Freilinghuysen's going to be a little longer. I think he's doing write-ins. He was going booth to booth, trying to borrow a pen."

"Where's Mr. Grosjean?"

"They're looking for him now. They know he checked in, because his name is checked off. They're peeking under the curtains, looking for his shoes, trying to fig-ure out which booth he's in."

Nadine Clanksy came out next, followed by Arthur Freilinghuysen, who had cookies for the group.

Jackie said, "Have they found Mr. Grosjean?"

"They found his booth," said Arthur Freilinghuysen "They're calling for him, but he won't come out. They're asking if he needs medical attention, but he won't respond. He's just in there, humming to himself. They're trying to locate a family member now."

An ambulance pulled up. The EMTs ran the gurney up the steps into the nature center.

Jackie said, "They seem to have the situation well in hand. Let's take these people home."

They went south to Grassy Knoll, dropping Nadine at her cottage and the oth-ers at the cube. They started back for Portsmouth on the coast road. Leonard tagged along, still hoping for a ride to Willingboro.

There were three museum rooms at the Gateway-to-the-Wetlands Nature Center. The line to vote snaked through them from the street doors, past the pay phones and a giant diorama called *The Marshes Before Man*. Jens shuffled with the others, briefcase at his feet, taking the odd pull off a bottle of Glucola. Word was coming down the line that there had been a medical emergency in one of the booths, a stricken voter or a claustrophobe, and help was on the way, which was why the line was stalled. Two EMTs bustled from the street a few minutes later, their belts and O_2 bottles riding on the bedding of their gurney, and after that the rumor stood confirmed.

Jens could see the women at the folding tables flipping through the multivolume voting rolls, A through E, F though L, M though XYZ. Voting was taking longer than Jens had expected. He was tempted to skip it, but he had already invested fifteen minutes in the line by then, and he was prepared to waste another fifteen minutes so that the first fifteen would not have been in vain.

The EMTs were standing by a curtained booth, trying to question the voter within. Jens saw a pair of Wallabees facing inward, away from the EMTs. All around, people gave their names, lined up for a booth, voted, had juice and cookies, or left right away. A priest joined the EMTs at the curtain and asked if he could help.

The line advanced. Jens gave his name to a woman who took names. The woman stamped his hand and he joined the nearest line. The priest and EMTs were standing at the center booth, talking to the Wallabees inside. The priest coaxed the old man out. Climbing on the gurney, the old man looked quite tired and relieved.

Food and drink were not allowed inside the booths, so Jens slipped the bottle of Glucola into the side pocket of his overcoat. He pulled the iron lever, closed the curtain with a clang. He stared at the options, the parties and the offices, the names in tiny type. He focused on his choice: the VP or the senator?

Peta had insisted that he vote ("Don't bother coming home if you don't vote," she'd said, smiling, that morning), which was just another way in which they were different: Peta so rooted, so engaged, so strong for the VP (in poll code terms, a four); Jens undecided (poll code five). Jens had declared this status to the first pollster who had cold-called the condo in the spring. He had stuck to his position through a hundred calls and canvasses since then. It was easy in the spring to express no preference between candidates because there were no candidates back then. There were many candidates, mentioned, rumored, or projected, but none of them declared, senators, ex-senators, governors, single-issue mavericks with small, fervent followings, some of whom were also ex–unsuccessful candidates for president, drubbed in past New Hampshire primaries. Jens saw these men on the nightly news, winking, hinting, being coy, refusing to rule out. He also saw them (sometimes the next day) on the streets of Portsmouth, or shaking hands at Monsey's Luncheonette, shirtless, tie loose, coat over the shoulder or held by an aide. Jens was prepared to shake the hand of any declared candidate, liberal, conservative, both parties. They shook his hand, sought his vote—it was honest and forthright. He wouldn't shake the hands of any nondeclared candidates he happened to run across (he felt that a governor of Texas or a senator from Delaware ought to declare his reasons for hanging out at Monsey's on a Saturday) —it was sneaky in a way, running undeclared. As the election neared and the field firmed up, pollsters called the house, pressing Jens: *Would it change your opinion, sir, if you knew that the vice president was soft on the economy?* Or: *Would it make you any less undecided if I told you that the senator has voted to put a nuclear waste dump about four hundred feet from your house?* This was called push polling, another sneaky tactic, campaign hirelings posing as true pollsters, spreading crummy information in their questions. Eventually Jens installed a voice-mail firewall to keep pollsters and fake pollsters at a distance, but this didn't block the rest of the barrage, the canvas vans, the TV spots, the radio, the mailings, the flyers and lawn signs, the billboards and the bumper stickers in the corner of your eye a zillion times a day. Jens had clung to his non-opinion through summer, fall, the holidays, and he found it hard, standing in the booth, to cast his long-defended undecidedness aside. The VP or the senator? He finished the Glucola, gazing at the names.

Peta found it funny, Jens and his dilemma. She called it their mixed marriage. She said that fives should never marry fours, it only led to nines or ones. She was satirizing Jens' indecision and his old programmer's bad habit of seeing things in logical or numeric terms—people, feelings, tendencies pseudo-quantified as code, four, five, OFF, ON, IF/WHILE. Peta said that nothing but the gas bill could be quantified in numbers, that nothing was precisely this or that. Peta could accept the gray of how things are, and, because she could, her political opinions were ironically quite black-and-white, this is who I am, this is where I'm coming from, this is what I think. Jens, seeking black-and-white, never found it, and wound up lost in gray. He had tried to analyze the question algorithmically, comparing the two candidates' positions on a number of issues, global warming, NATO, tax cuts, Russia, thinking that he would draw up a kind of tote board, his beliefs compared to their beliefs, with his vote going to the man who had the most checkmarks in his column when the process was completed. To do this, however, Jens first had to find out their positions, which turned out to be hard because their issue papers were vague and platitudinous. He also had to learn his own positions, which dragged the process out a lot. Russia, for example, was sprawling and chaotic, as a country and a subject. He stayed up late at the condo, trying to work on Monster Todd, failing in this effort, taking a quick break to cruise and study websites about Russia, the gangsters and decay, engrossing and disturbing, the short break from his monster often stretching toward the dawn.

When he shared his partial findings with Peta, she became exasperated, he became defensive, and sometimes they fought. Jens knew that they were really fighting about something deeper—their life as a whole, the work slump he was in, his problems at BigIf.

Jens stood in the voting booth: the VP or the senator? He was thinking about options. He had joined the game to make cool objects out of software, and, yes, for the money and the options, the chance to cash out young and return to pure research. He had built BigIf with Naubek and the others, and his options were waiting for the IPO, and everything was good, but was it what he wanted? He was undecided, a kind of cosmic five. On the one hand, there was Walter, so clearly disapproving in the months before his death. Jens had come to see his father's point. BigIf was immoral or amoral—the sheer scale of the killing, the product tie-ins with the frequent-flier miles, and the sinister new monsters (Postal Worker, Todd), the ones who look like us. This was the case for quitting. On the other hand, Jens knew it made no sense to leave BigIf now, after all his work, with his options vested.

He pulled the iron lever in the voting booth. The curtains leapt apart and Jens walked out.

"Hello," said Bradley Schwartz, "my name is Bradley Schwartz. I'm Naubek's replacement. Are these workstations being used or can I just pick one?"

Jens looked up from a screen of e-mails. Bradley Schwartz was a young man in loose chinos and a blue polo shirt. His glasses were gold-rimmed, moderately round. His chinos were slightly darker than most chinos at BigIf, more a light brown than a beige. Otherwise he seemed quite normal.

"Two of them are free," said Jens. "The rest are assigned. A few more may open up before the day is over. Naubek sat right here."

"Thank you," Bradley said. He sat at Naubek's terminal and looked at the keyboard. "Has this thing been cleared for booby traps at all?"

"I don't know," said Jens. "I'm not sure who does that. E-mail Digby. Digby probably knows."

"It's just that I heard that Naubek was a hard case," said Bradley Schwartz. "They say he's holed up with a cache of weapons, an actual cache. Is he the sort of guy who would take it personally, me replacing him?"

Jens said, "He was personally fired."

Bradley Schwartz logged on, triggering no booby traps. He pulled up the last draft of the Postal Worker, taking up where Naubek had left off.

Jens looked around the Bot Pod, doing a quick head count, making sure that he recognized his coworkers. Lu Ping was on the pushed-together bed, reconfigured as a love seat, wearing blue pajamas over a turtleneck and a green silk dressing gown, a gift from his bride, Phoebe Rosenthal, the artist-in-residence, on day two of their honeymoon. Phoebe was at her terminal, working on a likeness of Monster Todd. Prem Srinivassan was at the mirror in the corner, waxing his mustache. Bjorn

Bjornsson, across the room, was reprogramming his screen pets to have sex. The only Podders missing were the firees (Mayer, Naubek), Davey Tabor (trekking), and Beltran, who was due in from his mental health day. Jens relaxed, returning to his e-mails. Somebody named Carolyn had extra Celtics tickets, good seats on the baseline against Portland. Somebody named Chuck was turning thirty, cake and ice cream in the first-floor kitchenette at noon. Somebody named Pete needed a kidney. O-negative donors were asked to stop by his cubicle on two.

Across the room, Beltran signed in at the white board.

"How's the nervous breakdown coming?" asked Bjorn.

"Pretty good so far," said Beltran, who had learned to fit his breakdowns into weekends, holidays, and other forms of leave. "It's amazing what you can accomplish in a day. I took a scissors to my sheets, disinfected my apartment, binged and purged on cupcakes, smashed my television. It's all about time management. What's the word from Davey Tabor? How's Tibet treating him?"

"Nepal," said Bjorn. "He calls in once a day, like he's fooling anyone. My roommate from Berkeley saw him in the lobby at DigiScape in Mountain View. This was yesterday. Davey's such a bullshitter."

"DigiScape?" asked Beltran. "What do they do?"

"They design and manage various types of digiscapes," said Bradley Schwartz.

Beltran nodded and sat down. He said, "You're not Naubek."

"No," said Bradley Schwartz, "I'm Bradley Schwartz."

Jens said, "They fired Naubek. Charlie Mayer too."

Beltran cleared his throat and turned to Bjorn. "This DigiScape—they hiring?"

"I guess so," said Bjorn. "But they give shitty options. Slow vesters, says my friend. He's been there a month already. Everybody's looking."

Jens opened a file on his screen, the specs for Monster Todd. He was thinking of this room and how it had been when the game was in design. At first, the only coders were Jens and Naubek. Charlie Mayer came later and Lu Ping after that. They wrote the game here, eighteen million lines, wizards and rivers and moons. They knew that they were writing code for a war game. None of them—not Jens, not Naubek, not Charlie Mayer—had any right to claim surprise when the game became a silly, violent thing. They knew it on the first day, writing the first lines. But somehow, as they wrote more, they forgot more.

They plunged deeper into code with each passing day. As they fell in love with their creation, the world around their maze seemed to fall away. For a long time, in the heat of their creating, they knew and didn't know (they knew but they forgot) what the code was *for*. If a subroutine is beautiful—flexible and balanced, efficient, multithreaded, not one line longer than it needs to be— does it matter that its purpose is to make a cartoon fart? Jens remembered the night they wrote the sun. It was Naubek's project, and a challenge. Every game had a sun, Elfin, Napalm Sunday, Red Motorcade. Most of them were horse-shit suns, a crayon-yellow circle on the screen. It wasn't hard to write a sun, but it was very hard to write *the* sun. Naubek went to work, modeling a puls-ing, flaring, molten organ. He made it round; he made it move; he linked it to the cloud routines, sometimes behind them, sometimes burning through. Jens and Charlie Mayer were in the room too, working on their projects, and as Naubek coded, they came over and looked at his screen, and Jens had an idea for a haze-inversion module, a cool flattening effect, or maybe Mayer did, but it was Jens who wrote the mod, and Naubek who perfected it, and Mayer who debugged it, as Jens and Naubek hacked out the refraction math, a way to get the white of the sun turning yellow-orange-bloody-red as it descends. Jens knew that he would never feel that way again. None of them would ever feel that way again.

Jens had tried to tell his father that it didn't matter that the code was for a war game. Walter didn't understand, of course. How could he? He wasn't there the night they wrote the sun. Jens thought of Vi at the house. He thought of what she had said—not everything in your life has to do with you. He hadn't understood it at the time, but now he thought she'd meant that he ought to mind his own life and family, and not worry about BigIf, and whether it was good or bad, perfect or imperfect, the cartoons or the code. Give yourself a break, give Walter a break, don't worry about purity, just live. Peta could have said the same thing probably, but from Vi it carried weight. Vi had been there at the start. Vi had been there all along. Vi had seen the paper train derailed outside Berlin.

Lu Ping was doing tai chi, the flowing early moves, Raise Hands, Cradle Swan, Strum the Lute, Repulsing Monkey, nearly hitting Jens, who was heading for the door. Jens ducked under Monkey and went up to the second floor.

Meredith Shattuck was enthroned behind her desk of solid butcher block.

"How's Bradley working out?" she asked.

"He seems very nice," said Jens.

"Has he mentioned any preexisting medical conditions? Jaffe has to do the health insurance paperwork."

"Not so far, but I'll keep my ears open. May I sit? Thanks. Meredith, the reason why I wanted to stop by is I feel I ought to clear the air with you. I lost my head a bit yesterday. Vaughn Naubek was my friend and a great coder. Charlie Mayer was a friend too. I'm not going to sit here and tell you that I think it was a smart move, firing those guys, because I don't. I think it's a mistake in the long run, because whatever productivity dips they may have been going through, they had experience, Meredith, and that's important too—you can replace the old guard with the kids, but the kids don't have experience. So yes I was upset. And I admit I lost my head and I apologize for that. And I just wanted to make sure that we're fine, you and me, with our relationship. I know I haven't been the most productive member of the team either. Hell, I'll say it, Meredith: I've been in a slump. Monster Todd—he troubles me. I'm not sure why and I doubt you care. It's the damnedest thing, because I could always work. Remember when my dad died? And you sent those flowers, which was awfully nice of you. I handled the arrangements, and two days later, bang, I was right back at the code. Remember when I wrote the river algorithm? My son was born that night, that very night. I stood there in the delivery room in my booties and my desperado mask watching my child slide out of my wife. It was like nothing I have ever seen. Then she fed him, and they slept, and I came back here at three a.m. and the river just poured out of me. But it's been different with Todd. I couldn't work, I mean, I could—I could work on certain things. I wrote the shadow for the crater smoke, which is, by the way, a cool utility. Sometime when you get a minute, load it up and take a look. Then look at the file size. Less than a kilobyte, a single kilobyte. It's beautiful, it's *beautiful*, so tiny and complete, just like my son that night. There aren't a dozen men—people, sorry—who could have written that utility to compile as a k-byte. Let's see Bradley Schwartz do that, let's see goddamn Digby try to do that. I didn't come to pick a fight or grovel. I know we're living in the marketplace—that's fine and I accept it, which is why I didn't

make a big deal about SmoShadow. I know that you and Head and the twins have
prioritized Monster Todd, and, yes, I know Todd's overdue. I can't account for it. I
couldn't work or I couldn't work on Todd. It was like a flu bug, Meredith, like a
three-day flu, a head cold, a nothing stupid kind of thing, and yet you're totally
wiped out, you're good for nothing, and there's nothing you can do but wait until
it clears. What I came to say is that it cleared. Now I'm better. I feel like I can work
and that's why I thought I ought to clear the air."

Meredith said, "Yes. Thank you, Jens."

"*Yes?*" said Jens. "How can you sit there and say, *Yes?*"

Meredith spoke very softly, as if talking to a child in the dark. She said, "A corporation is a forest, Jens, and I'm the forester. In forests you have lightning strikes,
and fires, and many trees are burned, but the forest is renewed. But it's over now—
or it will be as soon as Davey Tabor shows his face and we can eighty-six his ass in
person. Relax, Jens, the fire passed you by. Do me a favor—go home and get some
sleep, or whatever it is that you need. I promise I'll look at your shadow later."

The roadblock was on Hanover Street, police cars nose to nose across four lanes of traffic, cops in yellow ponchos waving motorists away. Jens slowed, ran his window
down.

"What's happening?" he asked.

"Big rally," said the cop. "Where you headed?"

"To the square."

"Park it by the library. You'll have to walk from there."

Jens took the detour to the right, came all the way around again to the public
library, parked his car. He dropped three quarters in the meter, set it ticking with a
crank.

The sidewalks turned to brick coming into Market Square, the streetlights
turned to gaslamps, and the shops and offices took on the look of Dickens' Christmas without snow. A crowd was forming on the cobblestones and workmen were
assembling a scaffolding out of tube aluminum. Jens saw a news van parked the
wrong way on the street, a small dish antenna slowly rising on a mast.

Moss Properties was on the harbor end of Market Square, a building called the
Moss Block, a stately brick Bulfinch with a bow facade between the Aran Isle knit

store and the new patisserie. Jens stood outside the realtors for a moment, looking at the ships in the window, a model wooden frigate and a schooner named the *Sally Ann*, and the other toy-sized relics from the age of sail, a two-pound anchor on a coiled chain, brass cannons, and a polished sextant, and, higher up, a corkboard for new listings, snapshots of properties and two-sentence blurbs, stock phrases of the trade: *move in now—your country hideaway—stone's throw to the beaches.*

Peta was in her office with Daphne Jaffe, the rotundly pregnant wife of BigIf's corporate counsel. Daphne Jaffe was sitting in a rocker, one hand on her belly, leafing through a binder. Peta was on the phone, pacing back and forth.

Jens said, "Good morning."

Daphne recognized his face, he saw, but couldn't place him. She smiled slightly and went back to the binder, as Peta turned and looked at Jens and made a face like *You?* She was talking to a Kenny, somebody named Kenny, as she made the face at Jens.

"Kenny, it's a madhouse here," she was saying. "Just check your book and tell me if noon works for you. You're beautiful. Goodbye."

Peta did the introductions, Daphne Jaffe to Jens, Jens to Daphne Jaffe, a tongue-twisterish introduction, but Peta brought it off with her usual aplomb.

"Nice to meet you," Daphne said.

Jens said, "You already met me. At the BigIf Christmas party. I got your husband in the Secret Santa draw. I'm the one who gave him the case of Glucola."

"Yes of course," said Daphne.

"Don't mind my husband, Daph," Peta said. "Just go through the binder. I'll be back."

Peta took Jens into the corridor. She said evenly, "This is a surprise. Why aren't you at work?"

"Meredith gave me the day off."

"Why would she do that?"

"I think it's her idea of a peace offering," said Jens.

"Hope you locked your desk. I don't trust that wench one bit."

"Meredith's okay—we had a long talk. Let's get a cup of coffee, Pet. Better yet, let's get two—one for each of us."

It was an old Jens joke. He'd used it on their first, fourth, and eighth dates.

"Let me deal with Daphne," Peta said. "She's due any day now and she's renting presently. Hang out in the conference room. It'll be a couple minutes."

Noel Moss was in the conference room with his lobbyists, discussing what sounded like the overthrow of Cuba, so Jens waited in the corridor, looking at the noble oil portraits of the Mosses on the wall, Grampa, Noel's uncles and his father, five portraits in a line, middle-class conquistadores, storms on their foreheads, lightning in their eyes, pork chops on their minds. Jens had come to tell Peta that everything was going to be all right now. He felt it in his chest as he waited in the hall, new health and peace. He would get back to work and finish Monster Todd, the school shooter whom other kids could hunt through the halls.

Daphne Jaffe, showing great quickness for a woman of her size, left Peta's office, nodded at the secretaries and at Jens, and went out the door.

Peta stood behind her desk, doing seven things at once, making notes on Daphne's nascent househunt, pressing speed-dial B (Lauren Czoll's cell phone), kicking off her pumps, shouting around the corner to Claus, looking through her tote bag for the number of Anthony Bordique, the carpentry contractor, finding instead a dented can of seltzer. She opened the seltzer. Much shaken from her travels, it burst like a grenade, spraying seltzer on her lap. She left a message: "Shit!" —for the seltzer—"Oh hey, Lauren. It's Peta, honey, listen, I've found the perfect house. It's everything you're looking for, Greek Revival, sea views, a gazebo, humidor with net access. They have several offers, so we've got to shake a leg. I'm trying to organize a showing at noon. Page me when you get this, okay bye."

Claus came around the corner, dressed like a kommando, big black roll-neck sweater, polished boots and black cargo pants, bearing Peta's rolodex. They called Anthony Bordique, the old carpenter, on the speakerphone. Bordique was on a rush job for Moss Properties.

"What's the status?" Peta asked.

"We're getting there," said Anthony Bordique, talking over the sounds of table saws and nail guns, a gazebo with a sea view going up in record time.

"I have a call in to the client now," said Peta. "Tell me you'll be done by noon."

"I'll do my best," said Anthony Bordique, "but it won't be dry, the stain. Don't let her touch it, whatever you do."

"I'll handle it," said Peta.

As Peta talked gazebo with Anthony Bordique, Jens walked around her new and spacious office, Peta's reward for dealing with the madness at the Dental Building. Jens remembered when Peta was a junior broker for Noel Moss, camping in a cubicle, flogging unattractive fixer-uppers and vacant bodegas in North Portsmouth. He would come into town after an all-nighter at BigIf, or a double back-to-backer, forty hours at a terminal, writing rivers, moons, and monsters. He'd call Peta from a pay phone and say, "Let's go somewhere." They would sneak back to The Bluffs in the era before Kai, spend an hour in the bed in the afternoon. Later, as Peta climbed the ladder as a realtor, it was harder for her to slip away without a reason, so Jens would call Moss Properties posing as a client, doing funny voices, doing accents, using code names (Mr. Twillis was a favorite name), setting up an appointment to see a house. She would meet him at the listing (empty for a showing, Peta had the keys). They made love, made the bed, often without speaking, kissed and dressed and separated, Peta going back to Moss, Jens returning to his code. The houses grew bigger over time. They went to bed in palaces, almost, and this was how Jens knew that his wife was a success.

Peta finished with the carpenter. "Try Lauren at the fight gym," she told Claus. "I think she had a three-round bout against Chappie Xing this morning. Jens and I are going out for coffee. Beep me if you need me."

"Ya," said Claus. He marched back to his desk.

Peta was pulling on her raincoat, patting her hips to make sure she had her beeper.

"I think I'm getting close," she said.

Jens said, "Close to what?"

"To closing, babe, what else? Tell you what: if I get Lauren to commit, we'll find a sitter and go out for a steak. I'll wear that tight dress with the zipper up the armpit, the one that makes me look like a bargirl in Hong Kong."

"Yes," said Jens. He knew the dress.

He followed his wife out the door and into Market Square.

From the window of her room at the inn, Vi looked down on Market Square to the south and east. Vi was showered from the jog and semidressed. She wore a plain blue skirt, a red longjohn top, and a level three kevlar vest, standard-issue body armor for the agents on the ropes. The vest hung from her shoulders like a smock, white nylon velcro straps loose at her sides. Vi scratched her cheekbone absently, watching a crowd take shape below, people streaming up the alleys and the side-walks, converging on the square from ten directions.

Bobbie was sitting on the bed in pantyhose and camisole. She said, "Can I ask you something, Vi?"

"Sure," said Vi. "Help me with the vest."

Vi and Bobbie always dressed each other on the road, Vi first because she kept her gear in better order.

Bobbie stood behind Vi, cinching the vest tight. The vest was slate gray and smelled like damp putty. Vi hated the smell.

Bobbie said, "Too tight?"

If they wore the armor loose, it rubbed them raw all day. They wore it very tight.

Vi said it was good. She wiggled in the vest, getting it to sit right.

Bobbie said, "You ever have like—premonitions?"

Vi was buttoning her blouse over the vest. "Sure," she said.

"Really?"

"Sure—like once I was hiking with my dad. We were in the Whites, coming down Jim Liberty, and through the trees I saw these dry white boulders in a streambed, and I knew that I had seen this exact thing before."

Bobbie said, "That's déjà vu. Premonition's different. Déjà vu is when you see the past, premonition is the future."

"How do you know?"

"What do you mean, how do I know? That's the definition, look it up."

"But how do you know which one you're having? If I see white boulders in a streambed, does it mean that I was once there, or that I will be someday?"

"Did you ever go down that trail again?"

"No."

"Then it's déjà vu."

"But how do I know that I never will? What if I went back and checked to make sure my déjà vu was accurate? Then I've turned it into premonition."

"You just know," Bobbie said. "Some things you just know."

Vi felt a little edgy and was hoping that Bobbie would shut up for a while, so she could clear her head for the ropelines in the square. She tucked the blouse and longjohn top into her skirt, popped a clip into her Uzi, racked it once, and buckled it into the holster.

"I've been having premonitions," Bobbie said. "I'm in a crowd. I scan the hands, I see the muzzle coming up, I throw myself at the shooter and I take it in the face."

Bobbie clipped the comm set to the back of Vi's skirt, pressing a pair of thin black wires flat against Vi's spine.

Vi shivered a bit. She said, "It's just the stress, Bobbie. That's the job."

"Oh sure and I'm a hero and I go down in history, all the way down to a footnote probably, but what the fuck? I took the bullet like a good girl, and that's the fucking job—we plot against the plotters, right? Plan and counterplan. Only we didn't stop this plot, Vi, because the real target of the shooter was *me*. They planned that I would throw myself in front of the bullet."

The wires on Vi's body comm ran to a plastic brace on the back of her blouse collar. Bobbie fed the mike line over Vi's shoulder, under her arm, to a clip on Vi's right cuff. The comm, like the armor, was fitted to each agent by the Equipment Section, Beltsville. Vi plugged the receiver line into the earbud.

"Well?" said Bobbie.

"Well what?"

"Well what do you think it means?"

Vi could see that Bobbie was scared. Bobbie was always scared in the morning before a big outdoor event, a big crowd behind ropelines. Crowds were easier once you were inside them, scanning, vacant, ready. The hard part was getting ready to be ready, because you had to think about it. Vi considered Bobbie's premonition. It had a familiar ring, and Vi wondered if Bobbie had told her about this particular premonition at some point in the past. Bobbie averaged two or three premonitions per deployment and usually had four or more recurrent dreams recurring in a cycle at any given time. She also had hot flashes, sudden intuitions, many different déjà vus, and what she called the Creepy-Crawlies. Most of these involved her death, except her déjà vus, which usually involved ex-husbands. Vi brought her suit jacket from the closet, brushed the lint from the arms, and put it on.

"Wasn't that a movie?" she asked Bobbie. "'Cause, you know, it's sounds familiar. I really think it was a movie."

"What movie?" Bobbie said. "What's the title of this alleged movie that no one has ever seen but you?"

"I never said I saw it, Bobbie. But I think I might've seen the coming attractions."

"For my premonition? What are you, on crack?"

Vi was dressing Bobbie, the armor and the harness and the comm. Bobbie's comm was always snarled. Vi got it straightened out and draped the wires through the brace and down Bobbie's arm.

"See, there's this female agent, right?"

"In the movie?"

"Right. She's tied to a chair by this evil torture expert guy in the old abandoned oil refinery on the outskirts of town, and she has to shoot her way to freedom. She kills like fifty judo guys in turtlenecks. She can't get her hands free, so she has to shoot the gun with her mouth. She ulled the igga ike ith."

"That's preposterous," said Bobbie. "Was she pretty?"

"Really pretty."

"Did she die?"

"Nope," said Vi. "She survived and so will you."

Vi plugged Bobbie's earbud in. They were armored, armed, and all comm'd up. They left the room and started down the corridor.

"Maybe it wasn't a movie after all," said Vi. "Maybe they just did the coming attractions and never got around to making the rest. I'll bet that happens."

Bobbie said, "My second husband was like that."

"See?" said Vi. "It's nothing to freak out about."

Outside the VP's suite, the detail was assembling, the SWAT guys and the comm techs, Tashmo and Elias. O'Teen leaned against the wall, his florid face inside a book.

Bobbie said, "What's happening, O'T?"

"Waiting on Miz Gretchen," said O'Teen.

O'Teen was handicapping one of the major book awards, reading all the nominees. The book he was reading had a picture on the cover, a woman in the sunlight with two happy-looking pandas.

"Any good?" asked Vi.

O'Teen said, "It's going out at six to one on the Vegas line." He turned a page and sighed. "I'm not sure I'll make it until baseball."

Gretchen emerged from the VP's room. She saw Vi in the hallway and said, "Just the body I've been looking for. Come on, Violet, let's go prep the square."

Vi and Gretchen took the freight lift to the loading dock behind the inn and started up the sidewalk toward the square. Vi waited for Gretchen to say something about Vi's trip to C.E. the night before. Vi assumed that Gretchen knew about the trip— little happened on the detail without Gretchen knowing it, especially the petty derelictions which made the agents human and not robots, but which always put you on the wrong end of a blasting, Gretchen's famous rages, and sometimes got the people near you blasted too, Gretchen's rages being somewhat indiscriminate. Vi had heard Gretchen curse Tashmo over two stupid roadblocks, which Tashmo hadn't even been in charge of, and Vi's offense, flouting orders, going AWOL, was a lot more serious.

It was two blocks from the hotel to the square. They cut across a parking lot. Mounted cops cantered past. It had been raining off and on since the downpour of the morning. Now the rain had stopped, though it felt more like a pause than a stop.

"Go somewhere last night?" asked Gretchen.

The tone was chatty, but Vi was not deceived. Gretchen often started chatty, got her facts established, toyed with you a bit, before exploding.

Vi said, "Yes I did. I went to see my brother. I told you all this yesterday."

"You *asked* me. I said no. Or did I hallucinate?"

"No, I asked you."

"And what did I say?"

Vi said, "Just get it over with. Rip me ten vacation days. Fuck it, take 'em all. Dock my pay, hose me on my bonus, stick me on the ropelines until Christmas, I don't care. I'm sick of the cat-and-mouse. Every morning I get up, dress myself, dress Bobbie, then convince her that she's not going to *die* today, and only then can we leave the goddamn room. I caught O'Teen in the hallway reading about pandas. It's crazy, Gretchen. We're all going crazy."

Gretchen nodded and they walked along. She said, "What's your brother's name?"

Vi said, "What do you care?"

"Is it Jojo? It is Freddy? Is it Nick?"

Vi said, "It's Jojo. Jojo Asplund. Don't fuck around with me."

"Well okay," said Gretchen, "here's to good old Jojo. I rip you two vacation days. Next time I give an order, Vi, obey it for me, huh?"

They passed through a choke point onto the secured area behind the prefab stage. The stage was ten yards wide, plywood and tube steel, covered and enclosed on three sides by a canvas canopy, stripes of green and white, like a wedding tent. Hanging pieces of the tent were flapping in the breeze, the big sides filling like a sail, then going slack and sucking in, with each shift in wind. There were folding metal chairs against the back wall, half-filled with local dignitaries running through their speeches, some mouthing words in practice (eyes closed, it looked like prayer), others having sudden thoughts and scribbling on index cards. A podium stood out alone at the stage's edge, like a diving board—beyond it was a drop-off, space, and then the crowd.

Gretchen was conferring with a Portsmouth Parks Department supervisor. The stage had stairs at both ends, and Gretchen was explaining to the Parks guy why this wouldn't fly. They would bring the VP in by motorcade behind the stage when the rally was in progress, keeping his moments of exposure to a minimum. When he was introduced by the second or third speaker (Vi hadn't seen a program, but there were rarely fewer than three introductions at these rallies), balloons would be released as the agents walked the VP in a cordon a short distance through the crowd and up the right-side stairs. He would give his speech and exit by the same route. This made the stairs on the left Gretchen's blind side, in effect—not a blind side really, but she would have to mass her agents on the right, and she didn't need an extra access point. The Parks guy, bellyaching, said that the left-side stairs were bolted to the post supports, and he wasn't sure he had the tools to remove them. He started throwing around Parks Department terminology, like anybody gives a damn, Vi thought. Gretchen, who was paid to flatten all resistance to the Dome, told the guy that if the stairs weren't gone in three minutes, she'd call her welders, have the stairs cut off and delivered to his office in a heap. The Parks guy bought the threat, apparently thinking that Gretchen traveled with a team of metalworkers. He hurried off the stage to find his tools.

Vi looked out at the crowd. The rally, like the morning jog, was a high-threat event. Outdoor operations in a city center were generally bad. Shops and restaurants, offices and parking lots—the Service couldn't freeze all life for a mile square. In theory, they could do it. They had done it for the president in Pakistan (Islamabad a ghost town for two hours), but for that you'd need a thousand agents and a junta for a government. They would do as much for Market Square as you could do in such a place, overflights suspended from the county airport, the Coast Guard on patrol in Portsmouth Harbor, traffic detoured, a second gunship added for the morning. The troopers had the choke points, four of them arrayed around the square, designated red (north), blue (east), green (by the church), and gold (by the stage). The comm techs were on standby with the jammers; cops were working down the rooftops (checking each, posting guards to keep them sealed); a sniper team was climbing to the steeple of the church.

A yellow rent-a-truck backed into the area behind the stage. Two men in jeans and jeans jackets jumped from the cab and went to work unloading the balloons, four great rafts of balloons held together in four floating fish-net bags. Vi heard bluegrass music from the speakers. It was a cue. They were ready to begin.

The first speaker at the rally, the warmup to the warmup, introduced herself to sputtering applause as the state representative from Greenland-Belvedere, a straddle district down the shore. She thanked the sponsors of the rally, her good friend Tommy Monahan (the county party chair), the office of the mayor, and the Portsmouth Parks Department. She was swinging into her remarks when the PA system died, a shriek of feedback, followed by dead air.

Jens and Peta heard the PA die as they left Moss Properties a hundred yards down the square. They crossed the street together, walking side by side, close enough to hold hands, though they didn't.

Jens said, "How was volunteering?"

Peta said, "A clusterfuck. Someone owes me major chits. You vote already?"

Jens said, "This morning."

"Correctly, I assume."

"I couldn't vote for either of them, Pet."

Jens explained what he had done in the booth, how he had stared at the buttons by the names, trying to decide between the VP and the senator, and how, finally, unable to decide, he had pulled the big iron lever back without pressing either button.

Peta said, "What lever? I'm confused."

Jens started to explain again, but Peta cut him off. "Just tell me, did you vote or not?"

Jens said, "I voted, but for no one. I don't believe in either of those guys. If I picked one, I'd just be going the motions. It wouldn't mean a thing."

Peta said, "So instead you stood there and basically wasted an hour of your day. I'm sorry, Jens, but that's just *sad*."

"Sad how?"

"I don't want to talk about it."

"No—sad how? I can't *go the motions*, Pet."

"Yes," said Peta, looking down the square.

They were heading toward the new tabouli restaurant, which had eleven different coffees on its menu, counting the decafs. Jens had planned to wait until they were comfy in a booth, then have a short, important conversation with his wife. He was going to describe the conversation with Vi the night before, and with Meredith this morning, and how he felt certain now that his slump, his rough patch, was coming to an end. He had told her something like this several times before, but this time he was confident.

They got the PA up again, and the woman from the straddle district introduced the next introducer, a veteran state senator from Eatontown, who grabbed the mike and in a boomed voice thanked the party chair, Tommy Monahan (and his lovely wife Irene), the rep from Greenland-Belvedere (for her gracious introduction), and God, for the break in the weather.

"*Fold up your umbrellas, folks,*" he said, "*because I think I see the sun!*"

This mention of the sun brought the first real clapping of the rally, though the sun was nowhere visible.

Jens and Peta walked along the street. Market Square was packed by then, late-comers arriving through the gates. The tabouli place was down by the stage, past the bagelry, the wine shop, and the specialty tobacconist's. On the sidewalk, to the right, Jens saw a man in a postal worker's uniform, the sky-blue shirt, the blue-gray pants, and the white pith helmet. Jens had to look twice before he recognized Vaughn Naubek.

Jens said, "Vaughn?"

Naubek looked at Jens, quickly, sharply, then stepped off the curb, disappearing in the crowd.

The senator from Eatontown, having urged the crowd to vote and urge their friends to vote, brought his introduction to a climax: "*And now, and now, and now I'd like to bring up a friend, a dear friend, a leader and a patriot, a man who needs no introduction, and will receive none further—*"

Glancing at his notes, he introduced a congressman from Louisiana, who bounded up the stairs and launched into his speech, thanking Tommy Monahan, his lovely wife Irene, the mayor, the state rep, the state senator from Eatontown, God, and the good people of Louisiana and, of course, he added, veering from his blooper, other states as well.

"*My friends,*" the congressman began, his voice dropping an octave, growing grave, bouncing as an echo off the buildings in the square.

The motorcade had docked behind the stage by then, and Gretchen had her agents in position. She was standing by van one with Bobbie, Vi, and Tashmo. They would be the wedge. They would take the VP through the crowd. Gretchen drew this duty because she was never very far from the VP in a crowd. Bobbie drew it because Gretchen didn't trust her to run her own position, a choke point or the stairs. Vi and Tashmo drew it because they had seen the screamer at the Marriott on Sunday night and might know the face if they saw it here today. They were standing in a loose diamond formation, Vi in front, closest to the crowd, Bobbie at Vi's shoulder, Tashmo on the other, Gretchen a few steps to the back. They looked in their dark suits like a singing group with moves, the Pips or the Four Tops, left arms hanging loose, right hands at their belt lines as if covering their buckles. Gretchen was rechecking the perimeter. Vi heard it in her ear.

The snipers in the steeple said, *We're good.*

The comm techs were ready to start jamming.

Herc said, *My side A-Okay.*

Elias said, *We're standing by.*

The balloon wranglers gave Gretchen the thumbs-up.

"*My friends,*" said the congressmen again. "*Today, we—no, you—will send a message—*"

A cheer went up, spontaneous, unplanned, rolling from the back.

"No—no—no," the congressman modestly refusing the acclaim.

The crowd was pressing to the front. Jens and Peta, moving through the tight-packed bodies toward the tabouli place, reached a point where further progress was impossible. They were near the volunteers, Jackie Kotteakis and the other Texas teachers, Tim the lawyer from Rhode Island, the tort reform zealots, the global warming Deadheads, the football kids from Maine, the stricken women from Mothers for the Truth—a Napoleonic square of volunteers, waiting, gripping signs, primed to give it up for the VP as soon as someone introduced him.

The congressman boomed through a list of the VP's great achievements, his record of commitment, his deep belief in the binding causes of the day.

"*He believes—as I believe—in the future.*

"*He believes—as you believe—in tomorrow.*

"*He believes—as you believe—in the family.*

"*He believes—as we believe—in the family and the future of the family in to-morrow—yes—and so I ask you, friends—I ask: what do we want?*"

The phone-bank kids and volunteers whooped it up (they knew the chant). They shouted in two beats: "*Re-form!*"

"*I can't HEAR you,*" said the congressman. "*What do we want?*"

The answer was disorganized—no answer, many answers, a buzzing in the square.

The congressman bore down: "*What do we want?*"

The volunteers were shouting—others picked it up: "*Re-form!*"

The chant was slowly building, louder and more unified each time.

"*WHAT DO WE WANT?*"

One voice now: "*RE-FORM.*"

"*AND WHEN DO WE WANT IT?*"

Gretchen banged on the van door. Vi saw a shoe, a sock, a pant cuff riding up, a flash of white ankle, and then the man himself, the vice president of the United States.

The vice president looked out at the screaming crowd, firmed his jaw, and said, "Crazy weather, huh?"

"Yes sir," Gretchen said.

"Right here is where you want me?"

"Yes sir," Gretchen said.

"Which way do I face?"

"The same way we are facing, sir."

"*—to join me in welcoming a hero of reform, a friend of education, a tireless battler for tort sanity—a great man and the NEXT PRESIDENT OF THE UNITE-IT STATES—*"

The signs were dancing. The crowd was pressing in. The cops were linking arms. Vi was chewing gum, squinting at the steeple, casually unbuttoning her jacket.

Gretchen said, "All righty, Vi."

It was Vi who led them in. The others followed, moving in formation toward choke gold. O'Teen and the troopers were drawing back the barriers, steel across the asphalt, opening a gate.

Vi hit the crowd and cleared a path, parting bodies with her hands, bulling with her shoulders, freely throwing elbows. The agents tried to stay in touch; they were literally touching, the tips of Bobbie's fingers on Vi's left shoulder, Tashmo's hand on Vi's right haunch. The VP, sandwiched between Bobbie and Tashmo, reached past and over them to shake the outstretched hands, reeling off his greeting, *"Howyadoin, goodtaseeya, howyadoin."* Gretchen was behind him, forcing him toward the stairs up to the stage. The crowd surged around them and behind them, faces pressing in, hands reaching over arms to grab the VP's hands. Some people couldn't reach far enough and stuck their hands and wrists into the agents' faces. Vi knocked these aside, scanning hands and faces, moving bodies.

She tried to stay in touch with the other agents, but the people shaking the VP's hand were jostled from behind, and they lurched, pulling the VP a half step to the right or left, Tashmo's side or Bobbie's side, or pushing him back into Gretchen, and Vi, trying to plow a path, was also trying to hang back and stay in touch, but if she didn't plow full force, two legs and both shoulders, she felt herself loose ground. She heard *"Howyadoin, howyadoin, howyadoin,"* and greetings from well-wishers all around them, yelled encouragement, applause, bluegrass music, grunts of shoving, Gretchen saying, *"Move move move."* Just ahead, between the bodies, Vi saw a postal worker, who held some kind of helmet in his hand. Everyone was moving toward the VP or to the sides, or clapping, or yelling, or pumping a sign, except for this man, who wasn't clapping or moving. This was all Vi noticed about the man until he opened his hand and let the helmet fall. It clattered in the street and someone kicked it into someone else's feet and the helmet was kicked around at random until someone tripped on it, and nearly fell, and by then the postal worker had his hand inside his coat, and he brought it out with a magician's flourish, like when the magician pulls a rabbit from the hat or shows you that the four of clubs has been in your ear the whole time. Vi tried to put the gun over the comm, but her hands were pinned below her shoulders by the force of bodies pressing in, and she couldn't get her fist mike to her mouth, and the people were reaching and laughing and the VP was saying, *"Goodtaseeya howyadoin reallygoodtaseeya,"* and Vi went absolutely vacant—vacant even of her training—and she didn't move. Tashmo shouted, *"Gun gun!"* and yanked the VP back toward choke gold, which felt to Vi like a great and sudden loss of weight at her back. Gretchen put in the comm, *"Gun gun gun!"* and Vi heard the SWATs and snipers take it up, *Gun gun,* like an echo falling off, and saw Bobbie, curling across the VP's chest to block him from the shots, getting tangled in his legs as he tried to move. People in the crowd were starting to react, turning, screaming. Vi heard the snipers on the comm, barking something, what? Did they have a shot? She thought she'd see the man's head explode from a steeple round, but the balloons bumping upward through the air were blocking the steeple.

The man seemed quite calm. Vi pushed her way toward him; the strange thing was that his head was sitting unexploded on his shoulders. She hit him half-running, cross-checking him, and he felt soft and yielding for a moment, but then he dipped a shoulder and threw out an arm, knocking Vi off-balance, and people, running now, hit her from two sides, and she fell to the street, and was kicked in the ribs and the face and the knee by running shoes. The man with the black pistol was standing over Vi, his gun arm out, but he wasn't aiming or even looking at the VP. He was looking up, watching the balloons rise and disperse.

Vi was at the man's feet when the shots hit. The first shot hit him in the back. The second hit him in the head.

The agents ran the VP to the vans and evacuated Market Square. For the first few blocks, it was total pandemonium, sirens, squealing tires, aides and agents scream-ing, and every gun was drawn. Vi was bloody, face and blouse—was she hit? Was the VP hit? How many shooters was it? Did they get all of them, or both of them, or was there only one? The designated fallback for the rally was the parking lot of the public safety building on Hanover Street. They went there to regroup and assess the situation.

The VP wasn't hit. He said he wasn't hit and a careful check by EMTs found no wounds, no injuries of any kind except the cuts and bruises suffered when the agents had manhandled him to safety.

Vi was checked next. Gretchen found her sprawled out on the front bench of van two, shaking, pale, and groggy, splashed with blood and bits of bone, one shoe missing, her head in Bobbie's lap. The EMTs came up, but Bobbie, fierce-eyed and protective, wouldn't let go. Gretchen and Tashmo finally had to pull her off to give the EMTs some room.

Vi wasn't hit. The mess on her clothes had been the splatter of the head shot when the snipers neutralized the gunman in the square. The EMTs gave Vi a blue cold pack for her jaw.

Gretchen turned away, hailing Boone Saxon, who was with the gunman's body in the square. Boone said the scene was calm, the crowd dispersing quietly to the strains of bluegrass. He said it looked like two hits on the gunman, the head shot and a round through the chest.

Gretchen copied back. "You guys find a shoe? Lady's, blue. Vi's missing one."

The snipers joined the team a few minutes later, bringing a few souvenir balloons, and Vi's battered, flattened shoe, which Boone had found under a parked car.

The motorcade got rolling after that. The mood in the vans was oddly jubilant, Tashmo, Bobbie, and the others gabbing wildly, like a football team coming home from a big win, conducting a kind of group review of what they had been through, what each of them had done, or seen, or thought, or felt, at each unfolding moment in the square. Tashmo told the others how he saw the postal guy come out with the handgun, how he shouted *Gun gun*, which had started the alarm. The snipers picked the story up from there, how they heard *Gun gun*, waited for a break in the balloons, and took the shooter out. Bobbie told the others how she heard the warning, threw her body on the VP, helped run him toward choke gold, and so it went for twenty minutes in the van, stories and euphoria, and everyone took part, except for Gretchen, riding shotgun, and Vi, who held the cold pack to her cheek.

Behind the jubilation was relief and spent adrenaline, Gretchen knew. She thought it was best to let them play with the balloons and gabble on, and get it all out of their systems before the next ropeline. Gretchen thought they had a right to feel a little pride. After months of drilling, training, planning, and thousands of hours of gnawing, inconclusive tension on the ropes, they had finally met their Hinckley and defeated him. Gretchen knew her detail had never been especially close-knit, never had the semi-family feeling of some teams, no little pizza parties, no bring-the-kids-and-spouse cookouts at the chief-of-detail's house. Part of this was Gretchen's style, hard-nosed and remote. Part of it was Hinman, the great failure in the flood. After Hinman, the agents had gone their separate ways, or broken into cliques, as every losing team begins to fall apart. Gretchen listened to the snipers brag about their hits, and Bobbie laughing, and Tashmo bragging to O'Teen. She thought, well, here it is—we're all together now, Market Square undid whatever Hinman did to us. She watched them work the next event, a quickie ropeline on a village green. They worked it well, fluidly and jitter-free, and it was good to see her people moving as a unit.

They were closing this event and fanning toward the vans when Boone hailed Gretchen from the square.

"Shooter's name is Naubek, first name Vaughn," reported Boone. "Resident of Portsmouth, single, lives alone, no link, repeat no link, to the U.S. Postal Service. He's a computer programmer, laid off yesterday."

Gretchen saw her people pausing on the green, listening to Boone. Herc was nodding at O'Teen. Tashmo, one foot on the runner of the van, was nodding to himself. Boone was confirming something of importance to the agents. They recognized Vaughn Naubek as your classic shooter type, a loser with job trouble, a Hinckley or an Oswald, a shithead misfit who is pissed that history is leaving town without him. The Service existed to keep this type outside the margins of the story.

"We have his gun," Boone said. "Smith nine, no clip. Chamber's empty too. It makes no sense."

Gretchen wished that Boone had called her on the cell, rather than the comm, so that the detail would not have heard this. But it was too late now.

She shouted down the line of idling vans, "Move it, Herc. You too, Bobbie, get your rear in gear."

"Another thing," said Boone. "Naubek had a note in the pocket of his shirt. Snipers put a round through it when they blew his chest out, so what we've got is fragments here, I'm not even sure I've got the order right."

Boone read what he had—

To Whom It May Concern. . .
. . . no choice but to . . .
. . . test against . . .
. . . so that my message could be . . .
. . . I am not a "crazy". . .
. . . shuttle . . .
. . . O-ring . . .
. . . engineer . . .
. . . my mother and my sister Ruth . . .
Remember me.

                                      Vaughn Naubek

The aides and campaign handlers kept up their bright banter on the village green, but the agents in their midst were frozen, blank-faced, listening. The meaning of the empty gun was plain enough: in service of some muddled protest, Vaughn Naubek had summoned his community, and the VP and his press crew, to watch and film a public suicide.

The vans got on the road and the bodyguards were silent for a time.

"I don't buy it," Tashmo finally said.

Everyone agreed and the talking started up again, the round-robin storytelling, how Tashmo saw the gun and put it on the comm, how Bobbie covered the VP, how O'Teen cleared the route back through choke gold. It was a righteous shooting, clean, proficient, necessary. It was their will against Naubek's in the crowd. He had come to kill the VP; they had turned his will aside. The notion of the shooting as a suicide-by-Dome implied the opposite: Naubek had controlled them in the square.

"Probably the wrong gun," Tashmo said.

"Or they lost the clip," said Herc.

"That's what happened," said O'Teen. "The clip ejects when Naubek's struggling with Vi. It gets kicks around in the confusion and now it's down a storm drain and they'll never find it."

Gretchen said, "Forget about the clip. You did good work today."

"I saw a clip," said Bobbie. "Now that I think about it, yes."

Tashmo said, "Me too. I remember it distinctly."

Bobbie said, "Hey Vi, are you okay up there?"

Vi was in the first bench behind Gretchen and the driver. Vi's jaw was absurdly swollen. She said with a thick tongue, "I'm fine."

Bobbie said, "Did the clip pop out when you were fighting with that guy?"

"That's what happened," O'Teen said. "I took a class on crime scenes when I was in Crim. You reconstruct from data, see? The clip pops out and gets kicked down a storm drain. Did Boone even *bother* checking storm drains?"

Vi shifted the cold pack from her right hand to the left. She was trying to sort out what had happened in the square. She kept seeing the strange magician's flourish with which Naubek had brought the pistol out, and remembering the way his body had felt when she finally fought her way to him, the slack weight, the passivity—a living man—more like an empty bag.

She said, "There was no clip."

"Aw bullshit," Tashmo said.

"You couldn't see," said Herc. "You were on the fucking ground—you couldn't see one way or another, Vi."

Vi turned to face the other agents in the back benches of the van. She made this movement slowly, gingerly, because her head was throbbing.

She said, "All we did today was fulfill a wish."

The phrase was mincing, cruel, *fulfill a wish.*

They had left the coast by then, the string of village greens and ancient harbor towns. They were crossing through the mountains, sixty miles overland to Manchester. Halfway there, they encountered snow. The country disappeared into the gray of flurries and the darker gray of road. The vans slowed to a crawl. The agents, bored, turned their attention back to Vi who was facing front again and trying to nod off.

O'Teen said, "Yo Vi, let me ask you something, since you know so much—"

"She doesn't know shit," said Herc.

Bobbie said, "Don't pick on her. She can be wrong if she wants to."

Gretchen in the front seat thought, well, this is how it ends—we were almost all together for a minute there, but then they had to go and fuck it up.

"I'm not picking on her," O'Teen said.

"Your tone is not what I'd call pleasant," Bobbie said.

Tashmo said, "Oh please."

Vi stared straight ahead, ignoring all of them.

O'Teen said, "I'm serious. I've got a forensic question here. This will shed some light. Yo Vi, let me ask you— Yo Vi, turn around."